Kate Ellis was born and b̶̶̶̶̶̶̶̶̶̶̶̶̶̶ ̶̶ied drama in Manchester. Keenly ̶̶̶̶̶̶̶̶̶̶̶̶̶̶ ̶̶ory and archaeology, she lives in Cheshire with her family. *The House of Eyes* is her twentieth Wesley Peterson novel.

Kate has been twice nominated for the CWA Short Story Dagger and her novel, *The Plague Maiden*, was nominated for the Theakston's Old Peculier Crime Novel of the Year in 2005.

Visit Kate Ellis online:

www.kateellis.co.uk
www.twitter.com/kateellisauthor

Praise for Kate Ellis:

'A beguiling author who interweaves past and present'
The Times

'[Kate Ellis] gets better with each new book'
Bookseller

'Kept me on the edge of my seat'
Shots magazine

'Ellis skilfully interweaves ancient and contemporary crimes in an impeccably composed tale'
Publishers Weekly

CALGARY PUBLIC LIBRARY

NOV   2016

By Kate Ellis

A High Mortality of Doves

THE HOUSE OF EYES

OF EYES

Kate Ellis

piatkus

PIATKUS

First published in Great Britain in 2016 by Piatkus
This paperback edition published in 2016 by Piatkus

1 3 5 7 9 10 8 6 4 2

Copyright © 2016 by Kate Ellis

The moral right of the author has been asserted.

*All characters and events in this publication, other than those
clearly in the public domain, are fictitious and any resemblance
to real persons, living or dead, is purely coincidental.*

All rights reserved.
No part of this publication may be reproduced, stored in a
retrieval system, or transmitted in any form or by any means, without
the prior permission in writing of the publisher, nor be otherwise circulated
in any form of binding or cover other than that in which it is published
and without a similar condition including this condition
being imposed on the subsequent purchaser.

A CIP catalogue record for this book
is available from the British Library.

ISBN 978-0-349-40309-0

Typeset in Baskerville by M Rules
Printed and bound in Great Britain by
Clays Ltd, St Ives plc

MIX
Paper from
responsible sources
FSC® C104740

Piatkus
An imprint of
Little, Brown Book Group
Carmelite House
50 Victoria Embankment
London EC4Y 0DZ

An Hachette UK Company
www.hachette.co.uk

www.piatkus.co.uk

For Roger

And many thanks to Cornell Stamoran
who generously allowed his name to be used in
this book in support of a very good cause.

Prologue

April 1958

The infant reclines in his large new pram, shiny and black as a royal Rolls Royce and sturdy as a tank cutting through a battlefield. The sheets in the pram are pristine white and the soft blanket covering the small, precious body is blue, slightly paler than the sky. Blue for a boy.

The wide brown eyes stare at the dancing leaves above, watching the jewels of sunlight filter through the apple tree's blossom-filled branches. He kicks his chubby legs and chuckles. Fed, changed and warm, all is right in his narrow little world.

But a serpent crawls in his tiny Eden. A malevolence crouching in the outhouse, hidden behind the half-open green-painted door. The malevolence has been watching from its vantage point. It has seen his plump mother in her faded cross-over apron place him lovingly in the fresh air to sleep while she gets on with her household chores.

She thinks he's safe. The house is in the centre of the

village and there are no strangers around at this time of year. She hears a tractor chugging hypnotically in a nearby field and the gentle lowing of cattle. This is Devon; a place of nature and spring sunlight. There is no evil here.

The malevolence has a large basket, big enough to accommodate a small baby. It is essential to act before the infant becomes more aware of his surroundings. Before he learns to give names to the trees and the people around him. Before he is able to betray what is happening.

The malevolence pushes open the outhouse door and emerges from its hiding place, sneaking swiftly, crouching out of view of the sparkling windows. There is no sign of the mother. She is indoors. She will soon come out to check on her offspring but in the meantime the malevolence is free to do its work. It rushes to the pram and the infant fixes his large eyes on the unfamiliar face and gives a toothless smile.

But the malevolence is unmoved. Its heart cannot be touched by sentimentality. Sentimentality has been the ruin of the human race. Soft hearts stand in the way of progress.

It plucks the infant from his resting place, holding him gently so that he won't cry and alert his mother to what is happening. He is placed in the basket, covered by the blue blanket and carried away. By the time the malevolence has reached the lane, the child is perfectly quiet, soothed by the movement.

Soon the infant will serve a greater purpose. Soon he will know nothing but silence.

1

Richard D'Arles, his journal
  Volume the Second
  September 1786
  When I embarked upon this journey
it was my avowed intention to write in
this journal every day. However, after
recording my observations on the
medieval treasures of the Low Countries
and the beauties and cultural wonders
of France in my first volume, now
completed, posterity has sadly been
denied any further account of our
travels.
  So now I begin this second volume
with a brief mention of the
considerable discomfort we experienced
as we traversed the Alps. With the
necessity to dismantle our carriage

and find servants to carry our baggage, writing proved impossible and when we sojourned in Venice and Florence, the sights and spectacles of those remarkable cities and the solace of good society stilled my pen for a while.

Now that we have reached Naples, I am moved to take up my pen again. The demands of society are not so great here. Besides, there are certain matters that disturb me and setting them down will, I hope, help to make all clear in my mind.

The constable sat with his pen poised over the form. He was overweight and balding, nearing retirement, and beads of sweat were forming on his forehead. It was spring. Why couldn't they turn the bloody heating off?

'How long has Leanne been missing?'

The man sitting in front of him was pushing fifty. Close-cropped hair with no hint of grey; leather jacket and gold chain: Jack-the-lad type unwilling to let go of his long-lost youth. The constable had seen his kind many times before in the course of his long and undistinguished career.

'Two weeks.'

'And you're only just reporting it?'

'She's nineteen. Independent. You know what they're like at that age.'

'So what makes you think anything's wrong?'

'My ex rang to say she'd missed her birthday. I've never known her to miss her mum's birthday before.'

The constable wrote something on the form in neat, square letters.

'I'll need your details, sir. Name?'

For a moment the man hesitated. 'Darren Hatman. Three Riverview Way, Tradmouth. You are going to start a search, aren't you?'

'I'll pass the details on to our Missing Persons Unit,' said the constable. He sounded anxious to hand the responsibility to someone else. Hatman looked crestfallen, as though he'd expected him to assemble a team there and then to scour the surrounding countryside for his missing daughter.

The worried father rose from his seat and glowered at the officer. 'Pass it on? I don't think you're taking this seriously. I want to speak to someone in charge. I want to speak to a detective.'

The constable could hear the rising anger in the man's voice and he shifted back in his chair, eyeing the panic button.

'All in good time, sir. There are procedures . . .'

'Sod procedures. My little girl's missing. And there's something else you should know. She's got a stalker.'

The constable made a note of it and promised he'd make sure it was followed up.

Dr Neil Watson had been digging in the sandy trench for half an hour and now he stood up to stretch his back. His hair was damp with sweat, as was his T-shirt, and he took off his hat to fan himself, more used to digging in the Devon rain than the Sicilian sun. He could see the dog lying in the shade of an olive tree, apparently without a care in his canine world. Apart from a brief sojourn in Virginia, Neil had spent most of his archaeological career

5

in the UK, and he'd never before worked on a site where stray dogs were accepted as a fact of life. But many things were different in Sicily.

Theresa, the post-grad student from Palermo University who was digging beside him, looked across and smiled. 'Our dogs surprise you?'

She was olive-skinned, slender and beautiful, her only blemish being a nose that was a little too long for classical perfection. Her English was fluent, putting his attempts at Italian to shame.

'Archimedes just lies there and watches what's going on. I've never come across such a polite dog on a dig before.' He had named the dog on his first day there; it had seemed appropriate, Archimedes being one of the island's most famous former residents.

'One of the guides who works here says they're not stray dogs, they're free dogs. The temples are their home.'

'I've seen him feeding them,' said Neil. 'Looks like it's not only us Brits who are a nation of animal lovers.'

Theresa flashed him another smile, as though she took his observation as a compliment, and he squatted down again. In spite of the heat he wanted to carry on. This was an irresistible opportunity to get stuck in to some real classical archaeology after so many years directing excavations in Devon.

He still wasn't quite sure how he'd managed to wangle a fortnight digging in the Valley of the Temples, supposedly supervising a group of students from his old university, but somehow he'd done it through his professional contacts. Sunshine and Greek remains: what could be better for a jaded archaeologist who'd spent the winter buried in desk-based assessments and paperwork? However, he'd soon be back in England, taking charge of the community dig near Neston where his partner, Lucy, was already working.

A deep English voice suddenly interrupted his thoughts of home.

'Found anything interesting?'

The newcomer had stepped through the flimsy safety barrier erected to separate the dig from the wandering tourists, and was standing a little too close to the edge of the trench for Neil's liking. Dressed in black from head to toe, he was in his thirties, with piercing blue eyes and dark hair tied back in a ponytail. He had the look of an athlete who'd stopped training some time ago, lithe but beginning to expand a little around the middle, and there was a controlled watchfulness about him, as though he was viewing the diggers as specimens under a microscope, which Neil found a little disconcerting.

The man lifted his camera, a heavy, professional model with an elaborate lens. He never seemed to go anywhere without a suitcase full of expensive photographic equipment. 'What did you say this temple's called?'

'The temple of Olympian Zeus. Fifth century BC,' Neil answered before turning his attention to the section of temple wall emerging from the earth.

When they'd first met a few days ago the photographer had introduced himself as Barney Yelland and told him that he was over in Sicily taking photographs for a book he was working on – *In the Footsteps of the Grand Tourists*. It was to be a coffee table book of photographs, he'd said, confessing rather sheepishly that someone else was writing the text. The publisher who'd commissioned it had insisted that it would be a sure-fire commercial success. Sicily, with its magnificent classical ruins and rich history, was the final stop on his list of destinations.

Their conversation had rarely ventured into the realm of the personal but when Neil had asked whereabouts in England Yelland came from, he was surprised when the answer was South Devon. Neil himself had spent much of his working life in that area and when he'd mentioned this, the photographer had shown a polite but distant interest. Assuming Yelland was alone in a strange land, Neil had felt obliged to invite his compatriot to join the diggers at the trattoria in Agrigento they frequented each evening. Yelland had turned up a couple of times, sitting quietly, paying particular attention to one of the more beautiful female students but never speaking to her, almost as if he was appreciating a work of art in a gallery.

During one of their conversations, Neil had learned that Yelland was staying with a friend who taught English in Agrigento. However, the friend's name was never mentioned and it was clear the photographer preferred to talk about work rather than personal matters. But this didn't bother Neil and he became quite interested in what Yelland had to say about the Grand Tour, learning so much that, were he to be questioned on the subject, he probably wouldn't disgrace himself.

He resumed work, conscious of Yelland's snapping lens, and after a few minutes of silence the photographer spoke again. 'I'm going out to photograph a medieval site this afternoon. It's a place with a bit of a reputation. I've heard the locals keep away from it. Thought you might fancy coming with me if you can get away.'

Neil looked up, suddenly curious. 'Where is it?'

A hopeful expression appeared on Yelland's face, as if he

was eager for the company ... or maybe anxious not to go there alone. 'Just outside Naro. It's a small fortress dating to the first half of the thirteenth century. It's called the House of Eyes but I'm not sure why.' There was a pause. 'They say bad things happened there.'

'I can't leave the dig or I'd come with you.'

Yelland looked disappointed. 'Of course.'

'When are you going back to Devon?'

Neil told him.

'We're probably on the same flight. Mind if I hitch a lift to the airport with your group?'

'Shouldn't be a problem.'

Yelland took another batch of photographs before walking away.

DCI Gerry Heffernan entered the building. A couple of weeks ago the weather had been unseasonably balmy; now though there was a chill in the spring air so his hands were thrust into the pockets of his aging anorak. But the warmth of the police station hit him as soon as he crossed the threshold so he discarded his coat and muttered a complaint about the heat.

DI Wesley Peterson, walking beside him, was slightly taller and considerably slimmer with dark skin and intelligent brown eyes. He saw that Gerry was staring at a man who'd just emerged from the side door leading to the interview suite. The man wore a leather jacket in spite of the warmth and was accompanied by a plump, middle-aged constable. When he noticed Gerry he came to an abrupt halt, as if he'd spotted something alarming in his path.

Gerry stopped too and Wesley almost cannoned into him.

A wide smile spread across the DCI's face. 'Well if it isn't my old friend Darren Hatman,' he said in the distinctive Liverpool accent he'd never lost, despite all his years in Devon. 'Good to see you again, Darren. How's tricks? You've been very quiet since that post office job in Plymouth. Not taken early retirement, have you?' He looked the man up and down. 'I hope it's my lucky day and you've come to turn yourself in.' He turned to his companion. 'Wes, this is Darren Hatman. Getaway driver of this and many other parishes. Darren, I don't think you've met DI Peterson.'

For a second the man looked as if he was tempted to push past Gerry and make his escape, but he stood his ground. 'Plymouth was ten years ago and I haven't put a foot wrong since. I'm a respectable builder now. Got my own business.'

'I'm pleased to hear it.'

Wesley Peterson sensed Hatman's impatience, as though Gerry was obstructing him on some important mission and he was longing to knock him out of the way. Then he saw a look of relief pass across Hatman's face. And something else. Hope perhaps?

'I need help, Mr Heffernan. My little girl's gone missing.'

Gerry frowned. 'I didn't know you had a little girl. You've kept that one quiet.'

'My Leanne's nineteen now. Her mum's not heard from her for a couple of weeks, not even on her birthday. It's not like Leanne to miss her mum's birthday.'

'What about you?' Wesley asked. 'When did you last see her?'

'About three weeks ago. She's been busy.'

'Girls her age go off all the time,' said Gerry, a note of

10

sympathy in his voice. He had a daughter himself. 'She's probably off with some spotty boyfriend.'

Hatman shook his head. 'She was going out with a lad but they finished a few months ago. She made it quite clear to him that he wasn't wanted and he's been off the scene for a while. This just isn't like her.'

When Gerry didn't answer Wesley took the initiative. 'Have you tried her friends? Her work colleagues?'

'I'm not fucking stupid.'

'It's just that nine times out of ten missing people turn up safe and sound.'

Hatman put his face close to Wesley's. 'She could be any-where. He could have taken her and be doing God knows what . . .'

'He? Who are you talking about?'

'That bloody photographer. He's been stalking her. You should be pulling him in.'

'In that case, I think we should have a proper word,' said Wesley, taking the man by the elbow and steering him back in the direction of the interview suite.

2

I have so far failed to set out certain facts concerning my expedition. I travel with my cousin, Uriah, and our cicerone, the Reverend Micah Joules. We call Joules our 'bear-leader' as is the custom and my father has entrusted him with my welfare and education while we are abroad.

Joules is a rotund little man with a bald pate and a shiny face made luminous by the southern sun. Without his thick spectacles he can see little and misses much. He is curate of St Peter's at Turling Fitwell and, as the living of the church is in my family's gift, he could not refuse my father's request that he should accompany me on my travels. Yet he performs his duties with *a good nature of which I confess I sometimes take advantage.*

Joules has a fascination for the antiquities we encounter at each turn in this glorious country. I myself spend much time studying the art of the masters while my cousin, Uriah, pursues more dubious activities. Joules is quite unaware of this as he is one of nature's innocents. I suspect that even I do not see all.

'What are we doing about Darren Hatman's daughter?' Wesley Peterson sat on the chair in Gerry's glass-fronted office watching the DCI go through the papers that had arrived on his cluttered desk that morning. He saw him pick up each one and scan it with a grunt. Some he pushed to one side in the rough direction of his in-tray, others he scrunched up and aimed at the bin in the corner with a look of disgust on his chubby face. Soon the carpet was littered with balls of paper and Wesley, who had always been inclined to neatness and order, absent-mindedly picked them up and deposited them at their intended destination.

He had followed Gerry into the office after the morning briefing, curious to know what he thought about Hatman's complaint of the previous afternoon. The mention of a stalker had sounded alarm bells in his head and he had lain awake worrying about it before eventually getting to sleep at three in the morning. His wife, Pam, often warned him about becoming too involved. But how would he feel if his daughter, Amelia, was to go missing one day in the future? What would he do if a stalker was targeting her? Hatman might be an apparently reformed criminal but that didn't mean he didn't love his daughter. Yesterday his instinct had been to follow up the report of Leanne Hatman's disappearance immediately although Gerry, who appeared to know Hatman pretty well, had said it could wait till the morning.

'If she doesn't turn up I'll send someone over to have a word with her work colleagues. Who knows, she's probably off somewhere having a good time.'

'What about this stalker?' said Wesley.

'According to Darren, he's a photographer who put big ideas in her head and wouldn't leave her alone, but it's all a bit vague.'

'The mother might know more. We should have a word with her. And we can trace Leanne's mobile usage and see if she's used her credit or debit cards.'

'Hold on, Wes. Let's make sure she's missing first. I've known Hatman a lot longer than you have and he's always been inclined to panic.' He grinned, showing the gap between his front teeth he'd always claimed was lucky. 'If he's telling the truth about abandoning his life of crime, I reckon I know the reason why.'

'What is it?'

'He knocked an old lady over during his last job in Plymouth. She died a couple of weeks later in hospital.'

'I presume he was convicted?'

'Yeah. That was his last stretch inside. Nothing since.'

'Probably gave him a jolt.'

Gerry nodded.

'I'll go and speak to the mother if you like,' said Wesley.

'OK. But if her daughter's missing we've got to ask ourselves why the mum hasn't reported it herself. Maybe she knows something Darren doesn't.' He picked up a file off his desk. 'I've got a meeting with Aunty Noreen.' He rolled his eyes. 'Crime statistics.'

Wesley smiled to himself as he left the room. The boss always referred to Chief Superintendent Noreen Fitton as Aunty Noreen, as though he hoped the cosy domestic title would diminish her fearsome authority. Discussing dry crime statistics in her well-appointed office on the floor above was hardly Gerry's idea of bliss. In his opinion the fires of hell would be stoked with forms and paperwork.

As Wesley made his way back to his desk by the window, he heard DS Rachel Tracey calling his name. When he turned round he saw that she was standing up, waving a sheet of paper that he recognised as a Missing Persons Report.

'This report. Leanne Hatman. She's nineteen and not in any category that can be described as vulnerable. Why isn't the Missing Persons Unit dealing with it?'

'Because her father says she's got a stalker,' he replied, walking over to join her.

'That's not mentioned on the form.' She sounded annoyed about the omission.

Wesley frowned. 'Then it should be. The father spoke to the boss yesterday afternoon – they're old acquaintances . . . professionally speaking.'

'The dad's a cop?'

Wesley shook his head. 'Other side of the fence. Get-away driver – allegedly retired.'

He saw the disapproval on Rachel's pale face. Her fine blonde hair was tied back today but over the past weeks she'd been experimenting with various styles for her forth-coming wedding. There had been a time when he'd thought it might not go ahead; that her doubts about the wisdom of commitment would prevail. Now the wedding juggernaut seemed to be on track again.

'So we're following it up?'

'The boss reckons the father panics easily. Still, I'd like to pay her mother a visit and see what she has to say.'

A light of anticipation appeared in Rachel's eyes. 'Want me to come with you?'

'I was planning to take Trish. Leanne Hatman works at Eyecliffe Castle and lives in the staff quarters so it might be helpful if you went up there to speak to her colleagues. See if anyone has any suggestions about where she might be – or knows anything about this stalker her dad mentioned.'

'Fine,' she said, plucking her jacket from the back of her chair. 'I'll take Rob with me. He looks as if he could do with some fresh air.'

She nodded at a desk in the far corner of the room. A young man sat there typing something into the computer in front of him. He had a shock of fair hair and a look of frustrated boredom on his freckled face. Rachel took a step towards Wesley and whispered in his ear. 'He's like a caged animal when things are quiet. Always looking for things to do and making a nuisance of himself.'

'Think he's after your job?'

'No, I think he's after the boss's.'

'Nothing wrong with a bit of ambition.'

She didn't answer. Instead she clamped her mouth shut as though she could say more on the subject but thought it unwise.

As Rachel was preparing for her visit to Eyecliffe Castle to speak to the missing girl's colleagues, Wesley asked dark-haired, sensible DC Trish Walton to go with him to see

Leanne Hatman's mother. Trish seemed eager to get out of the office and escape her routine paperwork. Things had been quiet recently. Only a theft of farm machinery and a yacht reported missing from Tradmouth marina had clouded CID's horizon. However, all that would change once the holiday season began in earnest.

Marion Hatman, Trish discovered after a few phone calls, worked in a café in an upmarket part of Morbay but today was her day off. It promised to be a fine day, contrary to the weatherman's dire predictions Wesley had caught on breakfast TV before he'd left for work that morning, so he decided to take the car ferry over the River Trad. He loved the journey to the far bank of the river, chugging across the water, staring out at the yachts bobbing at anchor. During that all too brief crossing he always felt that he was in some liminal place between land and water where earthly problems melted away.

At first Trish sat silently in the passenger seat. Only when Wesley asked about Rachel's wedding arrangements did she become animated. She and Rachel shared a rented cottage just outside Tradmouth, not far from the farm where Rachel had grown up so, inevitably, she was the person Rachel tended to confide in. By the time they'd reached Morbay, Wesley had learned that the dress was purchased, the flowers ordered and the hymns chosen. Not once did she mention Rachel's fiancé, Nigel, almost as though the bridegroom was an afterthought, but she did chatter on about the difficulty of finding someone else to share the cottage once Rachel had moved out. When Wesley asked her about her own boyfriend, a dentist, her answer was evasive.

From Wesley's experience of working in the area, he

knew the genteel holiday resort of Morbay, ten miles from Tradmouth, concealed a dark underbelly beneath its smiling white villas and aspirational hotels. Away from the elegant seafront and its attractions stood the Winterham Estate, erected in the 1960s during the nadir of house building and shunned by anyone who could possibly afford to live elsewhere. There were areas of older housing too, converted into flats and bedsits: dusty streets of flaking stucco and overflowing wheelie bins in weed-filled front gardens. It was in one of these streets that Leanne Hatman's mother lived in a two-bedroom flat that occupied the ground floor of a large terraced house.

The house's sickly pink walls were stained with damp and moss and Wesley saw three unmatched cheap plastic doorbells beside the front door. The middle one dangled limply from the battered wood but fortunately the one with the name *Hatman* beneath it was still in place and working. When he pressed it, he heard a loud buzzing, as if a furious wasp was trapped in the hallway, and after half a minute the door opened to reveal a sharp-featured woman in a grey tracksuit. Her bottle-blonde hair was scraped back into an untidy knot and, as Wesley gazed upon her spreading waistline, he wondered why the most unfit people invariably chose to drape their bodies in sportswear. Perhaps they hoped that it would act like some magic spell and they'd wake up one morning with the physique of an Olympic athlete.

'Mrs Hatman?' he said, holding up his warrant card. 'May we come in?'

She led the way into a dingy hall. To the left of a flight of uncarpeted stairs a door stood open and Wesley and Trish followed the woman into a neat and airy room. Everything was spotless and the fireplace wall was covered in bright floral wallpaper. This was her space, her refuge from the troubles of the world – and she looked as if she'd had a few of them in her time.

'Is this about Darren?'

'We've spoken to your ex-husband,' Wesley said as he sat down, Trish taking her seat quietly in an armchair opposite. Her question had surprised him; he'd never before met the mother of a missing girl whose first thought wasn't for her child. Perhaps Gerry had been right after all.

Mrs Hatman looked exasperated. 'Look, as far as I know he's put the past behind him. And he's not my ex. We're still married ... officially. We're just separated.'

It was time to come to the point. 'Darren's reported your daughter, Leanne, missing.'

It was hard to read her expression but Wesley guessed she wasn't pleased. 'That's Darren all over. He still thinks she's a little girl.'

'So she's not missing?'

'Not as far as I know. I haven't heard from her for a couple of weeks and she did miss my birthday, which isn't like her at all, but ... '

'Do you know where she is?' Trish asked. 'We'd like to speak to her. Make sure she's OK.'

'She works at Eyecliffe Castle and lives in. Have you tried there?'

'One of our colleagues has gone there to follow up your husband's complaint. You're not worried?'

A shadow briefly passed across her face. 'She said she might have to go off to London at a moment's notice. She's had her portfolio done, you see. It's her big chance.'

'What is?'

'Modelling. She's been waiting to hear from one of the big agencies and if they've called to say they wanted her right away, she might not have had time to let me know.'

Wesley, seeing that her face had been transfigured with pride, couldn't help asking himself what sort of daughter would neglect to make a quick call to her mother to share her moment of triumph. It didn't add up and the only explanation that sprung to his mind was that there'd been bad feeling between them and Leanne had decided to punish her mother by ignoring her.

It was Trish who asked the next question. 'Did you and Leanne have a row?'

Mrs Hatman looked uneasy. 'Only the usual mother and daughter stuff. I nag her a bit about smoking. She said it helped her keep her weight down but it's bad for your health, isn't it. She said I was interfering with her life all the time. That's probably why she hasn't been in touch. She'll come round though. She always does.'

Wesley caught Trish's eye. It was beginning to look as if they were wasting their time, but he had a few more questions to ask.

'Your husband mentioned a stalker. A photographer.'

She shook her head in exasperation. 'That's all in Darren's head. The photographer who did her portfolio saw her in the street and followed her. She said she wasn't interested at first but he kept on texting her and then he turned up at the Castle. In the end I persuaded her to take him up on his offer. I told her it was the chance of a lifetime.' Her eyes were glowing at the thought of her daughter's burgeoning modelling career. 'She's a beautiful girl. Look.'

She bustled over to the mantelpiece and picked up a

silver-framed photograph of a stunning blonde with perfect, regular features. The face of an angel ... or, if you were feeling uncharitable, a Barbie doll. She handed it to Wesley proudly.

'Your husband brought in a photograph yesterday. She's very beautiful.'

Leanne was indeed beautiful; Wesley couldn't deny that. But he saw something else in that photograph kept in the place of honour like a holy icon. A spark of self-absorption, perhaps; a hardness and lack of empathy in the lovely eyes. Maybe there had been no falling out. Maybe Leanne was just the type who'd go off in search of riches without thinking to tell those who loved her where she was.

'I'd like to talk to this photographer, just to satisfy myself that she's safe. Do you have his contact details?'

She hesitated a few moments before struggling to her feet and disappearing into the next room.

'What do you think?' Trish whispered. 'False alarm?'

Before he could answer, Mrs Hatman returned with a business card which she handed to Wesley. 'There you are. Look, I don't want her to think I'm checking up on her. She hates me interfering.'

Wesley suddenly realised that the mother was afraid of her daughter; afraid of putting a foot wrong and causing her embarrassment. He felt sorry for the woman.

'Don't worry, Mrs Hatman. We'll be tactful,' he said before heading for the door.

Once outside the flat he looked at the small card in his hand. Barney Yelland. He'd never heard the name before, which was a good sign.

*

Even though Neil regretted that his break in Sicily was drawing to an end, he was looking forward to seeing Lucy again. He was even looking forward to getting back to the Devon rain and taking charge of the new dig.

At first he'd intended to spend that final evening packing. But it would have seemed churlish not to say goodbye properly to his fellow diggers from the University of Palermo, a friendly bunch who were always eager to practise their English on the willing visitors.

After he'd showered and changed, he made for the usual haunt: the trattoria with tables spilling out on to a narrow thoroughfare, as much a staircase as a street. The steepness of the place reminded Neil a little of Tradmouth – only Tradmouth rarely enjoyed the weather for alfresco dining.

They passed a convivial evening, consuming salad caprese, large juicy pizzas and several bottles of red wine. But by ten he was becoming increasingly aware that he needed to be at the airport early the next morning and he hadn't even packed.

During the evening he'd hardly given Barney Yelland a thought and nobody had mentioned him, even though he'd become a regular visitor to their excavation. Neil guessed he was spending his last night with the friend who was putting him up. Then he realised that he hadn't seen him since he'd set out for Naro and the strangely named House of Eyes, the place where superstitious locals feared to venture.

When the meal was over, nobody seemed to be in the mood to make a long night of it and they said their farewells with hugs, kisses, exchanges of email addresses and promises not to lose touch. Then Neil walked off into the night, making for the hotel with Theresa and a young man whose earnest, beautiful face wouldn't have looked out of place on a Roman mosaic. He could hear the distant buzz of motor scooters, as they strolled down a cramped street of old stone houses with rusted wrought-iron balconies at their upper windows. As they passed a small restaurant wafting out tempting odours of garlic and basil, Theresa broke the amicable silence.

'I wonder where your photographer friend's been for the last couple of days. I thought he might have joined us.' Neil had assumed that Theresa had taken no interest in Yelland but perhaps he'd been wrong.

'He said he was on my flight tomorrow so he probably decided to get an early night.'

'I liked him,' she said with a smile. 'Reserved but attractive. A man of mystery.'

The young man with them grinned. 'He'll be saying farewell to his lover tonight.'

'He's staying with a friend,' Neil said, amused that the young Italian was falling into the romantic stereotype of his nation.

They walked on a few yards and the young man came to a sudden halt. 'I saw him entering that house a few nights ago.' He pointed at the arched doorway of a tall ancient house, barely visible in the shadows. The ground-floor windows were shuttered but a window was lit on the first floor.

Neil couldn't resist having a quick peep at the illuminated name beneath the doorbell. It was an English one: Belamy.

But if Barney Yelland hadn't wanted to share the details of his personal life, it was none of his business.

Pam Peterson arrived home from work at four thirty. Her daughter, Amelia, attended the school where she taught so

23

they came home together to find her son Michael waiting for them, having trudged up the hill from the bus stop in the centre of town. He was at the grammar school now and, even in his first year, he relished his new-found independence and the anonymity of not being regarded as a teacher's son. A teacher and a policeman – hardly the sort of parents who endowed a boy rapidly approaching his teenage years with the necessary street cred to impress his mates.

Pam went upstairs to have a shower and get changed, relishing the luxury of having children old enough to be left unsupervised while their mother indulged in a bit of pampering. Wesley hadn't called to tell her he'd be late so, with any luck, he'd soon be home and they could enjoy a quiet evening in with a bottle of wine. Providing her mother didn't call with tales of some new calamity.

She undressed and climbed in the shower, shutting her eyes and letting the warm water flow over her body as she took deep breaths and smiled to herself. The citizens of South Devon had been surprisingly law-abiding in recent months so she'd seen more of her husband than usual. She tried to tell herself it would last but she'd never been a natural optimist.

Then, as the warm water cascaded down, her world suddenly changed. And half an hour later she was lying on the bed unable to move, paralysed with fear.

3

My cousin, Uriah, is two years my
junior and his mother, the widow of an
impecunious clergyman, was most
grateful when my father suggested that
he accompany me.

What can I say about Uriah? He is
tall with a pallid complexion which
matches ill his dark-blue eyes and the
black hair he inherited from his late
father. He is too thin and his face too
long to be thought handsome by the
ladies we encounter, and his manner
is taciturn. He has little conversation;
rather he misunderstands wit and jests
and would prefer to be alone than in
company. I do not find him an
agreeable companion and cannot help

but think that even Joules, with his genial nature, finds him difficult.

My cousin also interests himself in the macabre and his eyes shone with fascination at tales of cruelty in the arenas of Ancient Rome.

Wesley tried the mobile number on Yelland's business card several times but there was no reply. He walked into Gerry's office to share his concerns.

'I agree, Wes. It's worrying,' the DCI said with a frown. 'I've asked one of the DCs to get an address for him. Are Rach and Rob back from Eyecliffe Castle yet?'

'Not yet.'

But as soon as the words left his lips he saw Rachel arriving, a few paces behind DC Rob Carter who looked as though he was leading the way. Rob liked to give the illusion of being in charge and at times Wesley wondered how far the young man's ambition would take him – and who he'd be willing to trample on his way up to the chief constable's desk.

Rachel made her way over to join him.

'How did it go?' Wesley asked. Gerry was listening intently; in spite of his insistence that Hatman had been fussing about nothing, he seemed concerned.

'I spoke to Leanne's colleagues.'

'What did they say?'

Rachel considered her answer carefully. 'That she's got big ideas and she's set her heart on a modelling career.'

'Her and thousands of others.'

'Most of them assume she's gone off in search of fame

26

and fortune, although one person reckons she lives in cloud cuckoo land. Says she's gullible.'

'Who's that?'

Rachel took out her notebook. 'Mrs Mary Palmer, the mother of the present owner. Her late husband transformed the castle into a hotel in the nineteen seventies and I get the impression she has no intention of retiring.'

'Did you meet her son?'

'He's away at the moment. One of Leanne's colleagues at the spa, a Kirsty Paige, told us the photographer Leanne's dad accused of stalking her made her a portfolio of pictures which she's been sending round to modelling agencies.'

'This matches what her mother told us. Any of the agencies get back to her?'

'Nobody knows.'

'Did you take a look at Leanne's room?'

'All her things have gone so it looks like she's moved on.'

'She left without saying anything?'

Rachel nodded. 'I got the impression she wasn't particularly popular. She did a lot of boasting about her brilliant plans.' She glanced at Rob Carter. 'That never goes down well.'

'Anyone say anything about the photographer?'

'Kirsty Paige said he followed her in the street and kept texting her. Sounds like stalking to me.'

'The mother gave me his card. His name's Barney Yelland.'

'Is he known to us?'

Wesley shook his head.

'Can you contact all the London modelling agencies and see if they've heard of Leanne?'

27

'Right you are.'

'Did Leanne complain to her colleagues about this man stalking her?'

'On the contrary, she was excited about it ... flattered. She'd been going on about wanting to be a model for ages and nobody seems particularly surprised that she's quit work.'

'It still strikes me as strange that she took off without telling anyone.'

'You're right. If an agency's taken her on, you'd think she'd want to tell the world, wouldn't you. She didn't even hand in her notice.'

'Seems strange to me and all.' It was the first time Gerry had spoken. 'I want to see what this Yelland character has to say for himself. She's been reported missing so we'd be neglecting our duty if we don't get to the bottom of it.'

Wesley's eyes met Rachel's. They couldn't argue with the boss's logic.

It wasn't long before they had Barney Yelland's address in Neston. Wesley looked at his watch. Four thirty. If they went now, he could be home by six.

Rachel drove. She'd learned on her parents' farm when she was fifteen, taking her test soon after her seventeenth birthday, and she skilfully negotiated the twists and turns of the single track Devon lanes as only a native can. Those lanes had scared the life out of Wesley for years after he'd come from London to live there. At times they still did.

They made their way up the steep hill past the Naval College in third gear and took the Neston road. It was an A road but so narrow in places that two large vehicles had problems if they wanted to pass. As they drove Wesley gazed out of the window and once they'd passed the housing estate and the new superstore on the edge of town, he could see nothing but rolling countryside; green hilly fields folding into each other, edged by ancient hedgerows and copses of budding trees. He saw a solitary buzzard circling overhead in search of something to kill.

After negotiating miles of winding roads lined with fields and villages, they arrived in Neston. It was a pretty town, mainly Elizabethan, with a steep high street and a reputation for New Age inclinations. In Neston you were as likely to find a crystal healing shop as a butcher's.

Yelland's address turned out to be an Edwardian terraced house in a small street blocked at one end by the town's medieval wall. Wesley was surprised to see that the house was freshly painted and stood in a neat front garden. Somehow he'd expected something run-down like Mrs Hatman's flat.

There was only one doorbell, brass and solid-looking. He pressed it and waited.

The door was opened by a middle-aged woman with cropped fair hair and a long ethnic skirt. She smelled of patchouli and wore no make-up; only the network of lines around her eyes and a wrinkled neck betrayed her age. She looked Wesley up and down and he guessed she suspected their smart appearance meant they were selling something. It was probably only the colour of his skin that stopped her shutting the door in his face immediately; she looked the kind who feared being tainted with any whiff of racism. When he held out his warrant card and introduced himself and Rachel, a wary expression appeared on her face.

'How can I help you?' she said stiffly.

'Does a Barney Yelland live at this address?'

She frowned. 'Yes. But he's away at the moment.'

'Where is he?'

'Italy.' Her eyes widened in sudden concern. 'Has something happened to him?'

'Not as far as we know. May we come in?' Wesley asked.

The woman wavered for a moment then stood aside to let them enter. She introduced herself as Clare Woolmer and led them into a sitting room where Wesley noted the stripped wood floor, the original fireplace and the mellow antique furniture. Pam would love this house, he thought. Their own was built in the seventies but one day he suspected she would aspire to something more characterful.

'When did he go to Italy?' Rachel asked after they'd been invited to sit.

'Monday the twentieth of April – I remember because it was my birthday.'

'When's he due back?'

'I'm not sure. Why?'

'Have you heard from him since he left?

'No.'

'Is he there on holiday?'

'No. He's a photographer and he's working on a book,' she said with a hint of pride. 'Someone else is writing the text and Barney's providing the pictures. He's extremely talented.'

'Sounds fascinating,' said Wesley, hoping the woman would be more ready to open up if he took an interest.

His tactic paid off. Her eyes suddenly lit up with enthusiasm. 'It is. The book's about the Grand Tour. Wealthy young men used to travel round Europe to complete their education in the eighteenth and nineteenth centuries, you see. A sort of gap year, I suppose.'

Wesley smiled and nodded politely. He knew what the Grand Tour was but, in his experience, people like to show off their knowledge. And, after her initial wariness, she was beginning to relax.

'He's photographing the locations they travelled to as they are today, contrasting them with contemporary depictions. It's a long-term project,' she continued. 'Over the past eighteen months or so he's been over to Europe several times to cover the route. He would have liked to spend the year abroad and do the whole tour in one go but they've only given him a paltry advance for all that work and he has to earn a living as well so he's doing it bit by bit. This time he's concentrating on southern Italy and Sicily.'

This woman obviously took a keen interest in Yelland's affairs and Wesley waited patiently until she had finished speaking before he started asking questions, even though he sensed Rachel was growing impatient.

'Are you Mr Yelland's partner or . . . ?' As he was afraid of causing offence, the question was tentative.

'He's my lodger.'

Wesley thought he could detect a note of disappointment behind the statement.

'He has use of the upstairs floor,' she continued. 'Derek, my late partner, had a studio up there so it was ideal for Barney. The arrangement suits us both – and the rent comes in handy too,' Clare added with a sad smile, as though she regretted the necessity for money.

'Derek was a photographer too?'

'Yes. He worked in war zones and he was killed doing the

31

work he loved. It's good to know someone else is using his studio.' Her eyes began to glaze with tears. 'Sometimes when I hear Barney's footsteps up there I think ...' She took a deep breath. 'You haven't told me why you're asking these questions. I can't believe Barney's done anything wrong.'

Wesley chose not to enlighten her for the moment and left an appropriate interval before asking his next question.

'Have you ever seen Mr Yelland with any women?'

'He does portrait work. I've have seen girls go up to his studio from time to time but ...'

'Glamour stuff?' Rachel asked, an edge of disapproval in her voice.

Clare looked affronted. 'Of course not.'

Wesley placed a photograph of Leanne Hatman on the coffee table in front of Clare. 'Do you recognise this woman?'

'She's a model. Barney's been working on her portfolio. He has to take on things like that to fund his more serious work.'

'Things like that?'

'Portraits, like I said.'

'Families? Children? Couples? Pets? Do they come here?' As far as Wesley was aware, portrait photography wasn't normally confined to young, attractive females.

'Not usually. He does commercial work for companies too.'

'Weddings?'

'No. Never.'

'So it's mostly girls?

'Well yes.' She seemed a touch uneasy now.

'How many?'

'Four or five since he's been here.'

'This one's name is Leanne. Did you ever speak to her?'

'We were never introduced.'

'What about the other girls?'

'They were all blonde ... all the same type. I doubt if I'd recognise them if I saw them again. They just disappeared up the stairs; we never spoke.'

'Have you seen Mr Yelland's work?'

The wariness suddenly vanished. 'His landscapes are absolutely stunning. He's exhibited his work very successfully. I've seen some of the pictures he's already taken for the Grand Tour book and they're wonderful, really groundbreaking.'

Wesley suspected the fulsome praise was as much for the man as his work.

'Would you be surprised if I were to tell you that Leanne's father claims Barney's been stalking her?'

He watched Clare's face carefully as she contemplated the question in silence. 'That's ridiculous, Inspector, although I can understand how his intentions could be misinterpreted. He's a perfectionist, you see. That's probably why he's such a great artist. But he would never harm anyone.'

Wesley wondered whether she was prepared to ignore the obvious in order to be close to Barney Yelland. The fact that he shared her late partner's career probably made her feel there was a link to her dead lover, and there was also the possibility that she was in love with Yelland herself. His years in the police service had taught him that people's motives are often hard to fathom.

It was time to ask the question that was uppermost in his mind. 'Would you mind if we take a look upstairs?' It seemed that Yelland didn't technically have a separate flat so if she invited them to look round, it might save them the trouble of obtaining a warrant. He looked at her expectantly as he waited for an answer.

'I don't see why not. As long as you don't interfere with his things.' A worried look passed across her face. 'I'd like to come up with you.'

'Of course.'

Wesley let her lead the way. When they reached the landing only the bathroom door stood open, suggesting it was shared. There were no locks on the other doors and Clare opened them one by one. The spacious room at the front of the house was done out as a studio. Landscape photographs hung on the walls. Clare had been right: they were stunning. The place was cluttered with the paraphernalia of a professional photographer and Wesley could see nothing amiss.

He opened drawers and found some flattering portraits of young women, all beautiful, all with long blonde hair and slender bodies. Some were in a state of undress but there was nothing that could be considered pornographic. Rather they reminded Wesley of classical sculptures, or the slightly racy Victorian paintings of Alma-Tadema. Leanne Hatman featured in a number of the pictures, mostly dressed but in some half-naked, pouting and pointing her pert breasts at the camera. He wondered what her father would think if he saw them.

The second room was a living room, cramped but neat and surprisingly impersonal. When Wesley opened the third door he saw it was the bedroom. He wasn't sure what he expected to find. A red satin bedspread perhaps, or erotic paintings lining the walls? But there was no sign of decadence here. The double bed was neatly made, a pair of floral curtains hung at the windows and the wooden furniture had a plain, Scandinavian elegance.

He stood by the bed looking around. Then his eyes were drawn to a small patch on the brown cotton duvet, a darker brown that had stiffened the soft fabric, and he bent down to examine it.

'What is it?' Clare's question sounded anxious.

'Not sure. But please don't touch this room. I want to send someone over to take a closer look if that's OK.'

'In that case, you'll need a warrant,' she said with a hint of defiance.

Wesley tried his best to hide his disappointment. 'Very well, Ms Woolmer, that's up to you. When did you last see Leanne Hatman?'

'Hatman?' She repeated the name in a whisper as if it meant something to her, and the association wasn't a happy one.

'Is the name familiar?'

'No. He just said her name was Leanne.'

'You haven't answered my question. When was she last here?'

'It must have been a few days before he left for Italy on the twentieth. But I can't remember exactly when.'

'You didn't hear anything suspicious. An argument or . . . '

Her face suddenly clouded with worry. 'No. Nothing like that.'

'Would you say their relationship was volatile?'

'Not as far as I know. Why? Has something happened to her?'

Wesley didn't answer the question. 'Please call me the moment Mr Yelland gets back.'

He handed her his card and as she took it he saw that her fingers were shaking.

'What did you find?' Rachel whispered as they made for the car.

'I'm not sure. But there's a stain on Yelland's duvet. Might be blood.'

When Wesley returned to the office he found one of the DCs busy contacting modelling agencies in London. So far he'd had no luck tracing Leanne Hatman but Wesley told him to keep trying.

He walked into Gerry's room, hands in pockets. He'd feel a lot happier once they'd traced Leanne and made sure she was safe. It could be a big nasty world out there for an aspiring model.

Gerry looked up. 'Any luck at Yelland's place?'

'He's in Italy – left on twentieth of April. I thought we might find he's some seedy conman, taking naughty photos of gullible girls for his own satisfaction, but it turns out he's the real deal. He's exhibited his work and he's working on a new book about the Grand Tour.'

'What kind of grand tour?'

'You know, when young aristos swanned off to Europe and lived the high life while pretending to get a cultural education.'

'So he's kosher?'

'Looks like it. But that doesn't mean we don't need to speak to him. We found pictures of Leanne Hatman and some other girls. The landlady claims he does portrait work to bolster his income but *all* the pictures were of girls – same physical type as Leanne.'

'Weird?'

'Possibly. But none of the pictures were pornographic if that's what you're getting at.'

'Any luck with Leanne's mobile?'

'Switched off – which is worrying. No answer from Yelland's either. There is one thing ...'

'What?'

'There was a stain in Yelland's room that could be blood. If Leanne hasn't made contact by tomorrow I think we should get a warrant and make a thorough search.'

There was nothing they could do till the following day so Wesley made his way home on foot. He preferred to walk if possible; the demands of the job left him little time for gyms and fitness regimes and the hilly streets of Tradmouth provided a great cardiovascular workout. These days he could climb the steep hill to his house above the town without breaking a sweat.

When he opened his front door he was greeted by Amelia, who gave him a hug and asked him for help with her history project. Her affectionate greeting gave him a warm glow of happiness – until she added that she would have asked Uncle Neil only he was on holiday. His old university friend, Neil, was a frequent visitor to the house and, being an archaeologist, the children regarded him as an Indiana Jones figure, however much Neil tried to convince them otherwise. The lure of Hollywood heroes beat dirt and the back-breaking reality of excavation every time.

The thought that his children had become so used to his absence that they no longer thought of him as available made him uncomfortable. During his childhood his own father, a distinguished surgeon, had prioritised work and he remembered how he'd hated his long absences. Now history seemed to be repeating itself.

He found Michael upstairs in his room wrestling with a maths problem but there was no sign of Pam. When Wesley asked where she was, Michael said he thought she was in the kitchen.

Wesley was puzzled that he couldn't find her and when he went into their bedroom he was surprised to see her sitting on the stool by the dressing table, staring into the mirror. She turned round as he came in but there was no smile of greeting.

'You OK?'

'Why shouldn't I be?'

He thought she sounded distant, as if her thoughts were somewhere else.

'Want me to make the supper?' He suspected she'd had a heavy day in the classroom with the prospect of hours of marking and preparation ahead. The least he could do was take some of the domestic burden off her shoulders.

'Thanks,' she said softly.

He was about to leave the room but instinct drew him back. 'Is something the matter? Is it one of the kids?'

She stood up and fixed a smile to her face. 'Everything's fine. I had a text from Neil earlier. He's flying back tomorrow and he's asked if it's OK for him and Lucy to come round in the evening.'

'Photo time?'

'I guess so.'

'I've always fancied Sicily myself. Maybe one day when the kids are a bit older ...'

Pam turned her head away as though he'd said something hurtful. 'Maybe.'

*

The long queue for airport security was moving at the pace of an arthritic snail and Neil shuffled along, resting his rucksack on the ground and kicking it forward whenever the line began to move. In a few hours he'd be back in the UK and in a week's time the whole trip would seem like a dream.

He closed his eyes, running through the events of the past couple of weeks in his mind. The small statue of Aphrodite he'd found. His visits to the Greek theatre at Taormina and the Roman mosaics at Piazza Armerina. He felt like a child who'd been given the freedom of a sweet shop, and there was a lot he hadn't had time to see – the mysterious House of Eyes that Barney Yelland intended to visit, for instance. He hadn't seen Yelland since but, since they were booked on the same flight, he might get a chance to see the pictures he'd taken of the place.

The heat was becoming unbearable and as Neil listened to the crescendo of Italian voices he closed his eyes, wishing he could turn back time to the beginning of his trip. And yet he experienced a small thrill of excitement at the thought of going home. Back down to earth. But it was his earth. His patch.

He looked behind him, searching the queue for familiar faces. He could see the students who'd come with him standing in a huddle, looking as weary as he felt. But there was no sign of Barney Yelland.

And when the plane took off they were a passenger short.

When Darren Hatman had bought the barn from Eyecliffe Castle's present owner, David Palmer, with the intention of converting it into two desirable dwellings, he'd hoped to see more of Leanne. She was working at the castle's spa so the prospect of cosy father–daughter lunches was hardly an unrealistic fantasy. Or maybe it was. He and Leanne had never been close and since the split she'd always taken her mother's side.

Not that she treated Marion much better. These days she kept her distance from both her parents, which hurt Darren more than he'd admit. After the Plymouth post office job, he'd worked hard to build up his business so he'd have something to offer his little girl; something to prove to her that the mistakes he'd made in life belonged to the past. Now he was a builder and he was getting a lot of work locally. He even had two lads working for him now which meant he was an employer: a man of standing. And this barn conversion, in an ideal location halfway between the village of Turling Fitwell and the luxurious facilities of the Eyecliffe Castle Country Hotel and Spa, was the best job so far. Yet his hopes of playing happy families seemed to be coming to nothing.

But even though his daughter was missing he still had a living to make and he'd just thought of something that could bring easy money; a bonus while his men did the preparatory work on the barn nearby. The Dower House stood three hundred yards away, separated from the barn by an area of thick woodland. It was convenient and doing a bit of business might take his mind off Leanne's disappearance, which was buzzing away at the back of his mind like a troublesome fly, stopping him sleeping at night.

The Dower House stood in Eyecliffe Castle's extensive grounds and at one time widows of the lord of the manor were sent to live there to make room for their sons or other heirs. It had always been a place of loss; a place where the old waited for death.

The house was mostly Elizabethan with eighteenth-century additions; considerably smaller than the castle and a lot more comfortable. The black-clad relics of old probably moved there with some relief at no longer having to endure the discomforts of the huge, draughty castle at the end of the drive.

He knocked on the door again. He'd seen the woman on a few occasions. She was elderly with a regal bearing and snow-white hair tied in a neat bun, and she was usually accompanied by an aging black Labrador. He didn't know her name but he was good with old ladies. He knew how to turn on the charm, play the cheeky chappy and make them laugh. Or assume the role of the thoughtful, protective surrogate son issuing dire warnings against the cowboys of the business. Once he'd assessed the right approach, he'd soon win her round.

He knocked a third time and when there was still no answer he pushed one of his leaflets through the door, hoping she might get in touch with him and save him the trouble of the hard sell. He began to walk away. Then he changed his mind: if the house was empty it would do no harm to have a look round the back in the hope that he'd be able to point out some jobs that needed doing when he saw her – tactfully, of course. And then, once that contact was made, he might be able to get down to real business. Was she interested in selling the Dower House? It was far too big for one person, a burden, and she might be happier in a nice little retirement flat. Then he'd tell her he was willing to take it off her hands; give her a good deal which would enable her to buy somewhere more comfortable.

He walked along the side of the house, making plans in his head even though his worries about Leanne kept intruding, and looked in the windows, shielding his eyes, to keep the light from reflecting off the dusty glass. The interior was old-fashioned: an old person's house filled with chintz, dark wood and threadbare Turkish rugs. The furniture looked dusty and there were no fresh flowers. She wasn't much of a housekeeper.

He made his way past the back door and peered into another room, a sort of study dominated by a large, heavy desk. Then he saw something that made him catch his breath. A picture hung on the far wall, a dark oil painting of a man who was kneeling in a shaft of light that illuminated every sinew, every line of suffering etched on his long, sensitive face. His head was bowed in submission and around him were eyes. Disembodied eyes, watching, enjoying his pain.

It was the most horrible thing Darren Hatman had ever seen but he felt compelled to stare at it in fascination. Then he saw a movement; the door to the room was opening slowly. He ducked down and once he was out of sight of the window he tiptoed away, hoping he hadn't been observed.

4

We set off in daylight for Pompeii and
as we travelled I saw villages, farms
and vineyards ruined in the late
eruption of Mount Vesuvius and yet all
around nature at her most luxuriant
sprouted from the ashes.

Joules was in a state of such
excitement. He had heard much of the
ancient buried city and he had longed
for many years to see its wonders for
himself. He chattered on about the
glories of the Roman Empire while my
cousin Uriah maintained a sullen
silence.

I was somewhat surprised at my
cousin's reticence for I know him to be
an eager devourer of facts. Before we
embarked on our travels he spent much

43

time in my father's library scouring the volumes concerning the history of this region and yet the streets and buildings of Pompeii and Herculaneum appeared to leave him quite unmoved. It was only when he came across some remains of the unfortunate inhabitants, interrupted in their daily tasks by the call of death, that he displayed a spark of interest.

Although the staff at Eyecliffe Castle Country Hotel and Spa had been spoken to, Wesley thought it was worth having another word with those colleagues who'd worked closely with Leanne Hatman. He also wanted to see her room for himself.

As he drove towards the castle, he was surprised to see a van bearing the words *D Hatman, Builder*, parked at the side of the winding drive, not far from the entrance gates.

'What's he doing here?' said Gerry.

Wesley slowed the car. 'He might have decided to talk to Leanne's workmates himself. Maybe we should have a tactful word.'

Gerry made a noise of agreement, somewhere between a hum and a grunt.

But at that moment Hatman emerged from the trees at the side of the drive. Wesley cut the engine and when Hatman spotted them, a spark of hope appeared in his eyes.

'Mr Heffernan. Is there any news of my Leanne?' he said as Gerry got out of the car.

'Not yet. But they say no news is good news, don't they.'

Wesley wasn't sure whether the old cliché would offer the worried father much comfort but he saw Darren nod.

'We're going to speak to Leanne's colleagues,' said Wesley once he'd joined Gerry.

'So you're taking it seriously?'

'We take every report seriously.'

'I went to see her boss, Mr Palmer, yesterday. He said because Leanne went off without telling anyone, she was in breach of contract. I told him she wouldn't do something like that.'

'We'd appreciate it if you left things to us in future,' Wesley said. There was a note of sympathy in his voice. He could understand why the man wanted to do something.

'Nice van, Darren,' Gerry said, nodding towards the vehicle.

'Yeah. I'm converting an old barn into two dwellings – bought it from Palmer. Got a good deal.' He looked Gerry in the eye. 'See, Mr Heffernan, I'm a businessman now. Turned my life around.' There was no pride in his words. In fact Wesley detected a note of sadness behind the statement.

Gerry gave him a sceptical smile and got back into the car. Wesley was careful to thank Hatman for his help before joining him.

'That warrant to search Yelland's rooms should come through today,' he said. 'I'd like that stain tested. It looked like blood to me.'

'You're thinking the worst?'

'You know me, Gerry. Ever the pessimist.'

When they reached the castle Wesley parked in front of the building. There was a sign directing drivers to a car park round the side but Gerry told him to ignore it. They were there on police business.

Once he'd locked the car, Wesley stood for a while, staring at the great stone edifice, shielding his eyes from the morning sun. There was a medieval gatehouse, its two tall towers flanking an archway. Each tower had a pair of tiny windows to the first floor and arrow slits to drive off aggressors. A curtain wall ran from each side of the gatehouse, culminating on the right-hand side in a round tower. The other side was joined to a tall square building constructed of identical stone but clearly much later in date.

As he followed Gerry through the gatehouse he looked upwards and saw a groove in the archway between the towers, suggesting it had held a portcullis in more violent times. And he spotted a space where boiling liquid and missiles could be poured down on the enemy – a murder hole.

They emerged into a cobbled courtyard surrounded on three sides by an impressive stone mansion which Wesley guessed dated from the late sixteenth century, a period of Elizabethan confidence. Whoever had owned the castle back then had swept away the medieval accommodation and replaced it with the latest in status symbols, like a premiership footballer demolishing a house in a wealthy suburb and building a swish mansion on the site. To the left and the rear of the courtyard, the grand house boasted sparkling leaded windows but the wing on the right-hand side was a roofless shell and the blackened stones still bore signs of the fire that had destroyed it; the glassless stone window frames reminded Wesley of empty, staring eye sockets in a skull.

'Pity they didn't rebuild that bit,' said Gerry.

'It probably burned down during a lean period and they ran out of cash,' said Wesley. 'Aristocratic families frequently fell on hard times.'

They followed the signs to reception where a huge oak door stood open. Behind it a modern glass door opened for them automatically with a discreet hiss.

The young man behind the reception desk looked them up and down, making a swift assessment. When they produced their warrant cards, he showed no surprise and introduced himself as Sean. He was blond with an exaggerated quiff and a jacket that looked too tight. Wesley recognised a fashion victim when he saw one.

They asked him if he knew Leanne Hatman and he nodded.

'I don't know her well. I don't live in, you see.' He leaned forward as if he was about to share a confidence. 'A couple of your friends have already been here asking questions,' he said in a hushed voice, even though there was nobody there to overhear. 'I told them I hadn't seen her for a while – I presumed she was on holiday or something.'

'Is there anyone we should be talking to? Anyone she was particularly close to?'

He lowered his voice still further. 'Her and Kirsty work pretty closely together in the spa. She's in there now if you want a word.' He consulted a ledger. 'She's got a treatment booked at the moment but she should be free in ten minutes if you want to wait. Fancy a coffee? Or tea? Fruit tea?'

Gerry looked a little uneasy when Wesley said thanks, a coffee would be great. After a few seconds' delay, Gerry agreed gruffly to 'tea – strong – milk, one sugar.'

'What kind of treatment does he mean?' he asked Wesley when the young man had disappeared to order the drinks.

'It'll be massages, facials, body wraps, that sort of thing.' There were times when Wesley felt he was the worldlier half of the partnership and this was one of them. He sank into one of the squishy leather armchairs at the side of the entrance and Gerry did likewise.

'How do you know?'

'Pam's been to spas a few times with her friends.' He grinned. 'Pampering, it's called. I heard Rachel and Trish talking about coming here before the wedding.'

'It's a woman thing, then?'

Before Wesley could conjure an answer, Sean returned with their drinks. He seemed eager to please and Wesley wondered why this made him suspicious. Sometimes he thought he'd been a policeman too long.

The chairs were so comfortable and the heating so soporific that Wesley was glad of the coffee to keep him awake. After ten minutes, Sean picked up the phone on the desk and made a call, keeping his voice low and discreet.

'Kirsty's free now if you want to go through,' he said. 'Down the corridor to your left and you'll see the treatment suite. Just ask for Kirsty.'

Wesley stood up but Gerry was having difficulty raising himself from the chair's embrace. Wesley helped him up, hoping he hadn't been seen. It would hardly be a good advert for the police force if one of their senior detectives needed help getting out of a comfortable chair. And since the shooting the year before, Gerry had been sensitive about proving his physical fitness.

'Have a nice day,' Sean called after them as they disappeared down the corridor.

'No answer to that,' Gerry muttered.

The treatment suite was all glass and chrome; Wesley wondered what the original owners of the castle would have made of it. Another automatic glass door swished open to admit them and Gerry looked uncomfortable as they stepped into a world of perfumes and fluffy towels.

They asked the thin girl on the reception desk for Kirsty and she led them to a room that resembled the surgery of an upmarket physiotherapist. A pretty dark-haired girl in a pristine black uniform was rubbing lotion into her hands and she looked up as they entered, a look of uncertainty on her delicate, almost feline face.

'Kirsty?' said Wesley, presenting his ID.

'Yes.' She sounded nervous. But then many people are when the police come calling.

'We're investigating the disappearance of Leanne Hatman.'

'I've already spoken to the police. I told them everything I know.'

'I realise that but we were hoping you might have remembered something else. Leanne's a friend of yours, I believe.'

'Er ... yes. Look, I told the others, she hasn't disappeared. She's in London. She's signed up with a modelling agency. Her dad came round here and I told him just because she hasn't been in touch with him or her mum, it doesn't mean something's happened to her. Between you and me, she couldn't stand her dad and she said her mum was an idle bitch. If you ask me, she couldn't be bothered to tell them she was going.'

'Don't you think it's strange that she didn't give in her notice here?'

Kirsty shrugged. 'She left in a hurry. She said she was expecting to hear from a modelling agency in London any time. Then the next day she'd gone.'

'So she'd heard from an agency' said Gerry.

Kirsty looked at him with curiosity, as though he was some strange prehistoric creature that had suddenly turned up on her treatment couch. 'Suppose she must have done.'

'When did you last see her?'

'I've already told those other policemen.'

'Indulge us,' said Gerry.

'It was a couple of weeks ago ... Sunday evening. I remember because she didn't turn up for work on the Monday morning and she had clients booked.'

'What date was this?'

Kirsty walked over to a calendar on the wall. It bore a photograph of a blonde model with unnaturally perfect skin and the logo of a well-known make-up brand. She peered at the dates as if she was trying to work something out. 'Must have been the nineteenth of April.'

Wesley caught Gerry's eye. According to Clare Woolmer, Barney Yelland had left for Italy on the twentieth.

'What time did you last see her?'

'I went to my room after my shift – must have been around six. Her room's on the same corridor and she poked her head round my door and said ... ' She frowned, trying to remember the exact words. 'It was something like, "I can't wait to get out of this place. The sooner I go to London, the better." I asked her if she'd heard from an agency and she just smiled and said, "Might have done." Then she said she was going out. I asked her where but she didn't say. I never saw her again after that and I don't think anyone else did either.'

'Did she have a car?'

'No. She must have got a taxi – or a lift.'

'Who from?'

Kirsty shrugged. 'That photographer she's always going

50

on about? I don't know. David wasn't pleased that she hadn't handed in her notice.'

'David?'

'David Palmer. She fancied him ... kept flirting with him.'

'Really?' This was news.

'But she isn't his type. Anyway, Mrs P sacked the last girl who flung herself at him. Mind you, that girl did make a complaint ... said David couldn't keep his hands to himself – which was all lies, by the way. Mrs P knew she was making it up and gave her the push.'

'Mrs P?' Wesley asked when he could get a word in.

'David's mum. Nothing goes on here without her say-so.'

Wesley remembered it was Mary Palmer who'd described Leanne as gullible and he made a mental note to speak to her later. In the meantime, he had more questions to ask.

'Could Leanne and David Palmer have been having an affair?'

She shook her head. 'No way.' She sounded almost indignant at the suggestion. 'Like I said, she wasn't his type at all. Anyway, she had a boyfriend until that photographer came along.'

'Ever meet the boyfriend?'

'Never. For all I know, she might have been making him up.'

'How long have you worked here?' Gerry asked.

'Must be two years now.'

'And Leanne?'

'About eight months. She always made it clear this was a stepping stone.' Kirsty didn't meet his eyes and he sensed that she too had ambitions.

51

'What was she wearing when you last saw her?'

'Her uniform, same as mine. But if she went out, she would have got changed, wouldn't she.'

'Where were you that evening?'

'Once I'd eaten I watched TV in the staff lounge. There were only a few of us 'cause a lot of the staff who live in work in the restaurant. I went to bed around ten thirty.'

'Did Leanne ever use the lounge?'

'Not usually. She kept herself to herself.'

'Thought she was a cut above?' Gerry suggested.

The answer was a noncommittal shrug.

'And you're sure you didn't see Leanne when you went to bed or the next morning?'

Kirsty shook her head. 'I told you, I never saw her; never heard her. She probably went off while I was watching TV.'

'Is there CCTV around the castle?'

'Should be but it doesn't work. David said he'd call someone in but he hasn't got round to it.'

Wesley saw Gerry roll his eyes; he'd never had a high opinion of technology.

'You say she talked about Barney Yelland, the photographer?'

'Talked about him? I got sick of hearing about him and her bloody portfolio. He saw her in the street and followed her. You hear of models being discovered like that, don't you? He kept texting her and turning up here until she agreed to model for him.'

'Sounds like stalking to me,' said Gerry with disapproval.

'Oh no, it wasn't like that. She thought the sun shone out of his backside.'

'Did you ever meet him?'

She shook her head and Wesley thought she looked disappointed about the omission.

'Ever thought of taking up modelling yourself?' Gerry asked before Wesley could get the question out. Both men had noticed an undercurrent of envy. Leanne had made the big time while Kirsty, undoubtedly pretty but lacking Leanne's stunning looks, had more years to serve under the watchful eye of David Palmer's mother.

'I've heard it's quite boring really,' she said unconvincingly, studying her scarlet fingernails.

Wesley noticed a couple of her fingers were stained yellow with nicotine and he'd smelt a faint whiff of cigarette smoke. 'So you didn't envy Leanne?'

She shrugged. 'Why should I? I like my job here. Meet a lot of people – celebrities sometimes. Had a woman off *EastEnders* the other day: she booked in for the week and wanted treatments every day. And a man who'd had a part in the latest James Bond film stayed here last year. I did a hot stones massage for him.'

'Very nice,' said Gerry with mild puzzlement.

She looked Gerry in the eye. 'You look as if you're full of tension. You'd benefit from a massage.'

'Sure I would, love, but time's short. We'd like to see Leanne's room. Who do I ask?'

'Mrs P's got a pass key.'

'I understand Leanne took all her things.'

'Her door's been locked since she went so I wouldn't know.' She looked at her watch. 'Sorry, I've got a client in ten minutes. Is that all?'

Wesley knew that Gerry would have liked to say it wasn't; that they were the ones who decided when an interview was at an end. But the truth was that they had no real reason to detain Kirsty any longer. And Wesley was impatient to see Leanne's room for himself.

With Sean's help they located Mrs Palmer's office. It was oak-panelled and had the reassuringly solid look of an old-fashioned boardroom. She stood up when they entered and put out her hand, like the headmistress of an exclusive school greeting prospective parents. An imposing woman with a straight back and an immaculate helmet of blonde hair, she wore a well-cut blue suit and exuded an air of authority. This was her realm. Wesley guessed she was in her late seventies, although she might have been younger. A grey pallor was visible behind the face powder which had collected in the wrinkles around her mouth and eyes.

'I take it Leanne Hatman hasn't turned up yet,' she began. 'I've already spoken to your colleagues and I'm afraid I have nothing further to add.'

'I appreciate that,' said Wesley. 'However, we'd like to take a look at Leanne's room. I believe it's locked.'

As she resumed her seat Wesley thought she looked tired; weary about the whole business, perhaps. 'I'd be grateful if you could hurry things along.' She took a deep breath. 'All our staff accommodation will soon be needed with the summer season coming up. And, who knows, Miss Hatman might be back begging my son for her old job back when this modelling job of hers falls through.'

'You think it won't work out?'

The woman sighed. 'I've seen it before, Inspector. Silly girls taken in by men full of big talk and fancy promises. They generally come back sooner or later.'

'I understand you wouldn't allow her father to look at her room,' said Gerry.

'He had no identification. He could have been anyone

and I wasn't going to let a stranger wander about the staff quarters when there was nobody available to supervise. I'm sure you'll agree that you can't be too careful nowadays.'

Mrs Palmer took a bunch of keys from the top drawer of her desk and signalled them to follow her. As they walked with her through the hotel Wesley noticed that her eyes missed nothing. Staff she passed wished her good morning politely but there were no smiles.

Wesley had never been inside the hotel before and he couldn't help being impressed. The walls were stone, the carpets red and thick and the bedroom doors arched, gothic oak. The place oozed luxury and, from a brochure Pam had brought home from her day at the spa, he knew it was expensive.

They climbed a series of wide carpeted staircases until they reached what Wesley assumed was the top floor. Here Mrs Palmer pushed at an oak door which opened to reveal another flight of stairs. But these were bare stone and narrow: the servants' quarters. She grabbed the handrail and climbed more slowly, her mouth set in a determined line. The effort caused her pain but she wasn't going to show it.

The corridor at the top of the stairs here was half the width of its downstairs counterparts and the plain doors were painted a uniform white. When they reached the end of the passage Mrs Palmer flourished her keys and opened one of the doors, standing aside to allow the policemen to enter. Wesley flung open the room's thin curtains, dispelling the gloom. It was a small room with a single bed, and modern, chipboard furniture. Leanne's work uniform was hanging in the wardrobe but, apart from that, the rest of her clothes had gone.

Wesley turned to Mrs Palmer. 'You've been in here since she left?'

'I had a quick look when I was told she hadn't turned up for her shift then I locked it up. Why?'

'I take it she had a suitcase.'

'I believe so. One of her neighbours said it was a pink floral one. But, as you can see, it's not here.'

Wesley examined the shelves in the wardrobe while Gerry attended to the drawers. But all they found were some old glossy magazines in the bedside cabinet.

Wesley turned to Mrs Palmer, who was hovering in the doorway as if she was anxious to make her escape. 'Who else has access to this room?'

'Nobody. All the rooms have Yale locks so when the door's shut, you need a key to open it. The occupant has one key and I have the other. I promise you that nobody apart from your colleague has been in here since I first looked inside.'

'Did Leanne leave her key?'

'No. She probably forgot.' She sounded a little annoyed.

'Is your son about?'

'David's at an hoteliers' conference in Brighton and he won't be back for a couple of days. I can assure you he knows nothing of Leanne's whereabouts. Their paths rarely crossed.'

She seemed a little too eager to make the point which made Wesley keen to speak to the man if Leanne didn't turn up in the meantime.

There was one place they hadn't looked. Wesley felt underneath the pillow and his gloved hand came into contact with something hard. He drew it out carefully and saw that it was a hardback book, A4 size, with a dramatic monochrome image of a bleak landscape on the cover. There was a towering rock formation to the right of the picture and a network of dry stone walls in the foreground, creating a perfectly composed picture Wesley recognised as Dartmoor. The title on the front was *Devon Landscapes* and the name of the photographer was Barney Yelland.

They returned to the station to find that the DC who'd been contacting the London modelling agencies had spoken to several who'd received Leanne Hatman's portfolio, although none had summoned her to the capital. And as Leanne's phone was still switched off and no taxi firms had a record of picking her up from the castle on the night she vanished, Wesley thought it was worth going ahead with the search of Barney Yelland's accommodation.

When he arrived at Clare Woolmer's house armed with a warrant and a search team she stood aside meekly to let them in. She appeared to take the intrusion with good grace but he could see worry in her eyes, as if the reality of the situation had finally hit her. A girl was missing and so was the man who'd promised her a glamorous modelling career. Until they knew Leanne was safe, they had to follow every possible lead.

Gerry had returned to the station to co-ordinate things. Wesley knew he'd rather be there in the middle of the action but however much Gerry pretended that he hadn't been affected by the injury he'd sustained the previous year, Wesley saw through the act. It had been a reminder of mortality – a brief glimpse of the Grim Reaper's scythe. He only hoped it wouldn't encourage Gerry to take early retirement. Things wouldn't be the same without his blunt wit and wisdom.

He stood watching as Barney Yelland's rooms were searched, until Clare took pity on him and offered tea, which he accepted gratefully.

Downstairs in her living room he asked her, 'Did you see Barney on the night of Sunday the nineteenth of April – the night before he flew to Italy?'

'Yes,' she said. 'Or rather I didn't see him – I heard him moving around upstairs. He must have been packing for his trip.'

'Were you in all evening?'

'Yes.'

'Did he go out at all?'

'I'm sure he didn't. I would have heard the front door.'

'How did you feel about him bringing women back here?' he asked when he'd taken his first sip of the tea.

'They were just models, for his portrait work. Besides, he's an adult. It's his business.' Her words didn't sound convincing.

'You've a right to impose your own rules in your own house,' Wesley pointed out.

'Come on, Inspector. We're living in the twenty-first century. Look, Barney will be back from Italy soon. How long are they going to be?'

'Sorry, I'm not sure.' Wesley found himself liking the woman and regretted this intrusion into her home. He always tended to sympathise with people who became entangled in a police investigation through no fault of their own.

He let her talk, having learned long ago that some people often give more away over a cup of tea or a pint in the pub than they ever would in an interview room. She revealed that Yelland had answered an advert she'd put on the noticeboard of the organic wholefood shop in Neston – she'd thought anyone who went in there was guaranteed to be the right sort. He was from Devon originally but he'd lived in London for a while. She didn't inquire too much into his personal life – everyone's entitled to their privacy – and she knew little about his friends and family. They got on well but they didn't live in each other's pockets, she added with a hint of sadness.

'When I mentioned Leanne Hatman's surname, I had the impression it meant something to you,' he said, watching her face carefully.

'I don't know what made you think that.' She spoke convincingly but he was certain he'd seen that flicker of recognition. Though he wouldn't press the matter for now.

'Does Mr Yelland own a car?'

'Yes. A Toyota. It's parked outside.'

'Did you notice if he used it on the night before he went to Italy?'

'I told you before, if he'd gone out, I would have heard.'

He had just finished his tea when he heard someone calling his name out in the hallway. One of the CSIs was leaning over the banister while others in crime-scene suits passed him going up and down the stairs with boxes and plastic bags. Wesley joined him on the landing.

'We've found some memory cards but there's no sign of a computer,' the CSI said.

'If he was working in Italy, he probably took it with him,' Wesley said.

'And there were some photos hidden in a box at the back of his wardrobe. Artistic.' The CSI stressed the final word with heavy irony.

He made his way downstairs and handed the pictures to

Wesley. The glossy, coloured images weren't like anything he'd seen before in Yelland's studio. These featured four different women, including Leanne Hatman, and in each picture the subject was lying naked on a bed in an apparent state of sexual ecstasy. He wondered whether Yelland had taken these images for his own gratification or if he intended to share them with other like-minded people. They were pretty tame compared to a lot Wesley had seen in the course of his career, but there was something about them that made him uncomfortable.

'And there are these.' The CSI passed Wesley a box with three pictures of a fair-haired woman inside. This time she was clothed but in each photograph her face had been scored out with something sharp. Wesley stared at them, finding the violence of the mutilation shocking.

'Have you found an address book – anything to help us identify these women?'

'Not yet. He might have it with him, wherever he's gone.'

Wesley looked at the naked pictures again. Had Leanne Hatman been one of a long line? And if she displeased him in some way, would her pictures end up mutilated as well?

He was beginning to wonder how far she'd been prepared to go to get her beautifully pedicured feet on the rungs of the modelling ladder.

Darren Hatman had left work early to visit his estranged wife, Marion. He'd spent a couple of hours at her flat, talking at first, then sitting watching TV, hoping the travel programme on the screen would take their minds off their daughter's absence. But it hadn't.

The police had called to say they'd searched her room at the castle and found nothing to suggest Leanne hadn't left of her own accord. Darren feared this would mean they'd abandon the search; and that was the last thing he wanted. Even Marion, who'd been trying her best to ignore the uncomfortable possibilities, was starting to agree with him. Whatever the lure of a glamorous future in London, her daughter wouldn't have missed her mum's birthday. If she was OK, she'd have been in touch by now.

Before Darren left Marion's flat at six thirty, he'd suggested she come and stay with him at his new bungalow outside Neston; the one he'd bought for a song and renovated. Marion said she'd think about it. They'd had their differences in the past but now Leanne's disappearance had made all those niggling arguments seem trivial.

As Darren drove back from Morbay he passed a tasteful sage-green sign directing him to the Eyecliffe Castle Country Hotel and Spa. He turned his van into the narrow lane, intending to check whether the materials he'd ordered had arrived at the barn in his absence. The supplier had made promises but, in his experience, promises couldn't always be trusted.

While he was there, he was tempted to drive up to the castle to have another word with Leanne's workmates. The police were supposed to have done it but his prejudices convinced him that they would only have gone through the motions. To them she was just another girl who'd gone off to the Smoke to seek her fortune. It was only her father who really cared and he had plans: posters, appeals, social media – not that he knew much about the latter.

The weak sun was beginning to set and Darren switched on his headlights. The lane was single track with passing places and walled with high hedgerows on both sides and he drove a mile until he came to the little stone lodge that guarded the castle entrance. A couple of hundred yards up the drive he branched off on to the track that led to the barn. He knew he'd done well to buy the place because he'd heard that the owner's mother had raised objections. However, he'd learned long ago that most objections can be overcome with hard cash.

When he reached his destination he was pleased to see that the materials had been delivered as promised: great sacks of sand and cement and wood to replace the rotten beams. At least something had gone right today; but that couldn't still the nagging ache of pain and worry that knotted his stomach and ate away at his heart. His daughter was gone and there was nothing he could do.

He unlocked the padlock that secured the barn door and stepped into the great, roofless space, taking deep breaths and fighting back stinging tears. Although he'd clawed his way out of crime and oblivion all that would be meaningless if anything had happened to Leanne. Why did people always say *if something happened*? It was as if they were afraid of putting the reality into words . . . just as he was.

He could have waited until the next day to shift some of the lighter stuff out of the reach of thieving hands but decided that activity would distract him from his problems. He began to move things into the safety of the barn's interior, hardly aware of time passing. Until he heard the snap of a twig and a footstep on the rough gravel path outside.

5

I was much taken with the ruins of
Pompeii, imagining myself as a Roman
citizen walking the teeming streets
and stopping to refresh myself at the
public fountains.

I found some shade and sat for a
while sketching with Joules beside me,
fanning himself with a pamphlet he
had obtained in the city. He sweated
copiously and muttered constantly about
the heat, shooing off the stray dogs that
came to investigate this strange
English phenomenon.

There was no sign of Uriah and I
sensed Joules was uneasy about his
absence. He often vanishes from our
company without explanation and I
wonder where he goes on such occasions.

I suspect he seeks out wickedness as a moth seeks out light but I dare not say so to our cicerone.

More modelling agencies had come back to them, both in London and further afield, and none had offered Leanne Hatman work.

Wesley wondered whether Yelland had taken her to Italy with him – if he'd been telling the truth about his intended destination – and he asked DC Paul Johnson to check with the relevant airlines. The memory cards found in Yelland's room were being examined and they were trying to identify the other women in the photographs, particularly the one whose image had been mutilated. He'd also ordered an examination of Yelland's car but that had yielded nothing, apart from a few discarded parking tickets and a rusty can of de-icer. No evidence had been found to suggest Leanne had ever been in the vehicle, let alone that it had been used to transport her dead body. Gerry reckoned they couldn't do much more that day so Wesley decided to go home.

Pam greeted him with an absent-minded kiss and when he asked her if something was wrong, she answered 'nothing' with an enigmatic look. She'd seemed grateful when he volunteered to make the supper, melting away into the living room while he hurried towards the kitchen. He could make a mean lasagne but, from the restless way Amelia kept asking when supper would be ready, he knew he was under time pressure so he found some sausages in the fridge together with a packet of couscous and a tin of baked beans. It was an unusual combination, but it was healthy . . . ish.

It was almost eight o'clock by the time they'd finished

eating. Pam had said little during their impromptu meal, failing to comment on the unusual selection of ingredients. Once she'd eaten she returned to the living room to watch a documentary about Ancient Egypt on the TV while Wesley cleared up. But when he joined her he could tell she wasn't concentrating. And she looked exhausted.

At quarter past the doorbell rang and Wesley rushed to answer it. For the first time he could remember, he found himself hoping it was Pam's unpredictable and irresponsible mother. If his wife wouldn't confide in him, there was a chance she might tell Della what was bothering her.

But when he opened the door he saw Neil standing there wearing a wide grin, his face tanned to a golden brown. He'd almost forgotten that Neil had promised to come round but was glad to see him.

'How was Sicily?' he asked as they walked through into the living room.

'Amazing archaeology. We spent two weeks digging in the Valley of the Temples – Greek stuff. And we visited other sites as well. You would have loved it, Wes.'

Neil was full of his adventure and Wesley was relieved to see that, since his arrival, Pam seemed more animated, as though their friend had somehow infected her with his bubbling enthusiasm.

'I only got back a few hours ago and I've just dumped my things at the B&B we're using while we're working at Turling Fitwell.'

'You haven't brought Lucy with you?' Wesley asked.

This was usually the time when Pam would start probing, asking discreet questions about Neil's burgeoning relationship. But tonight she listened quietly and said nothing.

'She's gone to visit her mum.' A fond look came into

Neil's eyes. 'I'm joining her on that community dig tomorrow – the manorial water mill. Remember I told you about before I went away.'

Wesley nodded. 'It's near Eyecliffe Castle, isn't it?'

'According to the old documents I've seen, it was the mill for the castle estate. We dug some promising test pits before I left and the geophysics shows a complex of buildings.' He paused and Wesley saw his cheeks flushing slightly. 'Lucy and Dave have taken charge while I've been in Sicily.'

'Got any pictures of your trip?'

'Thought you'd never ask,' said Neil, taking a camera from his pocket. Wesley found the appropriate lead and plugged it into the TV before calling the children down, reminded of evenings in his childhood when his parents' friends or visiting relatives from Trinidad would arrive with boxes of slides and treat them to a show. In those days it had been a big event; aunties and uncles would provide a commentary and the grown-ups would make complimentary remarks.. The memory warmed him. Now here he was doing the same with his own children.

Neil kept up the explanations. 'Here's Salvatore, the site director, and this is the museum. Look at those amphorae. And that's the temple of Concordia. It survived so intact because it was turned into a church after the Emperor Constantine converted to Christianity. We were digging at the temple of Olympian Zeus – there we are. Look at the size of that Telamon,' he said as the image of a colossal stone figure appeared on the screen.

Pam yawned. She preferred pictures of people.

'Here's the Greek theatre at Taormina.'

Pam perked up at the word 'theatre'. In her distant student past she'd studied English Lit.

66

'This is Palermo. I took our students to visit the university there when we first arrived. Beautiful city. That's an eleventh-century palace. And this is the tomb of Frederick the Second, King of Sicily and Holy Roman Emperor who died in twelve fifty. Pope Gregory the Ninth called him the Antichrist and excommunicated him, but that didn't stop him getting a nice burial spot in Palermo cathedral.'

A picture of a red-brown curved sarcophagus surrounded by pillars flashed up on the screen.

'And this is Barney – don't know how he got in there. He's a photographer who's working on some book about the Grand Tour, turned up the second week. He's from Neston too. Small world.'

Wesley leaned forward, his heart beating a little faster. 'Barney. What's his second name?'

'Yelland. We got talking when he came to the Valley of the Temples. He'd been to Naples and Pompeii the previous week and then travelled on to Sicily. Told me it was the last place he needed to photograph – final stop on the Grand Tour.'

Wesley felt a rising excitement. It seemed this was his lucky day. He was tempted to share what he knew about Yelland with Neil but decided against it for the moment; there was plenty of time for explanations once he'd asked all his questions.

'Can I have a copy of this picture?' There had been no likeness of Yelland at Clare Woolmer's house so it was the first time he'd actually seen the man's face. He seemed both younger and better-looking than Wesley had imagined.

Neil looked puzzled. 'Sure. Why?'

Wesley didn't answer the question. 'Did Barney say when he was returning to the UK?'

'He was supposed to be on our plane coming back but he didn't turn up.'

'So he could still be in Sicily?' he said, suddenly wanting to be back in the office, tracing Yelland's whereabouts.

'It's possible. Maybe he changed his mind or he overslept and caught a later flight ... or an earlier one. I hadn't seen him for a couple of days before we left.'

'Where was he staying?'

'With a friend in Agrigento.'

'Did you ever see him with this woman?' Wesley took a picture of Leanne Hatman from his pocket and handed it to Neil.

'No. I would have remembered. He was always alone whenever he joined our group and he seemed to be more interested in his photography – didn't bother much with the social niceties.'

'How did he behave with the women in your group?'

'He wasn't a sex pest if that's what you're getting at. Why are you so interested in him?'

He looked at Pam and saw the same question in her eyes.

'His name's come up in one of our inquiries, that's all.'

Pam stood up. 'Sorry, I've got a headache. I'm going to bed.'

Before Wesley and Neil could say anything, she'd hurried from the room.

'Something up with Pam?' said Neil.

Wesley didn't know. But he intended to find out.

'It's a small world,' said Gerry when Wesley broke the news the following morning.

'I couldn't believe it when Neil mentioned his name.' He placed the picture of Barney Yelland he'd printed out the previous night on Gerry's desk.

'So he told the truth about going to Sicily. I was beginning to think it was a fairy tale he'd told Clare Woolmer to muddy the waters.'

'According to Neil, he wasn't behaving like a man who'd just abducted someone.'

'How does a man who's just abducted a woman behave? Maybe he's a good actor ... or a psychopath. What else did Neil say about him?'

'Only that he was quiet. Intense was how he put it.'

'Is it possible Leanne was there with him?'

'Neil never saw her. And Rob's found that Yelland took an outward flight to Naples and then on to Catania. There's no record of Leanne travelling with him.'

'Interesting that he missed the plane back.'

'I've asked Rob to check whether he caught another flight. It might be worth speaking to the Sicilian police to see if they can find out anything their end. Neil says he was staying with a friend, possibly called Belamy.'

'Sounds like an Englishman abroad,' said Gerry. 'I'll leave that to you, Wes. But don't you get any ideas about a jolly out there in the sunshine. The budget won't stand it.'

'I won't,' Wesley said with some regret. He fell silent for a few moments then spoke again. 'The Barney Yelland Neil described last night didn't sound to me like a man who's fled the country to escape justice. And Clare Woolmer said the trip to Sicily was planned so he didn't just up and leave without warning.'

'It doesn't mean he's innocent, Wes. He might have timed Leanne's murder to coincide.'

'We don't even know if anything's happened to Leanne yet. She could still turn up safe and well. Maybe we're getting this all wrong.'

'Any news on those memory cards?'

'Yes. They're mostly landscapes and other interesting shots. Nothing sinister. Just the kind of stuff you'd expect a professional photographer to have.

'What about those photos – the ones of the girls?'

Wesley shook his head. 'They're pretty tame, Gerry. Nothing you wouldn't find on a newsagent's top shelves. We're not talking hardcore porn – the Vice Squad wouldn't give them a second glance. And he hasn't got a criminal record. There's no history of violence.'

'I'm thinking about those mutilated pictures.'

So was Wesley, who couldn't get them out of his head. They suggested Yelland might be capable of violence when crossed.

'I'd like to speak to the friend he was staying with, Belamy. Yelland might have decided to stay on for some reason.'

Before Gerry could answer the phone on his desk rang. During the brief conversation that followed his expression changed from one of boredom to acute interest.

'You've tried his mobile?' Wesley heard him say. Then, 'OK. Leave it with me.'

He put the receiver down and stared at Wesley. 'That was Marion Hatman. Her husband left her flat at six thirty last night and said he'd phone her later but he never did and she hasn't been able to get hold of him on his mobile. She's spoken to the lads who work for him and they say his van's parked outside the barn. Apparently Hatman was expecting a delivery of materials to arrive after work yesterday and most of the stuff's been put inside the barn. But it's been left unlocked and Darren's usually very conscientious about security, as you'd expect from an ex-robber. Poacher turned gamekeeper. Anyway, Mrs G's worried.' He stood up. 'Perhaps we should get over there and see what's going on.'

They were interrupted by Rachel, who appeared in Gerry's doorway. 'I've just found out Yelland has a sister in Exeter. I rang her but she says she hasn't heard from him. Mind you, she said they weren't close.'

'Parents?'

'There's a father in a residential home. The sister says he hasn't been in touch with him for months either. She didn't sound too pleased about it.'

'Girlfriends? Ex-wife or wives?'

'There's an ex called Penny. They divorced a couple of years ago.'

'Does she have her contact details?'

'No. They've lost touch. But she thinks she's in the North-East.'

'Can you call her back and ask her if she's heard her brother mention anyone called Belamy?'

Rachel returned to her desk and reappeared a couple of minutes later. 'She thinks he was at university with someone of that name but that's all she knows. Sorry.'

'Not your fault, Rach,' said Gerry, standing up. 'It looks like Leanne Hatman's dad's gone walkabout and all so we're going to see if we can track him down. I just hope he hasn't decided to take the law into his own hands.'

Rachel sighed. 'Are you sure we should be putting so much effort into this? There's still no evidence Leanne's come to any harm.'

Wesley had to acknowledge that she had a point. The analysis of the stain in Yelland's bedroom still hadn't come through and, until it did or until her body was found, it was possible she'd turn up safe. However, Gerry seemed to share his gut feeling that they weren't overreacting. He had an adult daughter himself and knew the anxieties, just as Wesley would himself one day.

According to the glossy brochure, one of the main attractions of the Eyecliffe Castle Country Hotel and Spa, apart from its award-winning restaurant, was that it stood in extensive wooded grounds.

A couple of weeks previously Bev and Jim Hughes had enjoyed three nights there. Then, as soon as they'd returned to London, they'd used the internet to book in for a further four nights, bagging themselves a good deal because they were now regarded as loyal customers.

After a full English breakfast that negated the hours they'd spent on the machines in the fitness room the previous day, they decided to explore the grounds, having picked up a leaflet at reception outlining the history of the place. The first written reference to a castle on the site dated from 1470, the time when England was torn apart by the Wars of the Roses between the rival houses of York and Lancaster. The estate had belonged to the Fitwell family until the reign of Henry VIII when the family had fallen on hard times and sold it to a Thomas D'Arles, one of Henry's courtiers. D'Arles had demolished part of the castle, replacing it with a grand mansion, a place fit to entertain the king himself if necessary, though the hoped-for royal visit never materialised.

The brochure went on to say that the east wing was

perched above a steep slope that stretched down to a rushing river, and overlooking the river valley was a balustraded terrace, at present closed to the public, where the ladies of the house had once taken exercise when the weather was agreeable.

Over the years the fortunes of the D'Arles family had fluctuated and when the south wing was destroyed by fire in 1856, it had never been rebuilt. Henrietta D'Arles had inherited the estate in 1953; in 1970 she sold it to John Palmer, the present owner's father, who had gradually transformed the historic building into an exclusive and luxurious retreat for the discerning guest.

Inevitably, the brochure also mentioned the castle's two ghosts, both female. The first, the white lady, was a Fitwell and was said to haunt the gatehouse, carrying the baby she'd had by her own father sometime in the fifteenth century. The second was a grey lady who was often seen in the vicinity of the round tower. She'd allegedly been murdered by one of the D'Arles family in the late eighteenth century, although the truth of the story had been lost in the mists of time. Bev and Jim had looked out for these spectral residents even though neither of them believed in any sort of afterlife. However, it was fun in an ironic sort of way.

They walked down the gravel drive towards the woods. It was spring and most people would have found the birdsong and peace relaxing. But their thoughts were elsewhere: a fortnight ago they'd received a disappointment; a realisation that all their work and research had been in vain. Now however they had a fresh glimmer of hope.

When they reached the trees Jim stopped and put his arms around her. 'Come on,' he whispered in Bev's ear. 'Let's celebrate our good fortune.'

'Bit early for that. Anyway, it rained last night. The ground's damp.' Bev pushed him away.

'Then why did we bloody come here?' She could hear the peevish note in his voice. He could be like a whining child when he didn't get his way and she wanted his mind on the coming challenge. 'My coat's waterproof. We can use that.'

'Why not?' she said with a weary sigh.

He grabbed hold of her hand and led her into the trees, stumbling through the undergrowth, oblivious to her reluctance. The ground was covered in inhospitable bracken and to Bev it looked too uncomfortable for what he had in mind. Then, to her surprise, he suddenly stopped.

'What is it?'

'Look.'

She peered down at the ground and saw a denim-clad leg protruding from the bracken.

Jim edged towards the leg and saw that it was attached to the body of a middle-aged man, lying on his back and staring up at the canopy of trees with an expression of stupefied horror on his face, as if he'd seen a vision of hell itself.

6

There are some young men who will go
to great lengths to throw off their
bear-leader while travelling so they
can enjoy the excesses on offer in any
foreign town. But I do not share my
cousin's taste for whores and the oblivion
of opium and, besides, since the
unfortunate incident in Paris, I feel
somewhat protective of our chaperone. On
that occasion it was Uriah who was at
fault and I had to pay the girl
handsomely not to tell her father of
my cousin's assault. If Joules had not
interrupted him, the matter might
not have been so easily concealed. I
sense now that Joules is afraid of my
cousin. As I am at times.

   Uriah sleeps in the chamber adjoining

*mine and I lie awake at night and
listen. I do not wish him to melt into
the night and repeat his sins.*

Wesley sat at his desk, staring at his computer, so lost in his
own thoughts that the sound of Rachel Tracey's voice
made him jump.

'The report on that stain's come back. It's blood –
human. But without a sample of Leanne Hatman's we
can't make a match.'

'We can get a profile from her dad if necessary, or her
mum. Or maybe we should wait. We don't want to alarm
them unnecessarily.'

Rachel handed him a sheet of paper. 'Leanne Hatman's
mobile's switched off but here's a list of calls made and
received on her number. There's been nothing for a couple
of weeks but before then there were a lot of calls and texts
to and from Barney Yelland – the last one being when she
called him at seven o'clock on the night of the nineteenth,
an hour after she was last seen by Kirsty Paige. Looks as if
he was the person she was going to meet.'

'Clare Woolmer said he didn't go out that night.'

'Believe her?'

'Not sure,' Wesley answered. He'd been convinced when
Clare had said it but now he was starting to have doubts.

'All her other calls were to and from her mum and the
friends we've already spoken to. There are incoming calls
from her dad too but it doesn't look as though she ever rang
him back. Apart from the ones to and from Yelland, nothing jumps out as suspicious. The real mystery is why it's
switched off now.' She hesitated. 'I'm getting a bad feeling
about her, Wes.'

'Me too.' He looked up at her. 'How are your wedding arrangements going? Pam's looking forward to it. She's bought a new outfit.' He suddenly felt a small pang of unease. Pam had been unusually preoccupied over the last couple of days. He'd told himself she was tired, the term-time blues being an occupational hazard of her teaching job, but he'd been too busy with his own work to ask any probing questions. It had been easier to believe her when she'd said she was fine.

'I didn't realise getting married would be like a military operation,' Rachel said with a hint of irritation before returning to her desk. As she sat down he was aware of her watching him. But those days of attraction were gone. He was married and her wedding to a local farmer, the union of two long-established farming families, was imminent. They were friends and colleagues, nothing more.

The phone on his desk began to ring, distracting him from his ponderings.

'Tradmouth CID, Detective Inspector Peterson speaking.'

There was a moment of silence before the caller spoke. 'There's a man in the woods at Eyecliffe Castle,' the caller said, a tremor in his voice. 'I think he's dead.'

The activity set into motion by a suspicious death always reminded Wesley of a circus coming to town. Vehicles and tents pitched up filled with strangely dressed people, creating a focus of curiosity for any passing rubbernecker. He pushed this inappropriate thought to the back of his mind as he and Gerry struggled into their white protective suits. Gerry looked like a chubby snowman in his: all he needed was a pipe and scarf to complete the look.

'What have we got?' Wesley addressed DC Rob Carter who'd reached the scene before them and was talking earnestly to a couple in their forties.

'This is Mr and Mrs Hughes. They found the body.'

The couple had been sitting on a fallen tree trunk, looking stunned, and the man rose and shifted from foot to foot nervously. 'It's been a terrible shock,' he said. He had a London accent and was dressed as if he was preparing to play a round of golf. His wife was slightly taller than him, slim with bobbed blonde hair and a snub nose. She put her head in her hands as though the ordeal had been too much for her.

'How did you come to make the discovery?' Wesley asked.

'We're staying at the hotel and we decided to go for a walk in the woods after breakfast. He was just lying there. Gave us the shock of our lives, it did. I couldn't get a phone signal so I had to run back to reception to call you.'

'Ever seen the dead man before?' Gerry asked.

The couple shook their heads. Wesley believed them until he saw them exchange a glance and wondered if they were hiding something. On the other hand, shock made people behave in odd ways. He didn't see any reason why they shouldn't make their formal statements in the comfort of the hotel so he told one of the uniformed constables to take them somewhere more suitable. As it was, they were only getting in the way.

'We'd better take a look at this body then,' said Gerry, making for the cordon of police tape. After the crime-scene manager had ticked their names off on his clipboard they neared the focus of all the activity. Wesley looked round for Dr Colin Bowman, the pathologist who usually attended the scene of any suspicious death. For some time Colin had been talking about retirement and Wesley knew that Gerry in particular was dreading that dark day. Colin's genial nature helped to make even the most gruesome of post-mortems bearable. He had often wondered why the man had chosen forensic pathology as his specialist field of medicine when his bedside manner could have lightened the suffering of so many living patients.

But Colin was nowhere to be seen. Instead a young man with spiky dark hair was bending over the corpse making an examination. He looked round unsmiling as Wesley and Gerry approached.

'DCI Heffernan and DI Peterson,' Gerry said by way of introduction. 'Where's Dr Bowman?'

'On a cruise,' was the terse reply. 'I'm his locum. Dr Tennant.'

The man returned his attention to the corpse as if he considered their presence a nuisance. He lacked Colin's well-developed social skills and looked like a sixth-former on work experience, but Wesley always believed in giving people the benefit of the doubt until he knew otherwise.

'What can you tell us?' Wesley asked, looking round at Gerry who was standing behind him wearing a disappointed expression.

Tennant gave a heavy sigh and stood up, blocking their view of the corpse on the ground.

'Only that he's dead. There's a wound to his chest that was probably caused by a bullet.' He shifted slightly to one side and they saw the dead man's face.

Gerry stepped forward. 'I know him,' he said. 'He came to us recently to report his daughter missing. His name's Darren Hatman.'

'There's no sign of a weapon so I think I can rule out suicide if that's what you're getting at,' Tennant said quickly.

'It wasn't,' Gerry snapped. 'He never struck me as the suicidal type.'

'How long has he been dead?' Wesley asked.

Tennant rolled his eyes. 'You people should know by now that it's hard to be specific.'

'Humour us,' Gerry growled. 'Make a guess.'

'Probably late yesterday. These things aren't as easy to gauge as they are on the TV. PM first thing tomorrow. If you want to attend don't be late.'

'Can't you fit it in sooner if we ask very nicely?' Gerry said, giving the pathologist a hopeful look.

Tennant looked at his watch. 'It's lunchtime now. Might be able to fit him in at four o'clock. Would that suit you?'

'That'll do nicely, thanks,' said Wesley before the man had second thoughts. 'We'll see you there.'

'When will Colin be back?' Gerry asked. He sounded like a child who was asking how many days there were to go until Christmas.

'Not for a couple of weeks. He's doing the Caribbean.'

Gerry didn't reply but Wesley knew he was wishing Colin was there to conduct the postmortem; he wanted the familiarity of a friendly face he'd known for years, someone who would provide good-natured answers to his most naive questions. But they were dealing with a murder so they had to make the best of the situation.

Wesley gave Gerry's arm a nudge. 'We'll see you later,' he said to the pathologist, who didn't acknowledge him.

'Can't say I've taken to the new lad,' Gerry whispered loudly as they walked away.

'He's a bit ... brusque.'

'Downright rude. And I can't see him providing tea and biscuits at the mortuary like Colin does.'

'Life can't be one long round of pleasure,' said Wesley. 'I'll ask Rach to break the news to Marion Hatman and she can ask her to do a formal ID if she feels up to it. Poor woman. Her daughter goes missing and now this.'

'Wonder if Hatman went into the woods to look for Leanne. Maybe he was right and she was abducted. Maybe he was killed because he was getting too close to finding the truth. Mind you, someone with Hatman's record could have made enemies over the years.'

Wesley couldn't argue with that.

Rachel had stayed back at the station but Rob Carter, Paul Johnson and Trish Walton were hanging around the outer cordon awaiting orders. From time to time Wesley noticed Paul glance at Trish. They had once gone out together and you didn't have to be a detective to know that Paul wanted to rekindle their relationship. Rob stood in front of them, as though he was keen to be first off the blocks for any task assigned to them.

Gerry gave his instructions. Once a formal statement had been taken from the couple who found the body, he wanted everyone at the hotel interviewed. Someone might have heard a shot. And while they were organising that, he and Wesley would speak to Darren Hatman's workmen.

When Gerry began to stroll towards the castle where they'd left the car Wesley fell in beside him.

'What do you think, Gerry? Did Hatman decide to go looking for his daughter and come across someone with a gun? Or did he go there with his killer?'

'It'll be interesting to see how his workers take the bad news.

'They might already know,' said Wesley meaningfully. 'Nothing or nobody can be ruled out. Let's walk. It's not that far.'

They changed direction and found themselves on the drive, the gravel crunching loudly beneath their feet. Their crime prevention officers always recommended gravel as a deterrent to burglars.

When they reached their destination they were greeted by the sight of two men in work-stained jeans and T-shirts. One was several inches shorter than the other but both were well built with shaven heads and a fine array of tattoos on display. A dragon crawled up the arm of the taller man, its head hidden by his T-shirt sleeve, as though the creature was shy.

As the men watched them approach, Wesley could see suspicion on their faces and wasn't sure if this was because of the colour of his skin or the fact that they were recognisable as representatives of the law. He left it to Gerry to make the introductions and saw the men shift awkwardly from foot to foot as though they were anticipating immediate arrest.

'I'm afraid we've got some bad news for you,' Gerry began. 'Darren Hatman's dead.'

Wesley was sure that the shock on their faces hadn't been faked. 'Where? How?' the smaller man spluttered.

'Is there somewhere we can talk?' said Wesley

The barn door was standing wide open and the men led the way inside where some scaffolding planks and a few breezeblocks had been arranged to form a pair of benches, no doubt brought into use at tea-break times. They sat down and Wesley took out his notebook.

The taller man was Lee Varlow and the smaller Craig Gatting and both gave addresses in Morbay.

'I just can't believe it,' Varlow said. 'He was fine when I saw him yesterday. Well not fine exactly 'cause he was worried sick about his Leanne but . . . You know what I mean.'

'Do you know Leanne?' Wesley asked.

The two men exchanged looks and shook their heads in unison.

'Know of her but never met her,' said Gatting. 'Darren didn't see much of her. Used to go on about how her mam had turned her against him.'

'And that upset him?'

'Course it did. He bloody loved that girl. She's been missing two weeks, you know,' the man added as if he held Wesley and Gerry personally responsible. 'How did he . . . ? Was it a heart attack or what? He's been under a lot of strain. I told him, didn't I Lee? I said he should watch his blood pressure.'

'That's right. You did.'

He looked round at a pile of building materials stacked in the corner. 'And it looks as if he'd shifted this lot inside for safety. Suppliers said they'd deliver after we packed up for the night – Darren must have come back to check if they'd arrived. There's still a load outside so he might have felt poorly. Probably overdid it, poor sod.' He nodded with satisfaction as though he'd just solved the problem of his boss's death single-handed.

'We don't know for sure how he died yet,' said Wesley, not wanting to give too much away. 'There'll be a post-mortem later today.'

At this news both men bowed their heads, presumably in respect.

'Have you any idea what he was doing in the woodland where he was found?'

'Maybe he decided to go looking for Leanne,' Varlow suggested. 'I mean you hear of girls being attacked in woods and it's not far from where she works, is it, Craig?' He looked to his mate for confirmation.

'Yeah. Darren was dead proud when she got that job at the spa. She said she was going to London and I kept telling him that's where she'll be but he wouldn't listen, would he, Lee?'

'No. He wouldn't listen. He said some bloke was stalking her. Worried himself sick, he did.'

'Tell us about his plans for this barn.'

'He's doing it up to sell on but between you and me, I think he bought it so he could be near Leanne; get back in her good books; meet her for lunch, that sort of thing. And he's got – he had – his eye on another place and all – old house beyond those trees. Some old biddy lives there and he was going to ask her if she wanted any work done.'

Gerry was suddenly alert. 'And once he got his foot in the door . . . ?'

'He was sure she'd want to sell. I mean, a place like that is a burden when you're getting on a bit, isn't it. She could get a nice new bungalow, or one of them sheltered flats. My gran lives in one of them and she has the time of her life.'

'So Darren was planning to do her a favour?'

Wesley heard the scepticism in Gerry's voice. Neither of them liked builders who ripped off old ladies.

'Sure he was.'

'You should see the place. Roof shot. Windows rotten. Needs pointing. No central heating. He'd have given her a fair price for it.'

'I'm sure he would,' said Gerry. 'Let's get back to Darren. When did you last see him?'

'Yesterday. The materials hadn't arrived so Darren called to see what the hold-up was and they said they couldn't deliver till six. Around four he said we might as well call it a day and told us to go home.'

'Did he say if he had plans to see anyone – any business meetings? A call on the lady in the Dower House perhaps?'

'He said he was going to see his ex-missus but that's all.'

'We know about that. He didn't mention anything else?'

The two men shook their heads.

Gerry stood up. 'I'll send someone across to take your statements. Just routine.'

Wesley guessed the boss had come to the same conclusion as he had. It was unlikely, although not impossible, that this pair had anything to do with Darren Hatman's death.

'We'd like to know when the funeral is,' said Varlow. 'Pay our respects and all that.'

Wesley nodded. The men looked lost without their leader, unsure whether they were out of a job or if Hatman's estranged wife would take over the reins.

'Where to now?' said Gerry once they were out of ear-shot.

'I'd like to speak to the lady at the Dower House. If Hatman called on her after work yesterday evening and tried to make her an offer she couldn't refuse . . .'

'Maybe she didn't see it like that. Maybe she though he was threatening her home. See if she has a firearms licence, will you?'

'You think she shot him because he was offering her a dodgy deal?'

'When you put it like that, Wes, it seems unlikely. I'm sure this is linked to Leanne. Man's daughter goes missing then he's found dead. Too much bad luck.'

'Some people are just unlucky,' Wesley replied.

They started back towards the castle, this time taking a narrow pathway through a copse of budding trees where the only sound was birdsong. Wesley breathed in the air. It smelled of damp greenery: the scent of spring.

At the other side of the trees they came to an old house surrounded by a wall, high for privacy at the rear but only three feet tall at the front. A wooden gate separated the overgrown garden from Eyecliffe Castle's open parkland and it creaked loudly as Wesley pushed it open.

He stood back as Gerry raised the wrought-iron knocker. It was in the form of a grinning lion's head and Wesley thought it looked slightly sinister. As the knocker came down the sound thundered inside the house.

They heard footsteps then the door opened to reveal a tall woman with snow-white hair and bright sea-green eyes. She had a long, aristocratic face and Wesley estimated that she was in her seventies or possibly even older. She looked at them as if they were tradesmen who'd had the audacity to come to the front door instead of the kitchen entrance.

'We're sorry to bother you, madam,' said Gerry, holding up his ID. 'DCI Heffernan and Detective Inspector Peterson, Tradmouth CID. I wonder if we can have a quick word.'

It was hard to read her expression. She was of an age and class that considered the control of emotions a virtue.

'Sorry, I don't know your name, madam.' Normally Gerry would have called her 'love' but Wesley could tell he was on his best behaviour.

'D'Arles. Henrietta D'Arles. Please come in, gentlemen.'

She led them through to a drawing room that might once have been elegant but clearly hadn't been touched for decades. The colours of the wallpaper and drapes had faded to a dull brown and a layer of dust lay over all the surfaces.

On a shelf in the corner sat a row of dolls with hard glass eyes, porcelain faces and rosebud lips. They stared like a rapt audience but Wesley thought there was something cruel about them, like watchers at an execution. He noticed a dog bed in the corner. In it lay a black Labrador; an old dog who'd lost the appetite for barking at strangers and soliciting attention.

'That's Reginald. Like his mistress, he's not as young as he once was.' The dog stood up, ambled across to her and sat at her feet, gazing at her adoringly. 'I used to live at the castle until the upkeep became too much for me. I sold it to Mr Palmer in nineteen seventy and moved to the Dower House where they once put members of the family who'd outlived their usefulness.' There was a note of bitterness in her voice.

She sat down and invited them to do the same. Wesley perched gingerly on the edge of a velvet sofa that might once have been red but was now a greasy brown, Gerry beside him.

Henrietta D'Arles continued, 'Before you ask, I never married. There was just me and my younger sister and she lived abroad.'

Wesley had expected her to inquire about the purpose of their visit but instead she just seemed glad to have someone to talk to. This is what loneliness is like, he thought, hoping it was something he'd never experience.

'You haven't asked why we're here,' he said.

She looked him up and down. He knew that black police officers were rare in rural Devon but he hadn't expected her curiosity to be so blatant. 'Where are you from, Inspector?'

'Originally London. But my parents came to England from Trinidad to train as doctors.'

'I see.' She seemed satisfied, as though his well-bred accent and the mention of his parents' profession had reassured her. 'So why are you here? Is this about that girl who's gone missing? A couple of officers called the other day to ask whether I knew anything but I wasn't able to help them then and the situation hasn't changed, I'm afraid. You are quite welcome to search the house if you don't believe me.'

'That won't be necessary, madam,' said Gerry. 'This isn't about the missing girl this time. Her father's a builder. He's just started renovating that old barn on the other side of the woods.'

'Really? I wonder if he was the man who came round here yesterday. He pushed a leaflet through my door – Hatman's Building Services. I heard him knock but I didn't answer. I know what these builders are like with people my age. There's a slate missing so you'll need a new roof – that will be twenty thousand pounds, please. I have neither the time nor the spare money to bother with that sort of thing. And he went around the house looking in the windows. I wouldn't entertain such impudence.'

'Quite right, madam. Can you describe him?'

She provided a remarkably accurate description of Darren Hatman. Wesley wished all his witnesses were as observant.

'So you never spoke to him?'

'Why should I?' she said as though he'd asked a foolish question. 'Why are you asking about him? What has he done?'

'He was found dead in the woods this morning. We're treating his death as suspicious.'

Her hand fluttered to her heart. 'That's terrible.' She shuddered. 'Nowhere's safe these days. I'm sorry to hear the man's dead, of course, but, as I said, I never even spoke to him.'

Wesley assumed that this was all she was going to say on the subject. Gerry shifted in his seat as though he was about to stand up to go.

Then she spoke again. 'I said I'd never spoken to the man but I did overhear somebody else talking to him.' She looked at their expectant faces and Wesley suspected she was enjoying keeping them in suspense.

'When was this?'

'Yesterday, around seven. I was on the drive taking Reginald for his evening walk and I heard raised voices coming from the direction of the barn. Before you ask, I couldn't hear what was being said.'

'Was it men's voices you heard?'

'Yes. Definitely men. But I'm afraid that's all I can tell you.'

'What route did you take on your walk?' Wesley asked.

'Only from here to the lodge. Reginald isn't inclined to go much further these days.' She stroked the dog's head lovingly and he placed a paw gently on her knee.

'You didn't go into the woods?'

'It's not somewhere I care to go on my own ... and I fear Reginald wouldn't provide much defence against anyone with sinister intentions.'

'I'll send somebody round to take a statement from you, Miss D'Arles.'

She nodded, a smile playing on her lips as though she was looking forward to the company. 'Of course.'

Wesley looked around. In the gloom of the north-facing room, he hadn't noticed the paintings hanging on the wall at first. But now his eyes had adjusted he could see them better. In the days before he had transferred to Devon so that Pam could be near her widowed mother he had served in London, working in the Met's elite Art and Antique Unit, so he'd always taken an interest in such things, even though his degree was in archaeology.

'That's an interesting picture,' he said, pointing to a small watercolour. In contrast to the other paintings in the room which were all heavy Victorian oils elaborately framed in gilt, the one that had caught Wesley's attention had a plain wooden frame. It depicted a young man swimming beneath the sea surrounded by fish, a gold cup in his hand held out like a trophy. He was about to break the surface of the water; on the shore was a tower and a figure in a crown, presumably a king, surrounded by courtiers.

He thought Miss D'Arles looked a little uneasy about the interest he was taking in the picture.

'It depicts an old Sicilian legend,' she said. 'A young man called Colapesce was famed for his ability to swim under-water and one day King Frederick of Sicily set him a test. First he threw a golden cup into the sea and then his crown and both times Colapesce retrieved them. Then King Frederick threw in his ring but when Colapesce dived to get it, he didn't resurface. You see, the ring had gone much deeper and become stuck in an underwater crevice and when Colapesce reached the spot he saw that one of the three columns that supported the island was being burned away by a magic fire – some say it refers to Mount Etna – so he stayed down there, holding the column to stop Sicily falling into the sea. He sacrificed himself to save the island. It's a sad story.'

'A friend of mine has just come back from Sicily. Have you ever been there?'

She shook her head. There was a long silence before she spoke again. 'The picture was a gift from my sister. She spent most of her life abroad and worked in Sicily for a couple of years. She was a dancer – ballet. Those are her shoes.'

She pointed to a glass case in the corner of the room and Wesley went over to it. Inside he saw an arrangement of colourful programmes, all for ballet productions: *Swan Lake*, *Nutcracker*, *Giselle* and some he wasn't familiar with. In the centre lay a pair of pink satin ballet pointes, grubby and worn around the blocked toes; well used. Wesley found the sight of them rather poignant.

'Is your sister still alive?'

'She died abroad many years ago. A tragic car accident. I'm quite alone in the world, Inspector. The last of my line.'

After an awkward silence Gerry cleared his throat. 'Well if you remember anything more about this man who was talking to Mr Hatman, you will call us, won't you.'

Wesley watched as he handed Miss D'Arles his card. 'By the way,' he said casually. 'Would you mind telling us where you were yesterday?'

The woman looked affronted. 'I've already told you. I walked Reginald then I returned home and I didn't go out again. I'm afraid Reginald is my only witness so you'll have to take my word for it.'

'I'm sorry,' said Wesley. 'But we have to ask. It's just routine.'

'I understand.' She stroked Reginald's head. 'I thought we might walk down towards the river today, to see where those archaeologists are digging.'

'Make sure you lock up properly,' said Gerry.

'Don't worry, Chief Inspector. I will.'

When they took their leave she accompanied them to the door and stood watching until they reached the gate.

'Think she'll be OK there on her own?' Gerry asked.

'I don't think Hatman's was a random murder. He must have been targeted for some reason.'

'Pity she isn't the nosy type,' Gerry said as they turned on to the path leading to the castle. 'If she'd gone to investigate when she heard that argument yesterday, we might have had ourselves a witness.'

'The world is full of "ifs", Gerry.'

'Anyway, I think we can rule her out. I can't see her following Hatman into the woods and shooting him, can you?'

'Not really.' Wesley's phone made a jaunty sound announcing a text. 'That was the station,' he said when he'd read it. 'No firearms licence issued to the Dower House.

In amicable silence they walked towards the castle to check how the interviews were proceeding.

In reception they found Mrs Palmer and Trish sitting on a pair of winged leather chairs, deep in conversation. Standing in the doorway of the bar Wesley saw Jim and Bev Hughes, whispering and looking more like a pair of conspirators than an innocent couple who'd just stumbled across a dead body by accident.

As soon as they saw Wesley watching them, they vanished into the bar.

7

At times I wonder whether Uriah's
mother begged my father to let him
accompany me on my travels because she
was afraid that he might commit some
dreadful deed at home. Ever since my
father gave my aunt use of the Dower
House after her husband's death there
have been whispers amongst the servants.
I do not know what they whisper about
because they fall silent when they see
me, but before Uriah and his mother
came to Turling Fitwell the
atmosphere in the village and estate
was lighter and the servants more at
ease in their work. My father
understands none of this as he is adept
at ignoring the unwelcome, but I have
the sensitivity of an artist.

I know not whether it is mere strangeness in Uriah ... or the deleterious effect of the opium he is in the habit of taking. Or something worse - a taste for evil, perhaps.

An incident room was being set up in Turling Fitwell's church hall. When these things happened they happened fast and Gerry was confident they'd already have the phones and computer connections in. He told Wesley to stop off there because they needed to see whether any new information had come in before they drove to the hospital for Darren Hatman's postmortem.

The church hall was brick built and, even though it had seen better days, it was still used for Sunday school, scout and guide meetings, playgroups and pensioners' get-togethers. As soon as Wesley and Gerry arrived there, Gerry bagged the largest desk at the front of the room, nearest the stage. A massive noticeboard had been sent across from Tradmouth, already adorned with pictures of the main players. There were filing cabinets and cardboard boxes full of documents too: a whole police station, miraculously assembled in a small country village.

Gerry went through the messages on his desk. 'There's one here from a Commissario Lucetti of the Agrigento Questura – I think that's Italian for cop shop.'

'I'll give him a call. Got his number?'

Gerry passed him the message pad. Fortunately the commissario's English turned out to be a lot better than Wesley's Italian.

'Thank you for calling, *dottore*.' He knew that in Italy detectives are invariably graduates and therefore addressed as such. 'We are inquiring about a man called Barney Yelland. He has been staying in Agrigento and he failed to catch his flight home. We wish to interview him about a missing girl.'

'That is why I called you, *dottore*.' The man was returning the compliment. 'One of my men has spoken to Signor Harry Belamy, an Englishman who lives here teaching English. He and Signor Yelland are old friends from university and they share an interest in photography.'

'Does he know where Signor Yelland is now?'

'Signor Belamy told us he left his apartment a few days ago, saying that he'd decided to travel home early and had changed his flight. That is all we have been able to discover. My apologies that I cannot be of more assistance.'

'You've been very helpful, *dottore*,' said Wesley once he'd made a note of Belamy's number. '*Grazie. Arrivederci.*' He looked round to check whether anyone had overheard him; he didn't feel particularly confident in Italian, although, having studied Latin and French, he understood enough to catch the gist of the written word.

Hurrying over to Gerry's desk, he told him, 'The Sicilian police have spoken to Harry Belamy – the man Yelland was staying with – and as far as he knows, Yelland returned to the UK a few days ago; told him he'd decided to change his flight and travel back early.'

'Did the Sicilian police believe him?'

'They had no reason not to. I'd like to speak to Belamy myself. The commissario gave me his number so I'll call him when we've got the PM out of the way. We've only checked flights from Catania, not Palermo. I'll put someone on to it right away.'

Once Wesley had assigned the task, Gerry stood up

slowly, as though his limbs were stiff. 'Come on,' he said. 'Dr Tennant's expecting us ... if he's finished his homework and his mum lets him out.'

Wesley laughed. 'It's a sign of old age when you think the doctors are getting younger, Gerry.'

'I thought that was policemen.'

They drove to Tradmouth and, as it was a fine spring day, parked at the police station and walked to the hospital along the embankment. Seagulls shrieked overhead and the river was bustling with vessels, reawakened after a winter spent beneath tarpaulins. Fishing boats hung with nets and bright orange floats chugged back from a day at sea and the ferries scuttled to and fro to Queenswear on the opposite bank. Wesley breathed in deeply as he went, smelling seaweed and a faint aroma of fish and chips from one of the cafés overlooking the river.

When they reached the hospital they made straight for the mortuary, passing Colin's empty office with some regret.

The young pathologist was waiting for them, arms folded defensively. He glanced at his watch as they walked in.

'We're not late, are we?' Wesley said, preparing to apologise.

But the pathologist didn't answer. The assistant uncovered the body of Darren Hatman and Tennant began his observations, speaking into the microphone dangling above the steel table.

'Well-nourished man in his early fifties,' he began. 'No visible scars or abnormalities. Help me turn him over,' he said to the assistant. The word 'please' was lacking. Colin never forgot his manners.

Wesley expected him to continue speaking, but he'd fallen silent.

'What is it?' Gerry asked.

The doctor hesitated and Wesley saw his cheeks redden. 'It was impossible to see this when the body was found.'

'See what?'

'This.'

Wesley and Gerry circled the table until they had a view of the dead man's back.

'There's nothing?' said Wesley.

'That's the point. No exit wound.'

'The bullet's still in there?'

The body was shifted on to its back. 'I'll see what I can find when I open him up.'

'Better get on with it then,' said Gerry.

They stood and watched as Tennant cut into the body and removed the organs.

As he worked he began to look more flustered, and when he finally spoke it sounded like a confession. 'I can't find a bullet. I don't think he was shot.'

'So what killed him?'

'The heart was penetrated by a sharp instrument. The wound's about eight inches deep.'

'A knife? A screwdriver?'

Tennant shook his head. 'I don't think so. Whatever it is went in with considerable force because it's shattered a rib on its way towards the heart. And the wound looks wrong for a knife. It's round and very neat . . . similar to a bullet hole.'

The young man's manner had suddenly softened, as though the embarrassment of mistaking the cause of death at the scene had been a humbling experience.

'The wound's in his chest and he fell on to his back, which means he must have been facing his killer and fallen back with the force,' Tennant said. 'And there are no defensive wounds as you'd expect in a stabbing. He didn't put up a fight.'

'I'd like to take a look at the clothes he was wearing,' said Wesley.

They were bagged up on a trolley at the side of the tiled room. Wesley put on a pair of crime-scene gloves and took the items out one by one. In the largest bag he found the victim's sweatshirt, with a ragged hole in the front surrounded by a crusted circle of blood. He called Gerry over and showed him what he'd found.

Gerry stared at the garment, a puzzled frown on his face. 'From the state of the sweatshirt it looks as if the killer had some trouble pulling whatever it was out,' said Wesley. He turned to Tennant. 'Can you hazard a guess about the weapon – size, shape, length?'

At this stage in the proceedings, Colin Bowman would have been happy to speculate and probe the wound, discarding theories until he hit on one that fitted the facts. In contrast Tennant stiffened as though he suspected Wesley was trying to catch him out.

'I'll need to carry out more tests. You'll have to be patient,' he said, picking up a circular saw.

'OK,' said Gerry. 'But get on with it, lad. We need to know. In fact we'd like an artist's impression of whatever killed him by teatime.'

Tennant's face turned red and he began to remove the top of the skull in order to examine the dead man's brain. Apart from reciting his findings into the dangling microphone, he worked silently and Wesley was beginning to feel awkward standing there.

Eventually the procedure was over and Tennant turned

his attention once more to the wound in the dead man's chest.

'Well?' Gerry prompted after a minute or so of quiet contemplation.

Tennant shook his head, puzzled.'

'Could it be an arrow?' Wesley suggested.

'You might have something there.' Tennant walked over to the computer on the desk in the corner and began to bring up images. After a few silent minutes, he turned and spoke again.

'What about a crossbow bolt? A crossbow's easier to conceal than a bow and just as lethal. Whatever it was, the killer didn't leave it in there. Don't ask me why. That's your department.'

'When did you say Colin was due back from his jolly?' Gerry asked.

'Not for a couple of weeks.'

Wesley wondered whether Tennant felt insulted by the DCI's sigh of disappointment.

Pam arrived home at five thirty with Amelia. Michael had gone to a friend's house after school so it would just be the two of them … unless by some miracle Wesley arrived home at a reasonable time.

When she opened the front door she was greeted by Moriarty. She wasn't sure why Wesley had decided to name the cat after Sherlock Holmes's nemesis, the Napoleon of Crime, but somehow the name suited the aloof creature of unfathomable mystery. When Amelia made straight for the kitchen to feed the cat she was glad; she needed to be alone.

Pam entered the living room and stared at the phone.

She'd kept her secret to herself but perhaps it was time to seek reassurance —or learn the worst. This was something she couldn't put off.

She should be sharing her problem with Wesley but he'd texted earlier to say there'd been a suspicious death and he'd be late. Sometimes she wished he was still working in the Art and Antique Unit. But most of the time she wished that he wasn't in the police service at all.

Tears stung her eyes as she picked up the receiver and dialled her mother's number. To her relief Della answered after the first ring, as though she'd been waiting by the phone.

'Can't stay on long,' said Della. 'I'm waiting for a call. I've set up this date. I met him online and he's supposed to be calling this afternoon to say when and where. I asked him to ring me instead of making the arrangements online 'cause I wanted to hear his voice. The internet's so impersonal and you can tell so much about a man by his voice.'

Pam took a deep breath. This was typical of her mother, who was more of a teenager than the ones she taught at a local college. Why had she thought confiding in her was a good idea?

'Mum. There's something I need to talk to you about.'

'Sorry, darling. We'll speak tomorrow. I really must go.'

The line went dead. And when Amelia came into the room to find her, she did her best to fight back her tears.

Rachel had gone to Morbay to be with Marion Hatman. With her estranged husband dead and her daughter missing, the woman needed support. Marion had displayed remarkable stoicism when she'd identified Darren's body but now she was home, she was beginning to show signs that the strain was becoming too much for her. Rachel was staying with her that evening, just in case anything happened.

Rachel had arranged to see her fiancé, Nigel, at eight, but she'd put him off. If he intended to marry a police officer, she thought, he'd have to get used to her long absences. He was a farmer, used to working from dawn to dusk, but the erratic hours of a murder inquiry were different somehow; less predictable.

Although Marion Hatman's flat was cramped, Rachel could put up with anything for a short time. She had soon found her way around the tiny kitchen and located the essential tea-making equipment. A lot of tea flowed when she was acting as Family Liaison Officer.

She'd made another pot and placed a steaming mug in front of Marion. As well as providing support, it was her job to wheedle useful information out of the grieving relatives; to discover all she could about the victim and his relationships. Fortunately Marion seemed happy to talk but Rachel soon realised that her concern was more for her missing daughter than her dead husband. Every time Rachel asked about Darren the conversation somehow turned to Leanne.

Marion went over to the mantelpiece and picked up the photo of Leanne that stood in pride of place.

'Leanne's a beautiful girl,' Rachel said, careful to use the present tense. 'She must have had a lot of boyfriends.'

Marion gave a small, secretive smile. 'She's fussy.'

'Can you think of anyone she's rejected? Anyone who might bear her a grudge? Someone your husband might not have known about? Or someone he warned off?'

There was a long silence and Rachel took a sip of tea. It

was stewed. She'd left it to brew too long but her mind had been on other things.

'Not really ... unless ... well, I suppose there was Jordan.'

'Jordan?'

'Jordan Carnegie. Darren would have been furious if he'd found out.'

Rachel put her mug down and leaned forward. 'Found what out?'

Rachel went outside into the ground-floor flat's overgrown back garden so that she wouldn't be overheard and rang Wesley on his mobile. It was chilly out there and she pulled her sweater closely around her body for warmth.

'Marion Hatman's just told me something. Might be important.' She spoke quietly, casting occasional glances at the back door. 'Leanne has an ex called Jordan Carnegie. They split up around the time she started hanging round with Barney Yelland. Carnegie worked for Darren for a while but they never got on. Darren ended up punching him and sacking him from his job.'

'Did Darren take exception to him going out with his little girl?'

'Possibly, if he'd found out.'

'Where's Carnegie now?'

'In Exeter. According to Marion he's a loser – not good enough for Leanne.'

'Why hasn't he been mentioned before?'

'Marion thought he was off the scene so she never imagined he could have anything to do with Leanne's disappearance.'

'I'd hardly call Exeter off the scene. Hang on.' Wesley

went over to his computer and typed in Jordan Carnegie's name. 'Bingo. He's got a record. Affray. Actual bodily harm. Theft of a vehicle. Possession of class A drugs. He's been a naughty boy. I'll see if I can get an up-to-date address for him. We need to speak to him sooner rather than later.'

As he ended the call he looked at his watch. He suspected that when he broke the news about Jordan Carnegie to Gerry he'd want to go up to Exeter that evening. It was six o'clock and unlikely he'd make it home for supper.

He called the police station closest to the Exeter address on Jordan Carnegie's record and an officer there told him that Carnegie had been behaving himself in recent months – either that or he hadn't been caught, the man added cynically. He asked if Wesley wanted the Exeter police to conduct the interview but Wesley thanked him and said he'd come up there and speak to him himself. He'd never liked to rely on second-hand reports. He needed to see the man's face; take him by surprise and see how he reacted to questioning.

Gerry was going through reports but as soon as Wesley told him the latest developments he stood up and reached for his coat. 'Let's get up there, Wes. Darren's murder's going to be on the news now the press office has got its act together. We should catch Carnegie off guard before he's had a chance to think up a story.'

Wesley felt a pang of guilt. Pam hadn't seemed well that morning and he'd wanted to be home at a reasonable time. But he knew Gerry was right. 'I'll ring Pam to tell her I'll be late.'

'I better give Joyce a call and all.' Gerry fumbled for his phone, which was hidden underneath a pile of budget reports. 'We were supposed to be going to some film at the Arts Centre tonight but I did warn her I might be otherwise engaged.'

Wesley stood there while he made his call, sensing that Gerry's lady friend, Joyce, was a lot more understanding than Pam. She didn't have children to cope with and it probably made a difference. Then he made his own call and all Pam said was a sad-sounding 'OK.' He promised he'd be back as soon as he could.

The roads up to Exeter were fairly clear and when Wesley found a parking space outside Carnegie's address, Gerry commented that it was their lucky day. Carnegie lived in a district of the city popular with students; an area of Victorian houses and multiple occupancy not far from where Wesley had lived during his university days. There were bins outside Carnegie's house, overflowing with take-away pizza boxes, and in the front garden litter grew in place of flowers. The house was divided into four flats with Carnegie's name scrawled helpfully beside the top bell push.

They heard footsteps on uncarpeted stairs and the door opened to reveal a young man whose mousy hair stood up on his scalp in hedgehog spikes. His black T-shirt was emblazoned with a skull and his short sleeves revealed wiry, tanned arms decorated with a gallery of colourful tattoos.

Wesley asked if they could come in, making the request sound casual. But Carnegie's reaction to Wesley's request wasn't what he'd hoped for. 'You're not coming into my flat without a warrant.'

'In that case you can come with us to Tradmouth,' said Gerry, a hint of threat in his voice.

'I'm not under arrest. You can't make me.'

'We can arrest you if you like,' said Wesley. 'But we'd rather keep it unofficial at this stage. I understand you know Leanne Hatman.'

He stepped away, wary. 'Why?'

'She's missing.'

'That's got nothing to do with me.'

'Is it true you argued with her dad, Darren?' Gerry asked.

'Sod off,' was the reply.

'It's up to you, Mr Carnegie. Either you cooperate or we arrest you on suspicion.'

Wesley saw Carnegie making a slow calculation in his head, then he turned and began to climb the stairs. They followed him to the attic where the sloping walls of his small bedsit were covered in death metal posters. Gerry sat himself down on the grubby unmade double bed but Wesley preferred to stand, as did Carnegie.

'We'd like to talk about Leanne,' Wesley began.

Now he was in his home environment, Carnegie seemed a little more amenable. He slumped down on a hard chair by the window, his watchful eyes darting from one police-man to the other. 'You used to go out with Leanne Hatman.'

'So?'

'Why did your relationship finish?'

'She got big ideas. Met this bloke who said she could be a model. After that she didn't want to know me.'

'That must have hurt.' Wesley tried his best to sound sympathetic.

'She was a stupid cow. What makes you think she's missing? She probably just went off with this photographer bloke. It's him you should be speaking to, not me.'

'What do you know about him?'

'Not much. He was trying to get into her knickers if you ask me.'

'Where were you on the nineteenth of April?'

'How should I know? I don't keep a fucking diary.'

'The nineteenth was a Sunday – two and a half weeks ago if that's any help.'

A look of relief passed across his face. 'I was doing a gig in the Farmers' Arms. I'm in a band. Drummer.'

'Witnesses.'

'Loads. But I can't tell you their names,' he said, a challenge in his voice.

'Your fellow band members will do,' said Wesley, handing over his notebook.

Carnegie brushed it away. 'No use to me. I'm dyslexic.'

'Tell me then.'

Carnegie recited a few names and a couple of addresses. It was something they'd get someone else to check, a routine job for some hapless DC or uniform.

'Where were you yesterday – six thirty onwards?'

'Why?'

'Just answer the question,' Gerry growled.

'I was here all day. Off sick. Never went out.'

'Anyone confirm that?'

'No.'

'Did you use your computer at all?' Wesley asked, eyeing the laptop that stood on a shelf by the boarded-up fireplace.

'No. Didn't feel like it. I listened to music.'

'Any of your neighbours confirm that?'

'I used my headphones.'

'When did you last see Darren Hatman?'

There was an awkward silence before he answered. 'A couple of months ago.'

'We've been told you had a row.'

'Who told you that? Lee Varlow?'

'As a matter of fact it was Darren's wife.'

'Marion. She always had it in for me. Thought I wasn't good enough for her precious Leanne. I wouldn't be surprised if it was her who put all this modelling crap into Leanne's mind.'

'Why did you quit your job with Darren?'

'I got sick of travelling down to Morbay every day and I wanted more time to concentrate on the band. It was a crap job anyway, lugging stuff around on a building site. Being on your best behaviour in other people's houses. Didn't suit me at all.'

'You've got a bit of a temper,' said Gerry. 'Affray, actual bodily harm. Theft of a vehicle. Not to mention the Class A substances.'

'So?' His foot began to tap rhythmically; Gerry's line of questioning had got to him.

'We've heard you and Darren had a row and he punched you. That must have made you angry.'

'He gave me a slap and I left. End of story.'

'What was the argument about?'

'Work.'

'I presume Darren knew about you and Leanne?'

'No. We kept it quiet 'cause me and him didn't get on. Marion knew but Darren didn't.'

'Darren was found dead this morning. He died sometime yesterday evening – probably between seven and midnight.'

Wesley watched Jordan Carnegie's face, expecting a reaction. But he didn't see one.

'Aren't you're going to ask how he died?'

Carnegie shrugged his shoulders. 'I expect you'll tell me.'

Gerry opened his mouth to speak but Wesley stopped him with a sideways look. He wanted to keep quiet about the cause of death for the moment.

'We'd like you to come with us to Tradmouth police station and make a statement.'

There was no mistaking the panic on Carnegie's face. He suddenly sprang from his seat and ran for the door, hurtling down the stairs, his feet banging like a drumbeat on the bare wood.

Wesley began to follow him but when he was halfway down the stairs he saw the front door slam. He dashed down and opened it, almost tripping on a bike propped up against the hall wall, only to find there was no sign of Jordan Carnegie when he reached the street outside.

He returned to the top of the house to find that Gerry hadn't moved.

'He's gone. I'll get on to the local station – get them to keep a lookout. He'll have to come back here at some point.' He pointed at the shelf and grinned. 'He's left his drumsticks.'

Gerry levered himself off the bed. 'We might as well take a look round now we're here.'

Wesley knew this wasn't strictly by the book but he didn't see why not. They began to search the bedsit, opening drawers and poking around in the chipboard wardrobe in the corner of the room. In another corner stood a sink, a kitchen cupboard and a Baby Belling cooker and through a low door there was a tiny mould-stained bathroom set into the eaves. If Carnegie had attempted to stand up in the bath he would have banged his head on the ceiling.

'Here, Wes. Look what I've found in the bedside drawer.'

Gerry handed him a sheaf of papers, printed out from a website on a printer that was running short of ink. But the words and images were still quite clear: all kinds of crossbows at all kinds of prices, some models and packs of bolts circled in Biro.

Wesley made the call to the local station. He wanted Jordan Carnegie found.

8

Uriah returned late to our lodgings
with a bloody face and would offer no
explanation. Joules clucked around like
an old hen, saying he did not know
what action to take, so I took charge,
playing the bear-leader to perfection.

I left the reverend gentleman and
burst into my cousin's chamber to
confront him. I found him lying on
his bed, his eyes focused on the ceiling,
and he made no sign of recognition
when I addressed him. I shook him by
the shoulders and he turned his face
from me.

'What have you done?' I asked. But he
refused to answer.

When I rejoined Joules, I found him
speaking with a local man. The

stranger raised his voice and gesticulated wildly while Joules attempted to calm him. It is fortunate that our cicerone is fluent in the native tongue and was able to discover the cause of the man's distress. It transpired that Uriah asked the man's daughter to commit a most immoral act with him, as though he saw nothing wrong in such a vile request. The young woman's father beat Uriah for his impertinence, quite justifiably in my opinion.

Joules is most distressed. He has never before encountered such a thing in the course of his blameless life and thinks it politic that we leave Naples.

Wesley arrived home at ten o'clock, having already eaten – fish and chips guzzled hungrily in an Exeter street near the police station where they'd ended up after their abortive visit to Jordan Carnegie. With their discovery in Carnegie's bedside drawer, finding Leanne Hatman's ex-boyfriend had assumed a new urgency. Carnegie had been interested in crossbows. The question was, had he purchased one? And, if so, had he used it on Darren Hatman?

Wesley had called Dr Tennant who now had a better idea about the type of bolt used to kill Hatman, uttering the disclaimer that he couldn't be absolutely sure without the weapon itself there in front of him for comparison.

They'd taken the printouts away from Carnegie's flat to compare the bolts Carnegie had circled with the dimensions of Tennant's suggested murder weapon. It was a pity the killer had pulled the bolt out of the dead man's body and denied them that vital evidence. However, the catalogue was a start.

When Wesley opened his front door he was still feeling angry with himself for allowing Carnegie to escape so easily. Perhaps, he thought in a dark moment, he was losing his touch.

He found Pam sitting on the sofa in the living room, eating toast, a half-empty glass of red wine on the coffee table in front of her. She looked up as he walked in but there was no smile of greeting. When he sat down beside her and put his arm round her shoulders she put the remains of her toast down on her plate and turned to face him.

'Sorry I'm late,' he said. 'There's been a suspicious death up at Eyecliffe Castle. Has it been on the news?'

'Yes. A middle-aged man wasn't it? They didn't say how he died.'

'Believe me, you don't want to know.' He snuggled up to her and kissed the top of her head. 'Kids OK?'

'Fine.' She looked away.

'Something the matter ... apart from me being late, that is?'

There was a long silence as she picked up her glass and took a long drink of wine. 'I nearly called your sister earlier.'

'Nearly? Why didn't you? We haven't seen her and Mark for a while. When things quieten down at work ... '

'I chickened out.'

He looked at her, surprised. Wesley's sister, Maritia, was hardly the fearsome type. She was married to the vicar of a nearby village and worked part-time as a GP, and she and

Pam had always got along well. 'What do you mean, chickened out?'

'I wanted to ask her something.'

A worm of dread wriggled into his mind. 'What?'

Pam took a deep breath. 'I was in the shower and ... Well, I found a lump. They say you should always examine yourself and ... '

'When was this?'

'A couple of days ago.'

'Why didn't you tell me?'

'You were busy at work.'

Her words hurt like a punch in the stomach. She had been going through this alone and he hadn't even realised there was anything wrong.

'I'll tell Gerry I'm taking time off,' he said taking her in his arms, engulfed by a wave of guilt and shame.

She put a finger to his lips. 'I don't want you to fuss. It's probably nothing.'

'Have you made an appointment with the doctor?'

'They told me to call first thing tomorrow for an emergency appointment but it's awkward with school and ... '

'Don't worry about that. I'll ring your head and explain.'

'Not about the lump,' she said, horrified.

'Credit me with some tact. I'll just say you're ill. And I'm coming to the doctor's with you.' He looked at the phone. 'I'll give Gerry a call now.'

'I'll be OK going by myself.'

He stopped her words with a kiss and they sat, frozen, for a few moments. Then he drew back and saw tears welling up in her eyes.

'I'm coming with you whether you like it or not. I'll ask Maritia to come round and talk to you if you like.'

Before she could answer Moriarty jumped between them, looking for a vacant knee to settle on. As Wesley lifted the cat and put her back down on the floor, Pam began to sob.

Gerry Heffernan arrived at his desk early – seven thirty. At first he was surprised Wesley hadn't arrived before him, until he remembered the call he'd received the previous night. Wesley would be in a bit late. Something important had cropped up and he'd be there as soon as he could.

When his phone rang, he grabbed it, hoping it was news that would push the investigation along. But instead he heard Wesley's voice, sounding subdued, worried.

Gerry listened carefully to what he had to say and, for the first time in ages, he was lost for words. Afterwards he sat for a while staring at the phone. This was an unexpected shock. But Darren Hatman was lying in the mortuary and the investigation had to go on.

Next he put in a call to Exeter, but the news wasn't particularly good. Jason Carnegie's place was due to be searched properly that morning and someone was going to trawl through his computer history to see if he'd actually placed an order for a crossbow. But there was still no sign of the man himself. Gerry thanked his Exeter colleague and came out into the main office to give the morning briefing.

He didn't mention Wesley. He knew his friend wouldn't want all and sundry knowing his personal business so, if anybody asked, he intended to say he'd been delayed. Gerry might have a big mouth at times but years in CID had taught him to be discreet if necessary.

He stood in front of the huge noticeboard that almost

covered one wall of the hall. On it hung photographs of the main players: Leanne Hatman, the staff at Eyecliffe Castle, Clare Woolmer, Jordan Carnegie and Barney Yelland on one side. Darren Hatman, his wife and his colleagues, Craig Gatting and Lee Varlow on the other. No doubt their gallery would expand as more connections were discovered but this was as good a starting point as any.

'Right,' he began, scanning the faces to make sure they were listening with rapt attention. 'We need to liaise with Exeter on the search for Jordan Carnegie and find out if anything interesting turns up when his flat's searched.' He looked at Rob Carter. 'I'll leave that with you, Rob.'

Rob looked disappointed, as though he'd been hoping for something more exciting. Gerry sometimes felt he hadn't yet grasped that police work mostly involved a painstaking sift through the details.

After assigning tasks to the rest of the team, Gerry looked at his watch. 'I'm going to the castle. David Palmer's back today and I want to ask him about Leanne. Rach, you come with me.'

'Why's Wesley late?' Rachel asked as she followed the DCI out. 'He's not ill, is he?' She tried to make the question sound casual.

'He said he'll be in later,' said Gerry.

From the closed expression on the boss's face, Rachel knew he wasn't going to give any more away. She was curious though. Nothing usually kept Wesley away during a murder inquiry.

She drove them to Eyecliffe Castle. It was rumoured that Gerry had once passed his driving test but she'd never known him drive in all the time she'd worked with him. He saved his navigational skills for the water, being the proud owner of the thirty-foot yacht he'd renovated shortly after the death of his wife – something to take his mind off his grief. However, these days he didn't get as much sailing time in as he would like. His injuries had kept him ashore for a while, and then there was his workload.

'You've been here to use the facilities, I believe,' Gerry said as they approached the front entrance side by side.

'I had a girlie weekend with two of my sisters-in-law six months ago.' She smiled at the memory. 'It's a lovely place – done out like a country house. They've even preserved the old library. Roaring fires, the lot.'

'Do they do weddings?'

Rachel looked at him. 'Why, sir? Are you thinking of . . . ?' She noticed that Gerry's face had turned red. He'd been seeing Joyce for a while now and she'd wondered whether they might put the arrangement on a more permanent footing one day.

'No . . . er . . . I didn't mean . . . I was thinking of you. You didn't consider the castle?'

'We considered it but they quoted an arm and a leg. Times are hard in the farming industry, you know.'

'When haven't they been? What did you think of the place?'

'Nice.'

'Just nice?'

'Extremely nice. And before you ask, I didn't pay much attention to the relationships between the staff.'

'Pity. Leanne would have been working there then, wouldn't she?'

'I can't say I remember her.' She stopped walking and shut her eyes. 'Or maybe I do. I think it might have been her who did my mud wrap.'

116

'Mud wrap?'

'It's good for the skin.'

'I'll take your word for it. But wouldn't it have been cheaper to put on your cozzie and roll about on the river bank at low tide?'

This brought a slight smile to Rachel's lips but she said nothing. As they walked into reception, Gerry saw that Sean was on duty again behind the desk, his blond quiff standing erect on his head like a cockscomb.

'Is Mr Palmer back from his conference?' said Gerry, leaning on the desk, looking as relaxed as a drinker at his favourite bar.

'Yes, sir,' said Sean. 'I'll let him know you're here.'

'When did he get back?'

'Last night.'

'Where was the conference again?'

'Brighton I believe.'

Gerry gave the young man his crocodile smile. 'No doubt he'll tell me all the sordid details. Don't bother to let him know we're here, just point us in the direction of his office. We'll surprise him.'

Sean looked alarmed, as if he'd detected a threat behind the words, but he directed them meekly down the corridor to their right, as though too timid – or wise – to argue with a policeman.

Gerry and Rachel found the office easily enough. Its polished mahogany door had a brass nameplate: David Palmer. General Manager.

'Wish I had a door like that,' Gerry whispered as he raised his hand to knock.

Palmer's 'come in' sounded authoritative but Gerry, undaunted, opened the door and strolled in.

117

'DCI Heffernan and Detective Sergeant Rachel Tracey, Tradmouth CID.' They showed their ID and Palmer stood up to shake hands, his face serious as a funeral director's. He must have been in his forties; blandly handsome with immaculately styled dark-brown hair and an expensive, well-cut suit. He reminded Gerry of a shop window mannequin.

After the introductions Gerry sat down without being invited. Unlike Palmer's well-upholstered model, the chairs in front of the desk were hard and uncomfortable, minions' chairs for people who knew their place.

'You've been away, Mr Palmer,' Gerry began. 'Missed all the excitement.'

Palmer nodded solemnly. 'I've been at a conference in Brighton. Of course my mother called to tell me what had happened. I really can't believe a man's been murdered in my grounds. It was murder, I take it?'

'I'm afraid so. Which means we'll have to ask you a few questions. Your staff and guests have already given statements.'

'Then I don't think I have anything to add. I wasn't here when it happened.'

'But you do know the victim – Darren Hatman?'

'I wouldn't say I know him exactly.'

'You sold him the barn in your grounds.'

'That was all done through my solicitor. The first and only time I met him was when he came here to ask where his daughter was. He was the father of one of my employees who decided to leave her job without giving notice.'

'What can you tell us about Leanne Hatman?'

'She worked in our spa. She was popular with the guests so I was sorry to lose her.'

'You've no idea where she is now?' It was the first time Rachel had spoken and Gerry noticed that Palmer was looking at her, an appreciative smile playing on his moist lips.

'I'm afraid not.' The answer came quickly. 'I'd love to be able to help but ... '

Gerry cleared his throat. It was time to get down to business.

'We've heard that there was a complaint made against you a while ago. A member of staff accused you of being rather ... tactile.'

Palmer's face reddened. 'That was ages ago. A highly strung chambermaid developed what I can only describe as an obsession with me and made some hysterical allegations. All rubbish, of course. She didn't take the matter any further which rather proves she was making the whole thing up. She was asked to leave. It was for the best.'

There was a smug look on his face now, as though he was rather pleased with the explanation he'd come up with.

'What was your relationship with Leanne Hatman?'

'Employer and employee. I hardly knew the girl.'

'We've heard otherwise,' said Rachel. Gerry suspected she was rather enjoying herself. 'She fancied you ... kept flirting.'

'That's nonsense.'

'You were here on the night she disappeared.'

'Yes, but I didn't know she'd gone until she didn't turn up for her shift the next morning.'

'Would your mother know more?'

Palmer frowned. 'I'd be grateful if you didn't bother my mother. She's not been well.'

'She looked OK to me.'

'Appearances can be deceptive.'

There was a short silence before Gerry asked his next question.

'What about the night before last? Where were you?'

'I've already told you, I was in Brighton. I can give you the name of the hotel if you like.'

'Thanks,' said Gerry. 'And we'd like the names of the people you were with and all.'

Palmer scribbled down some names and handed the sheet of paper to Rachel.

'What did you think?' Gerry said quietly as they walked back down the corridor to reception.

'He thinks a lot of himself.'

'What about all these women allegedly throwing themselves at him?'

Rachel considered the question for a few moments. 'I suppose he's attractive . . . and he is the boss.'

'That's never helped me,' Gerry replied with a wide grin. 'Get those names he gave us checked out, will you?'

Rachel said she would as though she was positively looking forward to it.

Wesley had decided to confide in Gerry that morning. The boss was an old softie underneath all his bluster and, besides, he knew what it was like to lose someone close. His own wife, Kathy, had died in a car accident before Wesley had arrived in Tradmouth and his reaction to Wesley's news couldn't have been more sympathetic. Of course he had to go to the doctor's with Pam; he wasn't to worry about work. They'd manage. He hoped the appointment would go well.

Wesley asked him to call if there were any new developments in the case and felt slightly better when he agreed.

He was worried about Leanne Hatman. Did the fact that her father had been murdered mean she was dead as well? Or was she still out there somewhere alive ... possibly held by somebody who'd taken exception to her father's interference?

He couldn't help thinking of the photographs they'd found in Barney Yelland's room: the woman's face scored out with a violence that didn't bode well. If Yelland had developed an attachment to Leanne and then realised that she was just a vain wannabe using him to advance her career, who knew how he'd have reacted.

It had now been confirmed that Yelland had flown back from Palermo a day earlier than planned, which meant he'd been in the country at the time of Darren Hatman's murder. He hadn't yet turned up at his lodgings so the phrases 'lying low' and 'on the run' popped into Wesley's head.

Pam's appointment with the GP was in just over an hour's time. An hour of nervous waiting; of trying to fill the time with some activity while his mind was focused on just one thought – what would the doctor say? Occupying the time with work might help. Pam was sitting on the sofa turning the pages of the morning paper but he could tell her brain wasn't registering the printed words.

He picked up his phone. 'Mind if I make a work call? It's something I'm supposed to do today and I might as well get it over with ... if that's OK,' he said, a little wary of her reaction. This was alien territory and he wasn't sure how he should behave.

But Pam said it was fine; it would only be on his mind if he didn't.

Speaking to Yelland's friend, Harry Belamy, had been

high on Wesley's list of things to do until Jordan Carnegie had distracted him.

He went into the dining room and punched out the number he had for the teacher of English living in Agrigento who, apparently, knew Barney Yelland well enough to put him up while he was in Sicily. He had wondered whether Belamy would be at work but his call was answered after the first ring, almost as if the man had been waiting by the phone.

'Am I speaking to Harry Belamy?'

'You are.' The voice was deep and accentless.

Wesley introduced himself and was relieved when Belamy seemed happy to talk.

'Barney called me a week before he arrived and invited himself to stay.'

'Was that a problem?' Wesley's body tensed as he waited for Belamy to throw some light on Yelland's past. The missing link that might tell them what had become of Leanne Hatman.

'Let's just say I knew Barney from years ago and I was worried that he'd get too comfortable and outstay his welcome, if you see what I mean. '

'But you still agreed?'

'He told me he was working on a project and I thought it sounded interesting. Actually he left early so I needn't have worried – and he was remarkably well behaved. Must be old age.'

'What do you mean?'

'He was into all sorts in his younger days – drugs, girls. But this time he was a reformed character, just focused on his work. The commissario I spoke to said he was wanted in connection with a woman's disappearance. Is that right?'

'Does that surprise you?'

There was a long silence before Belamy answered. 'We were members of the same photography club at university. He had a real gift and I'm not surprised he took it up professionally. But ...'

'But what?'

'There was an incident. He became obsessed with the girlfriend of one of the other members: beautiful girl, slim, long blonde hair; gorgeous and way out of Barney's league. He kept trying to see her alone, saying he wanted to photograph her. She agreed at first but then her boyfriend took exception.'

'And?'

'The boyfriend warned him off but he wouldn't leave it alone. He started hanging round outside the girl's flat. In the end the boyfriend's mates in the rugby club roughed him up a bit so he got the message.'

'You kept in touch with him?'

'Not exactly but one of our group sends out a newsletter saying what we're all up to. That's how Barney found out I was in Sicily. He showed me the pictures he'd taken for the book he'd working on – about the Grand Tour – and they were impressive. Like I said, he's good. More than good – brilliant.'

'Did he mention a woman called Leanne Hatman? She's been modelling for him.'

'He never mentioned his sex life and I didn't particularly want to ask. I can imagine it could be pretty ... intense. I always thought he saw women as ...' There was a short pause while he searched for the right words. 'As works of art, something to be ... possessed. He always went for the same type – blonde and willowy. His perfect woman, I guess.'

'When did you last see him?'

'He was due to fly out on Wednesday morning but on the Monday evening he made a phone call to the author he was working with. On my phone – he'd lost his own soon after he'd arrived in Italy. Then he told me he'd decided to go back early because he'd got all the photographs he needed and he had to get hold of some extra material for the book. He managed to get on an earlier flight from Palermo and I took him to the airport.'

'Ever known him own or use a crossbow?'

'A crossbow?' Belamy sounded surprised. 'No, of course not. Why? Look, I think you've misunderstood me. When I told you about that girl I didn't mean to imply that he's ... I can't see him harming anyone.'

'I'm sure you're right, Mr Belamy, but we have to follow every lead. I believe he was married.'

'Yes, but it didn't work out. And before you ask, I don't know what happened. Look, I'm sure he can't have done anything to that girl.'

'Can you let us have the number he called on your phone?'

After a short silence Belamy recited a number and Wesley made a careful note of it.

'You've been a great help, Mr Belamy,' said Wesley before Belamy could say anything else. 'Thanks for your time.'

Wesley ended the call before Belamy could make any further protests of Barney Yelland's innocence, then called the office and spoke to Paul Johnson, relaying what he'd just been told. Paul promised to check Yelland's contacts and family again. Now they knew he was back in the UK they needed to find him.

Once he'd finished he rejoined Pam. It was almost time for her appointment and she was sitting on the sofa, staring ahead, fidgeting with her wedding ring. He sat down beside her and gave her a hug, feeling her body stiffen in his embrace. She hadn't bothered with her usual make-up or perfume. Worry kills all vanity.

They walked together to the doctor's surgery and while they sat in the waiting room Wesley watched her flick through a dog-eared magazine filled with pictures of smirking celebrities. They didn't speak but he reached out to give her hand a gentle squeeze, receiving a weak, brave smile in return.

It was twenty minutes before Pam's name was called; twenty minutes of terrified anticipation, her emotions veering from hope to despair. When she tried to stand up her legs felt weak and Wesley put a supporting hand under her elbow.

'You'll be all right,' he whispered in her ear as they walked towards the surgery door. She didn't look as though she believed him.

Kirsty Paige let her lady out of the treatment room, smiling smoothly and saying she was looking forward to seeing her again tomorrow for her next aromatherapy massage. But as soon as she was alone the smile vanished and she sat down, stretched out her arms and breathed in the lavender-scented air.

Then she walked over to the sink in the corner of the room and washed the oil off her hands. Her life had been busier since Leanne had gone but that wasn't necessarily a bad thing.

She looked at the watch pinned on the chest of her black

uniform, a quasi-nurse's outfit which flattered her slender body and made her feel efficient and sexy. There was now a gap between clients so she'd make the most of it and consolidate her position.

She left the treatment room, locking the door behind her because she didn't want any of the other girls to come in and borrow her equipment. That had been one of Leanne's irritating little foibles: she could never resist nicking anything that caught her eye and her sense of entitlement had irritated Kirsty and her other colleagues. That and her constant harping on about her brilliant modelling career. According to Leanne, she was going to take the modelling world by storm. She was going to be the next Kate Moss.

And Leanne's absence also gave her a chance to get closer to David Palmer. Like most men around the hotel, he'd been mesmerised by Leanne's beauty. But now Leanne was gone . . . and Kirsty had something to offer that she'd never had. Knowledge is a valuable commodity.

She checked her appearance in the large mirror hanging at the spa entrance, put there so that clients could see the near-miraculous effects of their treatments, in theory at any rate.

Walking down the corridor towards reception she switched the charming smile on again and said a cheery good morning every time she passed a guest. Staff she ignored or greeted with a curt 'hi'. She made straight for David Palmer's office, her head held high, exuding confidence, and when she knocked on his door she heard him say, 'Come in.'

'Can I have a word?' she said sweetly, shutting the heavy door behind her.

'Of course, Kirsty. Sit down. Is there a problem in the spa?'

Kirsty left a long silence. She'd seen it done in TV competitions to create suspense. And she wanted him on tenterhooks.

'I don't have a problem, David, but I think you have.'

He had been fidgeting with a pen, turning it over and over in his fingers. She saw him tense and the pen clattered on to the desk. 'What do you mean?'

She sat down and crossed her legs, her eyes fixed on his face. She could see she was making him uneasy but that was the intention.

'I think we should have a little chat about that secret of yours, David, don't you?'

James Garrard led the sort of life that hadn't brought him into contact with the police so he entered the portals of Tradmouth police station and approached the reception desk with some trepidation. The civilian woman posted at the desk didn't look as formidable as he'd expected. She was young with an open, freckled face, and she asked how she could help him, which was a good start.

He began by making it clear that he wasn't there to report a crime – well, not as far as he knew. However, he wanted to speak to someone about something strange that had occurred, or rather had been occurring for the past six months, ever since his picture had appeared in the *Tradmouth Echo*. He saw the sceptical look on the young woman's face and he knew he hadn't made himself clear. But it was a difficult thing to explain.

'So what exactly are you reporting, sir?'

He had no choice. He lifted the canvas bag he was

carrying on to the desk and took out a pair of pictures in gilded frames. They were small, around eight inches by six, and at first glance they looked like oil paintings. But on closer inspection it was clear they'd been created out of thousands of tiny pieces of coloured glass, microscopic mosaics of classical scenes made by an expert hand.

'You've found them? You suspect they're stolen property?'

She'd misunderstood and it was time to put her right.

'No. They were sent to me ... anonymously. In the post.'

She looked puzzled. 'Like a gift?'

'I suppose so. But they look rather valuable so I'm a bit worried. I want to report it.'

'Very well, sir. Name?'

9

Joules said we had no choice. We had to
leave that night and he had been
fortunate enough to find a berth for us
on a departing boat. Our destination
was the island of Sicily and our bear-
leader considered this most fortuitous
for it is the location of many
magnificent relics of the Greek and
Roman civilisations.

The prospect of Sicily so excited him
that he appeared to forget the
incident that caused our abrupt
departure from Naples and, for a
price, we secured the services of some
rough sailors who transported our
baggage from our lodgings to the vessel.
Uriah said nothing during the voyage
and yet I did not think his silence

*signified contrition. When he was told
that we were to land in Palermo, he
became suddenly animated and I saw
the light of hungry obsession in his eyes.*

Neil tried to call Wesley's mobile but all he heard was a disembodied voice telling him to leave a message on his voicemail. Though he'd left one as instructed Wesley hadn't returned his call, which was unusual. When he tried Wesley's work number he was told he was unavailable and, with further probing, he managed to winkle out the information that he wasn't in work that morning. When Neil called him at home there was still no answer, but he was too preoccupied to worry too much about it.

He'd driven from the B& B where he was staying for the duration of the dig to the site near the village of Turling Fitwell. His team from the Unit had already started excavating, along with some carefully selected members of a local community archaeological team. Neil had worked with the community group before and he was looking forward to joining them even though, in contrast to the Sicilian sunshine he'd enjoyed over the past fortnight, it had just started to drizzle.

When he parked in the castle car park he noticed that the woods in the grounds were sealed off with police tape. He'd heard on local radio that there'd been a suspicious death in the vicinity but details had been frustratingly sparse. No doubt when he finally managed to speak to Wesley, he'd find out what was going on.

The dig site was situated a quarter of a mile to the north of the castle, next to a rushing river. From the dig Neil could see the castle, standing above the precipitous slope that doubtless had provided extra defence in the Middle Ages. From the balustraded terrace overlooking the river valley the castle owners would have been able to see the water mill that once stood on their land, built far enough away not to disturb the gentry; a working building driven by the power of the rushing water.

When Neil had researched the site before his visit to Sicily, he'd seen sketches and paintings of the picturesque mill. It had fallen into disrepair at the start of the twentieth century and had eventually been demolished in the 1930s when modernity had promised the brave new world which had never really, in Neil's opinion, arrived.

The site no longer belonged to Eyecliffe Castle but it was accessible from the grounds via a path that snaked down to the water. Taking the equipment there hadn't posed much of a problem but lack of access for a mini digger meant all the trenches had been opened by hand.

In his absence Lucy and Dave, Neil's second in command, had carried out a geophysics survey and dug several test pits. When Neil arrived that day, he found them marking out a new trench with a couple of the volunteers.

He picked up a mattock and was about to start work when he realised he'd left his phone in the car. He swore under his breath and shouted over to Lucy, telling her he wouldn't be long.

As he passed Dave he noticed that he'd stopped work and was staring at the place where they'd sunk one of the test pits, only to fill it in again as soon as it had proved to contain nothing of archaeological importance. 'This pit looks as though it's been dug over again since we filled it in,' Dave said, scratching his head. 'But it could be my imagination.'

'Might be treasure hunters,' Neil replied. 'Or the castle ghost wanting a bit of exercise ... or exorcise ... get it?'

The team chuckled dutifully and Neil set off back up the steep path, his thighs aching with the effort. He'd always thought of himself as fit but as he trudged on, he realised that his break in the sun, eating and drinking far too much, had left him with a few extra pounds to carry.

Once at the top he paused for breath, thinking that if he did this climb every day, it would serve him better than a few hours spent in some expensive gym. When he reached the car park he saw that half the vehicles there belonged to the police and he looked around, hoping to spot Wesley – or, failing that, Gerry.

But there was no sign of either so he opened his car door and rummaged amongst the detritus that had built up inside the vehicle during the time he'd owned it. He'd lost count of the number of times he'd promised himself that he'd clear it out. When he heard someone saying his name, he backed out of the car, bumping his head on the door frame, and when he turned, rubbing the spot, he saw one of the volunteers standing there.

'I'm sorry, Dr Watson. Did I make you jump?' the man said with a worried frown, as if he feared he'd made some dreadful faux pas. He was a slight man with glasses, thinning hair and a general aura of neatness. Under normal circumstances, Neil was sure he would have looked like an off-duty chartered accountant but today he was wearing sturdy walking boots and digging clothes, as yet unsullied by the damp Devon earth.

'No, I'm fine, James,' said Neil bravely. He had worked with James Garrard before and knew him as a painstaking digger and recorder of finds. Archaeology had become his chief hobby since his early retirement from the civil service. The nature of his previous work was vague but, whatever it was, Neil was sure he'd have performed it diligently.

'I'm so sorry I'm late but I wanted to have a word with someone from the police.'

Neil raised his eyebrows. 'Oh yes?'

'I reported something but I don't think they took it seriously.'

'That's the police for you.'

'I visited the police station in Tradmouth and talked to some young girl on the front desk but I thought if I spoke to someone more senior . . . '

Neil heard a car draw up. The timing was fortuitous – for James Garrard at least. He watched as Wesley opened the car door and climbed out. Gerry Heffernan was with him, looking more earnest than usual.

He touched James's sleeve. 'Hang on. I just need to have a word with someone.'

As he began to walk towards the two policemen Wesley looked round but there was no smile of welcome.

'I've been trying to ring you,' Neil said, a hint of accusation in his voice.

He saw Wesley glance at Gerry. 'Sorry. I had something on this morning. How's the dig going?'

Neil could tell from the way he changed the subject that whatever Wesley had been doing that morning, he wasn't keen to discuss it. 'Come down and have a look if you've got time. What's going on over there?' He pointed at the distant trees cordoned off with blue-and-white police tape.

'A body was found in the woods. Suspicious death.'

'Who?'

'The father of a missing girl. We're working on the theory that the two cases are linked.'

Neil said nothing. His mind was on the archaeology that, hopefully, lay beneath the ground at the mill site, just waiting to be discovered, and besides, he could tell Wesley was in no mood for a chat. Meanwhile James Garrard was waiting patiently for the conversation to finish so at least he could do one good deed that day.

'James, come and meet a friend of mine. We were at uni together. Wesley this is James Garrard, one of our volunteers. He went to your police station to report something but he was fobbed off.'

'Your police station? You're a policeman?'

'Yes. Wesley Peterson – Detective Inspector.'

James looked sheepish as he shook hands with Wesley. Neil suspected that Wesley was in a hurry but was concealing his impatience out of good manners.

'Is there a problem, Mr Garrard?' Wesley asked.

'Er ... yes. It's actually rather unusual. I've been receiving these ... gifts. Anonymously.'

'What kind of gifts?' Wesley asked, suddenly intrigued.

'Perhaps you've got an admirer,' said Gerry who hadn't been able to resist listening in. 'A lady who's been pining for you from afar.'

'I'm a happily married man,' Garrard said, his cheeks reddening.

'When did this start?' Wesley asked.

'About six months ago. My wife and I moved back to Devon a couple of years ago. I was born here and lived in Turling Fitwell until I was seven when my family moved to London. I decided to return when I retired.' He paused. 'The ... things started arriving shortly after my picture

134

appeared in the local paper. I was helping to raise money for the Bloxham Lifeboat, you see.' He hesitated. 'The strange thing is, I remember something similar happening when I was little. Parcels used to turn up. Toys. My mother became quite worried about it but then we moved away and—'

'So you're not reporting a theft,' said Gerry. 'In fact it's the opposite.' He sounded interested, as if the report made a pleasant change from the usual run of violence and dishonesty they dealt with day in, day out.

'I realise that. But the trouble is, I'm finding it rather disturbing. I feel as though somebody's watching me.'

For a few moments Wesley said nothing. 'Well, unless an actual crime's been committed, there's not much we can do, I'm afraid.'

'But what would your advice be? You see, the things I've received are quite valuable and I feel awkward about keeping them. Is there a chance they might have been stolen? Is somebody trying to get me into trouble by dumping stolen property on me?'

'Tell you what,' said Wesley. 'If you're worried why don't you take the things to Tradmouth police station and ask somebody to check them against our register of stolen goods?'

There was no mistaking the relief on James Garrard's face. 'Thank you. That would set my mind at rest. But it still won't solve the puzzle of who's sending them.'

'Well, if they're not pinched, you can enjoy them with a clear conscience,' said Gerry. 'Now if you'll excuse us . . .'

Neil watched the two men walk away towards the castle entrance.

*

'What did you make of that?' Gerry asked as they passed under the gatehouse.

'I'm not sure.'

Gerry stopped. 'You sure you're all right, Wes?'

'Course I am.'

''Cause if you need any more time off to be with Pam or . . .'

'She's gone back into work. She says the worst thing you can do is sit at home brooding about it. The GP says the hospital should be in touch within a week.'

'Trouble is, with something like that eating away at you, it'll seem like a month.'

'I'm going to ask my sister to have a word with her. What's the use of having a doctor in the family if you can't make use of her?' He hesitated. 'I don't want to tell my parents yet; not until we know for certain that something's wrong.'

'What about Della? Surely Pam'll want to tell her own mum.'

'If anyone's guaranteed to make a bad situation worse, it's Della.'

When they reached the hotel entrance, Gerry suddenly stopped.

'I almost forgot to tell you – David Palmer lied to us about being in Brighton at the time of Darren Hatman's murder . . .'

'Did he?'

'The information came in while you were out. Rob Carter called the conference organiser and, apparently, Palmer checked out early. He's got over twenty-four hours unaccounted for, so I want to see what he has to say for himself.'

When they walked into David Palmer's office he looked like a frightened man but he rapidly rearranged his features to form the mask of the helpful citizen, anxious to help the police with their inquiries.

Gerry dispensed with any pleasantries and came straight to the point. 'You lied to us, Mr Palmer' he said, sitting down heavily. 'You said you were in Brighton but you left early. Went walkabout as they say down under. Where were you?'

For a moment Palmer was lost for words. Then he spoke. 'I assure you I wasn't killing people in the grounds.'

The answer sounded more confident than Wesley had expected. 'Then you won't mind telling us what you were doing.'

'It's delicate.'

Gerry leaned forward, his eyes shining. 'Go on. We don't shock easily.'

'I was with a lady.'

'We'll need her name. And don't worry, discretion is our middle name, isn't that right, Inspector Peterson?'

'She told her husband she was away on business and we checked into a little guest house. It wasn't ideal but a lot of the local hotel proprietors know me and . . . '

'We need her name.' Gerry was waiting expectantly. It was a tactic that rarely failed, and this time it worked as planned. Palmer bowed his head meekly and recited a name and an address in one of the more upmarket suburbs of Morbay.

'We'll have to speak to the lady,' said Wesley. 'But, as the DCI said, we'll be discreet.'

Wesley glanced back as they left the office. Palmer, sitting statue-still, reminded Wesley of a deflating balloon.

When they reached reception Wesley noticed that Sean was still on duty behind the desk. The lad looked bored but he straightened his back as they approached, as though he was hoping for some excitement; anything to brighten his day.

Gerry ignored him and marched past. 'We need to confirm Palmer's alibi,' he said when they reached the courtyard.'

'I'll organise it.'

They had just passed under the gatehouse when Wesley spotted a familiar figure walking in the dried-up dip once filled by a moat. It was Miss D'Arles and she had Reginald with her, the dog lumbering ahead, looking back at his mistress from time to time as if he was checking she was still there.

When the woman saw the two policemen she stopped and waited for them to reach her.

'Detective Chief Inspector Heffernan, Inspector Peterson,' she said once they were within earshot. Her voice was clear and commanding; the received pronunciation of the land-owning classes, so little heard in modern times. 'I saw the police cars and I was hoping to find you here,' she continued. 'I wanted a word.'

'What about?' Wesley asked. He watched the dog retrace his steps and sit obediently by her side. He'd always had a soft spot for dogs but Pam reckoned that the presence of Moriarty in his household prevented them acquiring one of their own. The thought of Pam produced another pang of anxiety. He put out a hand and stroked the Labrador's head, an action he found soothing, while Reginald looked up at him with adoring eyes.

'I've been thinking about that argument I overheard . . .

that poor builder who died. A very nice young lady came round to take a statement. DC Walton, was it?'

'Yes. You said you didn't recognise the voice.'

'I know but . . . I hope you don't think I was lying. It was just that I wasn't sure and I'd hate to get anybody into trouble.'

Wesley could tell she was having second thoughts. He saw Gerry opening his mouth to speak but decided it was best if he got in first. Gerry's intentions were good but he wasn't always the most tactful of souls.

'Why don't you tell us what's bothering you and we'll decide whether it's relevant or not,' he said gently.

'I might be completely wrong but I think one of the voices might have belonged to Mr Palmer, the son of the man who bought the castle from me. I'm not saying it was him, just that it sounded a little like him.'

'That's very helpful, Miss D'Arles,' Wesley said. 'Thank you for letting us know.'

'I won't get into trouble for not putting it in my statement, will I?'

Wesley could tell she was worried about finding herself inadvertently on the wrong side of the law so he reassured her that lots of people make a statement then remember something later. It wasn't a problem.

But it might be a problem for David Palmer.

Bev Hughes stood back and stared at the painting. A watercolour in a plain gilt frame, it hung in a corridor not far from their room.

'You're sure it's a Turner?'

'I was at the Courtauld, remember, before everything went pear-shaped.'

He never tired of telling her how he'd once studied art history at one of the country's most prestigious institutions. After a short time working at an auction house after graduating he'd decided to branch out on his own, setting up as an art and antique dealer. Then came the recession, followed by a few bad business decisions, and his dreams of independence and fortune had soured.

Bev had worked in the back office of the auction house when they'd met but she knew nothing about art. There were times when he blamed Bev for his misfortunes – he had to blame someone – but she'd stuck by him and sloth made them stay together.

'Turner visited these parts in eighteen eleven and eighteen thirteen and did a lot of work here,' Jim continued, staring at the picture hungrily. 'He did a series of drawings for an engraver as well as watercolours of local scenes. This is the River Trad at sunset. The style's unmistakable. This little picture could save our bacon.'

'If someone misses it . . . ?'

But Jim pretended he hadn't heard her. They were checking out in the morning, getting straight into the Range Rover and driving back to London. It would be ages before anyone realised the painting had gone; Bev was seeing problems where none existed.

He reached out and lifted the painting reverently off the wall. The spot was in shadow and if they replaced it with the cheap print they'd brought with them in Bev's large suitcase, its absence wouldn't be noticed for a long time – if at all. He passed it to Bev who looked down at it, awestruck as Jim hung the print of Constable's *Hay Wain* in its place.

'It's not quite the same size,' Bev hissed. 'You got the

140

measurements wrong. You can see where the other one's been.'

'No one'll notice . . . not until we're well away from here.'

'What about the other picture? The one we came for in the first place?'

'It obviously isn't here. We've looked everywhere.'

'But all that research you did . . . '

'The family must have sold it privately. It happens.' He spat the words at her with some venom. She was getting on his nerves again.

They heard the soft creak of ancient floorboards, padding footsteps on the thickly carpeted floor. Someone was coming. Bev tried to conceal the painting beneath the folds of her voluminous cardigan and they hurried away towards their room.

Since the commencement of our
journey Uriah has carried with him a
slim volume bound in worn brown
leather, a plain book lacking a title
on the spine. He carries it everywhere,
keeping it with him at all times. I
inquired about it on one occasion but he
stated most abruptly that it was none of
my concern.

The thought of this book has so
intrigued me that last night while he
slept, I crept like a thief into his
chamber. Although the book lay beneath
his pillow, I succeeded in easing it out
and I returned to my own chamber
with it. By the light of a candle I
began to read and found it to be an
account of that mighty Emperor,

Frederick II, who was once King of Sicily. He passed from this life in the year 1250 and now lies in a magnificent porphyry tomb in the cathedral here at Palermo.

I read on, fascinated, until I came to a passage that gave me cause to stop – a page Uriah had marked for special attention.

David Palmer simply denied that he'd argued with Darren Hatman. He hadn't even been at the castle at the time. Miss D'Arles wasn't as young as she was and she was mistaken, he said, implying that the former owner of Eyecliffe Castle was suffering some sort of delusion or memory loss. It was common at her age, he'd added unsympathetically.

Wesley didn't like the patronising tone Palmer adopted when he was talking about Miss D'Arles. However, Miss D'Arles herself had admitted that she couldn't be certain.

He had delegated the job of confirming Palmer's alibi to Trish Walton and he asked her to pay particular attention to his whereabouts at the time of the alleged argument. If he was lying, he'd be found out sooner or later.

Wesley and Gerry returned to the incident room in Turling Fitwell church hall to find a scene of frantic activity. Officers were talking on phones and typing into computers and more photographs had been added to the gallery on the side wall alongside a whiteboard bearing Gerry's observations and tasks to be actioned. Wesley was well aware of the team's frustrations. Barney Yelland was still missing and, as yet, there had been no word that Jordan

Carnegie had been found in Exeter, or anywhere else for that matter.

When Wesley checked what had come in during his absence, there was one piece of information he found particularly interesting. Jordan Carnegie had ordered one of the crossbows he'd circled on the print out they'd found in his room and it had been delivered to his flat, along with a number of bolts, a week ago. Wesley asked one of the uniformed constables who'd been drafted in to help to get on to Exeter to see if they'd made any progress with their hunt.

There was something Wesley wanted to follow up himself. Although he'd spoken to Harry Belamy in Sicily, he hadn't yet had any personal contact with the author who was collaborating with Barney Yelland on his Grand Tour project; the man he'd used Harry Belamy's phone to contact.

The author's name was Cornell Stamoran and he lived in Dorset. Paul Johnson had telephoned him the day before to ask if he knew Yelland's whereabouts but Wesley was itching to speak to the man himself. If the author had worked closely with the photographer, there was a chance he might be able to offer some useful insights into his history and his personality. Besides, he quite fancied a trip to Dorset.

As he set off with Gerry, he tried to convince himself that the journey would take his mind off his visit to the doctor that morning. The worry still nagged away at him but Gerry's chatter during the journey and his bad Liverpudlian jokes dispelled the clouds of gloom for a short while. He knew Gerry was making a special effort and he was grateful to him.

Cornell Stamoran lived in the town of Lyme Regis, not

far from the Cobb, the harbour wall jutting out into the sea made famous by Jane Austen in her novel *Persuasion* and later by John Fowles in *The French Lieutenant's Woman*. The realisation that Pam would have loved the literary connections brought uncomfortable thoughts bubbling into his mind again but he tried to banish them as they walked up the narrow street towards Stamoran's tiny stone cottage.

They rang the doorbell by the sage-green front door – a popular heritage colour that suited the property to perfection. Someone had taste.

Stamoran answered almost immediately. He was a tall American with a shaved head and a pleasant face. Dressed in a blue Breton smock with a row of ethnic beads hanging around his neck, he reminded Wesley a little of an actor taking on the role of somebody with artistic inclinations. He greeted them with a friendly smile and invited them in, offering coffee, seemingly a man with nothing to hide from the police.

'I've already spoken to one of your officers,' Stamoran began. 'I'm sorry I couldn't be more help but Barney hasn't been in touch since he got back from Sicily.' He frowned. 'Which is somewhat worrying. The publisher's given us another three months but I like to get everything sorted in plenty of time. I've never actually collaborated with someone else before; I've always thought it a little risky to rely on other people in a job like this.'

'Clash of artistic temperaments?' said Gerry, at his most jovial.

'Authors can't afford to have artistic temperaments, Chief Inspector. It's a myth. Wasn't it Thomas Edison who said that genius is one per cent inspiration and ninety-nine per cent perspiration?'

Wesley smiled. 'And Tchaikovsky said that inspiration is a guest who doesn't willingly visit the lazy.'

Stamoran looked gratified that his visitor had managed to top his quote. 'Quite. I can't say I ever really took to Barney, although the project's been fascinating to work on. I used to teach history back in the States, you see, but I gave it up to write. Fiction mainly these days, historical sagas. I write under the name Fenella Somerscale.'

He looked at Wesley expectantly, waiting for him to say he recognised the name. Wesley didn't. But Gerry did.

'Fenella Somerscale. My ... er ... partner loves your books. She's got all of them out of the library.'

This elicited a satisfied smile from the author. If he'd been a cat, thought Wesley, he would have purred with pleasure.

'So a factual book is a new thing for you?' said Wesley.

'Oh no. I've written a number of academic books about the Age of Enlightenment so when I was asked to write about the Grand Tour I grabbed the chance. The young people who undertook the expedition regarded countries like Italy like a candy store, grabbing all the paintings and treasures they could lay their hands on and shipping them back home to embellish their stately homes. It's a subject that's always fascinated me ... but it's Fenella who pays the bills, of course.'

'Who suggested this particular project?'

'It was my publisher. She'd seen Barney's work at an exhibition and thought it would be something different. The title's *In the Footsteps of the Grand Tourists*. I've seen the work he's done for the book so far and it's good. He's an extremely talented guy.'

'What about your bit?' Wesley asked.

'I've done as much as I can. I'm just waiting for some information Barney promised to send. I'll get that coffee'

Wesley had rarely seen a man so relaxed during a police interview. When Stamoran disappeared into the kitchen to see to the refreshments he began to look around the room. Two walls were lined with bookshelves. Titles by Fenella Somerscale took up one section but the rest of the space was mostly occupied by volumes on eighteenth- and nine-teenth-century history.

When the author returned with the coffee there was something else on the tray: a small brown book; probably very old.

'I wanted to show you this,' he said once he'd distributed the mugs. 'It's an account of the travels of a young man in seventeen eighty-six, shortly before the French Revolution and its aftermath plunged Europe into turmoil. He took the usual route through the Low Countries, France and Switzerland. The last stop he refers to is in Switzerland but he says he intends to cross the Alps and travel on through Italy. Barney tells me he's located a second volume and that's what I'm waiting for. Using a previously undiscovered contemporary account will give our book an original edge. It's written by a Richard D'Arles from South Devon. He was the heir to a place called Eyecliffe Castle.'

The mention of the name D'Arles and the scene of Darren Hatman's murder made Wesley sit forward and take notice.

'This first volume's interesting,' Stamoran went on. 'Richard travelled with his cousin, Uriah, who sounds like trouble on two legs. Richard's father arranged for a cicerone called the Reverend Micah Joules to accompany them. I can just picture him: a little fat middle-aged clergyman trying to keep a couple of young aristos in check. Can't help feeling sorry for the guy.'

'Where did Barney get the book?' Wesley asked.

'From a girl who was modelling for him. He said she found it at the hotel where she worked.'

'Did he say she had the second volume too?'

'He wasn't specific but I presume so. He said getting hold of it wouldn't be a problem.'

Wesley picked up the diary and flicked through it. It was written in neat, copperplate handwriting, fairly easy to read.

'I've taken a couple of photocopies,' said Stamoran. 'Would you like one?'

'That would be helpful,' said Wesley. 'Thank you.'

'We haven't got time for historical research,' Gerry whispered when Stamoran left the room.

'You never know what'll come in useful.'

Gerry responded with a sceptical grunt.

When Stamoran returned with the photocopy, Wesley drained his coffee cup and asked his next question.

'Have you any idea where Barney Yelland is at the moment?'

Stamoran sat down. 'I haven't heard from him since he called from Sicily. He asked me how the book was going and promised to get the second volume to me as soon as possible. He told me he'd got all the shots he needed so he was planning to catch an earlier flight and work on them at home. He must be back in Devon now but there's been no answer when I've been trying to call him.' For the first time he looked worried. 'I really need that source material if I'm to finish this book. You've been to his address?'

'He hasn't gone back there,' said Wesley.

'May I ask why you want to speak to him? The officer who called me said something about a murder inquiry. Is he a suspect?'

Wesley didn't answer the question. 'Did he ever mention the name Leanne Hatman?'

'I think the model's name was Leanne but he never mentioned her surname.'

'Or her father, Darren Hatman?'

Stamoran shook his head. 'Barney and I are just colleagues; I guess I know nothing about his personal life.'

'Can you think of anyone he might have confided in?'

'The only person he ever talked about, apart from the model, was his landlady, Clare. I've gotten the impression they're close.' He didn't exactly wink but there was an insinuation in his voice.

'She says she hasn't seen him.'

'Then I'm sorry, I can't help you. Wish I could.'

'If you remember anything else or if Barney contacts you, please give me a call,' said Wesley, handing the author his card. 'Thanks for the coffee – and the copy of the diary.'

'No problem.'

Gerry struggled to his feet. 'And keep writing them books. My Joyce loves 'em.'

When Stamoran saw them off the premises he seemed reluctant to let them go. There was no sign that anyone else lived in that house so perhaps he was glad of the company, Wesley thought, concluding that writing must be a lonely business. He was certain that Stamoran had been telling the truth when he'd said he'd kept his relationship with Yelland strictly professional. In fact Wesley had the impression that something about Barney Yelland made the author uncomfortable.

As they set off back to Tradmouth Gerry spoke. 'We should have another word with Clare Woolmer. I think she might have been lying to us.'

Wesley agreed. He'd been thinking the same. Clare Woolmer's would be their first stop when they got back, unless something happened to prevent them.

And it did. When they were ten minutes from Neston Gerry's phone rang again. This time it was Tradmouth police station to tell them a suspect had been brought in. He'd been taken down to the cells and the clock was ticking. What did the chief inspector want doing with him?

Gerry turned to Wesley. 'Jordan Carnegie's been brought down from Exeter and he's waiting for us at the station.'

Wesley steered the car towards the centre of town. Their visit to Clare Woolmer would have to wait.

Gerry suggested that Wesley and Trish conduct the interview while he watched from behind the two-way mirror. Trish had to make her way over from the incident room in Turling Fitwell so, while they were waiting, they talked to the custody sergeant who told them that the suspect had put up a fight when the officers from Exeter went to arrest him. Resisting arrest was one item on the charge sheet that couldn't be disputed.

As soon as Trish arrived at the police station she joined Wesley and Gerry in the CID office and, after discussing tactics, they made their way down to the interview suite. Carnegie was waiting for them with his solicitor, who was young and wore a sharp suit. Wesley hadn't met him before but he'd heard of him; they called him Mr No Comment.

Wesley sat down, switched on the tape machine and

announced who was present at the interview. The old days of Gerry's youthful memory when you could shout a suspect into submission in a smoke-filled room were long gone, something he suspected the DCI regretted on occasions like this.

Carnegie's attitude was enough to make even a tolerant man like Wesley yearn to land a punch.

'Your name is Jordan Carnegie?'

'No comment.'

'I must tell you that you'll be charged with resisting arrest and assaulting a police officer. And a quantity of class A drugs was found during a search of your flat. Heroin and cocaine, I believe.'

Carnegie looked away.

'But that's not why you're here. We want to question you about the murder of Darren Hatman.'

He produced the evidence: the printout with the circled crossbows and details of the order that had been dispatched to Carnegie's flat, all encased in see-through plastic folders. Carnegie examined them and smirked. 'No comment.'

'What would you say if I were to suggest that you purchased this crossbow and then used it to kill Darren Hatman?'

Carnegie whispered to his solicitor. Then he looked at Wesley and sighed. 'No comment.'

'You did know Darren Hatman?'

'No comment.'

'We know that a crossbow was delivered to your address on the twelfth of March. Where is it now?'

'No comment.' Carnegie looked at the two-way mirror and gave a little wave.

'Someone's checked out your alibi for the time of Darren

Hatman's murder. You said you were doing a gig but your fellow band members told us you failed to turn up. Someone else had to take over on the drums.'

'No comment.'

'What would you say if I suggested you drove down to Eyecliffe Castle that evening with your crossbow and killed Darren Hatman? You hated him, didn't you? You wanted revenge for the way he'd treated you.'

Carnegie glanced at his solicitor, who reminded Wesley of a cat who'd just knocked over the cream jug.

'I'd say prove it,' said Carnegie, putting his face close to Wesley's. His breath was sour.

'We will,' said Wesley. 'Unless you can tell us where you really were that night.'

'No comment.'

After another ten minutes of tedious questioning, Wesley and Trish gathered up their files and left the room. As the constable on duty shut the door they could hear Carnegie chuckling. To him, murder was obviously a laughing matter.

'It's wood.' Lucy prodded the object with the sharp end of her trowel. She was digging in the mud of the river bank, her knees protected only by a thin kneeling mat.

Neil had been studying a copy of an old tithe map but he folded it up and made his way over to her. 'What do you think it is?' he asked, staring down at the object in question.

'Well, it isn't a tree root. It's perfectly round and there's something attached to it – looks like corroded metal. Pass me my leaf trowel, will you.'

He obeyed at once, rummaging in the metal toolbox where she kept her equipment and handing her the small trowel she used for delicate work. 'Want a hand?'

'I think I can manage.' She worked away, carefully loosening the object from the mud which had preserved it.

It was a full ten minutes before Neil saw the thing emerge. He held a tray ready, aware that it would have to go for conservation sooner rather than later. It had spent years, possibly centuries, in anaerobic conditions but, once it was removed from its stable environment, it could decompose before their eyes if they didn't take great care.

Lucy didn't remove all the mud; instead she eased it free, still covered in a protective layer. She'd let the conservation people clean it properly. But the shape of the thing was unmistakable: a pistol, probably flintlock; eighteenth- or early nineteenth-century. Even with its muddy overcoat, Neil could tell it was a high-status object. Expensive in its day.

When he heard Dave calling his name he left Lucy's side and crossed the few yards to the neighbouring trench.

'I've got bone,' Dave said when he arrived. 'I thought it was an animal at first but . . . '

Neil squatted down and examined the long, stained object that had just been uncovered at the bottom of the trench. This was all he needed.

'Doesn't look like an animal to me,' he said quietly. 'Better carry on and see if there's any more.'

11

I asked my cousin about his book and I
was sorely shocked when he informed
me that the binding is made from the
flayed skin of an executed murderer.
The blood ran cold in my veins for I
have touched that dreadful book with my
own hands and I now feel polluted by
the thing. I was also greatly disturbed
by the manner in which Uriah spoke of
the cruelty behind the book's creation,
as if it were some great trophy; a
man's mortal body mutilated for his
pleasure.

Joules has been following my cousin.
That innocent man of God has trailed
him through the streets of Palermo,
keeping a good distance so that he will
not be seen. When he returns from

these expeditions, he appears pale and drained of life. I ask him what he has seen but he says it is better that I do not know.

Uriah and I rarely speak now. He has the chamber adjoining mine but at night he departs for the streets.

I try to continue as though all is well but I am afraid.

They left Jordan Carnegie languishing in the cells beneath Tradmouth police station. At least, with the charges that had already been brought against him, they could keep him there until he appeared before the magistrates the next morning. Even Mr No Comment could do nothing about that. Investigations were still ongoing in Exeter and Carnegie's known associates were being interviewed. Gerry was hoping to gather more evidence against him. That crossbow he bought had to be somewhere.

They returned to Turling Fitwell, frustrated by their lack of progress, and when Wesley told Gerry about Neil's call he rolled his eyes and told him he'd better go and see what was happening. Then they'd go to Neston and have another word with Clare Woolmer.

As the incident room was in the village, Wesley didn't have far to travel to the site of Neil's dig. His call had been intriguing. We might have found human remains. Want to come and have a look? His words hadn't carried much urgency so Wesley assumed that the remains in question were unlikely to be recent. But all human remains that turn up unexpectedly at a dig have to be reported to the police and the coroner. As they had been archaeology students together, Neil always liked to use Wesley as his first point of contact with the forces of law and order.

Wesley descended the steep slope leading to the river, regretting his choice of footwear. With the recent rain the ground had become soft and muddy, turning it into walking boots terrain.

When he arrived he saw that the discovery of the bones had halted work and the archaeologists were standing in huddles. Some were speculating and some were drinking tea from flasks. But they were all waiting for something to happen.

Wesley spotted James Garrard standing at the edge of one of the groups and saw an expectant look appear on his face, as though he hoped he'd come over to speak to him. However, Wesley knew he'd have to disappoint him.

Neil saw him and waved. Lucy was standing beside him and neither of them looked particularly concerned, more irritated at the delay to their excavation. As Wesley made his way over to join him, his phone began to ring.

'Is that Inspector Peterson?'

Wesley recognised the voice but it took him a few moments to place it. 'Sean. What can I do for you?' He hadn't been expecting a call from the young man on the reception desk at Eyecliffe Castle so he experienced a frisson of hope that he had something for them that would push the investigation along.

'Can I speak to you?' His voice was hushed, as if he was afraid someone might overhear.

'Of course. Shall I come up to the castle or . . . ?'

'No. I'll meet you somewhere.'

'Our incident room's in Turling Fitwell church hall. I'll see you there in half an hour. That OK?'

The answer was a whispered yes, immediately followed by the dialling tone. Wesley stared at his phone for a few moments; perhaps he should have told him to go to the incident room right away and speak to another member of the investigation team. He tried to return the call but there was no answer.

Neil was waiting to lead him down to an open trench not far from the river bank.

'It's just there. Can you see?'

Wesley stood and watched while Neil squatted down and scraped a little mud away with his trowel.

'This is what's bothering me,' he said, looking up. 'Dave thought it was animal at first but that's a femur, isn't it? And I'm sure this is a pelvis.'

Wesley climbed down into the trench and looked at the brown stained bones. At the bottom of the femur what looked like a patella protruded from the surface of the ground like a tiny mound. This was no animal.

'I thought I'd show you before we carried on. I think they've been here a long time. The course of the river might have changed slightly over the years so it might be someone who fell in ages ago and got washed up on the bank.'

'This was the site of a water mill, right?'

'That's right. Lucy made an interesting find earlier. Come and have a look.' The satisfied look on Neil's face told Wesley that whatever Lucy had found, it was something special.

He followed Neil over to the green gazebo erected to protect the finds and the diggers in the event of bad weather. Inside he saw a couple of makeshift long tables. On one stood a trio of plastic washing-up bowls alongside a pile of grubby toothbrushes – vital equipment for cleaning finds – and on the other there were several trays, lined with newspaper. One tray had been placed a little distance from its neighbours and inside Wesley could see a mud-shrouded object he recognised as a firearm. It was around eighteen inches long and bore little resemblance to the guns he'd come across in the course of his police career. He thought it was probably a flintlock pistol; possibly the kind used for duelling or a weapon a gentleman might carry to ward off highwaymen or footpads. Neil was sure to have contacts who would pinpoint exactly what it was.

'Very nice,' said Wesley.

'The mud's preserved the wood so we've got to be careful it doesn't dry out.' He tore his admiring eyes from his prize find and looked at Wesley. 'It was found not far from the bones.'

'Murder weapon?'

'You're the policeman. I'll assign a team to the skeleton trench and put the volunteers in trenches three and four, hoping that no more bodies turn up.' He grinned. 'I've called Margaret too. It's always useful to have her input.' Margaret was Neil's favourite bone expert. They'd worked together many times before and he felt comfortable with her; she was also extremely good at her job.

'It looks as if you've got everything sorted,' said Wesley, looking at his watch. 'I've got someone to see. Better go.'

'I was thinking of calling round tonight,' said Neil.

'I'll probably be working late.'

'Well Pam'll be in, won't she?'

Wesley hesitated. 'I'm not sure. She might have a parents' evening.' He felt bad about lying to one of his oldest friends but he wasn't sure whether Pam would want company.

'Another time then.' Neil paused. 'Anything wrong, Wes?'

'Just busy, that's all.'

He walked away and a feeling of desolation overwhelmed him. What if Pam was ill? What if his well-ordered life was about to be seized and shaken up by factors beyond his control? Suddenly he wanted to turn back and confide in Neil but when he looked round he saw that he was deep in conversation with Lucy and Dave. It wasn't the time or the place.

Sean was waiting for him in the church hall, perched on a plastic seat like a nervous patient in a dentist's waiting room. When he saw Wesley come in he stood up and Wesley noticed that his quiff seemed flatter today, giving him a crestfallen look.

'You wanted a word, Sean,' he said, leading the young man to the desk that was his for the duration of the investigation.

'Yeah,' Sean said. 'I think I've got some information. But I didn't want to say anything up at the castle.'

Wesley saw that Gerry was on the phone, looking in their direction. Once his call was finished, Wesley knew he wouldn't be able to resist coming over to join them.

He took out his notebook. 'What do you want to tell me?'

'It's about Mr Palmer. The boss.'

'What about him?'

'I was on my way to the restaurant – part of my job is helping with the bookings – and when I passed his office I heard him talking to someone. It was a woman.

'It was something like, "You've got a secret, David." Then he said, "I don't know what you mean. You're imagining things."'

'Do you know who the woman was?'

'I'm not sure. Someone came along the corridor so I went straight to the restaurant. I didn't want anyone to think I was eavesdropping, did I.'

'But you think you recognised the voice?'

Sean fell silent for a while, as though he was making a decision. 'It might have been Kirsty Paige but I can't be sure because I only caught a few words. I don't want to get anyone into trouble.'

'Except Mr Palmer. You don't like him much do you, Sean?'

'We all have to work with people we don't see eye to eye with, don't we?' He looked round the incident room.

'What do you think Mr Palmer's secret could be?'

'How should I know?' He suddenly sounded flustered, as though he'd begun to regret his visit.

Wesley sat back in his chair and gave him an encouraging smile. 'You work with the man. Take a guess.'

'Well it could be something he doesn't want his mother to find out about. A couple of months ago they had a big row about him selling some estate property and he's been treading on eggshells ever since.'

'What property was this?'

'An old barn. She said she had plans for it and he didn't consult her. She's not been well recently but she still wears the trousers. What she says goes. '

Gerry had finished his call and ambled over to join them. 'He's under mummy's thumb, is he?' he said, leaning on the back of Wesley's chair. 'Tied to the old apron strings.'

'Something like that,' Sean answered, giving Gerry a wary look.

'Could his secret be something to do with a woman?' said Wesley.

'I don't know.'

'About Leanne Hatman maybe?'

'I can only tell you what I heard. I'll make a statement but, like I said, I don't want to get Kirsty into trouble. I can't be absolutely sure it was her he was talking to.'

Wesley didn't believe him. He'd seen lots of people who backtracked after realising they'd revealed too much, but he decided to put him out of his misery and let him go.

'Let's have a word with Palmer's alibi ourselves, shall we,' said Gerry. 'And then perhaps we should have another little chat with Kirsty.'

Kirsty Paige had passed reception twice since Sean's return and both times he'd hardly been able to bring himself to say hello, let alone smile. His attempt to land Palmer in trouble had backfired and he felt he'd become a Judas, a betrayer.

If only he'd kept his big mouth shut instead of naming Kirsty. He could have said he hadn't recognised the voice. But now he knew they'd come after her, which was the last thing he'd intended.

He tried to busy himself by tidying up the shelves under the desk until the automatic doors leading to the corridor swished open and a middle-aged couple approached the desk. They had suitcases with them; wheelie cases trailing behind them like obedient dogs. One small, one large enough for a month's stay.

'Good afternoon. Can I help you,' he said with an obsequious smile.

'We're booked in till tomorrow but we'd like to check out early. Family crisis,' said the man.

'I'm sorry to hear that.'

Sean assumed a sympathetic expression but he didn't believe their story for a moment. He'd known it was only a matter of time before the murder in the grounds scared off the punters.

'Mr and Mrs Hughes, isn't it?'

'That's right.'

The woman smiled at him but the man seemed nervous, tapping his fingers on the top of the desk and repeatedly checking his watch as Sean printed out their bill.

Once they'd handed in their room key, they scurried off quickly. Whatever it was they were in a hurry.

'I hope you've enjoyed your stay,' Sean called after them, but his words were ignored.

It was half an hour before one of the chambermaids sauntered into the reception area and stopped by Sean's desk, glancing round as if she was fearful of discovery.

'Seen Ma Palmer?'

'Not today. Why?'

'I'm sure one of the pictures on the first-floor landing's been swapped. You can see a mark where the old one's been – looks a bit of a mess. I wondered if she did it for some reason.'

Before Sean could answer Kirsty glided into view and Sean felt his face burning red. He had more to think about at that moment than someone swapping pictures around.

12

My cousin has purchased a painting
although he will not say where he
obtained it. Uriah confides nothing to
me.

The picture is a work so strange that
whenever I look upon it, the blood
chills in my veins. It depicts a man
undergoing great suffering watched by
a wall of disembodied eyes. The title
beneath the painting is The House of
Eyes, which I believe is a ruined
fortification near the town of Naro in
the south-west of the island, which was
once a resplendent royal city in the
thirteenth century. Uriah claims that
the artist is the great Caravaggio
himself who once came to this island to
paint, although I doubt the truth of this.

163

I was unable to sleep last night as the image of the suffering man preyed upon my mind and in my sleepless hours, I lay listening for any sound from Uriah's chamber. I have replaced his book and I pray he is unaware of my interference.

I confided my thoughts to Joules and he assures me that he will keep a careful watch upon my cousin.

Wesley looked at his watch. It was six o'clock already and he didn't like to think of Pam coping alone with that terrible burden on her mind. He hadn't spoken with her since their visit to the doctor's that morning and he needed to reassure himself that she was all right.

Gerry was keen to interview the married woman who'd provided David Palmer with his alibi for the time of Darren Hatman's murder, but when Trish phoned to make sure she was at home, there was no reply. At Wesley's request she'd also called to check whether Kirsty Paige was at Eyecliffe Castle, only to be told that it was her evening off. Wesley knew he shouldn't have felt relieved, but he did, and told Gerry he was nipping home. He'd be back in an hour or so if he was needed.

He rang Pam's mobile and she answered after two rings, telling him she was at Maritia's with the children. This news made him feel a little better: if anyone could put Pam's mind at rest it was his sister. He said he'd be over there in fifteen minutes to pick Pam up though she told him there was no need as she had her car. But the offer was as much for himself as for her; he wanted to hear what Maritia had to say.

As he took his coat from the back of his chair Gerry's phone rang and, after a brief conversation, Wesley saw him stand up.

'That was Forensics,' he announced. 'That blood in Barney Yelland's bedroom is human and it's a familial match to Darren Hatman's. They always hedge their bets as you know, but they said it could be Leanne's and that's good enough for me. We should pay Clare Woolmer another visit.' He must have seen the expression on Wesley's face because he turned to Rachel. 'You and me, Rach. Let's get over there.'

Rachel closed down the screen on her computer and rose to her feet. Wesley had heard Trish mention earlier that she had an appointment to sample wedding cakes with Nigel that evening – one of the many burdens of the modern bride – but she didn't look too upset about missing it.

It wasn't far to Belsham Vicarage where his sister lived with her husband, Mark, the incumbent of Belsham and several other parishes in the area. It was a large, draughty Victorian vicarage; not a pretty building or the diocese would have sold it off as a desirable home years ago.

Maritia answered the door and greeted him with a hug. Although they were close this wasn't her usual style of greeting so the action made his heart sink. After telling him that Michael was at a friend's and that Amelia was in the other room playing a game on Mark's computer, she led the way into a comfortable living room filled with dark wood furniture and saggy chintz sofas. Pam was drinking tea, sitting in an old armchair with her feet tucked under her. As soon as she saw him, she levered herself up and once he'd kissed her, he held her for a few seconds, longing to ask what Maritia had said. It turned out he didn't have to wait long.

'I've been explaining the options,' Maritia said as Pam sat down again. 'Your GP's referred her to the unit at Morbay, which is very good. Mr Knight is the consultant breast surgeon there and I've sent a lot of patients to him myself. So many advances have been made recently and the prognosis is good.' She gave Pam a reassuring smile. 'You know I'm always here if you want to ask anything. Day or night. Right, Pam?'

Pam nodded. 'Don't know what I'd have done without—'

'Don't mention it.' She turned to Wesley. 'Told Mum and Dad yet?'

'I thought we'd wait till we'd seen the consultant.'

Maritia nodded. 'We've eaten, by the way, but there's some shepherd's pie left. Gift from one of Mark's fans in the Mothers' Union.'

It was hard to tell how Maritia felt about the grateful parishioner. Maybe she suspected the food was some sort of criticism of her domestic abilities – the working mum who didn't look after her saintly husband properly – but if she thought this, she didn't put it into words. Some of the older members of Mark's congregations had treated their young vicar's new wife cautiously at first, maybe because of the colour of her skin, or maybe because she had a career of her own and didn't fit the old-fashioned role of her husband's helpmate. It hadn't taken long for Maritia to win most of them over but there was still a handful who kept their distance. Wesley was hungry so he thanked her, saying he'd have whatever was going spare.

'I thought you'd be working late,' said Pam when his sister had left the room.

'I told Gerry I wanted to see you.'

She reached out her hand to touch his and he gave her fingers a squeeze.

'It's going to be OK,' he said. 'I know it is.'

But as Maritia returned with a tray, tears began to trickle down Pam's cheeks.

Gerry rang Clare Woolmer's doorbell three times, as if to emphasise the seriousness of their visit, while Rachel stood slightly behind him, her warrant card clutched in her hand. After a couple of minutes, the door opened a crack and Rachel stepped forward to announce herself. She'd told Gerry she'd met the woman before so she'd do the talking, at least at first. When the door opened Clare invited them in and they followed her into her living room.

'This is my boss, DCI Heffernan,' Rachel said. 'We'd like to ask you a few more questions.'

'I've told you everything I know.' There was a stubborn note in her voice.

'We've spoken to Cornell Stamoran, the author Mr Yelland's working with on his latest project,' said Rachel. 'He thinks Mr Yelland's back in Devon. Have you heard from him since we last spoke?'

'Well he's not been here and his car hasn't moved. Unless he's gone to relatives . . . or friends.'

'We've checked with his relatives and they haven't heard from him.'

'Then I can't help you,' she said, pressing her lips tightly together.

For a few moments nobody spoke. Then Gerry broke the silence. 'We've got some news,' he said. 'Remember we sent our forensics people round to have a look at Mr Yelland's rooms upstairs?'

'It's not something I'll forget in a hurry,' she said. 'They've sealed off his rooms with police tape. Can I take it down now?'

'Not just yet. We might need to have another look up there. They did some tests on a stain we found on his duvet cover.' He paused for dramatic effect. 'It turns out it's blood. And it probably belongs to that missing girl: Leanne Hatman. Are you sure you didn't hear Mr Yelland and Leanne Hatman arguing?'

She turned to Rachel. 'I've already told you I didn't. Don't you people write anything down?'

'Sometimes witnesses remember things later on . . . when they've had more time to think about it,' said Rachel.

'Having my home violated like this has been a dreadful experience. I've had police officers tramping up and down the stairs, delving into Barney's rooms and—'

'You don't seem particularly surprised that the missing girl's blood's been found upstairs?'

She looked away. 'If that's all, I'd like to make myself something to eat.' There was a finality about her words that told them they were being dismissed.

'The other girls who came here – do you know how we can contact them?'

She shook her head and Rachel and Gerry realised that until more information came their way, they had no reason to prolong their stay.

Clare Woolmer saw them off the premises and shut the front door. Then she stood in the hallway, leaning against the wall, taking deep, calming breaths.

After a while she made her way back into the living room

and took her mobile phone off the marble mantelpiece that had so attracted her when she'd first bought the house. She had the number on speed dial and her heart raced as she waited for an answer.

The investigation team's day always begins early during a murder inquiry and the fact that it was Saturday didn't alter that. Wesley had intended to go in late so he could stay longer with Pam but she'd told him to stop fussing and go. She couldn't stand being treated like an invalid. Until she saw the consultant there was nothing she could do and she wanted to carry on as normal. She didn't want the children to guess anything was wrong, but most of all she didn't want her mother told. If anyone was guaranteed to turn a drama into a crisis, it was Della.

He reached the incident room just before Gerry arrived and as soon as he walked in Rachel told him about her visit to Clare Woolmer's the previous evening, saying she was sure the woman was hiding something. He didn't mention his suspicion that Clare was a little in love with Barney Yelland, although her feelings probably weren't returned. Yelland went for a certain kind of beauty; a beauty that Clare, although attractive, definitely lacked.

Wesley had rather liked Clare Woolmer – but he'd found himself liking quite a few criminals in the course of his career; people who'd yielded to human weakness or been driven to extreme actions by events beyond their control. Hate the sin but love the sinner – that's what he'd been taught by his churchgoing parents. Perhaps that's why he so often felt sympathy for the wrongdoer.

'If we can spare the manpower, perhaps we should have her followed,' he said. 'I'll see what the boss says.'

As soon as Gerry marched in, shedding his old anorak like a chrysalis, Wesley joined him and watched as he began sifting through the messages that had come in overnight.

'You're right, Wes. I think it's worth putting a tail on Ms Woolmer,' he said. 'She's hiding something and if she's warned Yelland about our interest, he might be lying low somewhere. You never know, she might lead us to him.' He sounded optimistic.

'We can but hope.'

'Have we had any luck tracing Yelland's other women yet . . . especially the one in the mutilated pictures?'

'Not yet.'

Gerry examined a note he'd written to himself on a scrap of paper. 'After the briefing we're off to Morbay to have a word with David Palmer's lady friend. I don't believe this new alibi of his. I wouldn't trust him to tell me the time.'

'I suspect his mother's the domineering type so he'll be used to lying to dig himself out of a hole. Maybe we should speak to her as well.'

'I've read her statement and nothing flags up as unusual.'

'It was just a suggestion,' said Wesley. 'And don't forget we need to see Kirsty Paige again.'

'She's on the list,' said Gerry. 'What's Palmer's girlfriend's name?'

'Tabitha Sweeting. She sounds as if she should be in the same line of business as Cornell Stamoran.'

Gerry looked puzzled.

'Writing romantic novels.'

'See what you mean.'

After a few calls they discovered that Tabitha Sweeting worked on Saturdays in a waterfront gallery on the upmarket side of Morbay.

When they arrived Wesley's first impression of the Turnival Gallery was that everything looked bleached. The paintwork was white, the window display featured a lot of pale driftwood, and the shop sign was picked out on a snowy background in washed-out blue. The only brightness was provided by the paintings in the window, mostly seascapes, chosen to appeal to holidaymakers who would, with luck, take them home to remind them of their carefree break on the English Riviera.

Tabitha Sweeting's slenderness bordered on the skinny. Her long pale hair was tied back with an equally pale blue silk scarf and she possessed a remarkable pair of large grey eyes. She looked as if she was expecting them, so whoever had answered the phone at her home had, presumably, called to warn her of their impending visit. The gallery was empty and she was alone. Wesley turned the sign on the door to 'closed' to ensure they wouldn't be disturbed.

'My cleaner rang to say you'd been asking where I was,' she began. She sounded confident, even a little impatient. 'What's this about?'

'You told our colleague, DC Walton, that David Palmer was with you when he should have been at a conference in Brighton.'

She walked over to the glass shop door and gazed out on to the street, as if she was making a decision. Then, after a few moments, she swung round to face them. This time there was no mistaking the worry on her face.

'Look, if I say I lied would I get into trouble ... perverting the course of justice or something?'

Wesley sensed that they could either play this by the book or they could learn the truth and he knew Gerry would agree with his choice. 'People don't always remember

171

things accurately when a police officer calls out of the blue. They panic. They forget what they were doing when. But now you've had time to think about it . . . '

She gave him a grateful look. 'Yes, well, that's exactly what's happened. I got the date wrong. David wasn't with me on the night you're talking about. I don't know where he was.'

'So he asked you to lie for him?' said Gerry. 'Don't worry, love, you can tell us the truth. We're not going to haul you back to the station.' He grinned. 'I couldn't face the paper-work.'

She bowed her head. 'He rang me the day he left Brighton and said that if anyone asked, I was to say he was with me. It was something to do with the business – something he was desperate to keep from his mother.' She looked up and Wesley saw a spark of defiance in her eyes. 'He didn't give a toss about my position. I'm married with kids so I can hardly afford . . . To tell you the truth that was the last straw as far as I was concerned. I covered for him like he asked but then I heard on the news that there'd been a murder in the hotel grounds.'

'Did you believe his story?'

She considered the question for a few moments. 'I suppose I did at the time. He's always been very wary about upsetting his mother so . . . '

'But now?'

'I really don't know.'

'How did you meet him?' Wesley asked, suddenly curious about the relationship.

'Don't get me wrong, Inspector, I'm happily married but my husband's away a lot and when David and I met at an exhibition here in the gallery, he seemed so . . . '

172

'How long have you been ... ?'

'About a year. When Malcolm, my husband, was away we went out for meals and sometimes David would come round in the afternoons when the kids were at school. I used to hope he'd take me to his hotel – that we'd use the best suites – but he'd never let me near the place because of his bloody mother.'

Wesley suddenly felt sorry for Tabitha Sweeting. She was bored with her life and David Palmer had offered her a glimpse of excitement. He was just surprised that it had taken her so long to see through him.

'This trouble with the police is the last straw. I don't want any more to do with him now.'

'You've seen the light,' said Gerry cheerfully.

She gave him a curious look.

'Have you any idea what his secret business was?'

She thought for a moment. 'All he said was that his mother wasn't well and he couldn't risk her finding out.' She rolled her eyes. 'If you ask me, he's terrified of her.'

'Has he ever mentioned a Leanne Hatman?'

'That's the girl who's gone missing, isn't it? You can't think David's got anything to do with that, surely.'

'That's what we're asking you, love,' said Gerry. 'Leanne Hatman's father was killed on the night David asked you to lie for him. Do you think he's capable of murder?'

Her eyes widened in horror. 'I really don't know.'

When bones were discovered during an excavation Neil liked to get them lifted the same day. But this hadn't been possible before the light began to fade so he'd covered the trench with a heavy tarpaulin overnight and resumed the next morning, working slowly, careful not to disturb any evidence.

The bone expert, Margaret, and the forensic anthropologist she'd called in both agreed that the burial was considerably more than seventy years old and, therefore, of no interest to the police. However, Neil still wanted to know how and when the man had met his death.

The pelvis had been exposed, confirming that the skeleton was male, and now Neil and Dave were working on the ribcage while Lucy delicately scraped away the earth where the skull would be.

Dave spotted it first: a tiny metallic ball nestling among the ribs. On further inspection he thought it was probably lead. A bullet. Which meant they had a murder victim.

Wesley and Gerry returned to the incident room in silence, both thinking of David Palmer. Wesley tried to picture him with a crossbow and failed.

They'd asked Rob Carter to keep an eye on Clare Woolmer's house. The young DC still harboured illusions of the glamour and excitement of detection, but if anything was likely to bring him down to earth, it was a routine surveillance job. Gerry had told him to report back if Ms Woolmer made a move; as yet, however, there'd been no word.

Wesley took a seat beside Gerry's desk. Even here in their temporary incident room it had become cluttered with paperwork and files had begun to pile up on the floor.

'Any thoughts?' Wesley asked.

'We're still waiting for Exeter to come up with some evidence on Carnegie, preferably a crossbow hidden somewhere they haven't looked yet. In in the meantime, let's pay David Palmer another visit.'

Wesley nodded but Gerry knew that his mind was on

other things. At first he assumed that he was worrying about Pam, until he spoke.

'Do you think Leanne Hatman is still alive?'

'Don't know,' Gerry answered. 'If Yelland killed her he must have done it on the evening before he went to Italy so he wouldn't have had much time to get rid of her body.'

Their speculations were interrupted by the insistent ringing of Gerry's phone. He answered it and recited his name, then Wesley saw him scribble something in his notepad.

When he ended the call he looked up, the light of untold news in his eyes. 'That was one of the lads at the station. I asked him to get some background on Lee Varlow and Craig Gatting, Darren's workers, and he told me Lee's got a hobby. He's part of a re-enactment group. Medieval warfare.' He paused as if awaiting a drum roll to accompany his revelation. 'They use replica medieval weapons in their demonstrations – swords, bows and arrows ... and crossbows. He's sent someone to see if any weapons are missing from their stock.'

'Maybe we should have a word with Mr Varlow.'

'You took the words out of my mouth, Wes.'

Half an hour later Gerry had learned that, work on the barn having been suspended, Lee Varlow was working behind the bar in a Neston pub that afternoon. Gerry guessed that it was a casual arrangement – not a word to the taxman – but that wasn't their concern.

He looked at Wesley. 'We're going for a pint. Or rather I am. You're driving of course.'

Wesley had only been to the Cat and Fiddle once before several years ago in the course of an investigation, and he hadn't enjoyed the experience. It was a small pub in the middle of a row of terraced houses, well away from the

New Age atmosphere of the town centre. On the whole Neston was pretty law-abiding, but if you were seeking the town's small darker underbelly, the Cat and Fiddle was the place to look.

As soon as they walked into the pub, Wesley recognised the bottle-blonde standing behind the bar. She might have aged a few years since he'd last seen her but she was still displaying a vast expanse of cleavage as she pulled a pint for a thirsty customer. She was the only woman in the bar and the men all seemed large and wore tattoos like soldiers wore medals.

'I've heard they serve a good pint,' mumbled Gerry. 'But I've never actually checked it out myself. According to the lads at Neston nick, police aren't exactly welcome. I'll have a pint of Doom Bar,' he added absent-mindedly, scanning the bar for a familiar face.

As Wesley approached the bar he was aware that he'd attracted the attention of the regulars. He could feel their eyes on him and knew they'd be wondering what business a smartly dressed black man had in a place like this. He gave his drinks order confidently, doing his best to ignore the scrutiny.

Once he'd bought Gerry's pint and the alcohol-free lager that served as his tipple of choice when he was driving, he turned and saw Gerry talking to Lee Varlow, who had been collecting glasses at the other end of the pub. He joined them and they all sat down at a table near the window.

'I can't be long,' said Lee, glancing nervously at the blonde with the cleavage. 'Landlady's a bit of a tyrant.'

'We've been hearing things about you, Lee.' Gerry said in a low voice, looking round to make sure they couldn't be overheard. 'I believe you're handy with a crossbow.'

Lee's face flushed. 'Where did you hear that?'

'I'm told you do a bit of medieval re-enactment in your spare time.'

'Yeah but I don't have nothing to do with the weaponry. I'm armour.'

'So you've never handled a crossbow?' Wesley asked.

Lee's face reddened. 'I had a go once. They just use the bows and crossbows for demonstrations – target practice. It's too dangerous to use them in battle.'

'But you have access to them?'

'No. I mean, I never . . . ' He sounded as if he was starting to panic. 'Look, I had nothing to do with Darren's murder. Why would I want to hurt Darren? He's been good to me.'

'We can check with the group whether any crossbows are missing and get a warrant to search your address.'

'Do it, then. I've got nothing to hide.' This was said with a confidence that made Wesley think he was probably telling the truth. 'It's not me you should be looking at. Why would I want to put myself out of work?' He gave another nervous glance in the landlady's direction. 'If I was you, I'd be asking Darren's missus a few questions.'

'Why's that?' asked Gerry.

'She and Darren never saw eye to eye, if you see what I mean. And he's been keeping things from her. The business is doing well but he made sure she didn't get her hands on any of it. He got his accountant to cook the books so he didn't have to hand over half the profits like they agreed but now he's dead she'll get it all. The firm. The lot. Wouldn't surprise me if she'd lost patience.'

Wesley glanced at Gerry. It wouldn't be the first time a suspect tried to deflect suspicion on to someone else but

Marion Hatman had appeared to take the news of her husband's murder with remarkable sang froid.

'Anything else you'd like to tell us?' Gerry asked.

Lee considered the question for a moment. 'I reckon Darren made a few enemies in his time. I've heard he let a few people down when he decided to go straight. Then there was that old girl he knocked over. Maybe her family ...'

'We'll check that out,' said Gerry quickly. Wesley knew this was a line of inquiry that hadn't yet been explored; maybe it was time they pushed it up their list of priorities.

'Have you heard anything about Darren's daughter, Leanne? She's still missing.'

Lee shook his head. 'I've not heard nothing, Mr Heffernan. All I know is there are some very bad people in the world.'

Wesley couldn't argue with that.

13

In the early hours of this morning I heard a soft knocking and when I opened my door I saw Joules standing there. He was somewhat dishevelled and his clothes and hands were stained with blood.

I concluded that he had been set upon by rogues or that he had inadvertently become embroiled in some fight, even though it was against his nature. But he pushed past me, making straight for the basin which stood upon my chest of drawers, and as he washed the blood off his hands I saw the water in the basin turn a cloudy red.

'We must leave immediately,' he said in a frantic whisper. 'I pray you, pack now and do not delay.'

As soon as they returned to the incident room Wesley asked two of the DCs to follow up Lee Varlow's suggestion that the family of the victim of Darren's appalling getaway driving might have decided to seek revenge. He ordered a search of Lee's premises, just in case, and asked the leader of the re-enactment group to check whether any of their weapons were missing, careful to make the inquiry sound general. If Lee Varlow was innocent, Gerry didn't want to make unnecessary trouble for him. He remarked that a crossbow was an unusual weapon of choice, but Wesley pointed out that crossbows were silent – and they were also legal and relatively easy to obtain.

Rachel had been calling in on Marion Hatman every day to keep her up to date with their inquiries. But now, with Lee's hints that Marion was involved in her estranged husband's death, Gerry asked her to keep a closer watch on the widow. Rachel had observed that Marion was bearing up well in the circumstances. Perhaps Lee's accusation explained why.

Once Gerry's briefing was over Wesley perched on the edge of Rachel's desk. 'You know Marion Hatman better than any of us. Do you think she could be involved in Darren's death?'

Rachel sighed. 'How trustworthy is Lee Varlow? He might be trying to stir up trouble for her. He might even have hopes of taking over the firm himself,' she said. 'But I'm sure about one thing. Neither of Leanne's parents had anything to do with her disappearance. Darren was in a right panic when he reported her missing. And Marion's still trying to convince herself that she's in London leading the high life, although I can tell she's getting more worried with every passing day.'

Their conversation was interrupted when a uniformed constable burst into the church hall carrying a package and asking for the senior investigating officer. Gerry emerged from behind his desk, eyeing the parcel. The constable handed it to him and when he took it from its paper wrapper Wesley saw a plastic evidence bag containing a crossbow and another, smaller one containing a set of bolts.

'Exeter found them in a lock-up owned by a mate of Jordan Carnegie's. He said Carnegie asked him to keep them for him.'

'Get them sent to Forensic, will you. We need to know if this is the murder weapon.'

The constable hurried off with his trophy, looking pleased with himself.

'Carnegie's still in custody,' Wesley said. 'He's claiming he only did a runner because of the drugs in his flat but even Mr No Comment won't be able to get him out of this one if we find traces of Darren Hatman's DNA on any of those crossbow bolts. I've been wondering why the killer pulled it out of the body. Killing someone like that at a distance means you don't have to get your hands dirty but the killer risked getting blood on his clothes.'

'Perhaps he thought his prints would be on the bolt, or it could be traced back to him in some way.'

'How's Pam?' she said. 'I heard someone say she wasn't well.'

He couldn't bring himself to tell Rachel the truth, to put his fears into words, so he took the easy option. 'She's fine,' he said quickly, annoyed that the CID rumour machine had already ground into action. 'You'd better go and see Marion Hatman and do a bit more digging.'

Rachel looked at him. 'Sometimes it feels as if I'm betraying their trust, trying to catch them out like that.'

He watched as she prepared to leave. Whatever her misgivings, if anyone could wheedle the truth out of Darren Hatman's widow, it was Rachel Tracey.

He was about to sit down and go through the reports that had landed on his desk since their visit to the Cat and Fiddle when his phone rang.

'Is that DI Peterson?'

The voice was female and authoritative and it took him a few moments to place it. 'Mrs Palmer, how can I help you?' he asked smoothly.

'I want to report a theft.'

'What's been stolen?'

'A painting.'

'Valuable?'

'I didn't think so. It was just one of the many old paintings the owner of the castle left behind when my husband purchased it. We kept them because they suited the atmosphere we were trying to create but, as far as I know, none of them are of any great value.'

'How long has it been missing?' His mind was running through the possibilities. If Leanne Hatman had discovered it was valuable and taken it before disappearing . . .

'It was there yesterday. Someone's replaced it with a cheap print in a hideous plastic frame but you can see the mark where the original's been. It might have gone unnoticed but, fortunately, one of our chambermaids is a very observant girl.'

So much for his theory about Leanne's involvement, Wesley thought.

'Have you a photograph of the painting?'

'Yes. The entire contents were photographed a couple of years ago for insurance purposes.'

He looked at his watch. 'I'll be with you in ten minutes.'

When he turned the car down the long drive he had a strong feeling that Eyecliffe Castle was the epicentre of whatever was going on. And when he arrived he found Mrs Palmer waiting for him in reception, sitting on an upright chair, her ankles neatly crossed.

She rose and shook his hand in a business-like manner. Her silver hair seemed stiffer and more severe today and, at that moment, he could well believe that her son, David, lived in fear of her. His own mother was a doctor, a kindly and competent GP, but in spite of her apparent frailty, this woman would eat her for breakfast.

'Where was the painting taken from?' he asked.

'The first-floor corridor. Follow me.' The words were more of a command than an invitation.

She led Wesley up the thickly carpeted staircase, her knuckles bone-white as she clung to the banister. Once upstairs, he followed her to the end of the right-hand corridor. She stopped and pointed to a shadowy alcove where a poor-quality print of Constable's famous work hung a little askew. It was slightly smaller than the picture it had replaced and he could see a faint mark on the surrounding wallpaper.

'It was definitely there; a rather nice watercolour of a local scene. As I said, the previous owner left a lot of pictures behind because she didn't have room for them in her new home. I think my late husband paid her a couple of thousand for them and she seemed happy with that.'

'Were any of them valued?'

'She didn't consider it necessary. She took a few with her but wasn't interested in the rest.'

Wesley stared at the place where the picture had been. 'Why this one? Was there anything special about it?'

'Perhaps one of the guests took a liking to it.'

'But replacing it with another suggests a certain amount of planning,' Wesley observed.

He'd noticed a good many pictures hanging in the corridors and the reception area and, as far as he could judge, most of them seemed to be standard Victorian fare, predominantly oils with a few watercolours mixed in. There were also several larger works depicting classical ruins, the sort brought back by scions of many wealthy families from their Grand Tour of Europe. They were decorative but had no particular artistic merit. Art by the yard … or possibly the acre.

'The photograph's in my office. Judge for yourself.'

As he followed her downstairs he remembered he needed to speak to Kirsty Paige about her alleged argument with David Palmer, as reported by Sean. After he'd finished with Mrs Palmer he intended to visit the spa and seek her out. Discreetly.

Once they reached her office she sat down stiffly and Wesley saw her wince with pain as she drew out a thick file from one of the desk drawers..

The file was filled with photographs, and she sorted through them until she found the right one then pushed the picture over the desk to Wesley. 'That's the one. No plate, no signature.'

Wesley stared at it and something stirred in his brain. It was a painting of Tradmouth waterfront but, unlike Mrs Palmer, he could see its brilliance. The way the artist had captured the clouds and the movement of the water. The style was familiar. Perhaps someone else had recognised it too.

'Do you mind if I take this with me?' he asked. 'I'd like to make some inquiries with my former colleagues in the Art and Antique Unit.'

Mrs Palmer looked pleasantly surprised. 'That's very diligent of you, Inspector. To tell you the truth, I only reported it because it's a requirement of our insurance company.' She hesitated. 'You don't think it's valuable, do you?'

He could see the light of avarice in her rheumy eyes as well as a hint of anger that someone might have deprived her of a treasure. 'I'm not sure. Leave it with me.'

He left her office and followed the signs to the spa. It was time Kirsty answered some questions.

Neil knew Wesley was too busy to concern himself with a two hundred-year-old murder. According to the expert who'd examined the pistol, it dated from the late eighteenth century and the coroner had been happy to accept the forensic anthropologist's verdict that it was an old burial so there was no need to set a police investigation in motion.

Besides, the police seemed to have enough to do at Eyecliffe Castle. They still had patrol cars up there and he knew that Wesley and his team were using the church hall in the village as an incident room. However busy Wesley was, he usually made some excuse to pay regular visits to see what was going on at any nearby dig. But, unusually, Neil hadn't seen much of him.

The bones had now been lifted and taken to Exeter for further examination and, as the excavation progressed, he realised that the body must have been buried inside the building, possibly in some sort of cellar.

Neil was staring at the stone foundations of the old mill protruding from the damp soil in his trench when he heard

Lucy's voice, full of excitement. 'You'll never guess what they've just found in trench three.'

When he reached trench three he saw Dave standing there with a triumphant look on his face.

'We've got coins,' Dave said, grinning as though he'd just won the lottery. 'Gold ones.'

Wesley had been afraid of intruding on some half-naked woman caught mid-massage. But instead he found Kirsty Paige in the staff restroom with a mug of tea in her hand.

'Kirsty, have you got a moment?' he said after he'd knocked on the open door, trying his best to sound friendly and unthreatening. Suspects usually talked more openly when they were relaxed.

'What is it?'

'I've just seen Mrs Palmer. A painting's gone missing from the first-floor corridor.'

She looked affronted. 'Well, don't look at me. I don't know anything about it.'

'I never said you did. That's not what I want to talk to you about.'

She placed her mug on the draining board and folded her arms defensively, her whole body tense. Something was worrying her and it would take more than a relaxing massage to solve her problem – whatever it was.

'Since you gave your statement some new information has come our way.'

'What new information?'

'That you've been arguing with David Palmer.'

'Where did you hear that?'

Wesley thought he detected a touch of relief in her voice. 'Is it true? Yes or no.'

Kirsty closed the door as if she didn't want to be over-heard.

'Yes, it's true,' she said quietly. 'David's been hiding something and I was asking him what it was.'

'What makes you think he's hiding something?'

'He's been sneaking around. Making phone calls.' She paused. 'I didn't want to mention it before but David and I have become ... close recently and I don't like it when he keeps things from me.'

Wesley wondered whether she knew about Tabitha Sweeting. He thought not.

'I think it's something to do with the hotel,' she continued. 'Some scheme that Mummy wouldn't approve of.' She gave a small, fond smile. 'If he's raising two fingers to his mum, I wouldn't blame him. That's something we've all wanted to do at times.'

'You say you and David are close. Does Mrs Palmer know?'

'He's going to tell her when the time comes but not yet. We've got to get the timing right.'

So that was it: Kirsty had ambitions to achieve the position of Owner's Wife – Mrs Palmer's successor.

'Is it possible that his secret concerns Leanne Hatman?'

She stared at him, shocked. Then she shook her head vigorously. 'Of course not. That's ridiculous.'

Somehow she didn't sound very convincing.

'Could he have been sleeping with Leanne?'

'No. If anything like that was going on, I would have known about it.'

Wesley knew she believed what she was saying. For a split second he was almost tempted to tell her about Tabitha Sweeting; but it was none of his business. However, he needed to get to the bottom of David Palmer's alleged secret, and that meant talking to the man.

On his way out he asked the girl who'd taken over from Sean behind reception whether Mr Palmer was in but he was informed with corporate politeness that he was over in Portsmouth and she didn't know what time he'd be back. He asked her to call him as soon as he returned but the young woman arranged her features into an apologetic expression. She was sorry but she thought he wouldn't be back until late that evening. He might even decide to stay over.

Wesley thanked her and told himself there was always tomorrow.

Clare Woolmer was being followed at a discreet distance but Rob Carter had reported that her day so far had been completely uneventful. She'd met a female friend for lunch in Neston's Doggie Café – an establishment where dog lovers with no room or time for pets of their own could eat and drink in the company of a team of specially trained canines – a concept that was proving a great success with locals and tourists alike. After lunch, Clare returned home and didn't venture out again. From Rob's voice when he phoned in the report, Gerry could tell he was bored.

Gerry twisted round in his seat to stare at the wall behind him. Photographs of all the main players were pinned up there, along with observations and comments. On the whiteboard in the corner he'd scrawled the actions for the day: who was to be interviewed and what was to be followed up and by whom. Wesley had just called in to tell him about his conversation with Kirsty Paige, detailing what she'd said about David Palmer, but as far as Gerry was concerned this was just another loose end. They needed something concrete; something that would lead to an arrest.

He was contemplating his problem when he heard someone saying his name. When he turned round he recognised one of the young women from the forensic lab, holding a plain brown envelope.

'This is the report on the crossbow and bolts found in Jordan Carnegie's friend's lock-up,' she said.

Gerry looked at her hopefully. 'Good news?'

'That depends what you're hoping for. All the bolts have been examined and there are no traces of blood or Hatman's DNA. They came in a pack of six and there are still six there – no sign of any others. The crossbow and bolts were ordered off the internet and, as far as we can see, only six bolts were ordered along with a target, which was also found in the lock-up.' She paused. 'And, according to the pathology report, the diameter of these bolts isn't an exact match for the one that made the wound.' She must have seen the disappointment on Gerry's face because she added: 'Sorry.'

'Thanks, love. Not your fault.' Gerry watched as she hurried out of the room, as though she was half afraid he'd come after her, ready to wreak his revenge on the bearer of bad news.

He knew he couldn't put it off so he made the phone call to Tradmouth police station to say that they no longer had any reason to hold Carnegie on suspicion of murder. His solicitor, Mr No Comment, would no doubt be delighted but Gerry had no choice. They'd got Carnegie for possession of class A drugs and assaulting a police officer but if they were to pin the murder of Darren Hatman on him, they needed considerably more.

His day worsened when Paul Johnson reported that all of Lee Varlow's re-enactment group's weapons were accounted for, safely locked away and undisturbed. Then when his phone rang he feared it would be more bad news that would move the investigation back instead of forwards. This time though the voice on the other end of the line belonged to Cornell Stamoran, who was uttering what seemed to Gerry at that moment like magic words – he'd heard from Barney Yelland.

'He called this morning wanting to talk about the book,' said Stamoran. 'He's selected the pictures to go with my text and now he's processing them on his computer – says he'll email them to me as soon as they're ready. He hasn't been able to get hold of the second volume of the journal as he promised. I told him I needed it but he said it might take some time and I'd just have to wait.' He sounded annoyed.

'Did he say where he was?'

'I asked him but he dodged the subject.'

'You didn't tell him about our visit?'

'No. Should I have done?'

'You did the right thing. What else did he say?'

'Only that he'd lost his cell phone and he's got a new number ... and he said there'd been some trouble and he was having to keep his head down.' He paused. 'He did come out with something a bit odd. He said, "I'm being cared for by an angel." Does that make sense to you?'

Gerry had to admit it didn't.

14

We fled our lodgings by night.

As soon as Joules was cleansed of blood he gave orders for our baggage to be stowed aboard the cart and I saw that he was shaking. My cousin, in contrast, wore an expression of satisfaction, like one who has just partaken of a good meal. Neither said a word but as the cart drew away I saw Joules watching Uriah as a cat watches a mouse, alert and ready to pounce.

The monstrous painting is there amongst Uriah's baggage but I try my best not to look at it.

Wesley knew he should be hurrying back to the incident room but he'd never been able to resist a quick peek at any archaeology going on in his vicinity. So, on leaving the castle, he took the path down to the river bank where the water mill had once stood. He found Neil there, gazing at the contents of a finds tray and wearing an expression that came close to a miser's gloat.

'You look like a man who's just got his hands on the Holy Grail,' Wesley said as he approached his friend, carefully avoiding the trench that had grown considerably deeper since he'd last seen it.

'We've had an unexpected find,' Neil said. 'In fact I was going to ring you.'

Neil picked up the tray and presented it to Wesley with the pride of a new father showing off his infant. Wesley could see wonderful things, shining against a bed of newspaper. Five gold coins and six silver, all dating to the late eighteenth century – 1785 being the newest – and a fine gold-cased pocket watch. For a dig that was supposed to be uncovering the remains of a humble manorial water mill, this was treasure indeed.

'The coins were bunched together as though they'd been in a bag that had disintegrated over time. And the watch is by Thomas Mudge – hallmarked seventeen sixty-eight. Mudge was a Devon man who became watchmaker to George the Third. This is high-status stuff, Wes. And there's more. We found a lead bullet lodged in the ribs of that skeleton.'

'Is it still here?'

Neil shook his head. 'As soon as Margaret confirmed that it had been there more than seventy years the coroner gave permission for it to be moved to Exeter for further examination.'

Wesley nodded. He knew protocol demanded that human remains found at a dig were removed as swiftly and respectfully as possible. It wasn't done to allow them to lie unattended, at the mercy of ghouls or treasure hunters.

'May I?'

When Neil nodded his assent, Wesley lifted the watch out of the tray and saw that its case had been engraved with a coat of arms featuring three trees and something that looked like an eye in the centre.

'It's the arms of the D'Arles family,' Neil said as Wesley replaced it carefully. 'They used to own the castle.'

'So the victim might have been one of the family . . . or a thief who stole from the castle and was chased down here and shot.'

'If that was the case, surely the victim of the robbery would have retrieved his property.'

Neil had a point. He hadn't thought it through. Maybe he had too much on his mind.

His phone rang and when he answered he heard the boss's voice, sounding almost as excited as Neil had been.

'Do you want the good news or the bad news?' he began.

Wesley opted for the bad news.

'Jordan Carnegie's gone back to Exeter. Forensic couldn't find anything to link him to Hatman's murder.'

'Anything on Hatman's widow?

'Rachel's with her at the moment but she's not reported back.'

'What about the good news?'

'I've had a call from Cornell Stamoran. Yelland's been in touch and promised him the photos for his book'll be ready soon. Unfortunately he didn't say where he was but it looks like he's got his computer with him.'

'If he took it to Italy that's hardly surprising. Has he sent any emails?'

'Not according to Scientific Support. He's lying low. I'm getting his phone call to Stamoran traced so we should have something soon. Anything your end?'

'I've spoken to Kirsty Paige. She claims she's in a relationship with David Palmer and she says there's something he's been keeping from her – a secret – although she doesn't think it's connected with Leanne. She has no idea about Tabitha Sweeting, so it looks like Palmer's been keeping them both on the go.'

'Could Leanne have been involved with him and all?'

'Kirsty says not.'

'Maybe that's wishful thinking. Anything else?'

'That painting Mrs Palmer says has been stolen – I think it was targeted. I'm consulting my old colleagues in the Art and Antique Unit. And by the way, Neil's dug up a skeleton. But don't worry, it's old . . . not our problem.'

He heard Gerry swear under his breath. 'You nearly made my blood pressure shoot through the roof then.'

'There might be a link to our case though. Neil's found some valuables buried nearby that appear to be linked to the D'Arles family. Remember that lady we interviewed – Miss D'Arles.'

'Relevant?'

'Possibly not. But she might be interested and I'd like to ask her about this missing painting. According to Mrs Palmer, she left most of the art in the castle behind when she moved.'

'That's more your department than mine,' said Gerry impatiently. 'Don't get side-tracked, will you. When are you going to honour us with your presence back at the incident room?'

'Now. But I want to speak to Palmer when he gets back.

Something's going on at Eyecliffe Castle and I wouldn't be surprised if it has something to do with Darren Hatman's death.'

'What about Leanne?'

'There's still no real evidence that she's come to any harm. What do you think?'

Gerry didn't answer and Wesley was left there listening to the dialling tone.

As soon as Wesley returned to the incident room, he emailed a copy of the missing picture to one of his former colleagues at the Met. If it was offered for sale at any auction house or gallery could they let him know right away?

Half an hour later, Rachel walked in looking unusually subdued, like someone who'd just attended the funeral of a close friend. As soon as she sat down Wesley walked over to join her. 'How's Mrs Hatman?'

She considered the question for a moment. 'She doesn't exactly fit the stereotype of the grief-stricken widow.'

'Well, they were separated.'

'I know. But she's on edge – jumpy.'

'She's probably worried about her daughter?'

'She's still claiming she's in London. Says she'll be in touch any day.'

'Think she believes it?'

'If you ask me, she finds it less painful to bury her head in the sand.' She paused for a moment. 'I told her that none of the modelling agencies we spoke to had contacted Leanne but she said we've been asking the wrong ones. I didn't tell her we'd exhausted the possibilities. It seemed cruel to rob her of any hope. Am I getting soft, Wes?'

He touched her shoulder, a gesture of comfort. 'I think I

might have kept quiet too. I've suggested we do a thorough search of the castle estate.'

'You think Leanne's still there?'

'That's what we have to find out.' He hesitated. 'Do you think Marion's capable of arranging Darren's death?'

'What would she have to gain?'

'They're not divorced so she inherits his property unless he's made a will stating otherwise. She'll get the building firm and his house. And there's over fifty grand in his bank account. The firm's doing well.' He saw the surprise on her face. 'She hasn't mentioned it?'

'No. She's still going into her job at the café; counting the pennies.'

'Maybe Darren didn't tell her how well he was doing. Some men in his position try and keep their assets hidden from their ex to avoid paying a big divorce settlement.'

When Wesley returned to his desk he found he had an unopened email from the Art and Antique Unit in his inbox. As soon as he'd read it he made a call. 'I understand our missing painting's turned up.' he said once he'd got through to the right extension. 'That was quick.'

'It was a stroke of luck,' said the voice on the other end of the line. 'The minute we received your email we circulated the photo to auction houses and galleries and one got in touch immediately. The painting was brought in this morning for authentication and possible sale. The vendors believe it's a Turner.'

Suddenly the familiarity of the style made sense. 'And is it?'

'Let's just say the experts at the auction house are excited.'

'And the vendors?'

'They're a couple who claim they inherited it from a

grandmother who used to live in Devon. It's a depiction of the river at Tradmouth. You'll be familiar with that, I suppose?'

'Yes,' said Wesley, his heart beating faster. 'Turner did spend some time down here.'

'There'll have to be tests and expert opinions but at the moment it looks promising. But you say it was stolen?'

'From a local hotel.'

'How did the hotel get hold of it?'

'It was left in the building by the former owner.'

He heard a sharp intake of breath on the other end of the line. 'Who, presumably, didn't know its true value. The present owner will have to identify it as their property before we can act.'

'Of course.'

'We've already searched the couple's premises and we found some photographs of the painting. They claim they took them for insurance purposes but the colour of the wall in the background doesn't match anywhere in their home or place of business and neither place appears to have been decorated for a while. Suspicious.'

'Where are the couple now?'

'We've brought them in for questioning. They're called Brenda and Jeremy Hodges and they own a small gallery in Camden. I'm emailing you their pictures.'

There was a short pause while Wesley opened the new email of the promised photographs and, sure enough, the faces were familiar.

'Thanks – I recognise them. They were calling themselves Beverley and Jim Hughes when they were here.'

'They can never resist keeping the same initials, can they?'

'We spoke to them in connection with a murder case but they were eliminated from our inquiries.'

'Has our news changed that?'

'Not sure,' Wesley replied noncommittally. He ended the call. This small success had lifted his spirits a little, even though it was only one tiny victory in a sea of uncertainty. The identity of Darren Hatman's killer and the where-abouts of his missing daughter remained as elusive as ever.

James Garrard had enjoyed his day at the dig, although the most interesting trenches, the ones containing the bones and the gold artefacts, had been rapidly commandeered by the professionals and the volunteers put to work at the less exciting end of the site. James had felt irritated because he had discovered the first gold coin, only to be robbed of the thrill of holding it in his fingers by Lucy Zinara, who had shot across to 'help' as soon as he'd drawn attention to his find. Still, he'd been too polite to protest.

Dr Watson had suggested that the bones belonged to a robbery victim who'd been shot before the villain panicked and fled, dropping the valuables in the process. This sounded reasonable to James, who liked to daydream about historical events. During his childhood he'd done a lot of daydreaming. His mother had been too protective to let him out of her sight much so, rather than roaming and making dens with the other boys, he'd lost himself in the world of books and the imagination.

'Is that you, dear?'

His wife always asked the same question when he arrived home, using a half-fearful tone as though she was expecting to find an armed robber in the hallway.

'Yes. It's me.'

She came bustling out of the living room, a small, dumpy figure with a cloud of fair curls.

'There's another parcel for you.' She pointed to a brown paper parcel, about eighteen inches square.

He picked it up and stared at it. The address was neatly printed on the front in blue ink capital letters. The same as the others.

'Aren't you going to open it?'

He began to undo it, careful not to damage the packaging in case the police needed it as evidence. Inside was a plain cardboard box and he prised the top off gingerly, as if he expected a poisonous snake to slither out and strike at him with venomous fangs.

There, lying in a bed of white tissue paper, he saw four small silver bowls, beautifully crafted and polished to a shine. His hand shook as he lifted one out. It was hallmarked and he guessed it was very old, and valuable. At Inspector Peterson's suggestion he'd already paid one visit to the police station in Tradmouth and been told that none of the items he'd already received had been reported as stolen. This news, in his opinion, only added to the mystery.

'Is there a note?' his wife asked, hovering anxiously behind him, her eyes fixed on the gleaming bowls.

There had been nothing with the other things but this time he saw a square of thick, handmade paper lying on top of the tissue. James read the note out loud.

"'I'm so sorry.'"

'Sorry for what?' his wife asked.

James had no answer to that question.

15

Most of the souvenirs we have purchased during our journey have been sent on to England to await our return so now we travel with only our personal possessions, except for the hideous painting that Uriah insists on keeping with him at all times.

We have taken a boat to Corsica from where we will travel to the coast of France. There is such a change in Joules, our gentle bear-leader, as though he has seen a vision of hell itself, and when I try to wheedle out of him what he witnessed that night in Palermo, he says nothing, only that it is better I do not know.

My cousin too is silent. But I will discover the truth.

Wesley had been concerned about leaving Pam alone with the kids and her worries at the weekend, but when he arrived home on Saturday evening she appeared to be in good spirits. When he asked the inevitable questions, she said she'd been too busy to think about her problem – which was a good thing. If she'd had time to worry, she'd have been plunged into despair, imagining the worst that could happen.

That evening he did his best to distract her, but every so often a haunted look appeared in her eyes as her fears hit her afresh. Although she'd been told she wouldn't have to wait long for her appointment, every hour felt like a year.

On Sunday he knew the quietness of the day would allow her time to dwell on the situation; in contrast, during a major murder inquiry, days off for him didn't exist. He suggested that she go to his sister's for lunch but she insisted she'd be fine. This didn't stop him worrying and he felt more frustrated than usual when every lead they tried to follow that day hit a delay or a dead end.

As soon as he sat down at his desk first thing on Monday morning, he received a call from the Art and Antique Unit. Mrs Palmer had confirmed that the picture of the painting they had in their possession was definitely the one stolen from Eyecliffe Castle. Could Wesley possibly find out something about its provenance?

He was about to tell them that he was in the middle of a murder inquiry but he stopped himself. It would do no harm to pay Miss D'Arles another visit; she'd been interviewed when Darren Hatman's body was found and there was always a chance she'd remembered something useful. He also wanted to take another look at the barn Hatman had been working on. Lee Varlow and Craig Gatting had been laid off for the time being, which meant the place would be empty.

It was a fine May morning so he decided to walk to the Dower House and as he entered the Eyecliffe estate he passed the lodge. The small building had smart wooden blinds at the windows and he'd heard David Palmer had sold it to a private buyer for renovation. Just like he'd sold the barn to Darren Hatman.

He continued down the drive, thinking how the estate must have been a terrible burden for Miss D'Arles. She'd probably been relieved when Mrs Palmer's late husband had offered to take it off her hands, although her feelings must have been mixed. As the last custodian of the place, she would surely have experienced some guilt at being the one to let it go.

As he approached the Dower House he could see the roof, gutters and paintwork were in urgent need of attention. Perhaps Darren Hatman would have been doing her a favour after all . . . providing his price had been right.

At first there was no answer and he was tempted to go round the back and take a peek into the windows. It was an interesting house – a house with almost as much history as the castle itself – but before he could satisfy his curiosity, the door opened.

The stiff politeness of Miss D'Arles's greeting gave no clue as to whether or not he was welcome, but she led him into the drawing room where the dolls still sat watching silently from their shelf. Then his eyes were drawn to Reginald, who lay relaxed in his basket. The dog gazed up at him and his tail gave a small wag of greeting before he stood up and ambled over to his mistress.

'I'm sorry to bother you again, Miss D'Arles, but I have a few more questions.'

'Anything I can do to help the police.'

He took the photograph of the stolen painting from his pocket and handed it to her. 'I believe you left this painting at the castle when you moved out.'

She put on the reading glasses that were dangling from a chain around her neck. 'I left so many paintings behind. I didn't have room for them here so they were included in the price, along with most of the furniture. I only kept what I needed.'

'I've seen some of the paintings – the ones of classical ruins. Were they yours?'

'Yes, but I was told they weren't worth very much.'

'Grand Tour paintings?'

She frowned. 'I beg your pardon?'

'When young aristocrats did their grand tour of Europe a couple of centuries ago, they brought back souvenirs. Is that where the pictures at the castle came from – one of your ancestors?'

'I really have no idea,' she said quickly.

Wesley was familiar with evasion but he had no idea why the subject of the Grand Tour should elicit such a response. Or maybe something else was bothering her; perhaps the possibility that she'd left the Palmers in possession of a priceless art treasure by mistake.

'This painting was stolen from the castle and it's now been recovered by the Metropolitan Police. They think it might be a Turner.'

Her eyes widened. 'It was just one amongst many and I must say I thought it rather gloomy.' She sighed. 'Of course if I'd known it was a Turner I would have sold it separately.

The money would have come in useful. I suppose it belongs to the Palmers now.'

'I'm afraid so,' he said, wondering if Mrs Palmer's late husband had concealed its worth deliberately. 'Do you know how your family acquired it?'

'Turner used to visit these parts so perhaps one of my ancestors bought it from him.'

'He was here in the early eighteen hundreds I believe.'

'That would have been when Thomas D'Arles owned the castle. He lived to a ripe old age and did quite a bit to the place.'

'Was he the person who brought the paintings back from the Grand Tour?'

'No, that was his elder brother, Richard.' She gave him a curious look. 'You're a strange policeman, aren't you?'

There was no answer to that. He reached out his hand and stroked Reginald's head before looking at his watch. David Palmer would be back at the castle by now and he wanted to speak to him.

'I'm sorry, Miss D'Arles. I have to go.'

'Must you? I'm beginning to enjoy our little chats.'

When she smiled he could see that she had once been a beautiful woman and he couldn't help wondering about her past. As far as he knew she'd never married, but had there been lovers? Had she envied her sister who'd escaped to Europe to become a dancer while she'd been left behind with the heavy responsibility of the estate? All of a sudden he wanted to know more about her and what had brought about her present existence as the sad relic of a decayed dynasty.

He was about to leave when he remembered something else he'd wanted to tell her. 'A friend of mine is in charge of the archaeological excavation down by the river bank.'

'I'm aware of that. That mill belonged to the estate until my grandfather sold off that section of land just after the First World War. It was demolished long ago.'

'They've found a man's bones buried there. There's evidence he was shot. They also found some coins and a valuable gold pocket watch which date the burial to the late eighteenth century.' He paused. 'The D'Arles coat of arms is engraved on the case of the watch.'

'In that case the bones probably belong to a thief caught in the act and shot after hiding his loot. He was most likely buried in secret to avoid trouble with the local constable.' She smiled. 'But I doubt if you'll get to the bottom of the matter now, Inspector. It was all a very long time ago.'

Wesley looked at his own watch, a modern stainless steel model, so unlike Neil's exquisitely engraved gold find. It was time to move on. He said goodbye and stepped outside into the weak sunshine.

DC Rob Carter hadn't realised police work could be so tedious. He'd watched Clare Woolmer for most of the previous day and now DCI Heffernan had put him on the same job. He wouldn't have minded so much if the woman didn't lead such a boring life. What was she getting up to behind her closed blinds? Watching TV? On the internet surfing dating websites? She looked arty, the typical Neston type, so maybe she was painting or something equally creative. But whatever she was doing, it was hardly a thrilling spectator sport ... and it certainly didn't involve anyone else.

He managed to find a parking space opposite her address and sat waiting, glancing at her house from time to time while checking on the more exciting events playing out on his iPhone.

As it was he almost missed her door opening but he looked up just in time and sank down in his seat to avoid being seen. She was wearing a long velvet coat today and carrying an old-fashioned wicker basket – the type Little Red Riding Hood always carried in fairy tale illustrations. When she was halfway down the road he got out of the car and began to follow. She was walking quickly, as if she was in a hurry, and heading for the centre of Neston.

When he'd joined CID he'd hoped he'd be doing something more exciting than following some middle-aged hippie woman going shopping, but he put his hands in his pockets and kept her in sight.

Wesley called Gerry to say he was on his way to interview David Palmer but Gerry seemed more interested in the fact that Rob Carter had just rung with the news that Clare Woolmer was on the move.

He was still hoping she'd lead them to Barney Yelland but Wesley wondered whether Yelland would be that careless. Surely if he'd abducted Leanne Hatman and killed her father, he'd keep well away from Neston; and would a man who'd committed such crimes really be chatting to Cornell Stamoran about photographs as though nothing had happened? However, he knew that there was no accounting for the workings of the criminal mind.

'As you suggested, I'm extending the search to the entire castle grounds. I'm organising the team now,' Gerry said as he was about to end the call. 'Aunty Noreen's moaning about the expense but I told her it's got to be done.'

The chief super's concern about budgetary constraints came as no surprise to Wesley but, as far as he was concerned, they'd be neglecting their duty if a thorough search wasn't made. Unless Barney Yelland could throw some light on Leanne's whereabouts when they found him.

As he walked into reception, he found himself wondering how much the place had changed since Miss D'Arles's day. A great deal, he imagined. She wouldn't have had the resources for such elaborate renovations.

Sean was on duty again today and he gave Wesley a knowing smile when he asked if Mr Palmer was in. Before he could ring through to Palmer's office Wesley stopped him. He wanted to catch the manager off guard.

When he opened Palmer's door the man looked startled.

'How can I help you, Inspector?' He sounded nervous, probably recalling their last encounter.

Wesley sat down without being invited.

'Is this about the missing painting?' Wesley could hear his voice cracking with nerves.

'I've got good news. It's been found in London. Apparently your guests, Mr and Mrs Hughes, stayed here a couple of weeks ago under an assumed name. They probably saw the painting then and decided to come back and take it.' He hesitated. 'Are you aware it could be a Turner?'

This was obviously news to Palmer, whose face lit up with avarice. 'A Turner?'

'It's being scrutinised by experts at the moment but if they give it the nod then it's yours to sell if you wish. I understand your father purchased all the paintings in the castle when he bought the place. Miss D'Arles didn't realise what she had but, legally, there's no question that it's your property.'

It wasn't only greed Wesley saw on the man's face, it was relief.

'You look as if you've had the weight of the world lifted off your shoulders, Mr Palmer,' said Wesley.

'You could put it like that. This could solve a lot of problems.'

Wesley leaned forward. 'I've been told you have a secret.'

Palmer almost flinched. 'Who told you that?'

'Never mind who told me. It's my job to find out whether this secret of yours is connected to the disappearance of Leanne Hatman and the murder of her father.'

Palmer sat back. For the first time he looked relaxed. 'I can assure you there's no connection. It's a business matter . . . something I'm trying to keep confidential.'

'If it's not relevant to the case, whatever you tell me will stay in this room.'

'OK. I've been making inquiries about selling the hotel to a well-known international chain. We've been going through a bad patch recently and it was either remortgaging or conjuring up the extra cash some other way.' He sighed and looked around. 'I'm afraid Eyecliffe Castle has been a veritable money pit over the years. The gatehouse wing's still sealed off and completely untouched. I'd like to put more bedrooms in there as well as upgrading the swimming pool but the finance hasn't been there. My potential buyer's interested but negotiations are at a delicate stage. That's what my weekend meeting in Portsmouth was about, and that's where I was when I left the Brighton conference early.'

'Is your mother aware of this?'

Palmer's face reddened. 'I want to keep it from her. Her

health isn't good and she and my late father put their hearts and souls into this place so she'd be devastated if we lost control of the business. But I've no choice.'

'I've known people kill to protect secrets, Mr Palmer. I expect you'd do anything to prevent her finding out.'

'Yes but that doesn't include murder. You have to believe me.'

He looked almost pathetic; a weak man, dominated by his mother, who'd got himself into a mess. But Wesley knew that the weak can be as dangerous as the strong. Sometimes more so.

His face was suddenly transfigured by hope. 'If this painting's a Turner I can sell it and get the bank off my back. I can even forget the sale and make the improvements I've been planning.'

'Let's keep our fingers crossed then,' said Wesley.

Palmer bowed his head. 'You won't tell my mother?'

'She won't hear anything from me,' said Wesley. He had never thought he'd feel sympathy for David Palmer but life was full of strange surprises.

'She's walking along the river bank in Neston – near the old bridge.' Rob Carter held his phone in front of his mouth and spoke in a whisper, even though Clare Woolmer was too far away to hear.

He'd followed her through the town and when she'd descended the steps leading down to the river bank he'd followed at a distance, keeping his head down, slouching along with his hands in his pockets trying to look casual. He'd seen her stop by a small cabin cruiser tied up thirty yards from the bridge and lean over to knock on the cabin window. Then she'd gathered up her skirts and stepped aboard. The boat was called the *Fallen Angel* and, in contrast to its well-heeled neighbours, it had a neglected look.

'She's boarded one of the boats. What shall I do?' He'd been tempted to go straight in, use his initiative and make his mark, but after six months in CID he was becoming familiar with Gerry Heffernan's cutting tongue. If he cocked things up, he wouldn't hear the end of it.

'Watch and wait. Back-up's on its way.'

He did as he was told, leaning against a tree, dying for a piss, all the time keeping his eyes on the boat. Judging from the secretive way she'd knocked on the window there was someone else in there with her.

He waited fifteen minutes, his feet numb and his bladder bursting, and when Trish Walton and Paul Johnson appeared he felt a wave of relief.

'She's still in there. Are we going in?'

'Boss says yes,' said Trish. 'How are your sea legs?'

'Why?' Rob sounded wary.

'Because you're going on board first,' Trish replied with a grin.

Rob led the way to the boat, trying to stifle his apprehension and telling himself that maybe this was his chance to impress by making the big arrest. Without hesitating, he leaped on to the deck and pushed at the cabin door. It wasn't locked and opened with a crash.

Clare Woolmer was sitting at the table in the small cabin, nursing a mug of tea. Sitting opposite her a man with a dark ponytail had a laptop open in front of him as though he was working. Both of them turned their heads, the same look of startled alarm in their eyes.

'What the hell . . .' the man blustered, rising from his seat.

'Barney Yelland, I'm arresting you in connection with the disappearance of Leanne Hatman and the murder of Darren Hatman.' He recited the caution he'd learned by heart at police college and took his handcuffs from his pocket with a flourish as he heard Trish and Paul enter the cabin behind him.

This would give him some brownie points with Gerry Heffernan.

16

We are in France, lodged for the
night in a small inn near Nice. I
share a chamber with Joules as the
patron has many guests this night, but
Uriah sleeps alone. I would rather share
with our cicerone than my own cousin,
which seems a strange state of affairs.
And yet I fear Uriah's strangeness.

After we dined, I sat before the fire
with Joules who stared into his glass of
wine, lost in thought and saying little.
I asked what ailed him and I thought
he was about to confide his troubles when
he stood up, looking around in alarm
and asked, 'Where is he?'

When I did not reply he rushed
from the room, knocking over his glass
as he went.

His action disturbed me so I followed him but he was nowhere to be found and neither was Uriah.

People expected widows to be grief-stricken; to emulate Queen Victoria who mourned her late husband to excess and withdrew for years from public life. But Marion Hatman couldn't feel that way. For a long time she and Darren hadn't got on, although there had been no dramatic altercation. In the end their relationship had dwindled to indifference until eventually both had found it preferable to live their separate lives.

When they'd met Darren had been a petty criminal. Not a big-time mastermind, unfortunately – that might have impressed her in her younger days – but a getaway driver; a small cog in the criminal wheel. He'd spent time inside and regarded this philosophically as an occupational hazard. Until the day he'd been driving too fast away from the Plymouth post office his mates had just robbed and he'd hit an old woman who'd been crossing the road. When she died of her injuries his life changed, and on his release from prison he'd gone straight. He'd never admitted that the accident had caused his Damascene conversion to the straight and narrow: instead he'd told her that incipient middle age wasn't compatible with a life of crime. Getting your collar felt was a young man's game. Besides, he'd learned building skills inside and no lesson is ever truly wasted.

Darren had started his own business. He'd become an employer and Leanne had seemed impressed by her father's new standing in the community. She'd left Marion's flat to live with him for a while and, even though her daughter's rejection had gnawed away at Marion's soul, she'd tried not to show it. Then Leanne had started to treat her father with contempt as well, a state of affairs which gave Marion a degree of satisfaction, although she never actually said so.

Once Leanne flounced off to live in at Eyecliffe Castle Marion saw little of her, and now it looked as if the photographer she'd talked about nonstop during their increasingly rare meetings was responsible for her disappearance. All Marion could hope was that he was keeping her somewhere because the alternative was unthinkable. The family liaison officer who spent so much time at her flat providing endless tea and spurious sympathy had used professional tact to avoid the question of Leanne's fate. Marion wouldn't give her the satisfaction of seeing the tears she shed for her missing daughter in her private hours so she put on a brave mask. Nobody would see her grief.

But life went on so she'd already consulted a solicitor about her legal position. Since she and Darren had never actually divorced she reckoned his building company would come to her. She quite fancied the idea of being a businesswoman. Even though she'd left school at sixteen with no qualifications, she suspected she might be a late developer.

She'd sent away the family liaison officer, who said she'd be back later, just to make sure she was OK. Spying on her more like. Marion knew she was probably a suspect for her husband's murder but they couldn't prove anything against her. Besides, it stood to reason that whoever killed Darren had also abducted Leanne, and she had done neither.

As soon as she found herself alone, the tears came, tumbling uncontrolled down her cheeks, then after a while she took a deep breath and rinsed her face with cold water. It was time to go out. She had to think about the future.

She left the flat, locking up carefully behind her. Her car, an elderly green Fiesta with rusty sills and seats wrecked by a previous owner's dog, was parked down the street and she knew there wasn't much petrol in the tank but it would get her to Eyecliffe Castle and back. She wanted to view her new inheritance. Soon she'd be a woman of substance so maybe she'd replace the Fiesta with something more suitable when the money finally came through.

She drove to the village of Turling Fitwell and through the grand gates that stood at the main entrance to the Eyecliffe Castle Estate. She saw a sign telling visitors that it was now the Eyecliffe Castle Spa and Country Hotel. It was the sort of place Marion had never patronised, but from now on things might be different.

She knew the barn Darren had bought for renovation wasn't far from the entrance but it took her a few false turns to find it. When she parked she could tell that work had barely started. After Darren's death the lads who worked for him had abandoned ship, unsure whether they'd be paid or whether the project would go ahead and she could hardly blame them. Darren had said they were good workers so she'd make every effort to get them back on board as soon as everything was sorted out.

She walked round the half-ruined building. Bags of cement lay against the walls protected by tarpaulins and an orange cement mixer stood, waiting for action. Probably there'd be more materials inside the barn but the old wooden door was padlocked, and she didn't have the key.

As she was returning to the car she thought she heard a rustling in the nearby trees, but when she turned to look there was nothing there.

Then a memory flashed across her mind. This place had

a reputation for being haunted by a white lady and something else she couldn't quite recall from her childhood when she'd taken an interest in such things. However, she didn't believe in ghosts now ... and she refused to entertain the possibility that Darren might be watching; keeping an eye on her from wherever he'd ended up. It had been her imagination. Nothing more.

She climbed into her car and drove away. Too fast.

Wesley took out his phone, letting his finger hover over Pam's number. He felt a strong urge to speak to her but he knew she'd be at work in her classroom. Unobtainable.

As he made his way back to the incident room a trio of police cars passed him on the drive, heading for the castle, the reinforcements Gerry had ordered. The woodland where Darren Hatman's body had been found had already been examined but he wanted the search expanded to cover the whole area around the castle too. Darren Hatman had died there and there was no evidence that his daughter Leanne had ever left. All the local taxi firms had now been checked and, even though they'd considered the possibility that Leanne's abductor – if there was one – had picked her up in a vehicle, nobody had seen or heard anything to confirm that. She had simply vanished. Like a magician's assistant from a magic cabinet.

He had almost reached the incident room when he received a call from Gerry, who sounded excited.

'We've found Yelland in a boat that used to belong to Clare Woolmer's late partner. It's called the *Fallen Angel* – remember he told Cornell Stamoran he was being looked after by an angel? I'm kicking myself for not checking it out. As soon as Yelland got back to Devon, Woolmer tipped him off that we were after him and suggested he hide out there. She's been taking him food. We can have her for harbouring a suspect.'

'Where's Yelland now?'

'At Tradmouth waiting to be interviewed. I thought it would be best if we both did it.'

Wesley hesitated. If the interview dragged on, which it well might, he'd be late home again. But he heard himself saying, 'OK. Why not.' He'd call Pam as soon as her school day was ended and catch up. He hoped she'd understand.

'Where are you now?'

'On my way back to the incident room.'

'Have the search team turned up at Eyecliffe Castle yet?'

'Yes. I've just seen them. You're expecting to find Leanne, aren't you?'

'Aren't you?'

Wesley didn't answer but he shared Gerry's fears. Leanne's blood had been found in Yelland's room and he'd gone to great lengths to avoid arrest. He wasn't behaving like an innocent man.

In an ideal world, Gerry said, they'd have been able to await the result of the search of the castle grounds before they spoke to Barney Yelland. But the world was far from ideal and the clock was ticking. Besides, Wesley reminded him, if Yelland had killed Leanne he could have dumped her body anywhere. He had links with the river so he could have put her body into the water, in which case she'd turn up downstream eventually, floating face down and bloated with putrefying gases.

He drove back to Tradmouth with Gerry beside him in the passenger seat. Gerry was unusually quiet and Wesley knew he was thinking of the coming interview. In spite of all the other suspects who'd cropped up in the course of their investigation, Barney Yelland seemed their most likely candidate for Leanne's abduction. And because he'd returned home early from Sicily he was in the frame for her father's murder as well.

As soon as they entered the CID office Wesley's phone began to ring. It was Trish Walton, up at Eyecliffe Castle; he hoped she had news.

'The search team have found something,' he heard her say.

'What?'

There was a pause before Trish replied. 'I'm not sure.'

17

The following morning Joules said
little. He looked shaken and I
surmised that something had occurred
the previous night. But, whatever it was,
I was not privy to it.

Joules was anxious to be away and as
soon as we had broken our fast and paid
for our lodgings he saw to it that our
horses were saddled and ready.

As we were leaving the inn the
patron rushed up to us, seizing the
reins of Joules's mount and gabbling
swiftly in his own tongue, too rapid for
me to comprehend, even though I speak
French tolerably well.

I saw Joules press coins from his purse
into the man's hand before instructing
us to ride away at once. As he took the

reins of his steed I saw the blood had drained from his face so that he had the pallor of a dead man.

At the rear of the castle the terrace described in the hotel brochure overlooked the steep, grassy slope that ran down to the rushing river. It was guarded by a stone balustrade which had crumbled away in places so that one false step could send the stones and the straying individual tumbling down the hill beneath. It would never have satisfied any health and safety inspector, but then this part of the castle wasn't accessible to the public. It was also out of bounds to staff, although the presence of cigarette butts scattered over the uneven stone flags suggested that some used the place for a crafty smoke.

Trish had discovered that one section of the balustrade had collapsed and the worn, carved stones lay scattered on the slope below, leaving part of the edge unprotected. From the damaged state of the vegetation beneath the stones, she guessed the collapse was recent.

On Gerry's orders the terrace was sealed off and, after speaking with staff who'd admitted to using it as a smoking area, it soon became clear that the balustrade had been in that condition for a couple of weeks, although nobody had thought to link the collapse with Leanne Hatman's disappearance. It was an old building and bits fell off from time to time.

Wesley congratulated Trish on her powers of observation and told her it could be significant, especially as Leanne was a smoker. Although several of the hotel staff admitted to sharing her vice – including David Palmer.

Wesley stood on the terrace looking down at the river

below as it thundered towards the weir by the old mill. Leanne could never have fallen into the water from up there; it was a long way down and the shrubs and bushes would break her fall. But she might have tumbled from the terrace in the dark, and wandered, disorientated, towards the treacherous water. Or perhaps she'd had help. He had hoped the search would provide answers but all it had done was generate more questions.

As there was nothing more they could do there while the search was in progress they returned to Tradmouth police station to have a word with Barney Yelland.

Wesley wanted to do things by the book so the photographer was brought up to the interview room where the tape recorder and the video were set running. Yelland had a solicitor, a thin woman with short dark hair who had been contacted by Clare Woolmer, and she sat watching carefully, like a lioness ready to leap to her cub's defence.

'Why did you go into hiding, Mr Yelland?' was Wesley's first question after the formalities were complete.

'When I got back from Sicily, Clare said you were looking for me. I'd done nothing wrong so I didn't see why I should suffer the inconvenience of being questioned and, besides, I was working to a deadline. Clare suggested I stay on the boat for a while until the fuss died down. I had my computer and my equipment with me so work wasn't a problem. Cornell, my collaborator, was waiting for some material Leanne had promised to get for me but I had to tell him there was a delay. You can't imagine how frustrating it was when Clare told me she was missing.'

'Frustrating?' Wesley found the choice of word strange.

'Yes. Cornell needed the journal to finish his work ... and I wanted to take more pictures of her. The officers who arrested me said something about the murder of a Darren Hatman. Is he a relation of Leanne's?'

'You don't know?'

'No. Have you found Leanne? I need to speak to her.' The question sounded innocent. But suspects sometimes played games.

Wesley glanced at Gerry. 'When did you last see her?'

'About three days before I flew to Italy. It must have been Friday the seventeenth.'

'Where was this?'

'At my place. She arrived about seven and left at nine thirty.'

'Did she mention going away?'

'She was still waiting to hear from the modelling agencies but she didn't say anything about going.'

'She rang you on the Sunday evening before you left.'

'She told me she wanted a couple of her pictures redone – photoshopped. She said her eyebrows looked wrong. I didn't think so but I agreed to do it when I got back from abroad. She said she'd see me then.'

'She didn't say if she was going anywhere that night?'

'No.'

'Tell us about your relationship with Leanne Hatman.'

He thought for a few moments. 'I suppose I'd describe her as my muse.'

'Nothing else? You weren't sleeping together?'

'No.'

'Have you tried to ring her since you got back?'

'I was going to call her right away to ask about the journal but Clare insisted it was best for me to lie low for a while. She said you thought some harm had come to Leanne and she was worried I'd get the blame even though

222

I haven't done anything.' He looked up nervously. 'Shall I try and call her now?'

It was Gerry who answered. 'Wouldn't do much good. Her phone's switched off. What I can't understand, Mr Yelland, is why you didn't come straight to us when Ms Woolmer told you Leanne was missing. You might have been able to help us find her.'

'How? I've no idea where she is.'

'If someone close to me disappeared like that, I'd be at the police station making sure that everything was being done to find them. But you don't seem too worried.'

Yelland shook his head. 'Ours isn't a personal relationship, Inspector. She's beautiful and I like photographing her but I can't say I particularly like her. She's self-absorbed, vain, but she's the sort of woman you can't take your eyes off. I don't expect you to understand.'

Wesley opened the file that lay on the table in front of him. Inside was the mutilated photograph they'd found in Yelland's room. He picked it out and placed it before the photographer.

'We found this in your room. Was she another muse?'

'Not exactly. She's my ex-wife, Penny.'

'Why did you do that to her face?'

'Because she's a bitch. She betrayed me.'

'How?'

'With another man.' He took the photograph in his fingers as though it was contaminated and turned it over so he couldn't see the scratched-out face.

'Where is she now?'

'She moved up north with him. I don't know her address. She went back to her single name, Hill – and I think she might be in County Durham.

'We found pictures of other women too. Naked. They all bear a resemblance to Leanne Hatman. It's an obsession, isn't it – that physical type.'

'There is a type of woman I find aesthetically pleasing, yes.'

'We'd like to speak to these women. Can we have their details?'

Yelland meekly provided the names and Wesley glanced at the two-way mirror hoping that Rob Carter who was watching the interview would use his initiative and start to trace them right away.

'Do you own a crossbow?' Gerry asked.

Yelland looked affronted. 'Of course not.'

'Ever used one?'

'Never. Why are you asking?'

'Leanne's father, Darren Hatman, was found dead in the grounds of Eyecliffe Castle. He was killed with a crossbow the day after you returned from Sicily. I presume you've visited the castle?'

'Only when I first saw Leanne. I followed her there and asked her if I could photograph her. She told me she had ambitions to be a model, and agreed on the condition I make a portfolio for her.'

Gerry leaned forward. 'We found a trace of her blood in your bedroom. Can you explain how it got there?'

There was no sign of panic in Yelland's eyes, which Wesley found rather surprising.

'She had a nosebleed. She was getting changed in my bedroom and she slipped and hit her face on the side of the chest of drawers. She was worried in case the pictures were ruined but a little make-up did the trick.'

'When was this?'

'About a week before I went to Italy. She wasn't happy with some of her portfolio pictures and wanted me to take some more. She was very . . . demanding. A perfectionist.'

'Was there a lot of blood?'

'A fair amount. But it didn't spoil the pictures. You can see them if you like.'

'I'll ask you again, did you have a sexual relationship with Leanne Hatman?'

'I've already told you. She was my muse. It wasn't sexual.' His eyes flickered away and Wesley suspected he was lying.

However, when asked where he was on the night of Darren Hatman's death, he answered confidently. Clare had come to the boat around eight that evening to keep him company and he'd gone to bed as soon as she'd left around two in the morning. His car was parked at Clare's and he hadn't used it since his return. And he certainly hadn't been to Eyecliffe Castle. Clare had told him that Leanne was missing so he had no reason to go there.

There was something naive, almost childlike, about his answers and Wesley recognised the glow of obsession in his eyes. But had Leanne featured only as his muse, his idealised woman no more important to him than a beautiful marble statue? Or was their relationship more complex?

Could Leanne have done or said something that made him lose control? Could he have gone to the castle that night and killed her, disposing of her body somehow before going off to Italy as though nothing had happened?

As he looked into the man's unblinking eyes, he couldn't be sure.

A uniformed constable had asked Neil to suspend his excavation for a while, just when the search of the castle grounds was in progress. Then he'd returned, very apologetic, and told him the entire area would be sealed off for the rest of the day.

Neil's colleague, Dave, had moaned a bit but then he'd gathered up his equipment and gone home, as had the volunteers. Neil and Lucy had tidied up the site before making for the car park. Maybe a drink in Turling Fitwell's only pub was called for.

As he opened the car door he had an idea.

'The former owner of the castle lives in the grounds,' he said to Lucy. 'The estate was in her family for centuries so I think we should show her what we've found.'

Lucy looked at her watch. 'Why not?' She looked round. The car park was packed with police vehicles, including the Dog Unit. 'Do you know what's going on?'

'I'll give Wesley a ring tonight and see what's happening. I want to know when we can get back to the site.'

He took the cardboard box containing the coins and watch out of the glove box. Wesley, he knew, would have reminded him of the dangers of car crime and it had been stupid to leave them there. But this time he'd got away with it.

They walked to the Dower House and as he was about to knock on the front door, a woman came round the side of the house accompanied by an elderly black Labrador with soulful eyes.

'Can I help you?' she asked warily, as though she feared they might be trying to sell her something.

Neil looked down and realised how disreputable he must have looked, covered in soil with mud-caked boots and filthy hands. And Lucy wasn't much better. No wonder the woman looked apprehensive.

226

'We're sorry to bother you,' Neil began. 'Are you Miss D'Arles?'

The woman summoned the Labrador to her side and put a protective hand on his head. 'Yes. What do you want?'

'My name's Dr Neil Watson and this is Dr Lucy Zinara.' He thought the use of their full titles might put her at her ease. 'We're archaeologists and we're working at the site of the old water mill down by the river. I understand your family used to own the estate.'

She appeared to relax a little. 'That's right. I've heard about your excavation. A very charming young black policeman came up here to talk to me. He told me you'd found some interesting things.'

Neil hadn't considered that Wesley was bound to have been there before him but now he thought about it, it made sense for the police to interview everyone in the vicinity. He liked her description of his friend as being 'young', though he supposed most people seemed young when you reached Miss D'Arles's age.

'Inspector Peterson? We're old friends. We were at university together.'

This did it. Their credentials approved, she invited them into the house. The drawing room felt gloomy and Neil shuddered a little at the sight of the watchful dolls but he sat down beside Lucy and took the box of treasures from the largest pocket of his combat jacket.

'This is what we found. I believe this is your family's coat of arms.'

Miss D'Arles took the box from him, cradling it as if it was some precious baby. She opened it and picked out the watch, its gold undimmed by time or burial, and held it delicately between her thumb and forefinger.

'This is the D'Arles family crest. Your friend told me you'd found these things buried at the mill?'

'From the plans and photographs we've seen, we think they were in one of the outbuildings. I don't know whether he told you that we found a skeleton nearby. Male. Probably in his twenties. The bones have been sent away for carbon dating but, from the dates of the coins we found, we think they may be from the late eighteenth century. There was a firearm nearby too, a flintlock pistol. A lead bullet was wedged in the skeleton's ribs so we're assuming he was shot with that weapon.'

'I told your friend that the victim was probably a thief who fell out with his co-conspirators and paid the ultimate price I'm sorry I can't enlighten you any further.' It was hard to read Miss D'Arles's expression. 'Inspector Peterson also informed me that someone has stolen a valuable work of art from the castle. I left it there when I moved out, you see, thinking it was of no value, but now it transpires that it's by Turner.'

Lucy caught his eye and he knew what she was thinking. Someone had duped this old lady out of a fortune. But before he could say anything, Miss D'Arles spoke again.

'It's my own fault for not consulting an expert before I signed the contents over to the new owner.' She gave a regretful sigh. 'I fear that a lot of precious things were left behind. But we can't go crying over spilt milk, can we.'

'It must have been difficult to give up the castle,' said Lucy.

'Oh no, dear. It was far too big for me. I'm much better off here.'

During the awkward silence that followed, Neil searched

for something appropriate to say. But his mind went blank, so he was relieved when Miss D'Arles spoke again.

'Most of the books were left in the castle library but I did manage to retain a few histories of the family and the estate. Would you care to see them?'

'Thanks,' Neil said, struggling to his feet.

Lucy did likewise and walked across to the shelf to examine the dolls. 'These are old,' she said. 'They're probably quite valuable.'

'I played with them when I was small and some of them belonged to my mother before me so I couldn't leave them behind. They're part of my past.'

'It must have been wonderful growing up in a place like Eyecliffe Castle,' said Lucy.

The old woman's face suddenly clouded. 'Not really. There are too many ghosts up there.' She went out into the hallway and Neil and Lucy followed her to a closed door at the back of the house.

When she turned the handle the door opened with a loud creak to reveal a study dwarfed by a huge mahogany desk.

'It was my uncle's desk,' she explained when she saw Neil staring at it. 'My parents died when I was young and left my sister and me in his care.'

She crossed over to the desk and picked up a couple of dull brown volumes. When she handed them to Neil he saw that they were Victorian histories of Eyecliffe Castle; the work of local antiquaries.

'You may borrow them if you wish.'

'Thank you.'

Neil looked around. On one wall hung a dark painting, a horrible thing that seemed to suck the life and light from

229

the room. It depicted a man, a bruised and bloody victim of torture, being watched by a merciless wall of disembodied eyes. If he'd been Miss D'Arles, he would have been glad to get rid of it. The dramatic use of light and darkness reminded him of works he'd seen by Caravaggio, and as he studied it closely he could see that the artist had captured the essence of fear and terror. The power of the image disturbed him. It was the last thing he'd have wanted on his own wall.

'Tell me about this painting,' he asked. The horror of the thing had captured his curiosity.

Miss D'Arles stood beside him, staring at the picture as though she'd never seen it before.

'I was told it was bought in Italy,' she said quietly. 'The family have always believed it to be a Caravaggio. There's a small title plate on the frame. Can you read it?'

Neil bent forward to examine the small brass plate at the foot of the elaborate gilded frame. The artist wasn't named but the title of the painting was *The House of Eyes*. The name jolted something in his memory: Sicily. Barney Yelland, the photographer, had visited somewhere in Naro called the House of Eyes – somewhere with a bad reputation, avoided by superstitious locals.

Lucy, he noticed, was looking uncomfortable. She wanted to be out of there as much as he did.

'I've informed the authorities about the items we found and there's a chance they'll end up in a museum,' he said. 'Are you happy about that, Miss D'Arles?' As the things bore her family crest he thought he'd better ask out of courtesy.

'That land no longer belongs to my family, Dr Watson. What happens to them is no concern of mine.'

'I'll let you know if we discover anything about the bones.'

As Miss D'Arles saw them off the premises, Neil had the fleeting impression that she found the subject of the bones upsetting, although he couldn't think why this should be. Unless she already knew who they belonged to.

It had been left to Rachel Tracey to break the news to Marion Hatman that the latest search for Leanne had yielded nothing.

All CCTV from local railway and bus stations had been examined for a sighting of Leanne and her distinctive, colourful wheelie case. But there'd been nothing. It was as if she'd vanished in a puff of smoke.

The disused parts of the castle were being searched too. If she'd never left the premises, they'd find her.

Marion took the news calmly, interpreting it as proof that Leanne was in London and would be in touch when she was ready. Yet her apparent optimism was brittle, as though despair could replace hope at any moment. Not for the first time Rachel felt pity for her. In the meantime, Marion said, she had business to attend to. The secretive way she said the words made Rachel wonder what she was up to.

Rachel had been prepared to cancel her planned evening at a pub quiz with her fiancé, Nigel, but Marion insisted that she didn't need her. As she left she found herself looking forward to the evening, even though it wouldn't be a late one. She had to be at the incident room early and Nigel needed to be up for the morning milking.

Then she received a call from Wesley, with news that would change her plans.

Someone had checked out the relatives of the woman Darren Hatman killed in the Plymouth traffic accident and discovered that the elderly victim had had a daughter who'd married, only to divorce a year later. But, in spite of the brevity of the union, she'd kept her husband's name, even when she'd acquired a new partner. And that name was Woolmer.

Wesley said he'd meet her at Clare Woolmer's house in half an hour.

18

Joules hardly said a word when we rode
from the town. I could tell something
unspeakable had occurred and I guessed
that my cousin, who remained silent
for the whole journey, was at the centre
of it.

We rode for the whole day, stopping
only for refreshment, and when we
reached the back streets of a small
town with a name that escapes my
memory, we found a small inn where
the patron provided us with rooms and
made us most welcome. It was then that
I seized the chance to speak to Joules
alone and question him closely.

At first he said it would be better if
I remained in ignorance but when I
insisted, he revealed all he knew.

As soon as Joules realised that Uriah had left my company on that fateful night, he had followed, the responsibility my father had placed on him weighing heavy on his mind. Eventually he saw Uriah accost a woman of the night.

When she linked her arm through Uriah's and escorted him back to her mean lodgings, Joules followed, climbing the stairs after them on tiptoe and waiting on the landing outside her room.

After a while, feeling foolish, he prepared to depart. Then he heard a terrible scream, as if the devil himself had appeared before the woman to take her immortal soul.

When Wesley explained the reason for their visit, he saw a flash of defiance in Clare Woolmer's eyes.

'I don't see that this is relevant,' she said, giving Rachel a hostile stare.

'Darren Hatman killed your mother,' Wesley said gently.

'Yes,' she said, bowing her head.

'So when Barney Yelland brought a girl with the same surname back here, you must have wondered if she was related.'

'I suppose I did.'

'When did you discover Leanne was his daughter?'

'I asked Barney about her and he told me her father had been in prison.'

'So you put two and two together?'

She took a deep breath. 'I did some research and found out Hatman was doing well. He'd learned a trade in prison and turned himself into a builder and property developer. He profited from my mother's death.' She almost spat out the words.

'I can't blame you for feeling bitter,' Rachel said. 'I know I would in your place.'

Clare gave her a grateful look. 'But that doesn't mean I killed him,' she said. 'What would that achieve?'

'Revenge?' Wesley suggested. 'Justice?'

She shook her head. 'Not my style, Inspector.'

'Do you own a crossbow?'

'Of course not,' she said as if she found the question ridiculous. 'Is that how he was killed?'

Wesley didn't reply. 'Where were you on Wednesday night?'

A smug expression passed across her face. 'That's easy. I visited a friend in Neston. We had something to eat at six and I left around eight. On my way back I called in at the boat to see Barney and I ended up staying with him till two in the morning. He wanted to talk and I wasn't driving so I had a drink with him. My car was in the garage for repair; it failed its MOT. You can check.'

'You were on foot?'

That's right. Hatman was found up at Eyecliffe Castle, wasn't he? That's three miles away.'

'So it is. What's the name of your garage?'

She recited the name with a confidence that told Wesley she was telling the truth.

'I can't say I'm sorry he's dead,' she said as they were preparing to leave. 'But I assure you I had nothing to do with it.'

They drove back to the incident room and reported back to Gerry, who told Wesley to go home to Pam. She needed him. He didn't need telling twice. It was after six o'clock and he'd already called to tell her he might be late and ask how she was. She'd sounded quite cheerful in the circumstances but he suspected she was putting on an act for his benefit; trying to sound brave . . . rather like Marion Hatman.

Gerry asked if he could drop some forms off at Tradmouth police station on the way home and Wesley told him it wouldn't be a problem. He parked in the station car park and hurried into reception, keying in the code that allowed him access to the inner sanctum of the building. After delivering the forms to CS Fitton's office he made his way out again, keen to get home, but as he reached the automatic glass front door a man was blocking his way, carrying a small brown box and looking anxious.

'Inspector, can I have a word?'

If James Garrard hadn't looked as if he had all the cares of the world on his shoulders Wesley would have made some excuse to get away. But he couldn't help taking pity on the man.

'How can I help you this time, Mr Garrard?'

'It's happened again.'

'You were told that the things you received weren't on any list of stolen goods, weren't you?'

'Yes, but this time it's antique silver.' He held out the box he was carrying and opened the lid. Four silver bowls lay inside on a bed of tissue paper.

'I've taken them to an antique shop and the owner says they're rare. Early eighteenth century and by a top maker. He thinks they're worth around a thousand pounds. And there's a note.'

He passed Wesley a sheet of notepaper, deckle-edged and probably handmade. It looked expensive. The words *I'm so sorry* were printed on it in blue ink.

'Sorry for what?'

'I've no idea. This is getting beyond a joke, Inspector.'

Wesley knew the doorway wasn't an appropriate place to conduct a conversation like this so he led the way back into the reception area and they both sat down on a bench provided for the waiting public. Fortunately the place was empty apart from the young woman on the front desk and she was too far away to overhear.

'You told us you received things when you were a child and then the gifts stopped when you moved away from the area and started again when you returned?'

'Not as soon as I returned. It was after my picture appeared in the local paper.'

'So whoever's sending them presumably saw the picture and realised you were back ... unless it has something do with your fundraising? Perhaps the things are meant for the charity?'

'Then why not say? And what are they sorry about?'

'What do you want the police to do about it?'

'Tell this person to stop.'

'No crime's been committed. Besides, we don't know who it is, do we?'

'You can find out. I've kept the box. There's bound to be fingerprints and DNA.'

'I'm sorry,' said Wesley gently. 'We reserve that sort of thing for crime investigation and, as I said, this isn't a crime. If I were you, I'd go home and try not to think about it.'

Garrard looked quite crestfallen as he closed his box and tucked it under his arm. As he left the building, Wesley looked at his watch. James Garrard had only delayed him by ten minutes.

When he arrived home Pam rushed to the door to greet him, her eyes bloodshot as though she'd been crying. She seemed on edge, like someone awaiting the results of an important interview. He asked her how she was.

'I've got an appointment with the consultant at Morbay Hospital tomorrow. Twelve thirty.' She looked at him hopefully.

'Gerry'll understand if I take a few hours off,' he said quickly, anxious to assuage her doubts.

Tears began to trickle down her face and he took her in his arms and held her close.

Wesley spent a restless night and all sorts of dark thoughts ran through his brain as he lay awake beside Pam, wondering what the future held. To his surprise, she'd managed to sleep in spite of the situation and when morning came she seemed better prepared to face the day ahead than he did. After getting the children ready for school she announced that she'd decided to go into work for the first couple of hours then drive straight to the hospital. Wesley promised that nothing would stop him meeting her there.

But first he had to call into the incident room. When he arrived at the church hall Gerry was about to start his morning briefing and gave him a quizzical look as he walked in. Was everything all right? Wesley answered with an almost imperceptible nod. He'd explain about the appointment later.

Gerry assigned the jobs. The search of the castle was continuing and all the guests and staff who'd been there at the time of Darren Hatman's death were being traced, interviewed and eliminated. Wesley still had a bad feeling about Leanne, even though they'd found no evidence so far to suggest she'd come to any harm. That broken balustrade was bothering him. As was Barney Yelland.

Clare Woolmer's alibis were being double-checked and Gerry had officers poring over the customer lists of all suppliers of crossbows, looking for familiar names.

Gerry said cheerfully that they'd probably have more to go on once the search of the grounds was completed and Wesley wished he could share his Pollyanna-like optimism. He didn't bother mentioning his encounter with James Garrard the previous evening. The last thing they needed was a distraction.

Once the briefing was over he joined Gerry, sitting down on the uncomfortable wooden chair on the other side of his desk.

'Pam's got an appointment with the consultant at twelve thirty. Morbay Hospital.'

Gerry nodded. 'You take as long as you need, Wes. Hope everything's . . . you know.'

Before Wesley could reply Rob Carter appeared and cleared his throat.

'I've traced Barney Yelland's ex-wife. He was telling the truth about her living in County Durham. I spoke to her.'

'And?'

'She said her and Barney had a stormy relationship. He was always on the lookout for women to photograph, always the same physical type. She didn't think he slept with them; she said it would have been less creepy if he had. In the end she got sick of it and walked out.'

'Did you ask her if he owns a crossbow?'

'She says not. Sorry.'

'Not your fault, Rob. Any luck with his other models?'

'I've spoken to a couple of them. They said Yelland paid them and didn't give them any trouble. Liked to look but not touch. One reckoned he was a bit odd but the other said he was a gentleman.'

'Good work, Rob,' Wesley said, thinking a little encouragement never went amiss.

'Still think Yelland's our man?' Gerry asked when Rob had returned to his desk.

'There's no solid evidence to link him with Hatman's murder.'

'Yet,' said Gerry.

After a brief silence Wesley spoke again. 'I've been thinking about the theft of that painting. Bev and Jim Hughes stayed at Eyecliffe Castle when Leanne disappeared and they were there again when Darren was killed two weeks later. They found his body.'

'You think Leanne and her dad rumbled what they were up to?'

'If that painting's a Turner's it's worth millions and people have been killed for less.'

'There's too many ruddy suspects in this case. Yelland, Carnegie, Palmer, Clare Woolmer. Not to mention the grieving widow.'

Gerry looked round and his eyes rested on Rachel, who was talking on her phone. 'Rach,' he called over. 'Not going over to babysit Mrs Hatman today?'

Rachel mumbled something into the phone and covered the mouthpiece. 'She says she wants to be left on her own. Says she has things to do.'

'What sort of things?'

'Business, she said.'

'Worried about her?'

'I am a bit. She's still in denial about Leanne's disappearance. I think she could crack up once reality hits her. I might pop over later.'

'Keep an eye on her, won't you.'

Rachel nodded and returned to her call.

Wesley looked at his watch. He'd arranged to meet Pam in the hospital's reception area and time was moving on. Gerry must have seen the anxiety on his face because he told him to go.

As he drove to Morbay Hospital, he felt like a man going to his execution. More apprehensive than he'd ever felt before in his life.

Neil kept thinking of his visit to the Dower House. Lucy had found Miss D'Arles's predicament unbearably sad and she'd found herself torn between admiration and pity for the woman who'd lost her magnificent inheritance and now lived alone with the rotting memories of her ancestors and her long-dead sister. Lucy had a soft heart. Maybe that's why he liked her – he hesitated to use the word love because he felt he was too set in his ways to disrupt his well-ordered life with such a wild emotion.

They'd just opened another trench, hoping to uncover the mill's wheel pit, and the volunteers were digging away with gusto under Dave's supervision. Neil helped out for a while but at eleven o'clock, soon after they'd taken a break for coffee, he told Dave and Lucy he was going to the village in search of something that might identify their skeleton.

Through experience he knew that the best place to begin was the parish church; the repository of all local memories, grand and humble. As he walked to Turling Fitwell he saw several police patrol cars parked outside the church hall but there was no sign of Wesley, or any other familiar faces, so he carried on towards the ancient stone church.

He found the church door unlocked and as soon as he stepped into a cool, gloomy interior he realised that he wasn't alone. A middle-aged woman with curly grey-peppered hair was busy adjusting an elaborate floral arrangement in front of the painted rood screen separating the nave from the chancel. She looked round as he entered and gave him a wary smile.

'Is the vicar about?' he asked.

'He's in the vestry. Just go through.'

Neil made for the front of the church and knocked on an open door next to the organ.

'Come in.'

It was a voice he recognised. He knew that Wesley's brother-in-law, Mark Fitzgerald, was in charge of several parishes, such were the responsibilities of the modern rural vicar, but he hadn't realised that Turling Fitwell was one of them.

'Neil,' said Mark, his face lighting up with recognition. 'What can I do for you?'

'Maritia all right? And the little one?'

'They're fine.' There was something guarded in his reply. 'I hear you're digging near the castle.'

'That's why I'm here. I want some information about the D'Arles family.'

'Then you've come to the right place. You'll see their coat of arms everywhere. The family chapel's on the far side of the chancel but in the nineteenth century their tombs started to overflow into the nave and the more recent ones are out in the churchyard.'

'I've met Henrietta D'Arles. She lives in the Dower House.'

'I'm afraid she's not one of my regulars.' Mark gave a wistful smile which lit up the schoolboyish face topped by a shock of blond hair that made him the darling of the Mothers' Union. 'Have a look round and if you want to see the parish registers I can get them out for you.'

Neil thanked Mark and did as he suggested. There seemed to be D'Arleses everywhere, their memorials dotted around the building while their carved effigies reclined piously in their own private chapel.

When he'd finished his circuit of the church he rejoined Mark in the vestry and was pleased to find that he'd opened the huge safe in the corner in anticipation. The parish records now lay on the desk where generations of happy couples had signed the marriage register.

'I've got to visit a sick parishioner,' said Mark. 'Can I leave you to it? Mrs Cantrill will be working on the flowers for a while but I'll tell her you're here so she doesn't lock you in by accident. She can get a bit forgetful these days,' he added with what looked like a wink. 'Put the registers back in the safe and lock it when you go.'

As soon as Mark left Neil began to search through the registers of births, marriages and deaths for the late eighteenth and early nineteenth centuries. The skeleton at the dig might have been a thief but, on the other hand, the items bearing the D'Arles coat of arms might mean he was one of the family.

In the end he came up with four possible candidates, all D'Arles men who were born and baptised at the appropriate time but who hadn't been buried in the parish church.

Neil made a note of the names. Tracing them would give him something to do in his idle hours.

The staff quarters at Eyecliffe Castle were still being searched, as were the disused parts of the building that were normally kept locked. When Rachel arrived there, tasked with co-ordinating more interviews with the staff and guests, she found the search in full swing and the first thing she did was make for the terrace. It was only accessible from the staff quarters, the door from the main staircase having been blocked off when the castle had become a hotel, and as she emerged into the open air she was surprised that Palmer hadn't made use of this asset. The view was spectacular: the river valley below with rolling Devon hills and a patchwork of green fields beyond; but she was conscious of stone crumbling beneath her feet.

A couple of uniformed constables were out there, conducting a half-hearted search and bagging up cigarette ends.

'Found anything?' she shouted over to them.

'Lots of discarded fag ends. Nobody seems to have told this lot that smoking's bad for your health,' said a chubby sergeant, chuckling at his own joke. 'We found a shred of tartan cloth caught on that collapsed stonework.' He pointed to the section of the balustrade that had fallen away. 'It's been bagged up just in case but it could have got there any time.' The roll of his eyes told Rachel he thought this was a waste of time. 'Health and safety nightmare this. No sign of a body though, if that's what the boss is thinking.'

She approached the edge, not daring to get too close, and as she craned her neck to look over her phone rang. It was a message to say that the search of the disused part of the castle had turned up something interesting.

Rachel retraced her steps, making for the undeveloped part of the building across the courtyard. The west wing predated the main hotel by several hundred years and consisted of the rooms adjoining the old gatehouse, terminating in a round defensive tower. Although the gatehouse itself, with its little chapel and faint medieval wall paintings, was accessible to the guests, more as a historical curiosity than a hotel facility, the rest of the wing had been locked up and neglected for years. A while ago there had been talk of bringing it into use but it had never happened.

The huge oak door at the side of the gatehouse was normally kept locked, but today it was open. Rachel stepped through it and found herself in a corridor, lit only by arrow slits which threw daggers of sunlight onto the rough cobbled floor. The door at the far end of the corridor stood open and she could see the room beyond, lit with artificial beams from the CSI's temporary lighting. Once there she found herself in a large, vaulted chamber full of activity.

'Found anything?' she asked.

A young woman turned to her and pulled down her protective mask, her face serious. 'Next room.'

'The missing girl?'

The woman didn't answer her question. Instead she pointed to a box full of plastic shoe covers. 'Don't contaminate the scene, will you.'

Rachel took the hint and pulled the covers over her shoes, steadying herself on the cold stone wall. She made her way across the room, making for a smaller door set into the far wall.

She stood in the doorway, taking in the scene.

It looked like a dungeon. A prison: a windowless chamber with a bare earth floor. In a shadowy corner stood a large barrel and beside it she could see a woman's shoe and what looked like a knitted garment; a jumper or a cardigan.

But there was no sign of Leanne Hatman.

19

When Joules burst through the door he
was met with a terrible sight. Uriah was
leaning over a young woman who lay
prone upon the bed. The white cravat
my cousin had worn at his neck was
wound around her throat and Uriah was
slowly pulling it tighter so that her
face was a contorted mask of terror.

Such was the shock Joules felt that at
first he was unable to utter a word.
Then, summoning his wits, he went to
the woman's aid as was his Christian
duty, pushing Uriah out of the way with
as much force as he could muster.

My cousin, unprepared for the
assault, stumbled away and stood
motionless, staring as Joules unwound
the ligature and helped the woman as

*she spluttered and gasped her way back
to consciousness. But when he turned to
summon help Uriah barred his way.*

*'You ignorant dolt,' my cousin said.
'You have spoiled everything.'*

*Violence is not in our cicerone's
nature but he landed a punch on
Uriah's nose and sent him flying across
the room before raising the alarm.*

Marion Hatman had managed to get the police off her back. They were the last people she wanted around.

In spite of all their efforts, her Leanne – her baby – hadn't been found. But this had to be a good thing because it must mean she was alive. And once she knew that her father was dead and that her mother had big plans for their future, she'd be back – providing her modelling career hadn't taken off in the meantime. Either way, good times were coming and the argument they'd had before she'd vanished would be forgotten.

Marion left the flat and climbed into her car, trying to banish the fears and doubts that kept flitting into her head. Soon she'd get a better flat and a better car. The firm Darren had built up would be hers once the formalities were over. He'd kept his income from her but now she was going to get what was rightfully hers.

She'd seen the accountant that morning and now she'd arranged to meet Lee and Craig at the barn, telling Lee to bring his spare key to the padlock so that she could take a look inside. If Darren had employed them they must be reliable and she needed staff she could depend on. She'd deal with the administration while they did the construction work. And their first job would be the conversion of the barn into two dwellings which could be sold as weekend cottages to city people with more money than sense.

On reaching Turling Fitwell, she turned up the castle drive. This wasn't far from the scene of Darren's death but she ignored an unexpected pang of grief and regret, suppressing it with a determination she hadn't known she possessed.

She'd arrived half an hour early so she could take a look around and consider her strategy. For a while she sat in the car surveying her new empire. This would be the start of something big: M. Hatman Ltd, Builders of Distinction. She smiled to herself and switched on the radio. 'Things Can Only Get Better' was playing, which she took as a good omen.

When she left the car she slammed the door and the sound sent a flurry of birds rising in panic from the branches of the nearby trees. Then she circled the barn slowly, noting every detail: every frost-damaged brick, every missing roof slate and every piece of rotting timber. The place needed a considerable amount of work but when it was finished she'd sell it on at a handsome profit and never come near it again.

Her only potential problem would come if Darren had made a will in favour of someone else. But she wasn't aware of any other women in his life so who else would benefit? Only Leanne – and when she turned up she was bound to see the wisdom of her mother's plans.

She took the car keys from her pocket and was about to get back inside to wait in comfort when she heard a voice. Her first thought was that Lee and Craig had arrived early and parked the van elsewhere. She planned to tell them what was going on; to make sure they were on her side and lay down her own version of the law, but when she turned round she felt something hit her hard.

As she staggered backwards, the car keys she was clutching tumbled to the ground. She raised her hands in an automatic defensive reaction, then looked down and saw something that looked like a shortened arrow protruding from her chest. She heard herself gasp in horror, although she could feel no pain.

She managed to whisper the words 'Help me' to her assailant before her legs collapsed beneath her and she slumped against the car.

Gerry Heffernan found a message from Rachel waiting on his desk. Something had been discovered at Eyecliffe Castle. He looked at his watch, wishing Wesley was there with him to share ideas and speculation. But he knew these hospital appointments took time.

He cadged a lift back to the castle in a patrol car and as he sat in the passenger seat he couldn't get Wesley's problem out of his mind. When they'd parted earlier he hadn't been able to think of any reassuring words that didn't sound trite and clichéd so he'd just patted him on the shoulder and said nothing.

When he arrived at the gatehouse the rotund uniformed constable on duty outside told him that DS Tracey was waiting for him in the west wing.

He found Rachel waiting inside the disused building, examining her mobile phone.

'Right, Rach, what have we got?'

'Not sure. It's down there.' She pointed in the direction of the door to the first room. 'Looks like some kind of dungeon.'

'Used recently?'

'Not sure.'

'You don't seem sure of much today,' he snapped, immediately regretting the reproach in his words. Wesley's dilemma had put him on edge.

Rachel bristled. 'Nothing to do with me. It's the CSIs. They've found something but there'll need to be tests before they know whether it's connected to Leanne Hatman.'

'What is it?'

'A woman's shoe and a cardigan. There are some cigarette ends too. And a barrel.'

'Could the cardigan and shoe belong to Leanne Hatman?'

Rachel shook her head. 'They look as though they've been there for years. And I wouldn't have said they were her style.'

When Gerry entered the room he looked round, thinking Rachel had been right to use the word dungeon. He called one of the white overalled CSIs over, an earnest young woman in heavy-rimmed glasses.

'Let's see what you've found.'

The woman hurried off and returned a few seconds later with two packages. 'They've been photographed in situ,' she said. She handed over the packages but instead of returning to her work she hovered there, as if she had something else to add. Gerry could see the first package contained a dusty black court shoe and the second a rotting woollen garment. It was knitted, probably by hand judging from the imperfection of the ribbing, and although it might once have been green, it had now turned a muddy pale khaki.

'The cardigan looks very nineteen fifties,' the CSI said.

'It could have been bought from a vintage shop – there's a lot of them about now – but I think it's more likely that it's been lying here for years.' She paused. 'There appears to be a name tape inside . . . you know, the type your mum used to sew into your school things.'

'What does it say?'

'The first name looks like Linda and the second begins with SA. The lab'll be able to tell us more. The shoe's size four.'

Gerry turned to Rachel. 'Do we know Leanne Hatman's shoe size?'

Rachel shook her head. 'I'll call her mum.' She felt suddenly reluctant to ask the question that could bring Marion's world crashing down, but made herself punch out the number. She waited, the phone pressed to her ear, but after half a minute she gave up. 'No answer,' she said, trying to conceal her relief.

Gerry turned back to the CSI. 'Did you find anything else?'

'Cigarette ends . . . or what's left of them. It's dry in here so things have been well preserved but even so I think they've been there for years.'

'How many years?'

She shrugged. 'Hard to say.'

'What's this about a barrel?'

'It's over there, stood on its end. It's unusual. It's got a thick glass top and there are two small holes in the side, one sealed with a glass stopper and the other with a perished rubber tube. We've looked inside. It's empty.'

He thanked her and handed back the packages. If she was right about the age of their new discoveries, this wasn't his problem. Nevertheless he had to be sure.

He rejoined Rachel, who was waiting for him by the door.

'I want to ask David Palmer who has access to that room,' he said. 'And Rach . . . '

'Yes?'

'Get on to the station, will you. See if there's any record of someone called Linda with a surname beginning with SA going missing or being a victim of crime.'

Pam insisted on going back to school after her appointment. The last thing she wanted, she said, was to hang around brooding at home.

Once the tests, scans and X-rays were completed, Wesley sat with her waiting for the consultant to call them in, trying to think of the case, just to distract himself from what was going on. He even found himself telling Pam about it, asking her what she thought. She listened carefully, suggesting that Yelland had probably killed Leanne and hidden her body somewhere before he travelled to Sicily. Then her father had discovered what he'd done so he'd killed him as well. Wesley didn't altogether agree with her theory but it was good to see her indulging in speculation rather than sunk into the pit of worry that had threatened to swallow her during the past days.

It seemed like an age before they were called in and as the consultant put on his kindliest face and gave them the test results, Wesley clasped his wife's hand tightly.

When Wesley arrived at the castle it was just after four, too late for Pam to return to work. He'd taken her to Maritia's instead; the children were both with friends so she'd been able to talk to her sister in law about the prognosis. Wesley, overwhelmed with it all, had said he needed to get back to the investigation.

As soon as he appeared, Gerry greeted him with the inevitable questions, which had to be answered. Yes, they had seen the consultant and the news wasn't particularly good. He wanted to operate to remove a small lump that could be cancerous and there was the possibility of further treatment after that. Yes, Wesley would need to take some time off but hopefully they'd have the case wrapped up by then. In the meantime Pam was determined to carry on as normal. She seemed to be taking it well but he knew this might change once the reality had sunk in.

Gerry put his hand on Wesley's shoulder. 'It's amazing what they can do these days. She'll be fine.'

'The consultant said there's a high success rate.' He tried to sound confident but doubts kept intruding, however hard he tried to ignore them. He asked Gerry if there had been any developments in his absence, trying to focus his mind on work, and Gerry brought him up to date. The staff quarters at the castle were still being searched and he wanted to speak to David Palmer about the strange discoveries in the west wing. Did Wesley want to conduct the interview?

Wesley said he'd be glad to. First, though, he wanted to see that room in the west wing for himself. When they arrived there the CSIs were packing up and Wesley stood in the centre of the room, looking around at the rough stone walls.

'What do you think this place was used for, Wes?' Gerry said. 'Store room? Prison? Torture chamber?'

Wesley asked the CSI if it was all right to touch the barrel. Once he had permission, he began his examination.

'If it wasn't for the glass top, I'd say it was just an ordinary barrel,' he said.

'Looks like old glass to me.'

Wesley agreed. The glass, thick and marred with imperfections, was handmade, as was the stopper in the side.

Gerry stared at it, frowning. 'The seal's good. Airtight. But what would the D'Arleses want with a glass-topped barrel? Unless it wasn't the D'Arleses. Maybe it has something to do with David Palmer or his father.'

'It seems strange that the Palmers haven't made use of this part of the castle when they've spent a fortune on the rest of the place. The gatehouse and chapel are open to visitors so why not this bit?'

Gerry couldn't come up with an answer and they made their way across the courtyard in silence. When they reached David Palmer's office he rose to greet them as soon as they walked in, as if he'd been expecting them.

'What's happening with my painting? When can I have it back?'

'It's needed for evidence but it'll be returned to you as soon as possible,' said Wesley. 'If it's authenticated as a Turner will you sell it?'

'Probably ... if it really is a Turner.' He sounded as though he didn't quite dare to believe his good fortune. 'Have you finished in the staff quarters yet? Some people aren't happy about their rooms being searched.'

'If they've nothing to hide, they've nothing to fear.' Gerry trotted out the old cliché as if he'd only just thought of it.

'It's a terrible invasion of privacy.' Palmer's protest sounded half-hearted, as though he was aware of his impotence in the face of police authority but felt he had to make a token gesture.

'Your mother gave permission. They'll be finished later today and they'll let everyone know when they can return to their rooms.'

Palmer, looking peeved, muttered something that might have been thanks.

'We'd like to ask you about the west wing,' said Wesley.

'It's been locked up for years – apart from the chapel above the gatehouse, that is. There are a few medieval wall paintings in there which some of our guests are interested to see.'

'You've been in that wing yourself?'

'My father had most of it sealed off but when I first inherited the place I had a look in there. Sadly the funds have never been there to renovate it so it's kept locked. Health and safety. People can be very litigious if there's an accident as I'm sure you'll appreciate and our insurance company would raise merry hell if they knew we were letting our guests go anywhere that wasn't entirely safe. Our premiums would go through the roof.'

'Of course,' said Wesley. 'What about the room at the bottom of the far tower adjoining the burned-out wing?'

'What about it?'

'Did you see the barrel with the glass top?'

Wesley hadn't expected Palmer to smile. 'I assumed it had something to do with brewing beer. I believe all castles had their own breweries at one time. To be honest, I thought the place had a strange atmosphere. That's the part that's meant to be haunted, you know. The white lady – why are they always white ladies? Best keep the ghosts and the guests apart, don't you think?'

'Who has access to that part of the building?' Gerry asked.

'There's only one set of keys and your people have them

at the moment. They're usually kept in my mother's office but they're not locked away. Why are you asking all these questions? Have you found something in there? Something to do with Leanne?'

Before Gerry could answer, his phone rang. After a brief conversation he asked if he could have a word with Wesley in private.

They left Palmer's office and stood in the corridor outside. Wesley could see that Gerry had received news of the potentially exciting kind.

'That was Rachel back at the incident room. She's been looking at missing persons called Linda with a surname beginning with SA and she's come up with something on the internet – one of those unsolved case sites. In June nineteen fifty-three a sixteen-year-old girl called Linda Sangster went missing in Turling Fitwell. She's going to try to get hold of the case notes.'

Wesley stood silently for a few moments, taking in the news.'

'Well the Palmers didn't buy the castle till nineteen seventy. And David wasn't even born then.'

'In that case we'd better have another word with Miss D'Arles,' said Wesley.

Lee Varlow steered the white van down the gravel drive, branching off towards the barn. Craig Gatting sat beside him. This was make or break. Would they be in a job this time next week or would they have to look for something else? They'd always found Darren Hatman a good employer. Even though he'd had a dodgy past, he'd been fair. His wife, however, was an unknown quantity; so was working for a woman.

'Her car's here. She's early.'

'New broom. You know what they say about them. Bet she won't cut us any slack like her old man did,' Gatting said bitterly.

'I'm not worried as long as she keeps us on.'

'She'll need someone who knows what they're doing. She won't want to get her hands dirty, will she.'

Lee brought the van to a stately halt and they both got out. When there was no sign of the new boss Lee began to walk round to the back of the barn and Craig trailed behind. They still couldn't see Marion Hatman anywhere.

It wasn't until they were returning to the van that Lee spotted her. At first her car had blocked their view but now they could see her body propped up against the passenger door, staring with wide, startled eyes at the surrounding trees.

Lee ran towards her, thinking she'd been taken ill or met with some accident. Then he saw the small hole in her chest framed by a circle of crusted blood and he knew she was dead.

20

Joules paid the young woman handsomely before spiriting Uriah from the scene with an adeptness I found astounding in a respectable clergyman. It was almost as though he was accustomed to such deception.

As we made our way through France Joules and I watched my cousin most carefully, taking it in turns to keep vigil at night in case he attempted to prowl the streets with a view to repeating his outrage. We made for Bordeaux, a port that has done trade with Tradmouth for centuries, in the hope of finding a ship to carry us home.

We found an inn near the harbour and it fell to me to share a chamber with Uriah. I lay awake and watched

him sleep the sleep of the innocent,
unable to banish Joules' account of those
unfortunate events from my mind.
Uriah spoke little to me. Rather he
read the books he had collected on our
journey, smiling to himself as though he
was the guardian of some great secret.

When it was time to break our fast
the next morning he left the chamber
and I seized the opportunity to
examine once more the volume he
claims is bound in human flesh, careful
to cleanse my hands after touching the
terrible thing. The book is entitled
The Great Discoveries and Enquiries of
the Emperor Frederick II and as I
read I became ever more fearful of
what my cousin might do to emulate his
hero.

'You sure about this, Wes?'

'Miss D'Arles was living at the castle when Linda Sangster went missing. She must know something.'

As the two men walked side by side down the gravel path Gerry looked at his companion. He saw determination on Wesley's face, and something else: a temporary lifting of fear. For now the problem of Pam's health had been pushed to the back of his mind by this new discovery, but Gerry knew it wouldn't take long for it to resurface, bobbing up like a cork on water.

'How old would Miss D'Arles have been when Linda Sangster went missing?'

'Seventeen? Eighteen?'

'She might have known her.'

'She might.'

When they reached the Dower House it was a while before Miss D'Arles answered Wesley's knock, her hand on Reginald's collar. She looked almost pleased to see them, as if she welcomed the company.

'How can I help you this time?' she said. 'I've seen a lot of police cars going up to the castle. They drive so fast that I'm afraid to let Reginald off his lead in case he gets run over.'

'I'll have a word,' said Gerry, patting the Labrador's head. 'Can't have anything happening to Reginald, can we?'

'We're sorry to bother you again, Miss D'Arles,' Wesley said as she stood aside to let them in. 'I promise we won't keep you long.'

She led them through to the drawing room. Reginald walked beside Wesley with a wagging tail, sniffing Gerry's hand and soliciting a pat, and when they reached the drawing room Wesley tried not to look at the cold glass eyes of the watchful dolls on the shelf, instead focusing his gaze on the painting of Colapesce, the saviour of Sicily.

'You like that painting, don't you, Inspector?' Miss D'Arles said. Not much escaped her.

'I think it's charming.'

'It's rather primitive but I agree, there is something about it. And of course it's a reminder of my sister.'

'We'd like to ask you a few questions, if that's all right,' said Wesley.

'Of course.' She sat down, her gnarled hands neatly arranged on her lap, waiting for him to begin.

'Miss D'Arles, were you living in the castle in June nineteen fifty-three?'

'Yes. That was the month of the Queen's coronation. Why do you ask?'

It was Gerry who spoke next. 'Do you remember a room in the oldest part of the castle, the west wing? At the foot of the tower next to the burned-out wing?'

She hesitated, as though Gerry's question had resurrected uncomfortable memories. 'My sister and I were never allowed in that part of the building. Our uncle told us it wasn't safe and it was always kept locked.'

'What about when you inherited the castle?' said Wesley. 'Surely you were curious.'

'Yes, I was. But I was also a little apprehensive. In those days a woman came in from the village to clean and I asked her to accompany me when I went to explore that wing.' She took a deep breath. 'There's no lighting there so I took a torch. I remember seeing some rubbish in the room you mentioned but I locked the door and left it untouched. I don't know what Mr Palmer did with it but I assure you I just opened the door and shone my torch around. I certainly didn't linger.'

Wesley saw that she was staring ahead, directly at the dolls.

'Have you ever heard the name Linda Sangster?'

Again she hesitated before answering. 'She was a girl from the village who went missing from the coronation celebrations. It was in the newspapers at the time and I remember our housekeeper mentioning it.'

'Your housekeeper? Is she still alive?'

'I'm afraid not.'

'It must have been the talk of the village,' said Gerry.

Her cheeks reddened a little. 'We didn't mix with anyone from the village. My uncle preferred us to keep ourselves to ourselves. I realise that sounds rather snobbish by the standards of the present day but that was how things were in those days. We were the D'Arles family.'

'You didn't fraternise with the peasants,' said Gerry, half amused.

'If you want to put it like that but those aren't the words I'd use.'

'Did you know Linda?' Wesley asked. 'She must have been about your age.'

'As far as I'm aware, I never met her. I was sent away to boarding school, you see. After my parents died my uncle took very little interest in my sister or myself so I was one of those sad children who spent much of their holidays at school. There were a few of us – children whose parents were abroad or who couldn't be looked after for one reason or another. My uncle felt it was better for me to be amongst children of my own age so my visits home were brief.'

'A cardigan belonging to Linda Sangster was found in that tower room,' said Wesley. 'What you thought was litter was the missing girl's clothing.'

He saw her hand go up to her mouth in horror. 'How terrible.'

'There was an unusual glass-topped barrel in there too. Someone suggested it might have been used in brewing.'

'I wouldn't know.'

Wesley leaned forward. 'Tell us about your uncle.'

'Some people called him a recluse but he was a scholar, a slightly eccentric one at that. My sister was fortunate to escape to the Continent. When she was studying dance abroad she rarely came home and once she'd joined the ballet company I hardly saw her again. At times I felt bitter that she'd left me with Uncle and the responsibility of the estate but perhaps I should have had the courage to emulate her.'

'But as the elder sister you'd inherited everything,' said Gerry.

'I inherited a lot of debt and in the end I had to sell the estate to the Palmers. Uncle wasn't good with money. He preferred to pretend it didn't exist; the only thing that existed for him was the past. He was working on a history of our family when he died but it was never finished.'

'What happened to it?' Wesley asked.

She looked away as though the memory was painful. 'I burned it. At the time I blamed him for ruining my life, but now I see that it was my fault for not having the courage to escape like Gretel did.'

She shuffled over to the glass-topped cabinet where her late sister's ballet shoes were displayed and took out one of the theatre programmes with great care.

'There she is,' she said, handing it to Wesley and pointing out a name. 'Gretel D'Arles, soloist. Unfortunately she died before she could fulfil her true potential so she never made prima ballerina but she was a soloist at the age of nineteen. Uncle said it was her duty to come back here and help me to run the estate but I said it would be wicked to let a gift like hers wither and die.'

Wesley noticed that the programme was dated 1956 and that it was for a performance of *Swan Lake* at the Teatro Massimo in Palermo. Unlike her sister, Gretel had travelled widely.

'She must have trained hard from an early age to reach this standard,' he said, handing the programme back.

'She had private lessons then she attended a ballet school

in Paris. After my parents died she managed to continue her studies while I was placed in the care of my uncle.'

'You weren't close to your sister?'

'There was only a year between us and everyone said we looked so alike that we might have been twins ... but we were very different people. Very different,' she repeated as if she wished to emphasise the fact. 'In the end she went her way and I went mine.'

Wesley detected a bitterness behind those words. She must have envied her sister's freedom; the way her talent had allowed her to live her short life to the full.

'How did your sister die?'

'It was in nineteen fifty-eight – a road accident in Sicily. She was only twenty-one and she had a brilliant future ahead of her ... snuffed out in an instant.'

Wesley glanced at Gerry. The old woman's eyes were glassy with tears. Whether they were for her dead sister or for her own wasted life, he wasn't sure.

Miss D'Arles returned the programme to its resting place with almost reverent care and closed the lid. 'She was buried in Sicily. One of her fellow dancers sent me her personal effects but I didn't attend her funeral.'

'I'm sorry,' said Wesley. 'It must have been very hard for you.' He felt Gerry nudge his arm. They'd been sidetracked by this woman's personal tragedy while there were more urgent things to deal with. 'Can we talk about Linda Sangster? Were you here when she disappeared?'

'Yes. My school encouraged us to go home for the coronation. But I assure you, I know nothing of what happened to the unfortunate girl.'

'Who else apart from your uncle had access to that tower room?'

She thought for a few moments. 'Our housekeeper, I suppose, and there were various workmen and cleaners around. And there were the men who kept the grounds tidy. Not regular gardeners, you understand; by then the family couldn't afford such luxuries. As for their names, I'm afraid I don't remember. It was a long time ago. Another age.' She reached out to fondle Reginald's head then paused for a moment. 'If I hadn't destroyed my uncle's research, I might have been able to help that archaeologist who visited me about those bones that were found by the mill. They found a pocket watch bearing the family crest, you know.'

Wesley was surprised by the change of subject. 'You think the bones might belong to a member of your family?'

'I've no idea,' she answered. 'Perhaps my uncle discovered something in the course of his research into the family's history.' She smiled sadly. 'But there's no way of finding out now. As I said before, I burned the lot.'

Wesley raised his eyebrows. She sounded proud of her act of destruction. If she'd told Neil about it, he must have found it frustrating.

'I can't say I was fond of my uncle. He was a bachelor and he took more interest in his historical research than in two silly girls, as he called us.'

'Even though you were the heiress to the Eyecliffe estate?'

'I don't think he gave that a thought. He was an academic with his own concerns and obsessions.'

Her eyes flickered towards the watching dolls and Gerry moved to leave.

'I'll have a word with the patrol cars,' he said. 'Tell them to slow down a bit. Sorry to have bothered you.'

Wesley thought he saw relief on Miss D'Arles's face.

As they left the house his phone rang, and when he heard

266

the caller's news, he knew it would be a long day. Marion Hatman had been found dead.

'Who found her?' Wesley asked.

The constable standing guard over the scene nodded towards Lee Varlow and Craig Gatting. They were talking to Paul Johnson who towered over them, stooping a little over his notebook as he wrote down what they said. 'The Chuckle Brothers over there. Gave them a proper shock by the looks of it.'

The constable was right, Wesley thought. The two men looked stunned. Craig Gatting stared ahead, as though he was trying hard not to look at the place where they'd found the dead woman and Lee Varlow fidgeted nervously, scratching his head, unable to keep still.

'We'd better have a word,' said Gerry.

As they left the constable's side Wesley glanced over at the car. He could see Marion Hatman slumped against the passenger door, and Carl Tennant conducting his examination of her mortal remains while white-clad CSIs moved purposefully around him.

As soon as Gatting and Varlow spotted Wesley and Gerry, they assumed expectant expressions.

'I'm told you found her,' Gerry began. 'Must have been a shock.'

'I've never seen anyone dead before,' said Gatting meekly. 'I couldn't believe it. She'd asked us to meet her here, you know. She was taking over Darren's business and she wanted us to carry on doing up the barn.'

'She said our jobs were safe,' said Varlow. 'She was going to do the admin and drum up business and we were going to do the building work. She was planning to contact the tradesmen Darren used – had it all worked out.' He shook his head in disbelief. 'What'll happen now?'

Wesley didn't have an answer. He found himself feeling sorry for the men; work wasn't always easy to come by and they'd just had all their hopes of financial security dashed.

'When did she arrange to meet you here?'

'She rang me this morning,' said Gatting. 'Said she was going to see her solicitor then she wanted us to meet here to discuss the project. Asked us to bring the key to the barn door 'cause she wanted to look inside.'

'How did she sound?'

Varlow and Gatting looked at each other. 'Not worried if that's what you mean. More excited . . . as if she was looking forward to being the boss. Don't think there was much love lost between her and Darren.'

Wesley thanked them and left Paul to take their statement. They didn't seem to him like guilty men. But someone had killed Marion Hatman.

They clambered into their crime-scene suits then stepped carefully over the steel plates that had been laid down to protect any evidence on the ground. As they made their way over, the pathologist gave them a grunt of greeting.

'What's the verdict?' Gerry asked. Colin Bowman never committed himself until the postmortem proper but there was no harm in trying his luck with Carl Tennant.

'All I can tell you is that she's been dead about an hour and her wound looks remarkably similar to her husband's.'

'Crossbow again?'

'All I'm saying at the moment is that it looks similar. I'll know more tomorrow morning at the postmortem.'

'So we're looking for the same killer.'

For the first time Wesley saw Tennant smile. 'You're not going to get me like that. See you tomorrow.'

'Poor woman must have been surprised by her attacker,' Wesley said as they walked away. 'Just like her husband.'

'And the daughter's still missing. Is somebody trying to wipe out this family for some reason?'

'I'm finding it hard to believe Leanne's disappearance is related,' said Wesley. 'Unless . . .'

'Unless what?'

'What if Leanne's lying low somewhere? What if she resented her parents so much that . . . ?'

'I think we're straying into the realms of fantasy here, Wes.' There was a dramatic pause. 'You know who was released from custody while you were at the hospital, don't you? Barney Yelland. We didn't have enough to hold him so he's been bailed on condition he stays at Clare Woolmer's address.'

Wesley stopped. 'Has anyone checked where he was this afternoon?'

'I'm about to put someone on to it.'

Wesley watched Gerry approach Rob Carter, who was standing with Paul talking to Varlow and Gatting. When Gerry whispered something in his ear, Rob's face reddened and he hurried away. Wesley suspected Rob had tried to muscle in on Paul's interview in the hope of grabbing the glory if anything came of it.

When Wesley heard his phone ring, his first thought was that it might be Pam and his heart began to beat faster. But it was Trish calling from the castle.

'I'm in the staff quarters,' she said, her voice low as if she didn't want to be overheard. 'I think I might have found something interesting.'

'What?'

Before she could answer the line went dead.

As soon as Neil left the church he returned to the dig. It was some distance from all the police activity so they'd now been given permission to carry on, although he'd noticed a few of the volunteers drifting off from time to time, keen to catch some vicarious excitement. A rumour was going about that another body had been found but when he'd tried to call Wesley to find out, he'd just got his voicemail.

After digging for a while he took a break and strolled over to the trench where James Garrard had been hard at work since lunchtime.

'Did you ever solve the mystery of those presents, James?'

The man frowned and shook his head. The matter still seemed to be bothering him, in spite of Wesley's reassurance.

Neil was about to continue the conversation when his phone rang. He saw that it was Annabel, the archivist at the County Records Office. There was something of the detective about Annabel who, once she'd sunk her metaphorical teeth into a question, rarely let it go until she'd exhausted all avenues to uncover the truth. He'd given her the four possible names he'd gleaned from his investigations at the church and it seemed she already had news.

'I've traced three of those names,' she began. 'I found two of them in army records – two D'Arles brothers killed fighting Napoleon Bonaparte and buried abroad. One is recorded as being buried in Bristol. And a Richard D'Arles, the heir to the estate, was baptised in Turling Fitwell in seventeen fifty-seven and vanishes from all records about twenty years later. His younger brother, Thomas, inherited the estate but I can't find a reference to Richard's death. The disappearance of an eldest son and heir rings alarm bells, don't you think?'

Neil's heart began to beat faster. 'Richard wrote a journal – an account of his Grand Tour. I've only seen one volume but there might be others.'

'Perhaps he never came back from abroad,' Annabel suggested. 'I'll keep looking.'

Neil thanked her and told her he owed her a drink.

Trish was waiting for Wesley at the hotel reception.

'What's going on down at the barn?' she asked as soon as he walked through the swishing glass doors.

'It's Marion Hatman. Same MO as her husband's murder.'

'Crossbow?'

'Looks that way. You said you'd found something.'

'It's in Kirsty Paige's room. Nothing suspicious but I just thought you'd like to see it. And we've been contacting all the guests who were at the hotel at the time Leanne disappeared. I spoke to a couple who say that when they stayed here, they heard what they described as a shriek – probably female. It only lasted a moment so they didn't complain or investigate, and they couldn't remember which night it was ... but I looked in the hotel bookings and found that their room was just above the terrace. There was one particular night when they were the only guests in that corridor – the night of the nineteenth. The night Leanne disappeared.'

'A shriek? Nothing else?'

'No.'

'Do they remember what time they heard it?'

271

'Around eleven, they said, although they couldn't be exact.'

'So it may or may not have been Leanne?' He tried to hide his exasperation.

'No way of knowing. Sorry.'

'Don't apologise, Trish.' He paused. 'I'm thinking of that fallen masonry.'

'You think Leanne fell from the terrace? Perhaps she hit her head and wandered off. Perhaps she's got amnesia.'

'Why don't you show me what you found, eh.'

He allowed Trish to lead the way to the staff quarters. Leanne's room was still sealed off with police tape stretched across the door frame, but Trish walked straight past it and stopped at a door at the far end.

'The rooms next to Leanne's are empty – they use them for extra staff they hire for the summer season. This is Kirsty Paige's room.'

He tried the door but it was locked.

'Sorry,' said Trish. 'I'll go and get the master key from the search team. They're finishing off down the corridor.'

She hurried off, leaving Wesley staring at the door. He was trying to concentrate on the matter in hand but his thoughts kept straying to Pam. What would he do if the worst happened? He couldn't help cloaking the question in a euphemism – maybe because it was a way of sanitising the truth. As he thought of the children he began to feel a little sick. How would they react? How would they cope? He shut his eyes tight, trying to clear his head. He should be with his wife, not here. But a murderer was out there with a crossbow. Two people had been eliminated with a ruthlessness that meant the individual they were seeking was dangerous.

When Trish returned he forced himself to behave as he normally would, thanking her calmly and waiting while she turned the key in the lock.

He stepped into the room and looked around. It was neat and ordered, leading Wesley to think that its owner had a tidy, controlling mind. He opened the wardrobe and saw that the clothes inside had been sorted into colours: black at one end, white at the other with brightness in between. All the garments were on solid wooden hangers, not the usual hodgepodge of free wire and plastic that most people harboured in their wardrobes' crammed depths. Everything in the drawers was neatly folded too. When Wesley opened the top drawer he saw an assortment of expensive underwear and closed it quickly, feeling like a voyeur.

'It's in the jewellery box,' he heard Trish say.

He went over to the chest of drawers and opened a small white jewellery box sitting on top. As soon as the lid was raised a tinkling tune began which took him a couple of seconds to place as the overture to act two of *Swan Lake*. A tiny plastic ballerina pirouetted drunkenly inside the box, reflected in the mirrored lid. Wesley suspected the box had been a childhood gift, treasured and kept as a reminder of home and family. The jewellery was neatly arranged in compartments, with bracelets and earrings on the top layer and necklaces on the bottom. He removed the top section carefully and saw a few necklaces stored underneath. One of them caught his eye: an enamelled daisy pendant on a thin gold chain. It was a pretty thing and looked vaguely familiar. Perhaps Kirsty had been wearing it when they'd spoken.

'It's underneath the jewellery,' said Trish. 'I left it exactly where it was. I just thought of the book that author was looking for.'

He moved the necklaces aside, uncovering a small and very old leather-bound book. When he opened it he saw that the pages were filled with familiar copperplate writing. It was the last thing he had expected to find there.

Trish had done well.

21

Our time in Bordeaux has so far been without incident. Uriah behaves once more like a gentleman and Joules has convinced himself that the unfortunate happening was caused by a surfeit of drink.

I argued with him on the matter, saying there is an evil in my cousin that I have observed since childhood, but it seems he has forgotten the true horror of that dreadful night. I know there is no repentance. My cousin merely bides his time.

By good fortune we found a captain who sails tonight for Tradmouth with a cargo of wine. We will soon be home but I anticipate the voyage with dread.

My cousin cares nothing for God nor man.

Wesley found Kirsty in the spa, between clients.

'We found this in your jewellery box,' he said, holding up the book he'd found.

'I borrowed it from Leanne.' She looked more irritated at the intrusion than guilty but there was a defensive note in her voice, as if she suspected she was being accused of theft. 'She took it from the castle library to give to that photographer. It's a diary ... he wanted it for some book he's working on. I asked her if I could have a look, but the writing's hard to read so I gave up after a few pages. I was going to give it back to her but I never got the chance.'

'I'd like to look at it. I'll return it to the library for you when I've finished.'

'Thanks,' she said. She sounded bored, as if he was wasting her time.

'By the way, do you own a crossbow?'

The bored expression suddenly vanished and she gaped as if Wesley had just asked her if she rode unicorns on a regular basis. 'No. What would I want with a crossbow?'

'Do you know anything about the deaths of Darren and Marion Hatman – Leanne's parents?'

'Of course I don't.' She sounded indignant. 'Is that who got killed today – Leanne's mum?' She was blinking with disbelief, her scarlet lips slightly parted.

Wesley ended the interview and left, slipping the book into his pocket.

It was nine thirty by the time Wesley picked Pam and the children up from his sister's. At that late hour Amelia's

276

tiredness manifested itself in whining irritability but Michael, in contrast, seemed to be enjoying the change in routine. Neither seemed to be aware that anything was wrong in their sheltered world, for which Wesley was thankful.

When they reached home he put his arm around Pam and whispered in her ear, 'You OK?'

She squeezed his hand and told him her long talk with Maritia had done her good, leaving her feeling more optimistic. But Wesley knew it would only take one negative word, one adverse report on the TV news or one work of fiction depicting a death to plunge her into despair. He knew because he felt the same.

She asked how his day had gone and when he broke the news about the second murder he saw disappointment on her face, as though her hopes of getting him to herself again had just been dashed. He didn't have the heart to tell her they still had to uncover the truth about Linda Sangster. Had she been held in that strange room? Possibly murdered? Since the discovery of Linda's shoe and cardigan, she had been as much on his mind as the fate of the Hatmans.

When Wesley awoke the following morning, he held Pam in his arms, newly conscious of her fragility. As she rose from their bed he saw her hand travel automatically to her left breast, as though she hoped the problem had vanished miraculously overnight. While she dressed he saw a haunted look in her eyes and, when he held her, hot tears began to roll down her face.

Marion Hatman's postmortem was booked in for ten so Gerry had told him that it didn't matter if he turned up late that morning, promising to make some excuse to the team on his behalf. Wesley was grateful. He needed time with Pam, even though she was putting on a brave face and insisting she was going into work as usual. He tried to persuade her to stay at home and rest but she was determined. She needed to keep busy.

As soon as she'd left the house with the children he took the book he'd found in Kirsty Paige's jewellery box from his jacket pocket. He knew he should have given it to the exhibits officer to put with the other possible items of evidence but he'd forgotten, though he suspected his lapse of memory had been deliberate. From what he'd already seen, it appeared to be the second volume of Miss D'Arles's ancestor's journal – the account of the Grand Tour of Europe Cornell Stamoran was waiting for. So, after packing the dishwasher, Wesley sat down at the kitchen table and turned to the first page, pushing Moriarty off his lap. The cat looked up at him with an expression of pure disdain but Wesley wasn't giving in.

It seemed that the writer had abandoned his journal for a while and had only resumed his writings when the party reached Naples. In this volume the author wrote more about the character and activities of his companions than the places they visited, and Wesley soon became engrossed in the narrative. As Kirsty Paige had pointed out, the handwriting wasn't always easy to decipher but as he read, the people Richard D'Arles had travelled with began to come to life.

He turned the delicate pages but once the characters had begun to explore the ruins of Pompeii, he saw that time was moving on. He placed the book back in its protective evidence bag and reached for his coat, resolving to scan it and send a copy to Cornell Stamoran, returning his favour.

He reached the incident room to find it buzzing with activity. When he walked in he saw a glint of disapproval in Rob Carter's eyes, as if he was wondering why Wesley was strolling in halfway through the morning while the rest of them had been there since the birds woke up. The thought flashed across his mind that Rob was becoming too cocky for his own good.

Rachel looked up as he passed her desk. 'Everything OK?'

He halted, almost tempted to confide in her; but it wasn't the time or place.

He watched Gerry putting on his anorak, wishing he'd get a new one, something more likely to inspire respect in the criminal classes. Maybe he'd have a word with Joyce one of these days, but for now he had more urgent things on his mind.

'Ready for the postmortem?' Gerry sounded inappropriately cheery about the prospect.

'I'm sick of the sight of that mortuary,' Wesley mumbled, following Gerry out of the church hall.

'How's Pam?' Gerry asked as he climbed into Wesley's car.

'Up and down. Half the time I don't know what to say to her.'

'Nobody does, that's the trouble.' He patted Wesley's left arm. 'My brother's wife up in Liverpool had the same about ten years ago and she's fine now. I know it's easy to tell you not to worry but ... '

Wesley didn't answer. At that moment he wanted to forget and he'd only been able to do that while he'd been reading the journal; when he'd immersed himself in the past and the alien lives of those wealthy young gentlemen who could explore Italy without a care in their gilded world

Once they reached the mortuary Gerry walked ahead, passing Colin's office with a longing glance. When Colin was in residence he never stinted on his hospitality, however grim the situation. But today Carl Tennant was awaiting them, already in his surgical gown and wearing a solemn expression on his schoolboy face.

When the time came for the procedure to begin, Wesley and Gerry took their places behind the glass screen to listen to Tennant's commentary.

His words seemed routine. 'Well-nourished woman in her late forties. State of the liver suggests she enjoyed a drink.'

'Let that be a lesson to us all,' Gerry whispered to Wesley with a mischievous wink. Tennant started to examine the wound in Marion Hatman's chest, then, without a word, he left the corpse's side for a few moments and examined a file. After he'd finished reading, he turned to address the two detectives.

'I've checked the measurements and depths of her wound against Darren Hatman's and I'm confident it was caused by the same weapon. I'll need to conduct more tests, of course, but in my opinion whoever killed Hatman also killed this woman. Unless there are two lunatics going around South Devon armed with crossbows picking off members of the Hatman family.'

As they left the mortuary in silence Wesley went over the possibilities in his mind. Barney Yelland was out on bail and had been obsessed with Leanne. But what motive did he have to kill her parents, unless he blamed them in some way for depriving him of his muse? Then there was David Palmer; they still hadn't got to the bottom of his relationship with Leanne. And he couldn't forget Brenda and Jeremy Hodges, the art thieves. They were also out on bail but what would their motive be? Perhaps he should investigate Lee Varlow a bit further. Perhaps there was some as yet undiscovered financial arrangement between him and Darren that might have led to murder. Perhaps it was just a matter of business.

Wesley shared his speculations with Gerry on the short journey back to Turling Fitwell and when they reached the incident room the DCI gave orders that certain individuals should be looked at again in more detail. There was something they were missing: a link to Darren Hatman's business dealings perhaps.

Another possibility was nagging at the back of Wesley's mind but this time it was something he wanted to look into himself. When he told Gerry he was going back to Tradmouth for a while, the boss looked up from a report he was reading, a look of sympathy on his chubby face.

'Of course, Wes. Take as much time as you need. If anything new comes in, Rach'll let you know.'

Gerry obviously thought his temporary absence was connected with Pam's problem and he didn't put him right. He drove to Tradmouth and parked in the police station car park before heading for the CID office. Once there, he ordered two copies to be made of the journal found in Kirsty's room, one for Neil and one for himself, before emailing a copy to Cornell Stamoran, his good deed for the day.

After he'd finished he made a phone call to ask if the old files Rachel requested had turned up. The disappearance of a teenage girl back in 1953 was bound to have generated some paperwork which would now most likely be languishing in some long-forgotten cupboard or basement. It was a question of tracking it down.

It turned out they were still looking. However, he knew a place where the information might be a little more organised so he left the police station and made for Tradmouth's market place, walking fast as always.

It was market day and the cobbled square was bustling. He walked past stalls selling everything from cheese to jewellery, from sausages to waxed jackets. And when the meaty scent of hot dogs suddenly hit him, reminding him that it was almost lunchtime, he ignored his hunger and headed for the small cluster of permanent shops in the middle of the square.

The new offices of the *Tradmouth Echo* stood next door to a gallery selling paintings of local scenes. The editor he knew from his early days in Tradmouth had retired a year ago but he'd met his replacement on several occasions. Her name was Sonia Norris and she was making it her mission to transform the *Echo* from a local paper specialising in local events to a serious investigative publication. She'd already exposed a councillor with dubious business connections and a local restaurant employing illegal immigrants. Gerry reckoned she was trouble; Wesley wasn't so sure.

When he asked to see her, presenting his card to a young receptionist who looked as though she should still have been at school, Sonia Norris came out to greet him right away. At first sight she looked as if she was in her twenties, but the lines around her eyes betrayed the fact that she was considerably older. She was slender and blonde and her long ethnic skirt gave her a bohemian look. But her sharp eyes missed nothing.

'Detective Inspector Peterson,' she said his name with relish. 'To what do I owe this pleasure?'

'I'm looking for some help.'

'And why should I help the police?' The question sounded almost coquettish. She was flirting and he wasn't quite sure how he felt about that. Then he made up his mind: she was an attractive woman and he felt flattered.

He gave her a knowing smile. 'I'm not asking you to shop your nearest and dearest, Sonia. I just want a quick look at your back copies. I take it you've still got them all on microfilm?'

'We're a model of efficiency here at the *Echo*,' she replied. 'Coffee?'

'That'd be good.'

She led him into her office, which was larger than the editor's office at the old premises and considerably less cluttered. There she invited him to sit and poured two coffees from the filter machine standing on a filing cabinet in the corner.

'It's been a long time, Inspector Peterson.'

'Not that long.'

'Do you have a first name?'

'Wesley.'

She mouthed the name and nodded with approval. 'If I'm going to do you a favour, I expect something in return, Wesley. This murder case you're working on – the Hatmans. Any prospect of an arrest?'

Wesley hesitated. 'A press statement'll be issued as soon as we make one.'

'Oh come on, Wesley, can't you give me a hint? Do you think the daughter's still alive?' She looked at him quizzically, as though she was trying to read his mind. 'And if she is dead where is she and who would want to wipe out an entire family? It's a big story. Us being local, we should really have it first, don't you think?' She tilted her head to one side and smiled. 'Is it something to do with Darren Hatman's business? I've been hearing things since his murder.'

'What things?'

'Rumours. I've heard that his shady past might have come back to haunt him . . . and that he had a blazing row with his daughter's drug dealer ex. Any truth in that?'

'Is that all you've heard – rumours? Anything more solid?'

A look of disappointment passed across her face as she took a sip of coffee, all the time keeping her eyes on his.

'No. Just the usual tittle tattle and, believe me, I've had my staff out turning over all sorts of stones to see if there's anything nasty underneath. But the only thing we've got on him so far is his previous career as a getaway driver and that old woman he killed.'

'We're aware of that, thanks, and as far as we know he left all that behind and went legit. I'm sure that if there was anything to find, we'd have found it. As far as I know Hatman Construction was kosher. Unless you know otherwise.'

'What about his wife?'

'What about her?'

'Any jealous lovers who killed her husband and then killed her in a fit of passion?'

She was fishing again but Wesley didn't take the bait. 'Sorry.'

He sat back and took a sip of coffee. He knew she had nothing to tell him but he was reluctant to leave the comfortable office chair, the palatable coffee and the company. For a short while being flattered by an attractive woman had made him forget his problems.

'When anything happens I'll make sure you learn about it first.'

'How about a hint?'

For a moment he pondered the question.

'All I can say is that we're still looking for Leanne Hatman.'

She leaned forward, her eyes shining. 'Her disappearance must be linked to her parents' murders?'

'I really can't say.' The disappointment on Sonia's face was palpable; she'd hoped to get in before the opposition. But he couldn't help her.

She took a deep breath. 'You said you wanted to see our back copies. When for?'

'Nineteen fifty-three and maybe a few years either side.'

Sonia raised her plucked eyebrows. 'What are you looking for?'

'I'm not sure myself yet. Thanks for your help.'

'Any time.' She leaned towards him and winked. 'And I mean that. Doing anything tonight?'

'Sorry.'

'Can't blame a girl for asking.'

Ten minutes later he was sitting in another office in front of a machine, watching what seemed like acres of old news stories flash in front of his eyes. He wasn't quite sure what he was looking for but knew he'd recognise it when he saw it.

The account of Linda Sangster's disappearance on Coronation Day was easy enough to find. Then, scrolling back, he made another discovery. There it was in August 1952 – *Search for Missing Girl Continues. Where is Susan Thompson?*

He read the reports carefully and requested copies. Two local women had gone missing in the early 1950s, and they'd both vanished within two miles of Eyecliffe Castle.

22

Richard D'Arles - his journal
  Volume the third

  Now we are returned to Devon, I
have pondered long on the wisdom of
continuing this journal. It was, after
all, intended as a record of my
travels and yet it has become more
than that. Setting down events that
disturb me helps to make all clear in
my mind.

  Joules went back to the curate's house
and his church duties on our return. I
fear he has lost the exuberance that was
so particular to his nature before our
travels. There is a new wariness in his
eyes as though he has met with the
realisation that this world is not a
kind place for innocent souls such as

himself. Perhaps this is a lesson he should have learned many years ago but it saddens me to see his guarded demeanour.

My father greeted me most heartily on my arrival, thanking me for the treasures and souvenirs I sent on before us by carrier. Many of the classical landscapes I purchased in Italy now adorn the walls of the castle. However, my cousin's acquisition entitled The House of Eyes painted by that great artist Caravaggio has not joined them. My father called it an abomination and is glad that Uriah keeps it at his mother's home.

My cousin has gone to his mother at the Dower House. I met her while out walking yesterday and she asked me if Uriah had been in my company the previous night. When I told her I spent the evening with my younger brother, Thomas, and had not seen Uriah, I saw the shadow of anxiety upon her face.

'Another girl went missing a year before Linda Sangster, Gerry. Her name was Susan Thompson.'

'I don't see what this has to do with the Hatmans.'

Wesley knew Gerry was right. Even if they were to reopen the case of the missing girls, it had happened over sixty years ago so it was unlikely that anybody could be brought to justice now. However, he was reluctant to give up when there was a small possibility that the events of the past might be linked to their present-day case.

'Even so, Gerry, I'd like to see the files.'

'As if we haven't got enough to do.' Gerry had been doodling in the margin of an overtime request form; from where Wesley was sitting he thought it looked like a caricature of the chief super. The DCI's Biro suddenly stopped moving and he looked Wesley in the eye. 'I only suggested you take the time off so you could be with your Pam. You should be looking after your wife instead of poking your nose into ancient missing persons inquiries we've got no chance of solving.'

Wesley bowed his head. He knew there was truth in Gerry's words and he wondered whether he was using the newly discovered cold cases as a distraction from his troubles. When he was thinking of Linda Sangster and Susan Thompson, he wasn't fearing for his family's future.

'Indulge me,' he said.

Gerry looked away, exasperated. 'Do what the hell you like. Only don't expect me to cover for you if Pam rings and asks where you are.'

'Someone at the station's trying to find the case files. Look, Gerry, I think it's too much of a coincidence that these girls vanished in the same location as our murders. What if their bodies are there somewhere? What if someone doesn't want us to find them?'

'Who? Miss D'Arles? Can you really see her abducting girls? You might as well pull her Labrador in for questioning.'

'I agree, Gerry. But I want to know who the police suspected at the time . . . and whether they're still alive and in the area.'

288

Gerry sighed. 'You're wasting time, Wes, and wasting police time is a criminal offence. I'm thinking about bringing Barney Yelland in again.'

'Why? I don't think he abducted Leanne. And why would he want to kill her parents?'

'I still don't trust him, Wes. Then there's Jordan Carnegie? He likes crossbows and he had a grudge against the Hatmans. What do you think about Lee Varlow and Craig Gatting for that matter? They knew exactly where the Hatmans were going to be at the times they died. And don't forget Miss D'Arles heard Darren arguing with someone. Could it have been Lee or Craig?'

'They've given each other alibis.'

Gerry emitted another sigh, louder this time. 'Yeah. I read the report. Unless they're working together.'

Wesley shook his head. Somehow he couldn't see Lee Varlow and Craig Gatting in the role of murderous conspirators. 'All the Hatmans' other contacts, business or otherwise, have been spoken to. No sign of anything suspicious.'

They fell silent. They weren't making any progress. Then Wesley spoke again.

'What if this isn't about the Hatmans? What if it's about the location? What if somebody doesn't want that barn redeveloped?'

'In that case we can rule out David Palmer because he sold it to Darren Hatman to raise cash for the hotel.'

'But what about his mother? According to Sean, the receptionist, she objected to the sale. He heard her rowing with her son about it a few months back. She said she had plans for it and she was angry that David hadn't consulted her. The Palmers' private quarters haven't been searched yet, have they?'

'Can you see the old lady running amok with a cross-bow?'

Before Wesley could answer he heard someone saying his name.

'DI Peterson?'

'That's me.' Wesley and Gerry looked up and saw an anxious-looking young constable laden down with plastic boxes.

'These are the files you asked for. They've been in the station basement so I'm afraid they stink.'

Wesley thanked him and told him to stack the boxes up beside his desk. When he lifted the plastic lid, the smell of damp paper was overwhelming and he saw the officers in the neighbouring desks cover their noses and make wafting gestures with their hands.

'Sorry about this,' he said to nobody in particular. 'Can I have a volunteer to go through these with me? They're reports on two girls who went missing in the nineteen fifties and I'm looking for a common denominator.'

He looked round but nobody met his eye apart from Rachel, who left her desk and walked over. 'I could do with a break. I've contacted just about every seller of crossbows both here and abroad and I've drawn a complete blank. Apart from Jordan Carnegie and Lee Varlow, nobody connected with the case has ever owned a crossbow. Carnegie's bolts are the wrong size – it's been double-checked. And all Varlow's re-enactment society's weapons are kept strictly under lock and key and only the chairman of the committee has access. He's very health-and-safety-conscious.'

She looked dejected by her failure and Wesley imagined she'd be as grateful as he was for the distraction. He carried the boxes to the small stage at the end of the hall and when he climbed the steps he found himself elevated above the rest of the team. He pulled the cord at the side of the stage and the shabby velvet curtains swung open to reveal the scenery from some past amateur production had been left there: a painted drawing room with French windows open and a painted garden beyond. Wesley wondered if it was the set for a whodunit and the thought made him smile.

Two worn chintz armchairs standing centre stage looked made for the job. Wesley carried the boxes over to them and made himself comfortable while Rachel sat down opposite him.

'It was an Agatha Christie play,' she said, looking round. '*The Turling Players*. My mother came to see it because a friend of hers was playing the murderer.'

Wesley didn't answer. Instead he opened the first box and handed her a file that was musty and brown with age. 'Linda Sangster. Aged sixteen. Vanished on her way home from a dance held in this very hall to celebrate the Queen's coronation on the second of June nineteen fifty-three.' He opened the second box. 'Susan Thompson disappeared in Belsham on her way home from choir practice at the church in August nineteen fifty-two. We need to look through all these files and see whether any names crop up in both investigations.'

Rachel sighed. 'Better make a start,' she said as if she'd started to regret her offer to help Wesley chase his whim. After all, the DCI had said it was probably a waste of time.

Wesley looked at his watch and saw that it was four thirty. Pam would soon be home from work and he felt a sudden desire to see her. But he was sitting opposite Rachel, surrounded by a sea of paper, and if he broke off now he would probably forget which pile was which. He sorted through a set of reports on the disappearance of Susan Thompson in 1952 and one name in particular stood out. Someone who'd been interviewed several times.

'Any luck?' he heard Rachel ask, her voice distracting him from his thoughts of home.

'Does the name Barrington D'Arles-Cooper come up in the Linda Sangster inquiry?'

She picked up one of the files lying at her feet and shuffled through its contents before looking up with a glow of excitement in her eyes. 'Yes. He was interviewed in the Thompson case as well. One of the investigating officers in that inquiry has underlined his name in a couple of reports but he was never arrested because he had alibis for both incidents.'

'Who provided them?'

'His niece, Henrietta D'Arles. Her alibi put him in the clear.'

Wesley sat back in his armchair. 'Any suspicion that she was coerced into lying for her uncle?'

Rachel studied the report in front of her for a few moments before answering. 'Reading between the lines I don't think anybody cross-examined her too closely. The family owned the castle and people back then tended to be more deferential, especially in a rural community like this. It would take a bold policeman to even hint that she was lying, wouldn't it. Nobody challenged the uncle's story.' She hesitated. 'Apart from one detective constable who wrote a memo to his superior saying they should look into the activities of Barrington D'Arles-Cooper more closely.'

'And did they?'

Rachel shook her head.

'Do I detect a cover-up?'

'I suppose the best place to start is with Henrietta D'Arles. By the way, David Palmer's family are from the area too. I was talking to my parents and they told me the Palmers were a farming family before David's father went into the hotel business. They still have relatives farming nearby.'

'Then perhaps we should have another word with Mrs Palmer as well. Maybe we've been going about this investigation the wrong way. I'm afraid we've allowed ourselves to be distracted by Barney Yelland.'

Another thought suddenly occurred to him, something he'd suggested to Gerry earlier. 'What if the Hatmans were killed because of something connected with that barn they were planning to redevelop? I think we should take a closer look at it. And in the meantime I want to talk to Miss D'Arles and Mrs Palmer.'

He checked his watch again. Time had flown by and it was coming up to six. 'It's getting late,' he said. 'We'll do it tomorrow.'

'There's still time now.'

Wesley shook his head. 'I doubt if either of the ladies will be going anywhere.' For a brief moment he was tempted to confide in Rachel about Pam's problem; to tell her the true reason he wanted to get home. But something stopped him; maybe a reluctance to let the woman who'd once tempted him to stray glimpse Pam's vulnerability. Somehow it seemed disloyal.

'We'll visit them tomorrow morning after I've had a good look inside that barn.'

He left Rachel alone on the stage sitting in the flimsy approximation of a 1920s drawing room and made his way over to Gerry's desk.

Neil was conscious of unfinished business. The answer to the puzzle of the skeleton at the mill must lie somewhere, and he knew the church was the most likely place to find it, even though his last visit hadn't been exactly conclusive.

He drove to the village and parked outside the church. According to Mark there were more D'Arles burials in the churchyard so perhaps he'd find something there. He'd spent many happy childhood hours in churchyards, reading inscriptions about past people's lives – lives so different from his own. His parents had thought it a strange hobby but it had fired his passion for the past and set him on the road to archaeology.

It was twilight and the feeble glow of Turling Fitwell's few streetlights didn't reach as far as the rear of the church-yard, the north side where the poor, the wicked and the unfortunate were traditionally buried. Although he had already checked out the more prestigious south side and found a few D'Arles graves, it was always worth looking in unexpected places.

It seemed darker on the north side and Neil's feet slipped on mossy grave slabs as he walked. At first he saw no sign of the name D'Arles on any of the neat, well-tended graves. Then he came to one on the edge of the churchyard, in the shadow of a huge yew tree. The lichen-covered headstone had been toppled and lay smashed on the bare ground as if it had been broken with violence some years ago and the damage never rectified.

He picked his way towards it and squatted down to read

the name, taking the torch he'd brought with him from his pocket and pointing the beam at the carved letters: Barrington D'Arles-Cooper. Above the name was the now-familiar D'Arles coat of arms. Then he noticed that the eye in the centre had been daubed with what looked like black paint – as though somebody had tried to blind it to the act of desecration.

He took out his mobile and left a message on Wesley's voicemail.

It probably wasn't important but there was a chance he might be interested.

23

Today I received a note from the Reverend Joules asking me to meet with him as he wanted to speak in private. Not wishing my father to be privy to our discussion, I visited Joules at his house and found him in a state of great agitation.

One of his flock, a carter's widow, visited the vicar to tell him her daughter has been missing since last evening and nobody in the village knows her whereabouts. The girl's name is Jenny Warboys and she is but sixteen.

Pam rushed to the door to meet Wesley when he arrived home. Her next appointment had come through more quickly than she'd expected but, rather than being reassured, the speed worried her. If they thought it was that urgent, things must be bad. He held her in his arms for a while, his face buried in her hair, breathing in the sweet scent of her body.

'It's good they're acting so quickly,' he whispered, trying to convince himself as much as her. 'Everything's going to be fine. Don't worry.'

She didn't seem to be in the mood for talking so he kept up the flow of conversation by telling her about the case. Anything to take her mind off what was to come.

At nine thirty the phone rang and when Wesley answered it he heard his mother-in-law Della's voice. She sounded loud and in high spirits and his first thought was that she'd had too much to drink again. He covered the mouthpiece and asked Pam if she wanted to speak to her but she shook her head vigorously. She hadn't told Della and didn't intend to. Wesley thought up an excuse why she couldn't come to the phone, amazed at the ease with which the lie dropped from his lips.

He'd brought a copy of the journal home but didn't have a chance to read it. He didn't want Pam to feel neglected; he wouldn't give her the opportunity to brood while he immersed himself in the past.

That night neither of them slept well and Wesley woke the next morning with a tense headache. Keeping everything together for Pam's sake, and suppressing his worries, was a strain and he was horrified to realise that he was looking forward to escaping to the incident room and the distraction of the case.

As soon as he arrived at the church hall he looked through everything that had come in overnight. Neil had left a message on his voicemail the previous evening but he hadn't called him back because he hadn't been in the mood for a chat. But now he needed to speak to him because there was something he wanted to arrange. So, once he'd made sure there was nothing urgent to attend to, he made the call.

'Neil. I need your help.'

'Personal or professional?' The question sounded slightly wary.

'Professional. You tried to call me last night?'

'Yeah. But it's probably not important.'

'Go on. I'm listening.'

'I went to the churchyard last night and found one of the D'Arles graves smashed up. It looks as if it was done a while ago. Barrington D'Arles-Cooper, his name was. None of the other graves nearby had been damaged so I thought it was odd.'

As Wesley listened he had a strong feeling that what Neil had just told him was important, although just at that moment he couldn't think why.

'What do you want help with?' he heard Neil ask.

'I need someone who knows what they're doing to excavate inside a derelict barn on the Eyecliffe estate. Are you up for it?'

'What are you hoping to find?'

There was a short pause before Wesley replied. 'I'm not sure.'

'Fair enough. OK, I'm up for it, yes,' Neil said. 'Dave and Lucy can take charge at the mill site. By the way, I've got a possible name for my skeleton: there's a member of the D'Arles family who disappears from all records after seventeen eighty-six. Of course he might have gone abroad or—'

'Who is it?'

'It's Richard D'Arles – the guy who wrote the Grand Tour journal. There's no record of his death but his younger brother inherited the estate which suggests Richard's dead rather than living abroad.'

Wesley knew he should be concentrating on his case but Neil's words caught his attention. 'I've found the second volume of that journal, by the way. I've made a copy for you. In some ways it's more interesting than the first. Richard mentions having trouble with his cousin, Uriah.'

'Uriah Trelaven?' Neil said, his voice bright with recognition. 'He's in the baptismal register but there's no mention of him after that. There's a note in the register saying he was the son of Richard D'Arles's father's sister.'

Wesley thought for a while. He'd only managed to get through half the book so far and he suddenly wished he'd had time to finish it.

'You still there, Wes?' Neil sounded concerned by his silence.

Eventually he spoke. 'According to what I've read so far Uriah was a bad boy, fond of opium and prostitutes. Your skeleton might be someone he killed. It might even be his cousin, Richard. That would explain the watch you found buried with him.'

'I suppose it would. Where's this barn then?'

'Go down the castle drive and you'll see a track branching off to the left. Can you meet me there in half an hour? If you have any portable geophysics equipment, can you bring that as well as your spade?'

Neil said he'd see him there.

'You've told Neil to do what?'

'It's an idea I've got, Gerry. Indulge me.'

Gerry rolled his eyes to heaven. 'Don't I always. Aunty Noreen's already moaning about the budget for this investigation. We can't afford to go digging up the floor of somebody else's property on a whim.'

'I promise it won't cost us a penny, unless Neil finds something. He's using ground-penetrating radar equipment first and if that shows no anomalies, I promise I won't take it any further.'

Gerry grunted. Wesley knew he didn't agree with his theory that the Hatmans' deaths were linked to the barn, but he had to make sure.

'I told him I'd meet him there and I was wondering whether to call in on Miss D'Arles.' He explained what Neil had told him about the damaged grave. It belonged to her relative after all; the uncle who'd acted as her guardian during her teenage years. But Gerry reckoned that could wait. It was hardly an urgent matter; and, besides, it might upset her.

'I haven't asked you how Pam is,' Gerry said suddenly.

'She's got another appointment. It looks as if they're keen to start treatment. She's gone into work again. Says she couldn't stand sitting at home brooding about it.'

Gerry gave Wesley a sympathetic smile and told him he'd better get going.

He decided to walk to the barn and when he arrived he found Neil setting up his equipment.

'One problem,' he said as soon as Wesley was within earshot. 'If you want me to search inside the barn itself you'd better find a key to the padlock.'

Wesley produced the key Lee Varlow had left in the care of the police while the investigation continued. Once the padlock was undone, he pushed the rotting wooden door open and stepped inside the huge dusty space, looking around, Neil standing behind him.

When he'd taken a perfunctory look inside the barn before, his mind had been on other things. Now he took in his surroundings with new interest: the bare, trodden earth littered with rotting straw; the great wooden beams; the remains of long-defunct farm machinery and the building materials piled up at one end of the building. There was a faint smell of dust and decay and the old brick walls were crooked and half-collapsed in places. But with money, imagination and tender loving care, the place could be transformed into something impressive. No wonder Darren Hatman had been keen on the project.

'Where do you want me to start?' said Neil.

'I'll leave that to you. See if you can find anywhere that might have been dug up.'

'A grave?'

Wesley hadn't wanted to put his suspicions into words but Neil had said it for him. 'Yes. A grave. Or graves,' he added, thinking of the two missing girls. 'Give me a call if you find anything.'

'Will do.'

Wesley hesitated. There was a flaw in his plan: if his theory was right and somebody didn't want the barn examined too closely, it meant Neil could be in danger. He put in a call to the incident room and asked if a uniform could be spared, just to be on the safe side. The suggestion of a police guard made Neil laugh, but Wesley didn't like to think of his friend being alone there. Darren and Marion Hatman had gone there alone, and now they were dead.

When he emerged into the daylight he glanced at the

nearby trees. The woodland was thick enough to conceal an assassin. And that worried him.

He began to make his way down the rough path through the trees, walking more slowly than usual, enjoying the scent of undergrowth and the sound of the birds in the canopy of budding branches above his head. He stopped and shut his eyes, imagining himself in a place where death and sickness couldn't touch him – the safe place of childhood. At least it had been a safe place for Wesley and his sister; but his work had showed him that, for many, childhood wasn't the protective haven of family love it should be. Some had it tough, like Miss D'Arles, who'd lost her parents and been left in the care of an uncle who'd probably regarded her and her sister as an inconvenience.

He had just reached the drive when his phone rang. It was Rachel, sounding excited.

'I've been taking a look at the people who were around at the time those girls went missing,' she began. 'You know I said the Palmers were a local family? Well it turns out Mrs Palmer was actually brought up at the castle. Her mother was the housekeeper and she lived there when it was owned by the D'Arles family. She met her husband when he bought the place. They married and she never left.' She paused, as if she had something momentous to announce. 'She was interviewed about the disappearance of Linda Sangster because she knew her. In fact she was at the coronation dance on the night Linda disappeared.'

The lodge was in sight but Rachel's news made Wesley stop walking. 'I'll go up to the castle and speak to her.'

'Want me to come with you?'

He knew it would be better to go alone. 'No, thanks, I

can manage. Keep digging. By the way, what's Barney Yell-and up to at the moment?'

'Still at home with Clare Woolmer.'

'What about Clare's alibi for Marion's murder?'

'Her and Barney are backing each other up again. But people have been known to lie for friends.'

He retraced his steps and carried straight on to the castle where he found Mrs Palmer in her office. In the sunlight that streamed through the tall windows, she looked older than he remembered. Even her thick layer of make-up couldn't conceal the deep lines on her face and her pale blue eyes seemed sunken in her skull. Her thick snowy hair, he realised, was probably a wig.

'I need to speak to you, Mrs Palmer.'

'Anything I can do to help the police,' she said, assuming the helpful expression Wesley had often seen before on the faces of innocent citizens . . . and, at times, the duplicitous and clever.

'In nineteen fifty-three a girl called Linda Sangster went missing.'

Her intake of breath sounded like a gasp. 'Nineteen fifty-three is a very long time ago, Inspector.'

'She was a friend of yours.'

'I knew her a little but I'd hardly describe her as a friend. I told the police everything I knew at the time, which wasn't much.'

'You realise we've found items in the tower that might be connected with Linda Sangster's disappearance?'

'Yes.'

'And you didn't think to mention that you knew the missing girl?'

'I didn't know anything about it at the time and I don't

know anything now.' There was a stubbornness about her answer which made Wesley suspect she was hiding something. Or perhaps she was unable to face the terrible likelihood that her contemporary had suffered and met her death in there; sometimes the mind can only take so much horror.

'I understand your mother was the housekeeper for the D'Arles family. What can you tell me about that room?'

'Nothing. I was told it was unsafe – structurally unsound – so I was never allowed near it. And my mother used to say it was haunted, which was enough to keep me away in those days.'

'What about when your husband took the place over? Weren't you curious?'

'No.'

'I believe you didn't want your son to sell the barn to Darren Hatman.'

She seemed surprised by the change of subject and it took her a few moments to come up with an answer. 'My late husband had planned to make the barn into a function room and that was always my intention . . . once funds were available. I thought it unwise to sell a potential asset, that's all.'

'Tell me about Barrington D'Arles-Cooper.'

Her eyes flickered towards the door. 'I kept well away from him.'

'Why was that?'

'My mother told me it was best to avoid him and I did.'

'Why? What did he do?'

'I'm not sure exactly but I didn't like him.'

'His grave appears to have been vandalised. Do you know anything about that?'

'He wasn't popular in the village. But that was all a long time ago.' She pressed her lips together as though she didn't want to say any more on the subject.

'You must have been a similar age to his nieces. I expect you knew them well?'

'I was only the housekeeper's daughter so we didn't mix, and they were away most of the time. To be honest, I felt sorry for them. It can't have been easy for them being sent away like that . . . and then being stuck here with their uncle whenever they came back.'

He felt there was something she was holding back but he wasn't sure what it was. 'Which sister did you know best – Gretel or Henrietta?'

'Neither really.' She answered quickly, as if she wanted to change the subject.

'Henrietta lives in the castle grounds. I'm sure you must see her from time to time.'

'I know her to say hello to, that's all. The D'Arles family have always kept themselves to themselves.'

'You can't think why anyone would desecrate her uncle's grave?'

She looked him in the eye. 'He wasn't a nice man.'

Wesley leaned forward and lowered his voice. 'Did he abuse girls? Did he abuse you?'

She shook her head vigorously. 'I don't want to talk about it. Now if you'll excuse me, I have work to do.'

24

There is no sign of Jenny Warboys and I fear that Uriah, with his dark inclinations, knows something of her fate. With the help of my father's estate workers I set in motion a search of the castle grounds and at dusk the tragic discovery was made.

Poor Jenny's body was lying against a hedgerow in an outlying field, her dark eyes bulging, staring at the scene as though she had seen a vision of hell itself. As soon as word reached her father, he came to the spot and cradled her dead form in his arms and would not be separated from her until the Reverend Joules arranged for her to be returned to the church on a shutter in solemn procession, lit by

torches to dispel the gathering
darkness. I myself had joined the
search and I bowed my head in respect
as she passed by. But my cousin was
nowhere to be found.

I inquired of Joules later what
injuries the unfortunate girl had
suffered and he told me that marks of
violence had been found upon her neck.

Barney Yelland was the last person Wesley expected to
meet when he returned to the incident room. He found the
photographer talking to Gerry Heffernan and their discussion seemed to be growing more heated by the moment.
Gerry was repeating himself in a firm voice: 'You can't do
that. It's a crime scene.'

The rest of the team kept glancing up from their work,
no doubt wondering, as Wesley was, why the boss hadn't
chucked the suspect out straight away.

When Gerry spotted Wesley, a look of relief appeared on
his face. 'Inspector Peterson. A word if you'd be so kind.'
He waved his large hands in a beckoning gesture and
Wesley could tell his patience was wearing thin.

The trouble with the church hall was that it lacked privacy. There was, however, a separate kitchen area that lay
behind a door at the side of the stage. Gerry steered Wesley
towards it, leaving Barney Yelland staring at their vanishing
backs.

'What does he want?' was Wesley's first question.

'He wants to see the tower room. It's something to do
with that book you found in Kirsty Paige's room. He said
you sent Cornell Stamoran a copy.'

'That's right. I got it scanned and emailed it to him.'

Gerry scowled. 'When did you get time to do that?'

Wesley felt the blood rushing to his face. 'It didn't take long.' He knew he must have sounded defensive.

But to his relief, Gerry nodded. 'Sorry, mate. Didn't mean to sound ... Anyway, Yelland's asked if he can go into the tower to take photographs. He seems to think there's some connection with the man who wrote the journal.'

'What kind of connection?'

'Why don't you ask him?'

Wesley returned to the incident room and signalled Yelland to follow him outside. He didn't want an audience.

'I understand you've asked to take pictures inside the disused part of the castle. Any particular reason?'

Yelland answered almost in a whisper. 'It goes back to a man called Uriah Trelaven. When you read the journal you'll understand.'

'I've read part of it.'

'Well, I've read all of it. Cornell sent me a copy.'

Wesley was trying hard not to show his growing impatience. 'Look, if anything happened in the castle – and we're not sure it did – it was far more recent than the eighteenth century. There's no evidence of any link with this Uriah Trelaven.'

A smug smile appeared on Yelland's face. 'Yes, but he started it all. Others only followed.'

The cryptic nature of the words only increased Wesley's irritation.

'If you know anything about what happened to Darren and Marion Hatman, you have to tell me now.'

Yelland didn't answer.

308

'Look, as far as access to the castle's concerned, once we've finished it'll be up to Mr Palmer. You'll have to get his permission.'

For a moment Yelland looked as he was about to argue, then seemed to change his mind. 'I've had an idea for an exhibition based on Richard D'Arles's connection with the castle. I need photographs of—'

Wesley cut him off in mid flow. 'Like I said, you'll have to ask Mr Palmer.'

Yelland hesitated before giving a curt nod and turning to go.

Wesley rang Pam to ask how she was. She accused him of fussing but she sounded glad that he'd made the effort. He knew he'd become more attentive since she broke the news and the fact that it had taken a threat to his wife's life to move her wellbeing to the top of his list of life's priorities made him uneasy. What if they hadn't caught it in time? What if there was a risk of losing her? Every time he thought about it, he experienced a pain that was almost physical: a knotting in his stomach and an ache in his heart.

As he entered the incident room he saw Rachel looking up at him through lowered lashes. The memory of his attraction to her caused another stab of guilt. Even though all that was long over, it was still there, niggling away like a tiny piece of gravel in a shoe.

The copy he'd taken of the journal he'd found in Kirsty's room was still lying on his desk and he picked it up and started to read. He had just reached the final page when Gerry rose from his seat and lumbered over to him.

'What's that you're reading?'

The sound of his voice made Wesley jump. 'It's that journal I copied. In view of what Yelland said, I wondered if there might be some connection to the case.'

'What do you mean?'

'Not sure yet.'

'Anything new to report?'

'Neil's searching the barn. I've sent a uniform over there to keep an eye on things.'

'Is that the best use of police resources?'

'I think it's a wise precaution. We don't want another death on our hands.'

Gerry couldn't argue with that. 'I believe you've been speaking to Mrs Palmer.'

'Yes. She was living at the castle in the early nineteen fifties and she knew Linda Sangster. They were both at the coronation dance here in this very hall on the night Linda vanished.'

'In case you've forgotten, there's a nutter running about with a crossbow and two people are lying dead in the mortuary.'

'I realise that, Gerry, but the grave of the man who occupied the castle at the time the girls vanished has been vandalised. He was a suspect but his niece gave him an alibi. It's as if Barrington D'Arles-Cooper was regarded as an outcast and I'd like to know why, because I can't help feeling there's a connection. '

Gerry sighed. 'Come on, Wes, we know everything about the Hatmans down to what they ate for breakfast and their only link with the castle is that barn Darren bought to do up and flog on for a fat profit. Darren's an ex-con with a dodgy past. Then there's Yelland. If you ask me, there's something not quite right about that man and, let's face it, he was obsessed with Leanne so what's to say he didn't have a grudge against her parents? Or it might have something to do with the fact that Darren killed Clare Woolmer's mother. You're letting your imagination run away with you.'

He put his arm around Wesley's shoulder and led him into the privacy of the kitchen again.

'Look, Wes, I know things are difficult. You take some time off to be with Pam. We can manage. I'll square it with Aunty Noreen.'

Wesley said nothing. Gerry clearly thought the problem with Pam was clouding his judgement and for a few moments he started to doubt himself. Was he really losing it; seeing links with ancient crimes that didn't exist?

He shrugged off Gerry's clumsy attempt at sympathy and returned to the incident room where he stood staring at the photographs on the noticeboard: the victims and everyone involved in the inquiry. There was something he'd missed and he had the nebulous, frustrating feeling that if he started to look at things in a different way, everything would become clear.

Mary Palmer was doing her best to avoid her son. She'd heard it said that you always love your children but that doesn't necessarily mean you like them and she'd realised many years ago that she didn't like David very much. He had a history of making a fool of himself with the female staff by being unable to keep his trousers on. He was a weak man, just as her husband had been. She often wondered whether despising your own son meant you were a terrible mother; whether the whole thing was ultimately her fault.

She knew there was something she had to do, something she didn't want David to find out about. It was something she needed to keep from the police as well. During her youth at the castle she'd become used to subterfuge. She'd always been an expert in deception.

Because of her arthritis she walked with a stick, a situation she found frustrating because she'd always liked to move quickly. She made her way slowly down the stairs and left the building, straight-backed and determined, choosing to use one of the side doors rather than the main entrance. The fewer people who witnessed what she was about to do, the better.

She walked across the courtyard, her head erect. There had been a time when she'd longed to leave this place with its bad memories and its ghosts, but she'd never managed to escape and now she knew she never would.

It took her almost twenty minutes to reach her destination. And when she arrived her first words were: 'It can't go on. This has to stop.'

Then, for the first time in many years, she cried.

25

I went in search of my cousin and found him in the west wing, an abandoned part of the castle where he is wont to go when he wishes to be alone. I informed him of Jenny Warboys' tragic death but he claimed to know nothing of the matter. I suspected this was a lie for he proved when we were on our travels that he holds life cheap.

He swore to me that he had not been outside the castle for many hours because he was constructing an experiment. He invited me to watch and I went with him, dreading what I might see. When I reached the windowless room at the foot of the tower, I found it lit by many candles and I saw a wooden table upon which my cousin had set a large glass bottle attached with tubes to a pair of bellows. A bird, a white dove, fluttered in a cage in the corner of the room, panicking in its confinement, and I inquired of Uriah what he intended to do.

Without answering he took off his coat and rolled his shirtsleeves to the elbows as if he were about to undertake some onerous task. Then he opened the cage door and drew the bird out gently, stroking its trembling, soft feathers. He placed it inside the jar which he sealed with a large cork and then began to work the bellows.

I watched with horrified fascination as the creature fluttered, desperately at first as though fighting some invisible enemy, then more feebly. In the end it lay still, its feathers spread out like an angel's wings. And I knew that it was dead.

'I have removed the air from the bottle,' Uriah whispered. 'And with it I have removed the spark of life itself.'

When I asked him why he had done it he replied that such cruelty is justified if the knowledge of mankind is to be advanced.

'Next I must discover whether the same principle applies to a larger creature,' he said, the light of obsession glowing in his eyes.

314

Neil was so engrossed in his task that he'd quite forgotten about the policeman Wesley had asked to stand guard outside the barn. As far as he was concerned the precaution was quite unnecessary. Wesley wasn't usually one to overdramatise but he had been behaving a little strangely over the past days. Neil put it down to the strain of the case.

He worked away methodically, trundling the machine to and fro across the barn floor, and it didn't seem long before he had the results of the survey. There were two possible areas of disturbance – he always said 'possible' because he never liked to commit himself before he was absolutely certain of his facts – one large and one much smaller. He called Wesley's number and his friend answered after two rings.

'I've found two anomalies. They might be pits dug for some agricultural purpose and filled in. But on the other hand . . . '

'Can you start digging?' Wesley said. 'I need to know what's down there.'

He sounded so eager that Neil found it hard to refuse.

Mrs Palmer's patent leather shoes were stained with mud. It had been a mistake to walk through the trees, picking her way over bracken and last year's rotting leaves. She leaned on her stick. Walking was becoming increasingly painful. Good days and bad days. She'd thought this was a good day but she'd been wrong.

She knew her son would be angry with her for venturing so far but she was sick of restricting herself. Sick of the aging process with all its indignities and frustrations. Sick of her growing frailty. She felt a niggle of pain in her hip as she reached the edge of the trees but she took deep breaths and did her best to ignore it. The barn came into view some way ahead and her heart began to thud in her chest when she noticed that the door was standing wide open. Without hesitation she hobbled on. Somebody was in there. And whatever was going on she had to stop it.

When she reached the doorway she saw a man inside the building. His clothes bore traces of dried mud and his fair hair was long and unkempt. He was digging with a spade but he was working carefully, removing one layer of soil and then the next.

'Stop that at once and get out. You've no right to be here.' She was aware of the edge of hysteria rising in her voice but somehow she had to stop him.

He turned to face her, puzzled. But before he had a chance to reply, she heard another male voice behind her. She swung round and saw Inspector Peterson in the company of a young constable.

'Can we help you, Mrs Palmer?

She blustered for a moment. 'Yes, you can, Inspector. This man's trespassing.'

'He's here with my permission. I'm sorry you've been troubled.'

She stared at him, speechless. She'd lost control of the situation and there was nothing she could do about it.

She saw the inspector nod to the man with the spade. 'It's OK, Neil. Carry on.'

Once Mrs Palmer had gone, Wesley sent the constable away; probably an act of mercy as the lad was looking bored and the air was turning chilly. Besides, he didn't think the killer would dare to tackle Neil while he was there.

Wesley watched as Neil worked. After removing the first foot or so with his spade he squatted down and began to use his trowel. From the geophysics results he knew that whatever was buried there wasn't far beneath the surface.

When Wesley's phone rang he answered and heard a female voice that sounded familiar, although he couldn't quite place it.

'Inspector Peterson, this is Sonia Norris, *Tradmouth Echo*. I've been doing a bit of detective work of my own and I've found something interesting. There was another disappearance in Turling Fitwell in nineteen fifty-eight.'

Wesley pressed the phone closer to his ear.

'Only it wasn't a young woman this time. It was a baby. A little boy was taken from a front garden of a house on the edge of the village. His mother left him asleep in his pram and when she went out to get him he'd vanished. The garden wasn't overlooked so there were no witnesses.'

'Did they find him?'

'About eight hours later he turned up in the church. He was hungry and his nappy hadn't been changed but, other than that, he was OK.'

'He must have been screaming the place down.'

'That's how they found him. Someone heard him crying and went to investigate.'

'I presume the police got involved?'

'Oh yes. But once they had him back safe and well I get the impression the matter was put on the back burner. All's well that ends well. Just thought you might be interested.'

'I am. What was the baby's name?'

'James. James Garrard.'

*

According to Neil, James Garrard was down at the mill, digging with Lucy in trench three. However, Wesley was reluctant to leave Neil alone in the barn – not after what had happened to Darren and Marion Hatman.

If he'd been wearing suitable clothing, he would have given Neil a hand. They'd been on many excavations together in their student days and he had no objection to getting his hands dirty from time to time – it was only work and family commitments that stopped him volunteering to take part in a dig. The thought of home and Pam brought his troubles to the front of his mind again, like a twinge of pain.

'Hello, what have we here?' said Neil, distracting Wesley from his melancholy musings.

Neil was working on the smaller anomaly, a couple of feet from its larger counterpart. Wesley could hear the scraping of his trowel.

'There's something here. Bone.'

He fell silent and Wesley edged closer, leaning over to see what he'd found. For ten minutes he watched in silence, unwilling to distract Neil from his delicate work. When he'd mentioned bone, Wesley had assumed the remains belonged to an animal, a beloved dog some tenant farmer had buried with reverence in his barn perhaps. But as the white bones emerged from the dark earth, he saw with dawning horror that these bones were human. And that they belonged to a young baby.

26

After the incident with the bird I expressed my worries to my father but he dismissed them, saying that Uriah is a scientist, a pioneer of learning. It is no use protesting that I see the cold glint of cruelty in his eyes because he makes light of the incidents that occurred during our tour of Europe. He even suggests that I emulate my cousin's intellectual curiosity.

I fear that my father weaves a fantasy for himself when he says there is no evil in Uriah's deeds. He will not face the truth.

I confided in the Reverend Joules for he is the sole witness, apart from myself, to my cousin's depravity and yet he can suggest no solution to my dilemma.

My cousin has set up a large barrel in the chamber he calls his laboratory. It has a glass top he caused to be made for the purpose and a hole in the side which can be sealed with a stopper. Last night he killed a sheep by draining the air from the barrel with bellows inserted into the hole and watched its death throes through the glass. My father laughs about the matter and says we shall enjoy good mutton tonight.

When Wesley called the incident room to break the news to Gerry there was a long silence on the other end of the line before Gerry said he'd come straight over.

Rachel drove him there and Wesley greeted them as they emerged from the car.

'Where is it?' said Gerry, his face solemn. He often used dark humour to lighten a grim situation but on this occasion it seemed somehow inappropriate.

'Inside the barn and Neil's just started work on a second anomaly his geophysics showed up. He thinks it could be another grave.'

Gerry rolled his eyes. 'This is all we need. How long does he think the kid's been buried?'

'Don't know yet. Neil's talking about radio carbon dating if he doesn't find any dating evidence.' He paused. 'Do you remember I made inquiries at the *Tradmouth Echo* about those missing women? The editor rang me earlier to tell me that a baby was snatched from a garden in Turling Fitwell in nineteen fifty-eight. He was found in the church a few hours later, hungry and wet but otherwise unharmed.' He paused. 'That baby was James Garrard.'

'The recipient of the mysterious gifts?'

'That's the one. I think his abductor's been sending them. Guilty conscience.'

Rachel had been staring at the barn door but now she broke her silence. 'Could the baby in the barn be another child who wasn't so lucky?'

'That's exactly what I was thinking,' Wesley answered. 'In which case we need to put some effort into finding Garrard's benefactor.'

'You're right,' said Gerry. 'Better get the things he was sent over to Forensic. Could be fingerprints.'

'Neil says Garrard's down at the mill,' said Wesley.

'I'll send someone over to talk to him.'

Gerry made a call to Trish. As Wesley listened, he tried to envisage James Garrard as a helpless baby, and failed. But everyone had been that age at one time. It was a humbling thought.

'Mrs Palmer turned up here earlier,' Wesley said. 'She tried to stop Neil digging.'

Gerry raised his eyebrows. 'Maybe we should find out why.'

Before Wesley could reply he heard Neil's voice raised inside the barn. 'Wes. Come and have a look at this.'

Wesley walked into the gloomy interior with a feeling of dread, Gerry a short distance behind. Neil was kneeling next to the larger anomaly but Wesley's eyes were drawn to the baby's skeleton; the small cream bones standing out against the dark earth.

Neil looked up. 'We've got another skeleton. Adult this time. I've only just started to uncover it but, from the skull, I think it's female.'

Wesley looked down and saw the skull grinning up at him. Half of it was still in the earth but the face was clearly visible.

'She has fillings so we're not talking historical here.'

Gerry shook his head. 'I have to hand it to you, Wes, there could be something in that theory of yours about the Hatmans being killed to prevent them redeveloping this barn.'

'Nothing personal then. In which case we can rule out Jordan Carnegie once and for all – and probably Barney Yelland and Clare Woolmer too.'

'What about Leanne Hatman? Where does she come into all this?'

Wesley experienced a nagging feeling of inadequacy at the mention of Leanne's name. This new skeleton certainly wasn't her so it was still possible she was alive somewhere, unaware of her parents' deaths. Or she might be dead herself: the last of her line wiped from the earth, like the D'Arles family would be in the not-too-distant future when Henrietta passed away.

Neil examined the skull. 'She's been here a while. And these fillings could date back to the fifties. There are quite a few of them and dentists tended to be a bit drill-happy in those days.'

'In an ideal world we'd be able to get dental records for those missing girls,' said Gerry.

'If this skeleton dates from the fifties, they'd have been lost or destroyed years ago,' Wesley said. 'Unless we're extremely lucky.'

Gerry glanced towards the door, as if he was keen to get out of there. 'Why don't you and Rach go and talk to Mrs Palmer,' he said. 'I reckon she knows something about this.'

When Wesley told Neil he'd send a forensic team over, he

stopped digging and straightened up. When he resumed, he'd have to change into a crime-scene suit so he wouldn't contaminate the site. This was another suspicious death, and, as the bones might be less than seventy years old, just, it was the business of the police.

Once the barn had been sealed off as a crime scene and all the usual procedures had been set in motion, Wesley and Rachel were about to set off for the castle when Carl Tennant arrived in his Range Rover.

'What is it this time?' Tennant asked after he'd retrieved his bag from the back of the car.

'Two skeletons. A young baby and a woman with modern dental work. A couple of girls went missing locally in the nineteen fifties and it's possible this is one of them. Although that doesn't explain the baby.'

Tennant sighed. 'I'd better have a look. Pronounce life extinct.'

'DCI Heffernan's in there with the archaeologist who found her.'

'That's all I need,' Tennant muttered. Wesley knew the feeling was mutual. The sooner Colin Bowman returned from his cruise, the better.

He walked on with Rachel by his side and when they were halfway up the drive Trish called him to say she'd spoken to James Garrard, who'd known nothing about the strange incident in his babyhood. His parents must have kept it from him, a secret that had never been spoken of.

When Wesley and Rachel reached the castle they found Sean on reception. He told them in a loud whisper that Mrs Palmer had stormed in and headed straight for her private quarters without speaking to any of the staff, which apparently was unusual because she liked to be hands on in spite of her age. Wesley suspected 'hands on' was a euphemism for interfering.

They arrived at her apartment on the first floor, and Rachel knocked on the door. When there was no answer she knocked again more loudly to make it clear they weren't going to go away. Eventually the door opened a crack.

'May we come in, Mrs Palmer?'

The door opened wider and she stood aside to let them into a room filled with light from two large windows on the far wall. Wesley could see that they overlooked the river valley and the open countryside beyond and he guessed the terrace lay just below. He wondered whether she spied on the smokers from there.

Mrs Palmer's eyes were bloodshot and her usually immaculate coiffure was messed up, as though she'd been running her fingers through her hair. She was doing it now – a nervous gesture.

'Is something the matter, Mrs Palmer?'

She didn't reply. And she didn't invite them to take a seat.

'You seemed upset at the barn. Can you tell me why?'

She took a deep breath. 'I've been under a lot of stress.'

'Two skeletons have just been found buried there. A woman and a baby. Who are they, Mrs Palmer?'

Wesley thought she looked like a terrified mouse that had just seen a cat's paw poised above its head.

'I don't know.' Tears began to trickle down her face, ploughing dark tracks through her thick foundation.

Rachel opened her mouth to speak but Wesley put a warning hand on her arm. Bullying an elderly woman wasn't on their agenda.

There were other ways of discovering the truth.

27

I have no taste for my cousin's company
and yet it is necessary for me to
discover his intentions. For I fear his
curiosity might escalate into savagery of
the worst kind as it almost did on our
travels.

When I arrived at the Dower House
his mother, my aunt, greeted me
effusively. My father's sister is a good-
natured woman who sees good in all
men. My father has, in my hearing,
called her a fool. To my mind,
goodness is never foolish and yet hers
has blinded her to her beloved son's
shortcomings.

I asked her if she was aware of
Uriah's experiments and she seemed
most approving, saying he was a man of

science who was intending to prove the existence of the human soul. She expressed great pride in his achievements. Poor, naive woman.

Neil had asked Lucy to help him excavate the skeleton, leaving Dave to supervise the volunteers down at the mill site. As they worked he was conscious of Dr Tennant's impatience. But some things can't be rushed.

Dealing with the skeleton's hands was a delicate matter with all those tiny bones to uncover. Fortunately, after years in the archaeology business, Neil was used to exercising patience. He noted that the skeleton's hands had been neatly arranged, folded over the ribcage as if the dead woman had been laid out with some reverence. Even though her last resting place was a humble barn, somebody had taken the trouble to care.

'When will I be able to make my examination?' Tennant said, looking at his watch ostentatiously.

'When we've finished,' Neil replied without taking his eyes off the bony fingers emerging from the soil. 'Can't tell you how long that'll be, I'm afraid. In a situation like this we don't take short cuts. There are remnants of cloth. Looks like she was fully clothed when she was buried— Hello.'

Neil mumbled something to Lucy who was working on the skull, teasing the back of the head away from its damp-smelling resting place. She left what she was doing and squatted next to him.

'What is it?' Tennant suddenly sounded interested.

'She's wearing a ring. Looks like gold. Let me . . . '

He worked on the hand with a small leaf trowel for a few

minutes, brushing away the excess earth with a soft brush. Eventually, after asking Lucy to photograph the ring in situ, he lifted the finger bone delicately and slipped it off, handing it to Lucy who took it over to the barn door so she could see it better in the daylight.

'Neil,' she said. 'Come and look at this.'

He put down his trowel and brush and straightened himself up, stretching out his back. When he joined Lucy she placed the gold signet ring in the palm of his hand.

'Familiar?'

He studied it closely and nodded.

'What is it?' Tennant asked peevishly as if he suspected them of wasting his time deliberately.

Neil turned to face him. 'It's the coat of arms of the D'Arles family who used to own the estate. She might have been one of the family.'

Tennant stared, open-mouthed, as Neil took his phone from one of his many pockets and made another call to Wesley Peterson.

In Rachel's experience Wesley rarely gave up until he discovered the truth behind the lies and silent evasion, so she was surprised when he abandoned his efforts to question Mrs Palmer after five minutes or so and left the hotel. He made straight for the gatehouse and as soon as he got there he tried the old oak-studded door. When it opened he walked through and made his way up a spiral stone staircase to the room above.

It had once been used as a chapel and the plastered walls were still decorated with medieval paintings of saints, now dark, faded and barely visible. The east end of the room was screened off by a carved oak screen and behind it, in the light streaming in from a small stained-glass window, Wesley could make out another wall painting, better preserved than the others, depicting a nativity scene. But, much as he would have liked to stay and study the room further, he hurried over to an arched window filled with old leaded glass.

The window overlooked the drive and from there he saw Mrs Palmer emerging from beneath the arch of the gatehouse. She was walking with a stick but moving quickly which suggested to Wesley that wherever she was going, it was urgent. His gamble had paid off.

'What do we do now?' Rachel asked.

'We follow her.'

Without another word he descended the staircase and waited in the shadow of the gatehouse until Mrs Palmer was some way away.

His phone rang and he was tempted to ignore it. Then he saw the caller was Neil so he answered, hoping he'd have news about the skeletons in the barn.

'There's ID on the adult female.' Wesley could hear the excitement in his friend's voice. 'It's a signet ring with the D'Arles coat of arms, same as on that pocket watch we found near the bones at the mill.'

Wesley stood silently for a while, taking in the new development. 'Any indication of the cause of death?'

'Not yet.' He lowered his voice. 'The pathologist's here but I think he's losing patience.'

Wesley thanked him and ended the call. If they didn't follow Mrs Palmer now, they'd lose her.

But she was still in sight and Wesley held back, hoping she wouldn't look round.

'She's heading for the barn,' said Rachel.

'Where did you expect?'

They carried on down the path. Rachel was right. She was walking purposefully towards the barn. However, when the building came into sight she stopped suddenly, as though the sight of the police activity had made her reconsider her plans.

Then, without warning she turned and Wesley found himself face to face with her.

'You've been following me,' she said. She didn't sound shocked or angry, it was just a statement of fact.

'Why have you come here?'

'I wanted to see what's been found.'

'Why?'

For a while she said nothing. Then she straightened her back and looked ahead, like an aristocrat going to the guillotine. 'Because I killed her.'

Gerry decided to keep Mary Palmer overnight and resume questioning in the morning. David Palmer had kicked up a fuss but, in view of his mother's confession, it was the only course of action they could take, although Gerry had told the custody staff to make sure she was comfortable.

Wesley didn't sleep well. He lay awake, watching the glowing red numbers on the alarm clock, counting the dragging hours and listening to Pam's soft breathing. He turned over and wrapped her in his arms. At least at work he could strive to get justice for the victims of crime; but as far as his wife was concerned, he was helpless. He held her more tightly but she wriggled, loosening his hold on her. He turned over and lay with his eyes closed, trying hard not to envisage what life would be like if he lost her – if the children had no mother. In those dark hours all sorts of terrible thoughts danced in his head, each more dire than the last. He was relieved when the light of dawn seeped through the curtains and it was time to get up.

He was brushing his teeth when his phone rang. It was Gerry and his voice sounded solemn. For a few dreadful moments he feared it might be news about Mary Palmer; that she'd collapsed in her cell or even tried to take her own life. In the event it was bad news of another sort.

'A body's been found in the River Trad at Neston not far from Clare Woolmer's boat. It's female but she's been in the water a while. Get down here right away, Wes. There's a possibility that it's—'

'Leanne Hatman?'

'There are no other missing persons who fit that description. Our dead girl appears to be wearing pyjamas – or what's left of them. If it is Leanne, it suggests she didn't leave the castle that night.'

Wesley's mind had been clouded by lack of sleep but now he suddenly felt alert.

'She's not a pretty sight so I've asked someone to get hold of her dental records.'

'I'll be right down.'

When he reached the kitchen to grab a slice of toast, he found Pam sitting at the breakfast table. He asked her if she wanted him to tell Gerry he'd be late but she squeezed his hand and told him to go. Promising he'd be home as soon he could, he kissed her gently and left.

The morning traffic was thick and his journey to Neston was slowed by what seemed like a relay of slow-moving agricultural vehicles, taking it in turns to annoy the car-bound motorists. But once he reached his destination he found a parking space on the main road and joined Gerry and the forensic team in the park beneath the bridge. It was a pretty spot where the river flowed through the centre of the town and moored boats danced on the water. In the summer months the place would be heaving with tourists and locals but now it was sealed off and rubberneckers were standing on the bridge above, craning to see what was going on.

The body had been pulled from the water and it now lay some fifteen yards from Clare Woolmer's boat, the *Fallen Angel*, shielded from prying eyes by a white crime-scene tent. Carl Tennant had been called out again and when Wesley and Gerry entered the tent, covering their noses against the stench of decomposition, he looked up from his work.

'All I can tell you is that she's been in the water a couple of weeks. There are injuries on the body but they might have been caused postmortem as she was dragged along the bottom of the river by the current.'

'Leanne disappeared from Eyecliffe Castle,' said Wesley. 'Could she have gone in upstream and been carried down here by the river?'

'It's possible but I'm not a bloody clairvoyant. All I can tell you at the moment is that she's dead. I can't fit the post-mortem in before tomorrow morning.'

Wesley and Gerry watched in silence as he packed away his things and swept out of the tent.

'And goodbye to you too,' Gerry muttered once he was out of earshot. 'Come back Colin Bowman, all is forgiven.'

Wesley turned away from the body on the ground. He'd seen pictures of Leanne in life and he found it painful to look at her now. The jaunty tartan pyjamas, now sodden and torn, lent a pathos to the poor girl's mortal remains.'

'A piece of similar material was found caught on the fallen section of the castle terrace. Remember?'

Gerry nodded. 'We'll have to get a match.'

'Are we bringing Barney Yelland in again?'

'Might be worth having another word.' Wesley didn't sound convinced. 'And we need to speak to Mrs Palmer again. If she's a killer, it's possible Leanne's another of her victims.'

Wesley forced himself to look at the body again. An idea was forming in his mind but it might be completely wrong.

The sight of Mrs Palmer in a grey police-issue track suit made Wesley uncomfortable.

Gerry had asked Wesley and Rachel to conduct the interview while he watched from behind the two-way mirror. At first the prisoner seemed to think that a simple confession would seal the matter. But Wesley didn't work like that. He wanted to understand why she'd done what she claimed to have done, so he offered her tea and insisted that she accept the services of the solicitor her son had conjured up for her, not that she seemed particularly happy about his presence.

'Can you tell me who the bones in the barn belong to?' Wesley asked after he'd got the preliminary formalities out of the way.

'Her name is Jeanne Bordain and she was my husband's mistress. She was French. They met when she came to work at the hotel soon after it first opened.'

'And the baby?'

'That was hers ... and my husband's.'

'How did you kill her?'

'With a kitchen knife. I lost my temper and stabbed her

when she told me she was going away with John, my husband. I killed the baby too. I realise it was a very wicked thing to do.'

'Did you bury them in the barn on your own or did you have help?'

'My husband helped me. He didn't want a scandal. Once it was done we never spoke of it again.'

'The female skeleton was wearing a ring ... with the D'Arles coat of arms.'

'That came from the castle,' she said confidently. 'My husband found it in the library and gave it to her.'

'What about Darren and Marion Hatman? Did you kill them?'

'I had to stop the building work on the barn. I had no choice.'

'You used a crossbow.'

'That's right. I found it at the castle; part of the rubbish the D'Arleses left behind. I disposed of it in one of the large waste bins near the restaurant kitchens. It'll be at the tip now.'

'We'll send someone to look,' said Rachel.

'That won't be necessary. I'm willing to make a full confession.'

'What about Leanne Hatman?'

'She was a silly girl ... and nosy. Her parents came looking for her – that was another reason I had to get rid of them.'

'Tell me how Leanne died.'

A look of uncertainty passed across her face. The question troubled her. 'It was an unseasonably warm night and she was smoking on the terrace. I gave her a push. She fell back and tumbled down the slope and ended up in the river. The current's treacherous near the weir and she was swept away so I presume she didn't survive.'

'Why did you do it?'

'Because she said she knew I had a secret. She was an inquisitive girl – too inquisitive for her own good.'

Wesley listened carefully. Leanne had never been described as inquisitive before but perhaps Mary Palmer had seen another side of her. And there was no arguing with the fact that her statement fitted with what they knew about Leanne's death.

'So you confess to killing her as well?'

'I killed them all.'

She spoke clearly but Wesley thought there was a hint of martyrdom in her words. It crossed his mind momentarily that she could be covering for someone; her son, perhaps. The skeleton in the barn had been there far too long for him to have been involved in her death. But he still wasn't happy.

He heard a knock on the door. The constable standing on guard opened it and a few seconds later he handed Wesley a note. He unfolded and read it, surprised by its contents.

'Mrs Palmer,' he said gently. 'This is a note from the forensic medical examiner, the police doctor who examined you when you came in. He says he was concerned about your health so he contacted your GP.'

Mrs Palmer bowed her head.

'You're ill, aren't you? Pancreatic cancer.'

She looked up at him and he saw that the whites of her eyes were tinged with yellow. 'I only have months to live and I didn't want to die with all this on my conscience. Can I return to my cell now, please?'

*

Gerry sat back in his chair and it gave an ominous creak. 'She's confessed and we've no reason to disbelieve her.'

'If her son did it she has good reason to cover for him. She's got nothing to lose but he has.'

When Gerry didn't reply he asked Rachel what she thought.

'Her story fits with most of what we know so far. And her explanation about that ring on the skeleton in the barn is feasible.'

'Can you check this Jeanne Bordain? See if there's any record of someone of that name disappearing around that time.'

'If she was a French national it might take a while.'

'There must be a record of the baby's birth.'

'She might have gone home to France to have it and come back to show it to the proud father.'

Wesley thought Rachel had a point, but he wanted it checked anyway. Something about Mary Palmer's story made him uncomfortable. Or perhaps it was just the thought of a woman like her being able to kill so many people so readily.

'What about those girls who went missing in the nineteen fifties?' he asked.

Gerry shrugged. 'Let's face it, all we've found is Linda Sangster's cardy and shoe. For all we know she might have left them behind when she came up to the castle to meet some lad. That tower's supposed to be haunted. Maybe she went there as a dare, got spooked and ran. There's no evidence that either of those girls are dead. People disappear of their own accord all the time.'

Wesley knew Gerry could be right. They had no proof that any harm had come to those girls. For all they knew, they could have upped and left a rural village they considered boring.

'Leanne Hatman's postmortem's tomorrow morning, Wes. Get off home and see your Pam.'

Wesley didn't need telling twice. Their killer had made a full confession. Now it was just a case of dealing with the paperwork.

The following morning, Wesley and Gerry attended the postmortem on Leanne Hatman's body.

The young woman he'd seen in Barney Yelland's photographs had been flawless, but now her once-lovely face and body were in such a distressing state of decomposition that he found it difficult to watch. Even Gerry, who famously had an iron stomach, averted his eyes from time to time. Tennant's commentary was full of technicalities, unlike Colin's which he always tried to tailor to the layman – or the average police officer – and they almost missed the most pertinent point. Leanne had drowned, possibly after sustaining a head injury, but this wasn't certain as the injury might have been acquired postmortem.

In other words, Mary Palmer's confession could be true – at least as far as Leanne was concerned. Wesley felt some relief that her statement had been confirmed. He'd had an uneasy feeling that the whole thing was deeper, more complex, but now it looked as if he'd been wrong.

They returned to the station to charge Mary Palmer with five counts of murder.

'I feel sorry for her,' said Wesley as he drove into the station car park.

'She's a cold blooded murderer, Wes. You're too soft, that's your trouble.'

When they reached the CID office they found it practically empty. Most of the officers were still manning the incident room in Turling Fitwell; still amassing evidence and taking statements so that any prosecution would go smoothly.

However, Rachel was there because Gerry had asked her to conduct the next interview with the suspect. She stood as they entered as if she had something to tell them.

'David Palmer's been in.' She hesitated. 'He reckons we're making a big mistake – says his mother isn't capable of murder. And when I asked him if he knew about her finding a crossbow at the castle, he said he can't remember seeing one.'

'Did you believe him?'

She thought for a moment. 'I think he believes it. How did the PM go?'

'It seems to confirm her story.' Wesley fell silent for a few seconds. 'She'll die in prison, poor woman.'

'She murdered five people,' Rachel said with a hint of self-righteousness.

'Can I have a word, sir?' Wesley looked round and saw Rob Carter standing there. He'd thought he was at the incident room so he was surprised to see him there.

'What is it, Rob?'

'I've just been talking to the custody sergeant. He said the prisoner made a phone call.'

'And?'

'He couldn't help overhearing.' Rob went on to relay the salient points of the prisoner's conversation. Wesley looked at Gerry with disbelief. 'Is he sure he heard right?'

'Ask him if you like.' Carter sounded offended that Wesley hadn't taken his word for it. 'I've made a note of the number she called.'

Wesley examined the scrap of paper for a moment, then passed it back to Rob. 'Can you get this number checked out, please.'

Rob went straight to his desk while Wesley ran down the stairs to the custody suite.

When he returned to the CID office, Rob was waiting for him with the news. And it was something quite unexpected.

Wesley knocked on the door and the sound echoed, drowning out the birdsong in the surrounding trees. He knocked again, then a third time. But there was still no reply.

'Where are you going?' Rachel asked as he started to move away.

'I'm going to try round the back.'

'She's probably out walking her dog. We can either wait or come back.'

When Wesley ignored her words she followed, almost running to keep up with him. Soon they reached the back door but when Wesley tried the handle he found it locked. Then he noticed that one of the ground-floor sash windows was open a little.

He peered through the dirty panes into a study dominated by a huge desk. Almost immediately his eyes were drawn to a painting on the wall. An expertly executed study in suffering. He knew enough about art to recognise the style of Caravaggio: the characters picked out in glowing light against a background of dark shadows. But at this distance he knew he could be mistaken. It was more likely to be by somebody who'd copied his style.

'Bloody horrible painting,' Rachel whispered. 'Imagine living with that.'

Wesley didn't reply. Instead he hooked his fingers into the

small gap between the window and the frame and pushed it upwards.

'What are you doing?'

He put his finger to his lips and answered in a whisper. 'I've got to make sure Miss D'Arles is all right, haven't I?'

In view of his determination, she didn't argue, standing back while he climbed through the open window and then climbing in after him. When they found themselves in the study, their eyes were drawn to the painting on the wall. It was irresistible, like watching an accident or a horror film through splayed fingers.

'"The House of Eyes",' Rachel read from the plate beneath the picture.

'Michelangelo Merisi da Caravaggio,' said Wesley softly.

'Is it real?'

'The Hugheses said they thought there might be something spectacular here.' He stared at it, deep in thought. 'But it'd take an expert to confirm it.'

'Surely they meant that Turner they pinched.'

'I think that was a bonus. What if this is what they were really after?'

'How much is it worth if it's genuine?'

'Silly money. Millions. Tens of millions.'

'I still wouldn't give it house room.'

Wesley opened the study door and crept out into the hall. He could hear a gentle female voice coming from the drawing room. Miss D'Arles was speaking to her dog.

The door was shut and he stood outside in the gloomy hallway listening, sensing Rachel's impatience. Why didn't he go straight in?

But he preferred to listen, at least for a while. Miss D'Arles was talking to Reginald as she would to a child.

'Good boy, Reggie. We'll go for a walk later. You'd like that, wouldn't you.'

It was the voice of a lonely woman chatting to her sole companion and it made him feel bad about his next move.

As soon as he pushed the door open Miss D'Arles twisted round in astonishment, her hand to her heart.

'You gave me a shock, Inspector. I didn't hear you knock.'

'I'm sorry. The back door was open,' he lied. 'Mrs Palmer telephoned you earlier.'

She sank into an armchair and took a deep breath. 'That's right. She wanted to tell me what had happened. We've known each other for many years and ... I said I'd help in any way I could. Something terrible must have driven her to do such dreadful things, Inspector. Her husband—'

'You knew her late husband?'

'I did. He was a horrible man. A womaniser. I know it's no excuse but ... She must have been desperate, poor woman.'

'One of our officers happened to overhear what she said.' He paused. 'She called you Gretel.'

The colour drained from Miss D'Arles's lined face, leaving her flesh parchment-pale. She stared at Wesley, her mouth slightly open, as if she was about to speak. But no words emerged.

'You're Gretel D'Arles, aren't you? Your sister, the real Henrietta, lies buried in the barn. Am I right?'

'I don't know where you got that idea from. Gretel died in Sicily many years ago.'

'I think you and Mary Palmer know otherwise.'

Miss D'Arles didn't answer. With her eyes fixed on the

painting of Colapesce, she stood stiffly and walked across the room to where the dolls sat on their shelf. What happened next seemed to play out in slow motion. She pushed the dolls to one side, sending them tumbling to the floor, and Wesley watched, stunned, as she grabbed the loaded crossbow concealed on the wide shelf behind them.

He'd got it wrong. Badly wrong. And by the time he'd recovered from the shock the weapon was pointing straight at his heart.

'I don't think you want to do this, do you, Gretel,' he said, looking her in the eye. Keep her talking. Make her explain. 'Why don't you tell me what happened? Whose is the baby? Was it yours? Is that why you came back from Sicily, because you were pregnant?'

At the mention of the baby her body tensed and he feared he'd said the wrong thing.

'I had to stop her,' she said in a fierce whisper, lowering the weapon a little. 'I had to end it before it got out of hand.'

As he took a step forward she raised the crossbow again, her hands shaking.

'Help me understand, Gretel. I want to understand.'

'Don't come any closer.'

He was half aware of Rachel moving to his left, then he heard a soft cry and saw a look of horror on Gretel's face. The bolt was no longer in the crossbow.

He span round and saw Rachel on the ground, clutching her chest, blood trickling between her fingers.

Then Gretel D'Arles let out a piercing scream.

28

The blacksmith's daughter vanished when she left home to fetch eggs from a neighbour. All Turling Fitwell has been out in search of her.

There have been whispers about Marcle the miller of late. The villagers say he beats his own unfortunate daughter and they claim he cheats them when they bring their grain to the mill so he is not greatly liked. Some in the village say they should go to the mill and search for the girl. However, I felt it my duty to ensure that no hot-headed men took the law into their own hands so I rode to the mill and found Marcle there. Since he seemed quite unconcerned about the missing girl I began to share the villagers' suspicions and, without his permission, I searched the mill. I found nothing but I did not like the way he laughed at me, calling me a popinjay, which matters not for I have done my duty.

As I rode back to the castle I was minded to seek out my cousin and I went to the chamber he calls his laboratory. I found the door locked and I could hear noises of distress from within so it was with great apprehension that I hurried to seek the key in my father's desk. When I returned I unlocked the door and beheld the scene with horror.

My cousin was standing over the barrel in which he had killed the unfortunate sheep and when I drew nearer and peered into the glass I saw a young girl trapped inside, her eyes bulging, her face contorted and her arms reaching upwards in despair. I pushed Uriah aside and lifted the glass lid but I was too late. I hauled the girl out and held her lifeless body in my arms, my eyes filling with helpless tears.

'What have you done?' I gasped.

'I have done it,' my cousin replied, his eyes aglow with excitement and pride. 'The experiment works in human beings as in beasts. As the air left the barrel I saw the life leave her body.'

The Dower House was swarming with police officers. Wesley wasn't sure where they'd come from but he supposed he must have called them. In his dazed state he'd ceased to be aware of anything much . . . only Rachel lying on the ground, her life blood draining away, and Miss D'Arles standing, as if paralysed by the horror of what she'd done. The fallen crossbow lay on the floor beside her feet and she muttered the words 'I'm sorry,' over and over again.

Wesley knelt beside Rachel, reassuring her while she moaned in pain and hoping he was doing the right thing leaving the bolt in place. When the paramedics arrived he left her side reluctantly and watched as they attended to the patient, asking her constant questions and opening their bags of equipment.

He called over to them anxiously, 'Will she be all right?'

One of the paramedics, a young woman, answered. 'Let's hope so.'

He knew better than to distract them from their work so he turned his attention to Miss D'Arles, who was now surrounded by uniformed officers. One of them grabbed her wrists roughly, handcuffs to the ready, until Wesley caught his eye and shook his head. It wasn't necessary to restrain her. It was too late for that.

He himself took Miss D'Arles gently by the arm and led her out into the hallway, signalling one of the officers to accompany him, just in case. He escorted her into the study and instructed her to sit down at the desk. He sat at the opposite side where he couldn't see the Caravaggio and the constable, an overweight man with a hangdog expression, stood behind the prisoner. Wesley noticed he was staring at the painting with a snarl of distaste on his thick lips.

'You'll be taken down to Tradmouth police station soon to undergo a formal interview,' he said quietly. 'You understand that?'

Gretel nodded, shutting her eyes as if she was meditating.

'And you understand that charges will be brought?'

'Yes.' The word was whispered. Then the sea-green eyes opened wide. 'I'm so sorry about the policewoman. I didn't mean to fire at her. It was an accident. She will be all right, won't she?'

Wesley didn't answer. At that moment all he could see was Rachel with a crossbow bolt protruding from her chest, bleeding. In danger.

'I want to tell you everything. I want you to understand.'

For a few moments Wesley averted his gaze, unwilling to look at the woman who'd hurt his colleague, his friend. But he needed to know so he told her to continue. He was listening.

'Our parents died when we were young. I was thirteen and Henrietta was a year older. My sister and I were never close. We were very different people. She had always possessed a streak of cruelty and she was expelled from several schools for various incidents which were never made entirely clear to me. As a consequence she spent a lot of time here at the castle. My life was different. I lived for dance and, to tell the truth, I was glad to get away from my sister when I was sent abroad to ballet school at the age of eleven. Then when our parents died we were left in the guardianship of our uncle.'

'Barrington D'Arles-Cooper?'

She hesitated. 'Uncle Barry was a charming man. If you met him, you would never have suspected his true nature.'

'Which was?'

'He had a total lack of empathy with his fellow human beings and I suppose these days he'd be called a psychopath. My sister became besotted with him. They do say that when certain people have a chemistry between them they can goad each other on to unspeakable cruelties, don't they.'

'*Folie à deux*,' said Wesley.

'I studied abroad then I was taken on by a ballet company in Paris so I had no idea what was going on here. It was only when I came home for a week in the summer of nineteen fifty-two that I discovered the horror of what my uncle and my sister were doing.'

'What was that?' He noticed that she was staring at the painting, as if the sight of it conjured disturbing memories.

'A girl from Belsham had gone missing a few days before I arrived – Susan Thompson, her name was. I remember saying to my sister how terrible it was and that we'd have to be careful when we ventured out if there was some sex maniac about. Then she laughed and said it was nothing to do with sex. I didn't understand what she meant until ... ' She paused and bowed her head. 'We only lived in a small part of the castle in those days – the part that's now the main reception area and the bedrooms above. We couldn't afford to open up the rest. I've always been fascinated by the history of my ancestral home, Inspector. I loved the castle. I still do.'

'Understandable,' said Wesley.

'A couple of days after I arrived home I was bored so I decided to explore the oldest part of the castle, the rooms near the far tower.' She stopped, as though the memory was too painful to speak about, and bowed the head. 'And when

I reached the tower I saw the key was in the door. It had never, as far as I could remember, been locked before. I mean, why should it be? There was nothing in there. I turned the key and when the door opened I saw a girl lying on the floor. She was about my age and her wrists were tied with rope. I ran out to find the housekeeper and get her to call the police but when I reached the gatehouse my sister was there with my uncle. Foolishly, I told them what I'd found and said we had to call for help. They said I should ring the police so I went with them to the drawing room but . . . '

She fell silent but Wesley said nothing to prompt her.

'They kept me locked in my bedroom for several days,' she said after a while. 'Looking back, I'm sure they drugged me and they kept telling me I'd imagined the whole thing. They said I was ill . . . delirious. They even took me back to the west wing to show me the room was empty. They almost succeeded in convincing me I was going mad. Until I was alone with my sister one evening and she began to talk about one of our ancestors who'd gone on a Grand Tour of Europe in the eighteenth century and ended up in Sicily where the cousin he was travelling with developed an obsession with a king . . . an emperor.'

She looked straight at the painting.

'The cousin brought this home with him. There's a place in Sicily called the House of Eyes where this king used to carry out terrible experiments. It was called that because there were peep holes in each room where the king could observe his victims. He'd confine them in a barrel or a box and when they died he would watch, hoping to observe the souls escaping through a hole. In another experiment two captives would be fed then one was forced to exercise while

347

the other rested. Afterwards they were both killed and dis-embowelled to see which one had digested the meal better.'

Wesley suddenly experienced a feeling of dread. 'You think this is what your uncle was planning to do?'

'He'd read a journal written by the ancestor I mentioned. Well, let's just say there's bad blood in some families, Inspector, and the D'Arleses have had their share. My Uncle Barry fancied himself as a scientist but in reality he just enjoyed the cruelty ... as did my sister. The journal mentioned a book which was said to be covered in human skin, all about this king's experiments. I found out later that my sister and uncle used it as a sort of manual.'

'There was a housekeeper at the castle, Mary Palmer's mother. Did she know what was going on?'

'She was a simple, trusting woman and my uncle used to tell her to take time off when he ... '

'And Mary?'

'She knew to keep out of the way.'

'Didn't you tell anybody what happened?'

'They made sure I had no proof, don't you see. After my experience I returned to Paris, vowing never to go back. But I was only eighteen and Madame who was in charge of the company thought it would be nice if her little English girl went home for the Queen's coronation. She was being kind but ... '

She bowed her head.

'On Coronation Day – June the second – another girl went missing after a dance in the village and I couldn't help wondering whether my uncle and my sister were responsi-ble. I went to that room again and found it locked, only this time I couldn't find the key and I was sure it had happened again. When I asked my sister about it, she laughed as if it was a joke and I knew that if I said anything, they'd make out I was mad. They were so plausible, you see. Many years later after I'd inherited the castle, I found the key and went in that room again. There was some clothing in there with the missing girl's name.'

'But you still didn't tell anybody?'

She shook her head. 'No. I locked the door and left everything as it was. Henrietta was my sister – and a D'Arles. We deal with things ourselves.'

'What do you mean?'

'After Coronation Day I told myself Henrietta was gullible, easily influenced, and I postponed going back to Paris until … until I'd done what was necessary. I couldn't allow things to escalate and I convinced myself that once my uncle was out of the way … If I could just remove Henrietta from his influence … '

Wesley glanced up at the constable who was listening, fascinated. 'What did you do?'

'My uncle took medicine for his heart, digoxin. I put a little extra in his whisky. I did it for my sister. Who knows what depravities he would have led her into if I hadn't taken action.'

'You killed him?'

'His death was assumed to be natural and he was buried in the churchyard.' She shuddered. 'Later on I couldn't bear the sight of his name on the headstone so I smashed it up. Nobody in the village made any attempt to repair the damage.'

'What happened to your sister?'

'According to the terms of our father's will, she was old enough to inherit so I left her here in charge of the castle and returned to Europe. I deluded myself, Inspector, that my uncle had been the only source of wickedness in that partnership. Later I was to find out this wasn't the case.'

'If your uncle and sister killed those girls, what happened to the bodies?'

'It's a big estate, Inspector. I expect they're buried somewhere.'

'Not in the barn?'

She shook her head. 'Not there.'

'So who is? It's not Mrs Palmer's errant husband's French mistress and her baby, is it?'

She gave a mirthless smile. 'Of course not. That was something Mary made up. She's always kept my secret, you know. I suspect she too suffered at the hands of my uncle, although she never said anything. It's something she'll probably take to her grave.'

'Why?'

'Shame perhaps? Or she might have blotted it from her memory – married and tried to live a normal life. Who knows? She's a good woman. Loyal and selfless. She told me she was dying and she had nothing to lose so she was happy to take the blame. I shouldn't be made to pay for killing in a noble cause ... her words.'

'Whose is the body in the barn?' Wesley asked again.

She closed her eyes and breathed deeply as though she was preparing to go into a trance. Then the green eyes flashed open again. 'I joined another ballet company and I didn't return here for several years. Whether this was because I couldn't face the fact that I'd been responsible for my uncle's death or whether I secretly feared that my sister might not be the easily led innocent I'd convinced myself she was, I don't know. I claimed I was too busy to come back and I wrote her the occasional letter, just to let her know what I was doing.' A smile appeared on her lips, a proud smile as if she was recalling past triumphs. 'I worked for a couple of seasons at the Teatro Massimo in Palermo in Sicily, taking on solo roles in some of the major ballets and my career flourished. When I danced the pas de trois in *Swan Lake* I was told I was destined for great things and I loved Palermo.' The smile suddenly vanished. 'But when I visited the cathedral there and saw the tomb of Frederick the Second – the king who'd inspired my uncle's depravity – it brought the memories back. I didn't go in there again.'

'You must have been very talented,' Wesley said.

She smiled modestly. 'Those were the happiest days of my life, Inspector. I had friends. I had purpose. I loved dancing.'

'Then something happened?'

'My sister wrote, asking me to come home. She was pregnant.'

'Who was the father?'

'She wouldn't tell me but I felt I couldn't let her down so I left Sicily and came home. By the time I got back she'd given birth alone to a girl and she was living here in the Dower House. She'd dismissed the housekeeper as soon as she knew she was pregnant and locked herself away here. I tried to help but she wouldn't allow me to tell anyone. Funnily enough she seemed to be coping and I was eager to get back to Palermo. Then ... '

Wesley had a feeling that what she was about to say would be shocking.

'She started acting strangely then suddenly the baby wasn't there. I became worried and when I asked her where it was she said something about an experiment. She said she had to seize the opportunity while the baby was young and unable to speak. She kept talking about King Frederick, just like our uncle had done, and I could see that blank cruelty in her eyes . . . just like his. I knew she'd done something terrible and then she told me the king had experimented on babies to discover what would happen if they were kept in complete silence. Would they learn to speak? Would they develop their own language? I told her it was inhuman, and I said I wouldn't let her do it. But she'd hidden the baby somewhere and every time she went to feed it she made sure I was locked in my room so I couldn't follow her. After a day or so, I got wise and hid in the woods and when I saw her coming out of the house I followed her. I kept telling myself it wasn't her fault – she needed help. Some women can become ill after childbirth, can't they? But I knew in my heart there was more to it than that. There was a cunning about her. A coldness. She was determined to experiment on her own child and she saw nothing wrong in it.'

'What did you do?' Wesley asked.

'I followed her to the barn and demanded to see the baby, to satisfy myself that it was all right. She tried to stop me but I was as determined as she was and I pushed past her. When I got in there I saw a wooden box in the corner. The baby was in it but when I picked it up, it was cold and floppy. It was dead.' For a few moments she bowed her head as though the memory was painful. 'Henrietta stood looking at it. She didn't even ask to hold it. Just said the experiment had failed so she'd have to try again. Those words made my blood run cold, Inspector.'

'And she did try again. She abducted a baby from one of the cottages and brought it here. You rescued it and put it in the church.'

'Very clever, Inspector. That's exactly what happened.'

'You couldn't let it happen again, could you? Your sister was a danger to the whole community and you had two choices. Either you could turn her in to the authorities or you could kill her?'

'She was a D'Arles. I couldn't let her go to prison.'

'If she was ill she could have got help.'

Gretel shook her head. 'She wasn't ill, Inspector. She was evil.' She bowed her head. 'I've still got that horrible book. I keep it in my uncle's desk, just to remind me of what my uncle and sister were if I ever start to doubt that what I did wasn't right or necessary.'

'I presume you've read Richard D'Arles's journals?'

She nodded. 'I found them in the castle library.'

'I've read two. Are there more?'

She waved her hand towards the desk. 'I returned the first two to the library but the third volume is in that drawer along with that terrible book. There are some things that should be kept in the family. They're not for public consumption.'

'How did your sister die?'

'She'd never thrown away my uncle's medicine. Her death was peaceful.'

'You buried her beside her baby in the barn?'

'Mary Palmer and I had always been friends and we'd kept in touch while I was abroad. When I returned I needed someone to confide in and Mary was nearby. She'd always found my sister's behaviour disturbing so she'd kept well away. She understood, you see. I wish to make it quite clear that no blame attaches to her. The only thing she's guilty of is being a good and loyal friend. She helped me bury my sister in the disused barn. Then we had to think what to do; how to explain Henrietta's absence, and Mary suggested that I take my sister's place. She'd been a virtual recluse and never visited the village and we'd always looked so alike. That part wasn't difficult; what I found hard was casting off my old life. Leaving my career and friends behind broke my heart but it was necessary. I took over the castle and put it about that Gretel had died abroad. The deception worked perfectly until Mary's son sold the barn to that builder. I couldn't allow my sister's body to be found, you do understand that?'

'You killed Darren and Marion Hatman in cold blood so I can't say I do understand, Miss D'Arles.'

'I'd learned to use the crossbow as a child. My sister and I used to use it for target practice but I could only find one bolt when I brought it here from the castle. The rest must have been lost over the years, you see. That's why I couldn't leave it in the bodies. That was the hardest part – getting so close like that.' She raised her chin proudly. 'My aim is good. They didn't suffer.'

'But why did you have to kill them?'

'So that Henrietta and her baby could rest in peace.'

'And nobody would find out what you'd done.'

She looked at him with pleading eyes. 'I killed to save others, Inspector. Whenever I look at that picture of Colapesce I brought back from Sicily, it reminds me of why I gave up my life to stay here. I sacrificed my life to protect the people of Turling Fitwell. My sister wouldn't have stopped at one baby. To her people were disposable, like rats in a laboratory.'

Wesley could have argued with her. He could have pointed out that it would only have taken one call to the police to stop the evil and that there'd been nothing noble about murdering the Hatmans to avoid facing justice. But instead he left Gretel D'Arles in the care of the constable and went to see how Rachel was. When he reached the hall she was being carried out on a stretcher. She was conscious and managed a weak smile when she saw his anxious face.

He touched the hand that lay on the blanket and she grasped his finger like a baby seeking reassurance.

'You'll be fine,' he reassured her. They were the same words he'd said to Pam. And he just prayed they were true.

Gerry arrived a couple of minutes after the ambulance had left with its lights flashing and sirens blazing. He rushed into the Dower House, breathless.

'The paramedics are taking her to Morbay Hospital,' he said. 'I'll get up there, Wes. Have you spoken to Miss D'Arles?'

'She'll make a full confession. Both the Hatmans and a couple of poisonings we weren't even aware of.'

'And Rachel's attempted murder?'

'She claims it was an accident.'

'Where is she?'

'Study. She's been very talkative –even told me who killed those two girls in the nineteen fifties.'

'That'll do our clear-up rate no end of good,' Gerry said, absent-mindedly. 'What about Leanne Hatman?'

'She hasn't mentioned her yet.' He paused. 'Rachel was conscious when they took her out. She'll be OK, Gerry.'

Gerry looked round. Reginald was lying in his basket, watching the activity with interest. He squatted down and stroked the Labrador's head. 'I'd better get the dog unit in to take care of this chap. After we've had a chat to Miss D'Arles, do you want to go to the hospital?'

Wesley shook his head. 'I'd better get back to Pam.'

Gerry looked him in the eye. 'Right answer, Wes.'

Before Wesley could say anything, they heard a voice. 'What's happened?'

It was David Palmer and he looked worried. Wesley had almost forgotten that Mary Palmer was still in custody, held for crimes she hadn't committed. In due course she might face charges for her part in covering up the murders her friend had committed, but in the meantime Wesley thought it would do no harm to allow her to return to the castle.

After he'd sent Palmer to the police station to be with his mother Wesley touched Gerry's arm. 'Ready?'

They made for the study where Gerry sat down in the chair Wesley had vacated.

'I believe you're willing to make a full statement, Miss D'Arles.'

'Yes, Chief Inspector. Tell me, is that young woman going to be all right?'

'We don't know yet. One thing I want to ask you: do you know anything about the death of Leanne Hatman? Did you kill her as well?'

Gretel D'Arles shook her head vigorously. 'No.'

29

My father's sole concern was for the family name. No disgrace should besmirch the noble name of D'Arles and, whatever his sister's objections, he was minded to send my cousin away to some far-flung place, a plantation in the West Indies, perhaps. I asked how justice would be served by this but he refused to answer.

I left my father's presence and found Uriah walking in the grounds. He greeted me as though he had done nothing shameful or wicked and I knew then that if he behaved thus towards a girl from our own village, he would not hesitate to commit the most terrible atrocities upon the poor unfortunates enslaved on the plantations of the West Indies. My way was clear. It was my duty as a Christian to put a stop to such evil.

I was in the habit of carrying a pistol on my travels for the defence of my person and I had it with me now. I knew that my cousin has been visiting the mill on our estate, watching Annie Marcle, the miller's daughter. Her father might be a rogue but the girl is a simple innocent and I feared what he might have planned for her.

That day I followed him and saw Annie greet him humbly, as though she was dazzled by his superior station in life. Because of her father's cruelty, I fear she has been inveigled by my cousin's false kindness. A mouse in the presence of a cat.

Uriah was unaware that I was watching from the trees beside the mill. With the noise of the rushing river and the mill machinery, I regretted that I could hear nothing of his conversation with the girl but I saw him reach out and touch her face like a lovesick swain. He took her hand and started to lead her away and it was then that I emerged from my hiding place.

I imagined that my presence would deter him but he held her hand tightly as she, poor silly thing, gazed at him like a moonstruck calf.

'Leave her,' I said.

But he shook his head.

Then Annie spoke. 'I will not leave, him, sir, for he has promised to make me his wife.'

How can one rescue someone so reluctant from the snares of the wicked? Then my cousin took a pistol from his belt and raised it.

When Wesley arrived home that night it was late and he wasn't in the mood for conversation. He sat outside in the car for five minutes before he felt ready to go in. The curtains were drawn and he hoped Pam hadn't peeped out when she heard the sound of the engine and seen him from the window. If she asked him for an explanation, he wasn't sure he'd be able to find the words.

Eventually he climbed out and hesitated for a few moments at the front door. He hadn't done as Gerry had advised. Instead he'd gone straight to Morbay Hospital to see how Rachel was and now he couldn't get the image of her lying in that hospital bed, sprouting tubes, out of his mind. They were going to operate that night and they hadn't said much to reassure him that she was going to pull through. He was surprised at how numb he felt.

When he did go inside, Pam emerged from the living room to meet him.

'You look awful. What's happened?'

He knew he should be asking her how she was but he couldn't stop himself blurting out the thing that was foremost in his mind. 'Rachel's in hospital. We were making an arrest and she was shot with a crossbow.'

Pam's hand went up to her mouth and for a few seconds she said nothing. 'Is she going to be all right?'

Suddenly Wesley was aware of tears welling up in his eyes. The prickling sensation was almost painful as he made a great effort to blink them back but they came anyway, trickling warm down his cheeks.

Pam stepped forward and put her arms around him. 'I'm sure she's in good hands,' she whispered. 'Try not to worry.'

He wiped the tears away with his sleeve, unsure whether they were for Rachel or for Pam.

He could see the strain on her face; the dark shadows beneath her eyes. 'What about you?'

She gave a deep, shuddering sigh. 'I've got another appointment with the consultant next Thursday. Nine in the morning.' She paused as if expecting him to make some comment. 'Can you get time off?'

'No problem,' he said. 'We made an arrest for the crossbow murders today.'

'Who have you arrested?'

He led her into the living room. At least explaining the disturbing events at Eyecliffe Castle would take her mind off things for a while. He'd already eaten – a takeaway pizza at the station – so there was nothing else to do but talk, and they did so until the clock on the mantelpiece told them it was midnight. As they went upstairs to bed, Pam asked the question that had been nagging at the back of his mind. 'So if Gretel D'Arles didn't kill Leanne Hatman, who did?'

*

It was a community dig and some people could only make it at weekends so Sunday was like any other day. Neil and Lucy arrived early to get things ready. They'd seen a lot of police activity when they'd driven through Turling Fitwell the previous day but when Neil tried to contact Wesley to find out what was going on, he'd had no luck.

So he was surprised when Wesley turned up at the dig, just as he was taking the tarpaulins off the trenches. There had been rain overnight and Wesley had to raise his voice to be heard above the sound of water rushing over the nearby weir.

'Any news on those skeletons?' was Neil's first question.

'Yes, we've made an arrest.'

'Good. How's Pam?' Neil asked. 'Lucy and I are thinking of calling round one evening. When's best?'

For a few moments Wesley didn't answer. Then the whole story flooded out, as if he was relieved to share his troubles. 'She's got another hospital appointment next week,' he said. 'They're going to decide on treatment.'

Neil gave him a hug. It was the first time in all their years of friendship that had happened and it took both of them by surprise.

'Rachel's in hospital too,' Wesley said. 'She was shot yesterday while we were making an arrest. Crossbow.'

Neil gaped in astonishment.

'They say she'll pull through.'

'Thank God for that. Who have you arrested?'

'Yes. You've met her – Miss D'Arles.'

'The old lady with the Labrador?' He shook his head as though all his most dearly held beliefs had been shattered.

'And I've found something that'll interest you – the third

361

volume of that journal. It identifies your skeleton. Case closed. I'll get you a copy.'

'Thanks,' said Neil. As he recovered from the shock of Wesley's news, his eyes suddenly became hungry to see the promised treasure.

'Look, I need a favour,' said Wesley. 'Do you remember Lucy saying she thought someone had been digging in one of the trial pits that had been filled in?'

A look of recognition passed across Neil's face. 'I remember her saying something about incompetent treasure hunters: they'd chosen an empty trench. Hang on.' He shouted Wesley's question over to Lucy who was a few yards away, examining finds. She came over to join them and greeted Wesley with a kiss on the cheek.

'I thought the soil looked as though it had been disturbed, that's all,' she said once Neil had explained.

'Will you dig it out for me?'

She looked at Neil. 'There was nothing in it, that's why we closed it down.'

'Humour me.'

'Sure. Why not?'

She was about to call over a couple of the volunteers but Wesley asked her and Neil to do it. If his suspicions were correct, the empty trench might now contain evidence of a delicate nature.

Wesley noticed James Garrard watching him with curiosity. Now he knew the truth about the gifts he'd been receiving, he wondered whether to share it with him. But it wasn't urgent and was something best done in private.

Neil and Lucy assembled their equipment and began to dig. After five minutes they hit something hard.

'There's something in here,' said Lucy with disbelief.

They continued until the thing had emerged from the earth. It was a floral suitcase. Just like the one Leanne Hatman had once owned.

Wesley had taken the precaution of donning crime-scene gloves before touching the case and placing it on the tarpaulin Neil had provided. When he'd opened it he'd found it packed with clothes, presumably the ones Leanne was supposed to have taken from her room And her phone was in there too.

Whoever had buried the distinctive case in the fresh, easily dug soil had cleared Leanne's room to make it look as if she'd gone away. In order to do this he – or she – would have needed access to the staff quarters of Eyecliffe Castle, which ruled out Barney Yelland once and for all.

He'd arranged for the case to be sent to Forensic in the hope they'd be able to lift some fingerprints. In the meantime something was jarring in the back of his mind. A small, seemingly insignificant memory.

He left Neil and Lucy to seal off the small, square trench for examination in case it held more clues, and drove to Neston. He could have asked someone else to do the job for him but this way would be quicker.

When Clare Woolmer opened her front door he could feel her hostility. To her he was the officer who'd persecuted her innocent lodger and a representative of oppressive authority. Now, though, he needed to convince her that his intentions were benign ... and urgent.

He asked if Barney was in, saying he needed his help, and at first she seemed unwilling to admit him. When she finally relented and allowed him upstairs he found Yelland going through photographs on his computer.

363

He gave a token knock on the open door and Yelland glared at him as he entered the room before returning to his task. Wesley couldn't really blame him; it wasn't easy being accused of something you hadn't done. He watched for a few moments and recognised the landscape on the screen from Neil's holiday pictures. The photogenic ruins of Sicily captured for posterity.

'Have you been told that we've found Leanne's body?'

After a few seconds of silence Yelland turned to face him. 'Yes, but I had nothing to do with it.'

'We know that now. But I need your help. Can I see all the pictures you took of Leanne?'

It was hard to know what Yelland was feeling as he looked away.

'You want to help us catch her killer, don't you? Please.'

The photographer turned back to his computer and replaced the sunny images of Sicily with pictures of Leanne. As he scrolled through them Wesley looked over his shoulder and eventually he told him to stop and asked if he could blow up a section of one particular picture.

He now knew who'd killed Leanne Hatman. And once the forensic evidence on the case came back he hoped he'd be able to make an arrest.

Wesley called Gerry and asked him to come to Eyecliffe Castle. It was urgent. The two men met at the gatehouse rather than in reception, because Wesley feared Sean might be on duty and he wasn't in the mood to face his questions. If Sean chose another path in life, he might make a good copper, he thought. He had the necessary curiosity about his fellow human beings.

'Are we sure about this, Wes?'

'Everyone at the castle had their fingerprints taken as a matter of routine and Forensic phoned through half an hour ago. They've found a match.'

He went on to tell Gerry about his visit to Barney Yelland and the DCI nodded gravely. 'That clinches it then.'

In the end Sean couldn't be avoided. He was stationed at the reception desk as usual but they hurried past him before he could ask anything.

After they'd obtained a pass key from David Palmer they made straight for the staff quarters. Mary Palmer was nowhere to be seen and Wesley wondered where she was. She had been released pending further inquiries and last time he'd seen her she'd looked ill and traumatised by recent events – a victim of evil and its repercussions.

When they reached the room he gave a token knock before unlocking the door and stepping inside. Wesley knew exactly what he was looking for and when he found it he handed it to Gerry along with a copy of the photograph Barney Yelland had given him. Gerry examined both items then nodded in understanding.

They returned downstairs and Wesley hesitated before entering the spa, hoping their arrival wouldn't bring embarrassment to some hapless soul. But they were in luck. An overweight woman with brassy hair burst from the room, her flesh unnaturally pink. When she saw the two policemen looking at her she put her nose in the air and pulled her towelling robe closer round her body, as if she feared they were a pair of perverts on the prowl.

It seemed they'd timed it perfectly.

The room smelled of lavender, the oil used for relaxation. The fluffy towel covering the couch in the centre of the room was rucked up, suggesting that it had recently been vacated by the pink woman, and Kirsty Paige was standing beside a trolley, sorting through bottles of oils.

She looked up from her task and her calm, self-absorbed expression suddenly changed. 'Can I help you?' she said.

'Kirsty Paige, I'm arresting you in connection with the death of Leanne Hatman.' Wesley went on to recite the familiar words of the caution, watching her face. If the evidence didn't suggest otherwise, he would have said that this was the last thing she expected.

They took her out by a back entrance, denying Sean his frisson of excitement, and she protested her innocence all the way to Tradmouth police station.

Wesley found himself wishing that Rachel was with him to conduct the interview. But instead it was Gerry who followed him into the interview room with a determined look on his face.

Kirsty was sitting beside the duty solicitor in her black uniform, looking stunned, as though she couldn't quite believe what was happening. When Wesley placed a plastic evidence bag containing the necklace he'd found in her jewellery box in front of her, along with a photograph of the same necklace around Leanne Hatman's slender neck, she stared at it in horror.

'We found this in your room,' Wesley began. 'It belonged to Leanne. Can you tell us how it came to be in your possession?'

'She gave it to me.'

'When?'

Kirsty's eyes flickered left and right, as though she was searching for an escape route. 'The evening she left.'

'And you never thought to mention it?' said, Gerry who was glowering at her from the other side of the table.

When Kirsty didn't reply Wesley tried again. 'A suitcase belonging to Leanne Hatman was found buried at the archaeological site near the castle. We've tested it for fingerprints and found Leanne's – and another set. Yours.'

'I helped her carry it once.'

'These were all over it, inside and out, as if you'd packed it then manoeuvred it into the hole. What have you got to say about that?'

Kirsty bowed her head. 'I don't know.'

Wesley recalled the collapsed section of balustrade and the shred of cloth from Leanne's pyjamas. Leanne had been out there, probably smoking, and he guessed Kirsty had been with her.

'Were you outside on the terrace with Leanne having a cigarette? Did you argue with her? Did you push her or was it an accident?'

He hadn't expected it to be so easy but she took the escape route she'd been offered, grabbing it eagerly like a thirsty man would grab a water bottle in a desert.

'It was an accident. She tripped and fell over the edge and I panicked.'

'Tell me exactly what happened.' He leaned forward like a sympathetic family doctor asking what the trouble was. Perhaps he should have followed the family tradition of entering the medical profession after all, he thought fleetingly.

'When I went upstairs she came out of her room and said she was going out on the terrace for a last smoke. Did I fancy coming with her? I said yes but she was getting up

367

my nose, going on about her modelling career and her photographer. She said that once she'd heard from one of the big agencies she was quitting and going to London. I asked her to see if her photographer would do a portfolio for me but . . . '

'She refused?'

She looked away. 'She said she wouldn't embarrass herself by asking. Said I didn't have the looks.' Wesley could see from her face how Leanne's words had wounded her.

'Where were you when this conversation took place?'

'Out on the terrace like I said. She'd already changed into her pyjamas – it was really warm that night, you see. I gave her a bit of a shove – nothing hard – and she lost her balance. Part of the balustrade gave way and she toppled over.'

'What did you do?'

'I tried to climb down after her but the drop was too steep so I ran out of the back entrance and went round the side. It was dark so I couldn't see her on the slope. I thought she must have rolled down into the river.'

'Our pathologist said she suffered a head injury.'

'That must have happened when she fell. I know I should have got help but I panicked. I was scared I'd get the blame.'

'We've spoken to Barney Yelland, the photographer. He says she always wore the necklace we found in your room. She took it off for most of their photo sessions but she told him she normally wore it all the time, even at night.' He held the evidence bag up to the light. 'She told him it was a present from her late grandmother – hardly something she'd just give away.'

No answer.

'I put it to you that after she fell you went down to the river bank and found her there. You helped yourself to her necklace then you rolled her body into the river. Only thing is, Kirsty, she wasn't dead. She suffered a head injury which probably rendered her unconscious but the actual cause of death was drowning.'

She thought for a moment. 'Then perhaps I didn't kill her. Perhaps someone else was watching us below the terrace and killed her when she fell – it was dark so there's no way I would have seen anyone down there. Someone else might have pushed her in the water . . . or she might have fallen in by accident.'

'Then how do you explain the necklace?'

Kirsty suddenly broke down and began to sob uncontrollably. 'It was an accident, I swear.'

30

It was a moment of madness, a sudden loss of control. I pointed my own pistol at Uriah and for a moment I feared that I lacked the courage to shoot a man in cold blood.

Then I looked at the maid and saw that, in her naivety, she still clung to him. 'Don't you know what he is?' I shouted to her. 'He thinks nothing of killing and torturing God's innocent creatures in his twisted search for knowledge. If you go with him you will die.'

He told her not to listen to my words and questioned my sanity. So plausible was he that she smiled as he began to lead her away. I knew then I had to save her. His was a dangerous madness, inspired by that terrible book and the vile painting he obtained in Sicily, and he had to be stopped.

He lowered his pistol and walked ahead with Annie following him like a faithful dog and I had to act. I raised my pistol and fired. Then I saw my cousin stagger before turning to stare at me in amazement. He stood for several heartbeats before falling to the ground.

Annie became hysterical and her piercing screams brought her father from his mill. I had already shared my fears with him and, although he is a rough and simple man, he understood my meaning.

As Annie lay sobbing, her father spoke. 'I have a place for him,' he said, picking up the body like a sack of grain. He carried Uriah away and buried him in a far outhouse while I tried to soothe Annie.

The miller swears neither he nor Annie will speak of what happened and I have told my father that my cousin has embarked on further travels. He appears to believe my story as the matter has never been mentioned again within the castle, although Uriah's mother has taken to her bed in grief that her only son has departed without a word.

And yet I am uneasy for I have taken a human life and I fear I will be damned for my great sin. Or will there be forgiveness because I committed a dreadful act in a noble cause?

Should my crime come to light, I would face the gallows. So, as I write this, the last page in my journal, I prepare for another life. My kin will think me dead but I have no choice if I am to escape the hangman's noose.

I will take a ship from Tradmouth and retrace my journey through Italy and assume another name. Richard D'Arles is dead. In the city of Palermo I shall become a new man.

The jury believed Kirsty Paige's account of events and when she was convicted of manslaughter the judge imprisoned her for three years. Although Wesley knew she'd be out in half that time.

He hadn't been convinced by her story. As far as he was concerned, she was guilty of murder. Her jealousy of Leanne Hatman had been out of control and she'd killed her, possibly in the hope of taking her place, using Barney Yelland to advance her ambitions. Gerry, however, had reckoned manslaughter was a result. Be thankful for small mercies, he'd said.

In contrast Gretel D'Arles had been told she'd die in prison. The murders of Darren and Marion Hatman to prevent the discovery of her past crimes deserved life, the judge had said. She'd displayed considerable dignity when she'd been led from the dock and, in spite of himself, Wesley had found himself admiring her, although this feeling had been swiftly suppressed. Those who kill never deserved admiration, even though it appeared that her first murders had been committed for the best of motives.

The third volume of the journal and the skin-bound book about Frederick II had been returned to the castle library. Wesley hadn't mentioned the unusual nature of the binding. Some things are best left unsaid.

Summer had arrived, bringing with it the usual blend of sunshine and rain, and the threat of major crime appeared to recede. Thieves targeted boats; burglars stole from holiday cottages and a local cash point was ram-raided but there were no more deaths. However, in spite of making a full recovery, Rachel had postponed her wedding again and set a new date in December.

Pam too had done her time in hospital. The initial operation to remove the lump had been successful and even though the tissue the surgeon removed proved to be malignant, the cancer hadn't spread. She'd had radiotherapy just to be sure, which had left her feeling weak and sick. But she'd dealt with her ordeal bravely and come through ... for now. The doctors would give no concrete assurances.

Whenever Wesley looked at her he thought of what might have been – what might still be.

Now her treatment was finished, they planned to go away in late August; maybe to Sicily, leaving the children with Wesley's parents in London. A week of Sicilian sunshine sounded good, Pam said. And the destination came highly recommended by Neil.

One day Wesley returned home from work to find a package waiting for him. Pam had left it unopened on the kitchen table and he was surprised that she'd been able to contain her curiosity.

When he tore off the cardboard packaging he found a hardback book inside, *In the Footsteps of the Grand Tourists* by Cornell Stamoran with photographs by Barney Yelland. He flicked through the pages, enjoying the moody shots of European cities and landscapes. Towards the end of the book, one image in particular caught his attention. It was a tower, a ruin set in hilly countryside. And beneath it was a caption: The House of Eyes.

Kirsty Paige knew to keep her head down. Survival was the name of the game in prison, and survival would be her priority when she got out. She was counting the days. And making plans for the future.

She was allowed to write letters and this one would be important.

Dear Mr Palmer, it began. I have been considering our arrangement and I have a proposal. She liked the word proposal – it sounded businesslike. I am willing to keep our meeting of 19th April and its conclusions confidential on the condition I am offered the partnership I requested previously. Please let me know if this is acceptable to you. Yours sincerely, Kirsty Paige.

He owed her this reward for keeping his part in Leanne's death a secret. She hadn't told the police that after the altercation on the terrace that night, she'd run to find David to tell him what had happened. She hadn't told them that he'd brought a torch and they'd gone in search of Leanne on the slope leading down to the river. She hadn't told them that when they found Leanne unconscious and bleeding, she'd been sure she was dead. She hadn't said that she'd told David it would be better to push Leanne into the water so that her body would be carried away by the river's strong currents and her death wouldn't be linked with the castle. David had done the pushing so, according to the police evidence, he'd been the one who'd actually killed her.

She'd heard he was building a nine-hole golf course in the castle grounds, which probably meant he'd sold that Turner that had been hanging, unnoticed, in a corridor. She'd also heard that a couple of skeletons had been found during the construction of the golf course. The TV news had said they dated to the 1950s and the police weren't looking for anyone in connection to the find: police-speak for they knew who the bones belonged to and what had happened.

When she was released she'd return to Eyecliffe Castle and run the place with David. His mother was ill and she'd heard Mrs Palmer hadn't long to live.

Soon she'd be in charge. And David would never betray her. Not if he knew what was good for him.

AUTHOR'S NOTE

Today young people often embark on a 'gap year' to travel and, hopefully, gain new experiences. But this concept is far from new. From around 1660 until the advent of the railways in the 1840s, the sons, and occasionally daughters, of British nobility and gentry travelled to the cultural centres of Europe as an educational rite of passage. This also had the advantage of allowing young gentlemen to indulge in such high-spirited activities as drinking, gambling and illicit sexual liaisons without inconveniencing their noble families.

Gentlemen (and sometimes ladies) usually travelled in the company of a tutor or cicerone, often referred to as the bear-leader. These long-suffering companions were often impoverished clergymen entrusted with the care of their young charges who, I imagine, couldn't wait to give them the slip.

The Grand Tour usually began in France, and from Paris travellers would make their way to the Alps and then on by boat to Italy where they visited the great cities of the

Renaissance and the excavations at Pompeii and Herculaneum. Sicily wasn't always on the route but, with its stunning classical ruins, it no doubt proved popular with those who ventured that far.

The travellers came home with crates of souvenirs and would also send furniture and paintings on ahead. In most of the stately homes of England you will see paintings, often featuring classical ruins, which were acquired by some young scion of the family on his (or her) Grand Tour.

It is some years now since I first read about Frederick II (1194–1250) who ruled as Holy Roman Emperor and King of Sicily. Frederick spoke six languages and was an avid patron of science and the arts. A contemporary chronicler called him *stupor mundi* (the wonder of the world) and many historians have called him the first modern ruler, establishing in Sicily and southern Italy a centrally governed kingdom with an efficient bureaucracy. But his disputes with the Papacy resulted in his excommunication and Pope Gregory IX went so far as to call him the Antichrist. Nevertheless this didn't prevent him being buried in a magnificent porphyry tomb in Palermo Cathedral. The House of Eyes referred to in this book doesn't, as far as I'm aware, exist, although the town of Naro itself was a splendid royal city during Frederick II's reign.

There was a dark side to Frederick's thirst for knowledge. A Franciscan friar, Salimbene di Adam, recorded some of the king's cruel experiments in his Chronicles and I have referred to them in this book. His cruelty wasn't confined to experimenting on prisoners. Possibly his most famous experiments were conducted on young infants who were raised without human interaction to see what kind of language they would develop.

However, one of the experiments I describe in this book was inspired, not by Salimbene di Adam's account, but by a painting by Joseph Wright of Derby which can be seen in the National Gallery in London. It is entitled *An Experiment on a Bird in the Air Pump* (1768) and it depicts a white bird dying in a bottle as a scientist pumps out the air. It is the reaction of his audience that most interested me; the contrast between the relish with which some witness the creature's suffering and the horror on the faces of others. It reflects the eighteenth century's preoccupation with science, commonly called the Enlightenment, but also poses uncomfortable questions.

The story of Colapesce is a well-known Sicilian legend and I couldn't resist using it in *The House of Eyes*. Neither could I resist creating the Eyecliffe Castle Country Hotel and Spa (very loosely based on the ruined and uninhabited Berry Pomeroy Castle in Devon – English Heritage) because I developed a taste for castles when I stayed at the lovely (and definitely not murderous) Peckforton Castle in Cheshire for my son's wedding. Happy memories!